BREAKING
FAITH

Nason Nichols Mysteries

Breaking Faith
Trade Secrets

BREAKING FAITH

Featuring Nason Nichols, P.I.

MAYNARD F. THOMSON

POCKET BOOKS
New York   London   Toronto   Sydney   Tokyo   Singapore

M

POCKET BOOKS, a division of Simon & Schuster Inc.
1230 Avenue of the Americas, New York, NY 10020

ISBN: 0-671-74900-5

First Pocket Books hardcover printing October 1996

10 9 8 7 6 5 4 3 2 1

POCKET and colophon are registered trademarks of
Simon & Schuster Inc.

Printed in the U.S.A.

JUN 1 4 1997

To Laura

Acknowledgments

I am grateful to many people for help in producing this book. Among them are:

Detective George Lotti, for his explanation of Boston Police Department organization and procedure; Joseph Kelly, a lifelong "Townie," who generously guided me through the haunts and ways of the Boston Irish; the Krotinger family of South Natick Village, for the warm "home base" they provided while I did research; Chilton and Janet Thomson, for teaching me to read, the first step in writing; Shirley and Bill Shapero, for their generous financial and emotional support; Jim Shapero and Joan Tryzelaar, who provided medical insights; Deborah Kelbach, who once again gave her free time to get the manuscript out; Fred Hill, for brokering the deal and knowing when it was time to check my manic tendencies; Jane Chelius, for being the first to say I had a book, not just a manuscript, and for then editing my work into something far better than it was; Pat Golbitz, for showing me how to cut out clutter; Peter Wolverton, for knowing where additional work was needed, and when to leave well enough alone; and Katherine O'Moore-Klopf, whose copyediting spared me much embarrassment.

BREAKING
FAITH

prologue

The Boston Hub
August 1, 1994

DEVELOPER BLASTS DISTRESS RUMORS,
PLEDGES MAJOR PROJECT

BOSTON—Responding sharply to rumors that recent declines in the Boston market have jeopardized his real-estate interests, developer Timothy R. "Tip" Finn yesterday assured financial analysts that his company, Quahog, Inc., was "fundamentally sound" and that cash flow is "more than adequate to service existing debt and develop new projects." Denying "categorically" reports that Quahog's Seaside Complex, a thirty-story office and retail development adjacent to Boston Harbor, is in distress, Finn assured the group "we have signed leases or bankable commitments for substantially all of Seaside. Seaside is very profitable."

Finn then announced a major new development, which he said was made feasible by the "businesslike and responsible" administration of Mayor Conor O'Conor. Finn promised that land acquisition would commence "within days." He declined to say where the project would be located, asserting that acquisition costs would rise prohibitively if the project's location were disclosed before Quahog representatives could acquire the land.

Finn also took the occasion to announce that he was endowing the Sean and Colleen Finn Scholarship, to be awarded annually to a high-school senior from South Boston, the still largely Irish, blue-collar neighborhood minutes from downtown where Finn, the grandson of Irish immigrants, began work as a mason's apprentice almost fifty-five years ago. The scholarship is named after Finn's parents and will be given each year to a member of the graduating class at South Boston High School who, in the opinion of the faculty, "best exemplifies the qualities of decency, hard work, and community spirit that characterized Sean and Colleen Finn."

While Finn now lives on a twenty-acre farm in Dover, outside of Boston, where he and his second wife Elaine raise prize-winning horses and host gatherings of the city's business and political elite, he remains close to the South Boston community, where he still attends mass every Sunday. He has been a vocal supporter of Mayor O'Conor's administration, and the mayor repaid the favor by joining numerous other civic leaders at the luncheon.

Accepting the scholarship on behalf of the city, Mayor O'Conor said: "With this generous gift, Tip Finn reminds us all of the spirit that makes Southie such a special part of Boston and Tip Finn such a special son of Southie."

chapter 1

THE MAN IN THE BACK SEAT OF MY TAXI HAD A
soft voice and I had trouble hearing him over the din across
the street. "Keep going."

"Can't—they've got it blocked off." I took one hand off
the wheel and gestured at the barrier, a blue-and-yellow
sawhorse with BOSTON PD stenciled on the crossbar.
"Seems like something's going on in Washington Park."

I rolled down the window and peered across the street.
There were floodlights on in the park and a loudspeaker
system issued sound blobs every few seconds. I couldn't
make out a word and couldn't imagine who'd choose
Washington Park on a Friday night for a rally. "Better back
up and go around. Don't worry—I'll turn the meter off."

"Keep going, dude."

I looked up into the rearview. At first all I saw was the
big man's dark glasses and the cowl of the sweatshirt pulled
up around his face; then I saw the little chrome-plated

automatic in his fist. He flicked the back of his hand at me just to make sure I hadn't missed it.

"Right. But if I try going through here, the cops'll be all over us." I pointed at the barricade, where a motorcycle trooper stood facing the park. Somewhere in the distance, a bullhorn crackled, and I had to raise my voice. "I'd better back up and turn around."

I turned in my seat, slowly, and looked inquiringly at my passenger. He had the automatic folded into his hand so only the muzzle protruded as he waved it at me.

"You do that, man—real slow." His soft, pleasant voice and half-smile hadn't changed since I'd picked him up, which scared me more than if he'd sprung six-inch fangs.

"You did say Bowdoin Street?" I stalled, hoping the cop would turn around. I reached my hand toward the meter to flick on the trouble lights. "I'll just turn this off."

"Leave it, Jack, and move out slow. I'll tell you where to stop."

I should have demanded an address, of course—they'd told me that the first day: "Never take a fare who won't give you an address; last guy did almost got hisself a new smile two inches lower than the old one." Well, at least I wouldn't be cut.

"Whataya think about the Hinson trade?" I started to back the cab so I could swing the tail into an alley and turn around. I was looking straight at the man as I backed.

"What you talking, man?"

"No lie. Hinson for Jimenez—they just announced it. You didn't see the paper?" I shook my head and stopped the car.

"Hey, man—just keep driving." Again, the little flick of the wrist, reminding me.

"Here—take mine." I picked up the copy of the *Sporting News* that had been lying on the seat next to me, handed it back to the man.

"Don't want that. Just haul ass, hear?"

"Okay, okay. Sorry." I dropped the paper and accelerated,

hard. The red-and-white shot back ten feet until it
slammed into the front of the truck pulling up behind us.
My passenger's head snapped back and his hand flew up.

"Watch it, mutha—"

"Sorry." I shifted into drive, stood on the accelerator, felt
the g-forces press me into the seat as the cab surged toward
the barricade with a shriek of rubber and a fusillade of
flying gravel. I thought I heard shouts, and then I slammed
on the brakes, but not quite soon enough, because the car's
hood limboed under the barricade. Then the crossbar was
flying through the air, up over the hood and down. I got to
see the motorcycle cop's terrified expression for a fraction
of a second before the windshield exploded into a million
beads. Then the wheels locked and we nose-dived into the
pavement, hard enough to get the rear airborn.

The man's face shot over the back of my seat, where it
met my elbow, which I drove into his nose as hard as I
could. A shock like several thousand volts shot up my arm,
and then he was pressed back against his seat and I was out
of the cab, with the gun I'd had under the paper now
pointed at the blood blooming between the fingers pressed
against his nose.

"You think it's sore now, try taking one of these in it." I
was hyperventilating and my right hand was numb. The
trash talk came rolling out as I switched the gun to my left
hand and lowered my aim to the man's chest. "Now push
that gun over or they'll be hosing you out."

I was trying to get control of my breathing when a
nervous voice barked behind me: "Police! Don't move! Put
your hands up!"

It almost startled me into a mistake, but my better
instincts won out and I didn't jump. I did chance a slow
look over my shoulder, which revealed the motorcycle cop,
six feet away in a shooting stance, with his Glock describ-
ing unsteady circles on the small of my back.

"I'm a P.I., Officer. The man in the cab's carrying.
Don't—"

"Put your hands behind your head—now!"

I darted a look at my fare. He had composed himself and was sitting in the middle of the seat, seemingly mindless of the blood dripping from his shapeless nose. The dark glasses were awry but still shrouded his eyes. The half-smile drew the corners of his lips up toward his ears. He'd lowered his hands to his lap and I couldn't see the automatic. I glanced over my shoulder again. "He's got a gun. If I . . ."

Now I could see the sweat on the white face under the helmet, the rapid rise and fall of the patrolman's chest under his black leather jacket, and I knew he was close to panic state. The muzzle of the Glock looked as big as the Callahan Tunnel. "Officer, he'll—"

"I'm not telling you again: get those hands behind your head—now!"

With a last glance at my man, I brought my hands up, slowly, sidling sideways so at least the man in the cab wouldn't have a straight shot at my gut. The corners of my eyes took in the crowd moving uneasily around us, but my attention stayed fixed on the policeman advancing crab-fashion, the big, black automatic leading the way.

Then the hard muzzle probed my neck for the second it took him to snatch my gun from behind my head. "Up against the car!" He gave me a hard shove to get me started.

"That won't be necessary. I can vouch for him."

We both looked around. The dark-molasses voice had come from a tall, black man in a blue blazer with his gold shield hanging over the breast pocket, standing a few feet behind the patrolman.

The uniform looked from me to the new man and back to me. Finally, he nodded but kept his weapon on me. "Yes sir, Lieutenant. But he almost killed me. He—"

"I'm sure he did, Corporal—whatever you say. He's sorry. You *are* sorry, aren't you, Nase?"

"For Chrissake, Bernie—there's an armed man in the back of the cab."

Lieutenant Lawson slowly lowered his head to peer past me into the cab, then straightened and shook his head. "Nope. There's nobody in the car."

"Shit." Forgetting about the patrolman, I stepped over and looked in. A trail of dark drops led across the seat to the open door on the far side. "Damn it—he's gone, Bernie."

"And no tip?" Lawson's face was as impassive as a bowl of Indian pudding.

"Some guy's been jacking cabs out of Codman Square the last six months—company hired me to see if I could take him down. You might send someone looking for a black male about your size, Patriots sweatshirt, nose like a pancake. He's got a gun—little silver automatic."

Lawson looked around the crowd surrounding us and snorted. "That'll set him apart. Oh, well . . . Parker"—he nodded to the patrolman—"call in a backup; see if anyone has any idea where Mr. Nichols's fare got to."

He turned back to me: "When'd you get back in town, Nase?"

"Few months ago." I scanned the crowd, but my man hadn't hung around. "Damn it."

"Heard you were down in Brazil, someplace like that."

"Someplace like that."

"Well, good to have you home. Cab looks like hell, though."

It *had* achieved a distinguished level of distress, even for Roxbury. Pedestrians strolled slowly by, casting nervous looks back and forth between us and the shattered vehicle. Three teen-age girls, arms around each others' waists, brushed back tears long enough to look at me, the cab, and Bernie, then resumed snuffling as they ambled past. A couple slowed, eyed me suspiciously, shook their heads, then hurried on. A placard on the woman's shoulder had GOD BLESS THE CHILDREN printed on it in big block letters. The man carried a piece of white cardboard with LUKE 18:16 scrawled in red crayon.

"What's going on here, Bernie?"

The amused look faded. "They're calling it a rally for life: 'SOS Roxbury'—'Save Our Sons,' something like that. Reverend James, some of the other movers and shakers thought it might help pick folks up after the Whitmore killing."

"Who's Whitmore—a homicide?"

He nodded, slowly. "Kid, bought it a couple nights ago—Purnell Whitmore. Pulled his body out of a Dumpster yesterday, few blocks over."

"How'd he draw the turnout?"

Lawson's face showed something, then recovered its impassive mask. "You mean, what's the big deal, another dead black kid?"

"Come on, Bernie—I meant this is unusual, that's all. That guy in the cab took *me* out, you wouldn't be holding parades."

Lawson let the thought work until the corners of his eyes crinkled. "Maybe a small one, but okay—I overreacted. Thought there wasn't a single damn thing people could do to each other that could get to me anymore, but maybe this one has." He sounded disappointed in himself.

"How'd it go down?"

"Oh, nothing special about that—nineteen-year-old black male with his head stove in, tossed in the garbage. Around Roxbury, that's death by natural causes."

"So what's different about this one?"

"It's who Whitmore was." He shook his head, looked blankly around at the thinning crowd. "*What* he was, I guess I mean. Some kind of symbol, maybe." Lawson's voice trailed off, as though uncomfortable with the abstraction.

"Symbol of what?"

"Ah, I'm getting carried away. Spent too much time listening to Reverend James. What I meant is, this kid was something else, from all I hear. Straight-A student, all-world in every sport you can think of. Went to Latin on a scholarship. Active in the church, good to his mama, just finished his freshman year at Yale, full ride. Yale University—can you believe that?" He shook his head in disgust. "Not your average ghetto crime statistic, see?"

"Not average anywhere."

"You know what someone like that means to someplace like this?"

"I can guess; I can't know."

He thought about that, then shook his head. "No. No, you can't. Well, let's say whoever took this kid out took a pretty big piece out of a lot of other people at the same time." His tone shifted. "I grew up near here, you know?"

"I didn't, no."

"Yeah." He looked around again. The rally must have broken up, because more and more people were streaming by. Some of the people were crying, and there was a lot of loud talk and occasional bursts of laughter, quickly stifled. "Mostly Jewish then. By the time I joined the force, the place was getting toward all black. Now it's there. Some of the kids I grew up with have gone someplace civilized. The ones who've stayed, the unlucky ones—you know what they say to me when I come back here, like tonight?"

I shook my head.

"The mothers introduce me to their kids, tell 'em: 'Officer Lawson a big man with the police. He grew up here but now he live out with the white folk. He even got white folks *working* for him. You be good and stay in school, someday you can grow up and run the police department.' Bet you didn't know I was a role model, did you?"

"They could do worse."

"Lot of 'em will. Lot of the role models around here deal crack, ride a limo, and have a hell of a funeral before they're thirty. That's why losing a Whitmore hurts so much."

"I understand. It's a shame."

"He was *there*, Nase," Bernie said with more passion than I knew he had. "Right there, ready to say to the man, 'Move over, Jack, I'm coming through.' Instead, he gets out in a box, same as the others. People walking around like they been kicked in the head. It's just too damned much."

He blinked, shook his head, then stepped aside as a maroon Lincoln Town Car slid slowly by. A large black man sat in the back seat, his white clerical collar a disembodied halo in the dark. A long arm extended from the window, grasping hands extended by passers-by. I heard the man say, "Bless you, brother" before the car passed.

I shook my head: "Reverend James sure didn't take a vow of poverty, did he?"

Bernie watched as the big car drew away. "Took a lot of quarters in the collection plate, all right, buy that baby." He scratched his head: "Still, I never thought I'd say this, but Reverend James actually made sense tonight. Maybe even helped a little."

"You're kidding."

"I know, I know—it amazed me, too." He laughed to himself, a soft, melodic sound. "But like I say, I had to take my hat off to him tonight—man cooled a *bad* situation."

"I'm glad to hear it; I had him down as just another guilt merchant."

Bernie made a disgusted noise in the back of his throat. "All that jive about 'no justice, no peace,' whipping on the cops every time there's a bust? Yeah—gives me a red ass. But not tonight—tonight he was right on. Told 'em it was time to start tending to their own messes, stop blaming you honkies for everything. Really laid into 'em—stop the doping, stop the killing. Said if they didn't, Whitmore might as well never have lived. Had *pimps* crying, for Chrissake. That kid was carrying a lot of bets, and James said the right things."

"Any leads, Bernie?"

"Nothing."

"Any guesses?"

He pushed his hat back and scratched his forehead.

"Well, it doesn't smell like robbery—almost a hundred bucks in the kid's wallet. Maybe he looked at someone wrong; 'round here, that's a capital offense. I don't know." His voice trailed off.

"How you working it?"

"Homicide's on it, standard stuff. Try to catch some breaks before next week's quota gets filled, pushes Whitmore to the back burner."

"The new patrols helping any?"

"Some. Takes time. Don't forget—until Flanagan took over, Roxbury was treated like a drug dealer's enterprise zone. Can't turn it around overnight. The *Hub* says we're running terror squads as it is."

"The *Hub* thinks you should carry water pistols. Anything to their beefs?"

"Hah! Sometimes I wish." Bernie spat on the pavement. "Flanagan laid it down the day he became commissioner: all the force that's necessary, and not one ounce more. And any cop who crosses the line'd better not look to the department for cover. I've already demoted one guy who didn't believe him, gave some scumbag a little too much help getting into the wagon. None of the excess-force complaints have amounted to a hill of beans. Don't sell as many papers with that story, though."

"That's what I figured."

"I know what I'd like to do—bring the U.N. in, patrol the place like the other Third World countries."

A traffic cop approached. "Pretty well thinned out, Lieutenant. Let 'em through?"

"Sure. Think you can drive that hunk of junk, Nase?"

"Probably. Don't think you'll pick my man up, huh?"

"A brother walking around with a bloody nose and a piece at eleven o'clock on a Friday night in Roxbury? I can round up five of 'em in the next ten minutes, if you're not picky."

"Good point."

"Why don't you head back to Codman Square? Your guy may be ready for a lift again." He stepped back and waved the traffic through.

The Boston Hub
August 15, 1994

ROXBURY CLERGYMAN DECLARES WAR ON CRIME
FOLLOWING WHITMORE SLAYING

BOSTON—In the wake of the unsolved beating death of nineteen-year-old Purnell Whitmore, the Rev. Theophilus James, pastor of Roxbury's African Apostolic Temple Of Glory and a leading voice in African-American affairs, last night demanded that Roxbury organize for "total, unceasing war on crime and those who engage in it." James promised to forge alliances throughout Boston "with all races, creeds, and colors" to assist the police in attacking crime throughout the city.

Speaking at a Washington Park rally following the discovery of Whitmore's body in a Roxbury alley Thursday, the Rev. James told the somber crowd, "As Christ drove the money-changers out of the temple, we can and will drive the killers out of our community."

Whitmore, who attended the Rev. James's church and was on his way to a youth gathering at the church when last seen alive Wednesday night, was an honors student and star athlete home for the summer following his freshman year at Yale University. Whitmore's murder has blanketed Roxbury, a warren of crumbled buildings and blasted lives, in an almost palpable sense of despair. The rally in Washington Park was an attempt to restore a sense of hope to a neighborhood that has little else.

Although there is as yet no evidence that Whitmore's murder was drug-related, the Rev. James directed many of his remarks at Roxbury's endemic drug trade, declaring that "the drug culture is a death culture; drugs have fostered an atmosphere of violence and permissiveness in our community that killed Purnell Whitmore as surely as if a drug dealer's gun had done it. None of us is safe until this scourge is driven out."

Calling upon Roxbury to "take its destiny into its own hands," the Rev. James promised to offer a concrete program for attacking the crime problem within days. He added that crime is a disease that "infects the morally weak and preys on the morally complacent," and said that many African-Americans had for too long refused to acknowledge the role that illegitimacy, broken homes, and personal irresponsibility play in fostering crime.

In the past, the Rev. James has frequently suggested that crime in the African-American community is largely a symptom of underlying economic hardship and racial injustice, but his remarks at the Washington Park rally and afterward indicated a marked change in emphasis. "It's time to stop making excuses," he said. "Crime in Roxbury is about black people killing black people, and black people have to accept their responsibility to stop it in Roxbury and to work with people of all races to stop it in their neighborhoods."

The Rev. James drew sustained applause when he declared, "Whatever my differences with [Boston Police] Commissioner Flanagan in the past, in this war we will serve together." A frequent critic of the Boston Police Department, the Rev. James earlier this year referred to Commissioner Flanagan's controversial "Blue Tornado" street sweeps, directed primarily at inner-city drug traffic, as "night-riders in uniform," targeting African-Americans without reasonable cause and with excessive force. Asked after the rally whether he still held this view, the Rev. James said that he was certain he could work with the commissioner to ensure that the raids were "effective, fair—and frequent."

The rally culminated with the Rev. James leading the crowd in singing "Onward, Christian Soldiers."

chapter 2

A LITTLE MAN WITH AN IMPENETRABLE SOUTH Boston accent was telling me why it was *essential* that Corky McSquiggin become our next registrar of deeds. Or maybe he was explaining why under *no* circumstances should Squiggie McCorkle become our next county recorder. It was hard to tell, because the little man was carrying a lot of ballast and Amrhein's was packed to the rafters with two hundred well-lubricated members of the South Boston Democratic Club, many taken with loud song. It also didn't matter, although I was too polite to tell the little man.

I looked around for Bucky and snagged another Harp from a passing waitress. The little man tapped my lapel with a rolled-up handbill. "On my sainted mother's eyes . . . John Kennedy his own self. That close, he was. So Michael Kilbane—told you about Michael; my da's cousin was deputy registrar of motor vehicles in Medford—he says . . ."

Bucky's cascading mop of black Brillo appeared over the little man's shoulder, capping a howl that could be heard even in Amrhein's: " 'We'll all be *out* together, at the risin' of the moon.' What's the matter, limey? You're not singing." The pint of beer pinched between his thumb and forefinger looked like a shot glass in a normal-size hand.

"Rather talk to a man who talked to a man who stood that close to the late great. Can we go now?"

"Not yet. Want you to meet somebody."

"I spend five nights a week looking for thieves. You've got me surrounded by them on my night off."

"Cute. Now come on." He snagged my elbow, shouldered us through the crowd, past bathrooms and pay phones, past thinning knots of men and scurrying waitresses, until we came to a door a few steps from the kitchen, the percussive clash of dishes punctuating the drone of voices seeping from the room on the other side. Bucky knocked, then murmured something to the face that popped out. After a few seconds, the door opened, a man came out, and the greeter beckoned us in.

The room was a microcosm of the restaurant outside; a half a dozen men were sitting around a table strewn with ashtrays overflowing with butts, glasses, beer bottles, and a liter of Bushmill's, and as many more stood around them. The air was ripe with bodies and booze, smoke and talk. "Behold." Bucky beamed as though he had brought me to the Godhead.

With the door shut behind us, I could hear for the first time that night. Bucky pushed past me as one of the seated men rose to his feet and came around to meet us, big teeth displayed in a weathered, angular face. "Well, I'll be damned—if it isn't Bucky Hanrahan, large as life!"

"Dapper, you ugly old mick!" They clasped hands and tousled each others' hair, two huge men whose bulk seemed to reduce the rest of us to leprechauns.

Bucky pried his hand loose and turned the man to face

me. "Nase, we have here none other than the redoubtable crime fighter and second-best acolyte in the history of St. Mary's Parish, Charlestown—Police Commissioner Francis X. Flanagan. Nason Nichols."

"*Best* acolyte in the history of St. Mary's Parish, Bucky. You lost out when you put the Tabasco on the hosts, turned the mass into a revival meeting. A pleasure, Mr. Nichols." He had a high, light voice for so large a man, though it was said that when he was a beat cop he had only to whisper "I wouldn't" to stop an assault half a block away.

"Nice to meet you, Commissioner."

"Dapper, my friends call me." His mitt swallowed mine. "I'll be wanting you as one of them, you being with Bucky. Come on, then."

He led us around the table to a man as trim and well turned out as the plastic groom on top of a cake, who stood as we approached. "You'll recognize the fella with the cheroot, which he sneaks back here because tobacco is the one thing the fancy folk he hangs around with now don't smoke: our mayor, the most prominent Townie of our time, Conor O'Conor." The commissioner's exuberant gesture took in the slender, black-haired man with green eyes and the best voice in American politics.

"The day a man can't smoke a cigar with his friends in the back room at Amrhein's, that'll be the day I become a Republican. Good to meet you, Mr. Nichols."

It seemed remarkable that a machine of such relatively modest dimensions could produce so luxurious a sound, a rich, baritone purr with just enough edge to cut effortlessly through the aural backwash. He gave me the practiced politician's quick, spare-the-grip handshake, then fixed Hanrahan with an artless smile. His attention seemed to narrow as though Bucky were the only person in the room, and I felt his magnetism as he closed the gap between them.

"By God, Bucky, I haven't seen you since you got out of grade school. Must have been thirty years . . ."

"Too long ago, Conor. Or should I call you Mayor?"

"Back then, you called me twerp; Conor's a big improvement."

"Hey—when you're in the sixth grade at St. Mary's, you call *all* the fifth-graders twerp."

"You're right there. Anyway, great to see you again—and fit as a fiddle, from the look of you." O'Conor took a quick grip on the roll around Bucky's waist.

Bucky sucked in his gut. "You're looking good yourself—long pants become you."

An old priest who'd been hidden behind the crowd gathered around the mayor stuck his head between the two men in front of him and wagged his finger at Bucky. "So that was you, corrupted the communion wafers, was it, Phillip? I might have known. And all these years, I worried they burned like that because I'd harbored lustful thoughts about Sister Mary Immaculata."

"Father John!" Bucky hurried around to the tiny figure and all but picked him up. "I didn't know *you'd* be here. Nase—come meet the best teacher in the history of St. Mary's."

"Wheesh—by the time you were twelve, I'd nothing more to teach you. Now, if I could have gotten you to seminary, the Jesuits would have beaten you into a formidable priest."

Bucky clamped his arm over the old priest's shoulders. "And where would the next generation of Catholics have come from, then, if such a thing as a celibate Hanrahan were even imaginable?"

"How many is it now, Phillip?"

"Seven, Father, last I counted."

"Only seven? Why, you might as well be a Presbyterian." The priest feigned a scowl.

"The night's young, Father."

"And I don't doubt you'll take advantage of it—you always were a hard worker." He smiled paternally at the three men. "You've all worked hard, and done well, and

made me proud. Like my own sons, you are." He patted
Bucky's waist. "Look at you, Phillip—you who wouldn't
learn your times table no matter how many times Sister
Theresa rapped your knuckles—a rich man, with a
banker's belly on you. And Conor, going from class president to mayor to Lord knows what's next. And you, Francis
Flanagan—the day you smacked Dinky Wilson on the
earhole for throwing a spitball at Father Fahey, I knew you
were born to join the force, but I never dreamed you'd
become commissioner."

Flanagan linked his arm over Bucky's, so that the old
priest's head was all that could be seen of him. "And I never
would have if Conor here hadn't pulled me out of the heap,
God bless him. But seeing as how confession's your trade,
Father, I have to admit I clocked Dinky Wilson for *missing*
Father Fahey. Hit your target—always been my motto."

One of the butt boys that attach themselves to politicians
like remoras to sharks called out, "By God, Dapper, you've
hit a few of 'em, too, and that's a fact. I hear they're still
blotting up that fella in Savin Hill."

"Dap heard those ads, figured he'd 'reach out and touch
someone,'" added another.

The others laughing and echoing the line didn't include a
thin, feverish-looking bearded man in a tweed jacket who
was seated at the table. He'd been looking simultaneously
out of place and supercilious since we'd arrived, but now he
just looked as though he'd found a toe in his beer. He
cracked his knuckles, cleared his throat, took the moment
when the buzz died: "Maybe you've hit a few too many
targets, Commissioner. You *and* your men. We're getting a
lot of negative feedback, you know." He glanced at the
mayor out of the corners of his eyes.

Flanagan looked at the man curiously, as though wondering what he was. His big hand smoothed his thin, yellow-
white hair. "Dave, is it?"

The man worked his knuckles, bobbed his head once,
jerkily. "David. David Foster. Community Relations." He

had a prominent Adam's apple that popped through the red
beard as he spoke, disappearing between words.

"Come over from some college, did you?" Flanagan
sounded genuinely curious.

"I taught at BU, if that's what you mean."

"Um." Flanagan ran his hand over the planes of his face,
then sighed. "What's that you're saying, then?"

"We . . . we've had to field a lot of complaints from
community leaders since you started those Blue Tornado
raids. And when you shot that boy in Savin Hill last week, a
Latino delegation called on me and demanded an investigation." His larynx danced in indignant recollection of the
occasion. "No due process at all, they said, and it was no
wonder the department was terrorizing people of color, if
the commissioner himself didn't—"

A flush began on Flanagan's neck and rose like the
mercury in a thermometer thrust into flame. His jaw
muscles bulged under the surface of his face, but his voice
stayed soft and slow. "Hold on there, son."

He only had a few years on Dave and there probably
wasn't another man in the room who could have gotten
away with the *son,* but it sounded right coming from
Flanagan. He rested his knuckles on the table and looked at
the man with more sadness than heat. "Hold it right there. I
think you've been misinformed." He lowered himself into a
chair, carefully folded his hands on the table in front of
him, dropped his voice to little more than a raspy whisper.

O'Conor started to say something, but turned it into a
vague smile as he sank into his own seat and leaned back,
pulling lightly on his cigar. His eyes twinkled, or maybe it
was my imagination.

"I may be commissioner, thanks to His Honor here, but I
was a cop first and I'm still a cop. And when I'm driving
down the street and I see some punk pistol-whipping an old
man, he by God had better not make the mistake of
pointing his piece at me when I tell him to stop. They want

to play with grown-up toys, they'll play by grown-up rules. That's all the 'process' they're due. And that 'boy' you're going on about was twenty-two years old, had half a dozen felony arrests, and already served eighteen months in Walpole. Your 'community leaders' tell you that?"

The man thrust out the beard defiantly. "No, but that really isn't relevant. He had rights. . . ." He looked over at the mayor, but O'Conor had his hands locked behind his head and was staring pensively at the ceiling.

Flanagan's jaw muscles tightened suddenly and the flush that had sunk back below his chin suddenly darkened his entire face. "Rights?" His hand slammed on the table; ashes erupted into the air from the overflowing ashtrays, then drifted slowly earthward. The bearded man's eyes bulged, and he looked down at the floor as though searching for an escape hatch under the table. "You're worried about the fuckin' 'rights' of some animal like that? What about the rights of the old man who had three teeth knocked out in front of his wife? What about—"

"Now, Francis—control yourself. I taught you how to behave. Shame on you." The old priest wagged a scolding finger in front of Flanagan's sharp nose.

Flanagan stopped as abruptly as if he'd been slapped, twisting in his seat like an errant eight-year-old. "Sorry, Father." He nodded to the bearded man and continued in a tight, controlled voice. "Sorry. Father John's right. I apologize. I shoulda said there are a lot of people in that neighborhood sleeping a little better, now that Jorge"—he pronounced it "Hor-gee"—"Gonzalez has gone to his maker. Just like there are a lot of people all over Boston sleeping a little better, now that we got some of the drug scum too busy running to be bothering decent people. You want to worry about rights, how about the right to live without being raped, robbed, killed, or just shit-scared all the time? Don't know if that's in the Constitution, but by God, it ought to be, Dave—*is*, in mine."

He tossed back the last inch in his glass of beer. "Now, I don't know about those 'community leaders'; don't much care, either. Probably live in Cambridge or someplace like that." He shook his head wonderingly.

I live in Cambridge, so I understood how he felt.

Dave swallowed hard, the Adam's apple surfacing in all its glory. "I didn't mean . . . I mean . . . well . . . we need those people, Commissioner. They can make or break a candidacy. They raise the money. You don't seem to . . ." Dave's nervous eyes roamed the mayor's face, but if they were looking for encouragement, all they found was the half-smile that might have meant anything, or nothing.

"Ah, hell, sonny—now you're talkin' politics." Flanagan flipped his hand dismissively, congeniality returning to his voice. "If I understood politics, I wouldn't've been stuck as a zone commander when Conor here appointed me. Like I told him then: you worry about the political stuff, let me worry about getting the dirt off the streets. Remember, Conor?"

The mayor, who'd been working on his cigar through the exchange, exhaled a stream of smoke, his eyes following it upward. "I do, Dap—indeed I do. Let's see"—his tone grew bemused—"I believe your exact words were 'I'm no politician, Conor,' only you said it the way someone would say—begging your pardon, Father—'Sorry, but I don't diddle sheep.' Then you said, in that quiet, diplomatic way of yours, 'If that's what you want, give the job to some sniveling kiss-ass like Moriarty.' I remember it well."

"Did I call him that?" Flanagan looked embarassed as the others hooted. "Well, that's about right, judging from the way he kisses up to me now. And you said, 'Dapper, all I ask is that you run a clean department that enforces the law fairly and follows the rules. You do that, and I'll handle the politics.'"

"That's what I said, all right." O'Conor looked at the shrinking cigar, tapped the ash, shook his head. "My very words. And you said"—the mayor lightened his voice, mimicking Flanagan's lilt nicely—"'Oh, I'll run a clean department. We'll enforce the law fairly, and when we kick ass, we'll kick it by the rules.'" He returned to the burnished register of his natural voice. "Of course, I thought the part about ass-kicking was meant to be a joke."

Everyone except Dave and the mayor were chuckling appreciatively when a knock on the door announced a phone call for Flanagan.

"Feel free to refresh those drinks, gentlemen." The mayor resumed the Teflon bonhomie of a few minutes before.

Tension oozed out of the bearded man's body as Flanagan's back disappeared through the door. "The commissioner just doesn't get it, Mayor. He's liable to do or say anything, ruin our outreach efforts." He sighed, gave O'Conor a palsied smirk. "As I was telling you the other day, our supporters in the suburbs, the minority leadership . . ." He shook his head: "The man's a . . . a"— he stabbed at the air as he searched for the word— "Neanderthal."

O'Conor's eyes narrowed momentarily. "He's a damn fine man, Dave, and a damn fine cop. And that Neanderthal, as you call him, has a hell of a following. Should've heard what they were saying about him at that Commerce Club lunch for Tip Finn the other day."

The tone was light but the message clear, except to Dave: "I just meant, with the governorship coming up, and you—"

A new voice cut in, all adenoidal vowels and swallowed r's: "Exactly. Dapper's doing a hell of a job, and the voters know who put him in." Smelling blood, the fat, bald ward-heeler sitting on the other side of O'Conor flicked the tip of his tongue across his lips, leaving the trace of a smirk in its wake as he leaned toward his prey. "Fact is, Dave, people *like* what Dap's been doing with the department. Like he was sayin' about the beaners bein' happy he blew away that

shitbag, see? That bunch that came around bitchin' about it
to you, they pro'ly said we shoulda got the asshole a job,
didn' want him bangin' on people, so it's our fault, right?"

One of the bit players piped up. "Well, Dap got him one,
all right—as an organ donor."

Dave winced at the chorus of guffaws and looked from
O'Conor to the fat man and back, then blundered on.
"What *you* don't seem to appreciate, uh, Jerry, is that a lot
of . . . important people are fed up with Flanagan's simplistic approach to things. Opinion leaders, I mean, and financial backers, too. It's not just the Gonzalez case. I spent
hours last month—I can't tell you how many—cooling off
that Corey Webster, some of the other activists, after that
drug raid in Roxbury smashed that house to kindling. Why,
they could back Newell—"

"Dave, Dave—get what I'm saying: you can take that
fruitcake Webster, all the other little girls, all the ministers
and professors"—he laid a heavy sneer on the last—"and
you know what? They couldn't get their sisters elected
homecoming queen at a gang bang, they make Dapper an
issue. You want 'outreach'? Dap's right: ninety percent of
the voters in this town—I don't care what they are—
they're tired of getting the shit kicked out of them every
time they go out on the street. We could put Attila the Hun
out there: the average voter—white, black, brown or
yellow—gonna kiss our asses. *That's* outreach."

"Well, maybe you should talk to Webster and some of *his*
supporters and you'd understand why we're concerned."
Dave kept flicking looks at O'Conor but found only the
distracted gaze at the ceiling. "They're—"

Jerry snorted. "They're scared shitless they're gonna
hafta go out and get a real job, people in the ghetto figure
out it isn't white guys turning their neighborhoods into
free-fire zones and it isn't assholes like Webster finally
doing something about it."

"Webster represents—"

"A bunch of rich guilt-suckers jackin' off out in the

'burbs, got no idea what people—our people—is sayin', any more than you do. Get outta that office, stop worrying about a buncha jerks couldn't find their asses with a road map, spend some time in the precincts, you'd know. And not just Southie, neither. More and more, I hear the spoo—I mean the *African-Americans*—sayin' they're seein' cops in their neighborhoods for the first time ever, and they *love* it. That right, Hiram?"

A black man sitting across the table nodded. "Wouldn't surprise me if Dap's maybe the most popular man in my ward. White man, anyway. I wouldn't want to run against him."

Jerry jumped back in. "There you go. Why, just yesterday—"

"You know, Jerry, you're right, although it would be nice if you could stop talking like a sewer smells." The mayor let just enough cigar smoke go to drive the fat man out of the bearded man's face. "I'm hearing the same thing, and I'm not surprised. I appointed Dapper because I knew people wanted firm, fair law enforcement, and that's what Dapper has provided." He looked at the cigar turning between his thumb and forefinger.

The bearded man was routed, and he finally knew it. "I just thought, you know . . . when you asked me the other day . . ."—he looked as though he wanted to swallow the beard—". . . about how the Gonzalez shooting was playing with our supporters, and whether maybe Dapper was . . ." Dave's mumble disappeared into a wad of phlegm. "I thought you meant . . ."

"Sure, Dave. You misunderstood me. Just leave the politics to me, okay?" O'Conor gave him a playful punch on the arm. "Just leave—"

We all looked up as Flanagan's bulk filled the doorway. "I'd better be taking my leave, I'm afraid."

"Anything I should know about, Dapper?" The mayor rose and came around the table, then rested his hand on the commissioner's shoulder.

"I suppose maybe you'd better. You know the Whitmore killing, young man murdered in Roxbury couple nights ago?"

The mayor nodded, adding the politician's reflexive mantra. "Tragic thing."

"Well, Davis and Malone—been working the case—just came up with something not so good, thought I'd better know."

"Yes?"

"They located a witness, a woman who lives near where the body was found. She remembers seeing the boy the night he was killed, outside the alley where he was found."

"And?"

"She saw him go back in there with a man."

"Well, isn't that a lead?"

"It is."

"What's the part that isn't so good?"

Flanagan unfolded the story the way he'd been taught to testify, a fact at a time, and I could see the mayor's impatience as his fingers tightened on Flanagan's shoulder.

"The woman says the man was a police officer. A uniformed, white cop. There was a Blue Tornado sweep going on nearby; we've got to consider the possibility the kid was done by one of the men on the sweep."

"I see." O'Conor dropped his hand but showed no emotion beyond the sudden tightening of his jaw. "What now?"

"I'm heading down to headquarters; we've got to find that man fast." With his hat on it, the top of his head almost brushed the lintel on the way out.

chapter 3

"THANKS, BUCK." I CRADLED THE SCARRED WHITE mug. "Flanagan's quite a guy. Glad we stuck around." Except for the sullen counterman leafing through a *National Enquirer* and a drunk snoring in a corner booth, the all-night joint at Park Square was deserted.

"Huh? Oh, yeah—sure. Thought you'd like that." Bucky loaded another teaspoon of sugar into his coffee and stirred it slowly.

"Bad news, if a cop did the Whitmore kid."

Bucky's scowl deepened. "Terrible. Terrible for the city. Bad enough it happened at all, but if a cop on a Blue Tornado operation did this kid, people could turn around on Flanagan mighty quick." He broke off a piece of Drake's coffeecake, plunged it in the coffee, then inhaled the soggy mass.

"They'll get this guy, whoever he is. A cop had anything

to do with this, he's a dead man. Flanagan's spent too much time trying to convince people that the law doesn't come in colors to let one bad apple ruin it."

"Yeah, but have you been reading the *Hub* editorials? You'd think Flanagan was the Grand Kleagle and the department one big klavern. Think what they're gonna say now."

"That what's bothering you? Hell, the *Hub*'s been baying for Flanagan ever since he sent in the SWAT team against those cultists in Jamaica Plain, left the place looking like Sarajevo."

Bucky pouted. "Good day's work, far as I'm concerned."

"My point exactly, Bucktooth. You and me—most people—said, 'Nice start; just don't quit when you're ahead.' Nobody without initials after his name pays any attention to *Hub* editorials. They're for people who drive Range Rovers, think a criminal is someone who doesn't recycle."

"O'Conor's pretty tight with that set." He began tearing a napkin into tiny pieces.

"Of course he is, Buck. Any young, Democratic pol who doesn't carry a picture of George Wallace in his wallet is going to be pretty tight with that set—he needs their money. So every now and then he gets his ticket punched: that's why now you and your boyfriend can go to City Hall and come out married. Or like last year with the Patriots, when O'Conor wouldn't show up at the Redskins game because the logo insults Native Americans. Remember that?"

"The *Patriots* insult Native Americans. Insult all of us."

"Right, right. Anyway, a little of that stuff and the *Hub* talks about how *caring* O'Conor is and the suburban goo-goo money comes rolling in. Meantime, O'Conor's been doing a pretty good job looking out for the things that really matter to the people who can actually vote in Boston, like not appointing Willie Horton police commissioner and

keeping taxes a little short of total confiscation. So everybody's happy. Besides, Flanagan's a big boy—he can look
out for himself."

"That's where you're wrong—Dapper Flanagan is the
least likely commissioner in memory, precisely because he
has the political skills of a night stick. Shit, he's still the kid
who whaled the snot out of me in the third grade, then kept
mum while Father Clarence beat him silly for causing a
ruckus."

"Why?"

"Why'd he keep quiet?"

"No—why'd he pound you?"

"He said I took his lunch."

"Did you?"

"Promise you won't tell?"

"That's what I thought."

"That's why I worry about the guy—he's got no more
guile now than he did then." He wadded another chunk
into his mouth and started grinding.

"No doubt he's a target for the grievance pros and
reflexive cop haters, but I don't think they'll get him—too
many people are tired of being scammed. God, this coffee's
vile. And how can you eat that thing? I bet it glows in the
dark."

"It's not bad—I may have another. But I have a feeling
Dapper'd better watch his back, that's all."

"'Cause of what that cretin Dave was saying about
negative feedback?"

"Right." He flicked a little napkin ball onto the floor.

"Guy's a meatball. You heard what the fat guy . . .
um . . . Jerry said. Flanagan's a huge asset."

"Yeah, I heard."

"Well, he's right—Flanagan's made the whole city feel
safer, and O'Conor knows that's the hot-button issue these
days."

"O'Conor's a good man, but at the end of the day he's still

a politician. He may know Dapper's popular in the neighborhoods, but that doesn't mean there aren't plenty of
people after Dapper's scalp, people with weight. You listen
to the stuff Reverend James slings?"

"Not if I can help it."

"You should." He tucked his thumbs behind his
lapels and beetled his brows: "'Blue Tornado is black
genocide.' Then there's 'Francis Flanagan is the Bull
Connor of Boston.' And my favorite: 'If the man in blue isn't
black, we don't want him coming back.' That makes sense,
huh?"

"Like the fat guy said, Buck—people aren't buying
slogans anymore." I remembered what Bernie Lawson had
said about James's speech at the Whitmore rally. "I think
maybe even James is beginning to figure that out."

"Nase, you got people out there whose whole careers are
built on hustling guilt. Hell, the commissioner before
Dapper subcontracted security in the public housing projects to the gangs; they got payoffs and he got awards for
creative policing."

"Well, actually he got indicted for creative accounting,
Buck."

Bucky flapped his big hand in my face. "My point is,
Flanagan's cutting into business opportunities for everybody from the drug dealers to the buttholes who get federal
grants to write papers proving criminals are just poor
people with initiative. To say nothing of the suburban
element that thinks Dapper's just too, too *crude* for words."

"Look, even if O'Conor went nuts and wanted Flanagan
out, the law says he can be removed only for cause.
Otherwise, he's in for five years, mayor or no mayor. I don't
think annoying drug dealers and their lobbyists are considered cause. At least not yet."

"You sure about that?"

"Absolutely. And that's why he has more job security
than the pope."

"I only hope you're right." He called to the counterman. "*Garçon—un autre Napoleon, s'il vous plaît.*"

The Boston Hub
Editorial
August 16, 1994

WHITMORE CASE DEMANDS INDEPENDENT REVIEW

An eyewitness's statement that a uniformed, white police officer was the last person seen with homicide victim Purnell Whitmore, 19, murdered in a Roxbury alley Wednesday night, raises serious questions about the Boston Police Department's controversial street-sweep program, "Blue Tornado," questions Bostonians cannot count on the police department to answer.

The street sweeps, introduced last year by newly appointed Police Commissioner Francis X. "Dapper" Flanagan, supplement conventional patrols in high-crime areas with strike forces taken off administrative duties. Driving unmarked cars, Blue Tornado teams sweep down on concentrations of suspected drug traffickers, forcing them to flee or face interrogation and possible arrest. The object of the program, according to Commissioner Flanagan, is to raise the pulse rate of the drug community: "We'll make a buy a natural high," as the commissioner put it in his distinctive way.

The street sweeps have produced numerous arrests, and many residents report the virtual disappearance of drug sales in areas long plagued by dealers. This can only be welcomed.

What cannot be welcomed are the reports of excessive force used by police involved in the arrests, and any program that encourages the police—overwhelm-

ingly white—to view two African-Americans on a
street corner as a crime waiting to happen is a formula
for police brutality.

Corey Webster, director of People of Color Advan-
cing Together, or POCAT, an alliance of local African-
American and Hispanic advocacy groups, said that the
program "targets people of color because of their color,
and is no different than the racial cleansing in Bosnia."
The Rev. Theophilus James, long a voice for the
African-American community, warned last year that
Blue Tornado turned "BPD into KKK." In a cruel irony,
Whitmore was on his way to a youth gathering at the
Rev. James's church the night he was killed.

Regrettably, Commissioner Flanagan has derided
these concerns, dismissing POCAT as "a three-piece
band with only one tune," and calling the Rev. James
"a thirty-minute mouth with a thirty-second message."

When Commissioner Flanagan instituted Blue Tornado, this newspaper said it would withhold judgment
until it could be determined whether the street sweeps
were both fair and effective: "Laudable as the goal of
stemming the plague of drug-related crime may be,"
we wrote then, "it must not be allowed to serve as the
basis for indiscriminate police harassment of the
African-American community. Commissioner Flanagan is a blunt-spoken policeman of the old school. All
too many African-Americans remember that school,
and want nothing to do with it unless the commissioner takes steps to ensure that Blue Tornado is devoted to
getting criminals off the streets, not black men—
contrary to what many of our police believe, they're
not the same thing."

Now, tragically, it appears all too likely that our
worst fears may have been realized. It is imperative
that Mayor O'Conor appoint an independent investiga-

tive body to determine whether Blue Tornado and other Flanagan initiatives have resulted in a rogue police force's oppressing, not protecting, minority citizens. Should it be determined that a police officer involved in a Blue Tornado operation was implicated in the death of this fine young man, Commissioner Flanagan will share the guilt for releasing demons he was unable, or unwilling, to control.

chapter 4

I TORE OUT THE COUPON GOOD FOR THIRTY PER-
cent off on steroid-engorged chicken and tossed the Star
Market flyer on the floor. I shoved the sample tube of
toothpaste back in the mailbox and riffled the bills. I was
about to put them back, too, when I saw the letter stamped
with a comic-opera picture of a beribboned dictator and
recognized the handwriting. An invisible hand grabbed my
esophagus and shut it down hard.

It was an airmail envelope, thin and crinkly, and all I
could think was that I'd done so well to forget and now I'd
have to start all over and I wasn't ready, which was why I
was going out to serve summonses at one hundred dollars
per and it wasn't fair of her, not fair at all, not with all the
work I'd done to get over it, so many memory cells trashed
in the effort. I was tempted to tear it up and toss the pieces
onto the rest of the litter, but of course I didn't, but I didn't
read it, either, because Manny had given me another bunch

of summonses to serve and if I got involved in the chase enough, I'd found, I didn't have to think about it and maybe it would still work, even with the thin, crinkly letter with the absurd stamp and that topsy-turvy handwriting in my pocket, the same as the writing on the other letter, the one I *had* torn up but hadn't been able to evict from the memory cells, no matter how many times I flushed them out with alcohol. The one that began *Dear Nase, Wouldn't it be better if . . .*

The first customer on my list was easy enough, a Greek in a garage on Huntington Avenue who filled my tank and wiped the scratched windows and even offered to check the air, then stood wiping his hands with a greasy rag while I fumbled for my wallet. "Nice service. You Nikos?" I pointed at the name over the door.

"That's me." He was so proud.

"Here." I handed him a ten, he handed me my change.

"And here's your change, Nikos."

"Huh?" He looked down at the paper: "You are commanded . . . fail not upon penalty of . . . such and such a time, such and such a place, grind you up, spit you out, such a business, welcome to America . . .''

"I think your kids want you to write. Checks, you know? 'Bye.''

The next one was a little trickier, a huge woman in Roslindale who came after me with a leg of lamb when she saw I hadn't really brought her a present from the Lottery Commission. Her boyfriend made the mistake of trying to grab what he thought was his ticket out, and I fled while she was escalloping his head with dinner.

I did two more before lunch, an Italian sub on Brighton Avenue. I had extra hot peppers, but they didn't help, and the oil on my fingers left more and more fingerprints on the thin paper as I sat in the car and turned it and imagined her fingers on it, and then I tore it open and got it wrong so that I had to turn it again to read it.

Dear Nase:

No, I guess it wouldn't be better after all. At least it hasn't been for me. If it has been for you, then I'm . . . happy, I was about to write, but that's not true. I want you to be happy, but I want to be, too, and I'm not. Frankly, if you are, I'm even more unhappy—furious, if you get right down to it. Remember—I warned you I wasn't the selfless helpmate type.

The problem, as I see it (and I'm the educated one), is this: you're hell to live with, and hell to live without. If I'm living with you, I can always live without you; if I'm living without you, I can't be sure I'll always be able to live with you. Ergo . . .

I screwed up, big time, and I'm awfully, awfully sorry. Let's try it again—only this time as though we meant it. I promise: I do. And if you do, too, then we can both say I do. You know what that means—I hope.

Love,
Rachel

I slammed my hands against the wheel, again and again, until they were numb. Then I smoothed the paper, folded it carefully, and put it in my pocket. There were six more summonses in the bundle, and plenty more where they came from, and with enough of them, and the other jobs, I might not have to think much. Now I had so much more to think about, and I really didn't want to.

The next victims were child's play, docile targets accepting with bovine resignation the indignity of a stranger walking into their workplace or home and thrusting a court paper in their hands, just one more steaming heap on the treadmill of their lives, but they were scattered all over town and I ate up time in traffic. By seven, I was ready to knock off for dinner before reporting to the cab company, but since I was in Allston anyway, I couldn't resist taking a run at the Quark.

The Quark—a.k.a. Norman Wilkins—had, in a few short

months, become a legend in Boston process-serving circles. The FBI had Abu Nidal; we had the Quark.

Wilkins' celebrity began simply enough. He had a wife; she discovered that she was not the first and that he had not observed the amenities before she became the second. The two Mrs. Wilkinses, concluding that tenancy in common was not a viable state, asked the courts to sever their respective interests. The popular press found this mildly amusing and, in reporting it, provoked yet another woman sporting the Wilkins surname to come forward and proclaim that no, she held the dower rights.

The several Mrs. Wilkinses, engaging counsel, sought Mr. Wilkins's attendance in a domestic-relations tribunal, but he proved rather more retiring than would have been expected of one so recently at ease in three simultaneous conjugal relationships. Wilkins disappeared, absconding with several of the marital assets, including Bootsie, a gray cat with white paws, the love child of Wilkins and Wife III, who was not pleased to learn that the missing feline bore Wilkins's pet name for Wife II.

So it happened that three lawyers, laboring under the burden of an archaic Massachusetts law requiring personal service of divorce papers, came to engage the cream of Boston's process-serving community.

Wilkins, a manufacturer's representative otherwise distinguished only by surpassing ordinariness, proved, against all odds, elusive prey. The good gray Wilkins slipped the net, week after week, earning for himself the sobriquet devised in frustration by one of my competitors, a moonlighting high-school physics teacher: the Quark, a subatomic particle, existing only as a hypothesis.

He was a mirror's image in a mirror, the season's first snowflake, a sense of déjà vu, a transient memory, the echo of a whisper, a politician's promise. There were holographs easier to grasp, moments of ecstasy more readily retained.

So spectral was the Quark, so sensitive his radar, that process servers boasting no more than a sighting endured the skepticism awaiting those claiming contact with a Yeti. The Quark was the ultimate quarry; immortality awaited the man who served the Quark. I meant to be that man. It was long past making any economic sense, but it distracted me, and I needed distraction, now more than ever.

For a modest bribe, a contact at New England Telephone had given me three months' new listings, and I'd gotten the criss-cross directory at the library and cross-checked every name with the initials N. W. I'd found a possibility in one Norton Wilson, newly resident at 167 Antwerp Street, Allston.

Allston, a tired, lower-middle class expanse of three-deckers and low-rent apartments, was prime Quark cover: drab, faceless, and—what drew me to Norton Wilson— home to Mother Quark, to whom he was obsessively devoted, according to the daughters-in-law. The widow Wilkins resided at 32 Holton Street—which happened to be right around the corner from Antwerp.

Oh, we'd all staked out 32 Holton, of course, the little band of brothers one step above repo men, shivering in the rain and trading smokes while praying for Quarkly filial feeling to relieve us of our posts. I'd had enough of that, and enough of dogging Mother Wilkins, whose taxi rides, MBTA trips, and disappearances in department stores could have served as a CIA training film. I was ready for extreme measures.

I pulled up in front of the decrepit bulk of number 167 a little before eight. The mailboxes told me that N. Wilson occupied apartment 3-A. I went back outside and looked up: light streamed out of one set of third-floor windows; those on the other side of the building were dark. A woman came out the front door and I slipped back in and went through the foyer door before it swung shut. I climbed the steps to the third floor.

Apartment 3-A was the one showing no light under the door. I listened for a few seconds; not a sound. I crossed the

hall to apartment 3-B and knocked. Cabbage smells and
game-show cheers came through the door. Bolts shot, the
door opened, a suspicious, bloodshot eye peered through
the crack the chain allowed. "Yeah? What is it?"

"Sorry to bother you, ma'am, but I'm looking for Norton
Wilson."

"Who?"

"Norton Wilson. Haven't seen Nort in years, but I was
passing through and thought it would be fun to surprise
Nort and Tina."

"Maybe that fellow lives over there." She pointed through
the crack with her chin whiskers. "Don't know about no
woman—ain't seen one."

"Hmm, that's odd. Say—there were a couple of N.
Wilsons in the book. This a tall, skinny guy, blond hair?"

She sucked her teeth and eyed me up and down. " 'Bout
tall as you. Fatter. Ain't got much hair left. Don't look
blond."

Could be, could be—the last wedding photo showed a
mousy man my height, two-fifty easy, a Rogaine candidate.
"Heck, I bet this isn't the Nort Wilson I know at all.
Thanks, ma'am—knew I shoulda called first."

I went back outside and circled the building; an old-
fashioned exterior fire escape passed one of 3-A's windows.
There was good cloud cover and the twilight left deep
shadows across the back of the building, so I pulled down
the swing-up ladder and scrambled up to the third-floor
landing and peered through the two inches of window not
covered by a shade.

It was too dark to see anything in the apartment, so I
chanced my pencil flashlight, but the glass reflected it and
it was worse than useless. I flicked it off and an ephemeral
wisp brushed across the glass, no more than a fleeting flash
of white. I turned the light on again, playing it over the
glass, and the specter followed it faithfully. And then the
beam caught something yellow, and it stared at me: a nice,

yellow eye, two inches from the glass, trying to help its
owner decide where the little star that was so much fun to
chase with the little white paw had come from.

Norman/Norton had latched the window, so I said good
night to Bootsie and returned to earth. If I hadn't found the
Quark's lair, I'd found someone who was trying out for the
lead role in *The Norman Wilkins Story*. I looked at my
watch; time to go. I'd be back.

The Bay State Advocate
Editorial
August 17, 1994

HEED OUR RISING VOICES, MISTER MAYOR

A coalition of community leaders gathered yesterday in
the Dorchester headquarters of POCAT, or People of
Color Advancing Together, and called on Mayor
O'Conor to dismiss Police Commissioner Francis X.
Flanagan and appoint an independent citizens' panel to
investigate the circumstances of last week's savage
murder of nineteen-year-old Purnell Whitmore of Roxbury.

Whitmore's battered body was found last Thursday
in a Roxbury alley, near the house where he lived with
his mother, Rose. When last seen alive, he had been on
his way to a youth fellowship outing that was to leave
from Roxbury's African Apostolic Temple of Glory
church, shortly after a Blue Tornado raid swept down
on a nearby gathering. A police spokesman acknowledged that a witness claimed to have seen Whitmore
pushed into the alley by a uniformed policeman the
night he was killed, prompting POCAT's Corey Webster to convene the meeting of prominent black and
Hispanic leaders to demand Flanagan's ouster.

It has long been obvious that inner-city crime reflects a despair that only a comprehensive jobs program can relieve. Flanagan's contemptuous retort? "I've got a jobs program—making license plates at Walpole State Prison. You want some twenty-five-year-old gang-banger doing brain surgery, I know some brains they can start on." This is not the man to lead the department into caring, community policing.

Blue Tornado treats the symptom, not the cause. With the murder of Purnell Whitmore, apparently the victim of a monster encouraged by Commissioner Flanagan's inflammatory rhetoric and indifference to the warning signs, it should be clear to all that the wrong hand is steering the police department.

Heed our rising voices, Mr. Mayor: Commissioner Flanagan must go—now!

chapter 5

HANRAHAN WAS WEDGED BEHIND A BACK TABLE
at Jacob Wirth's, his nose buried in the *Clarion*. I elbowed
past the throng of suits bracing for the commute home and
slid in across from him.

"Evening, Buckleberry. You're looking in the pink." His
spheroid face was flushed a deep red; he'd been reading
something that disagreed with him.

"Unbelievable. Un-fucking-believable."

"Sorry, but I told you I had to pick up my check from the
cab company. They were a little upset—seemed to think I
owed them for some body work. Took longer than I expected."

"Not you, idiot—this!" He pushed the paper across to
me and stabbed a forefinger into the story he'd been
reading: QUINCY WOMAN, 26, PRUNES SLEEPING MATE'S
PRIVATES.

The first paragraph captured the essence:

Mary Boylan of Quincy has been charged with assault for attacking Patrick O'Malley's groin with a pair of garden shears while O'Malley, an unemployed forty-three-year-old dock worker, was asleep on a couch in the house they share at 147 Prospect St. "Now I'll always know where it is" was Boylan's only explanation. O'Malley was taken to Quincy City Hospital for treatment. Neighbors report that Boylan and O'Malley have been living together for about two years but have had a troubled relationship.

I pushed it back. "So? Friends of yours?"

"It's a feature story! The market takes the biggest tumble in three years, the Isros and ragheads about to go at it again, and they run a little Irish courtship ritual as a feature. Unbelievable. Un-fucking-believable."

"What do you expect, buy that rag? Want to read about World War III, get the *Times*." I signaled to the old waiter. "Coffee regular. And a Bratwurst. Two. You having another beer?"

"Shit." His full lips writhed as they replayed the story.

"That's a yes, waiter." He shambled off. "Why do you buy that garbage, gets you all stirred up?"

He shook his head. "I dunno, Nase. It's like I've got an obsessive-compulsive disorder. I keep thinking, maybe this'll be the day I'll pick up a Boston newspaper and there'll be this big lead: HARVARD PROF'S SHOCKING CLAIM: HUB CITY PART OF LARGER WORLD."

"Never happen; Harvard's the last place anybody'll buy that. They think Dukakis is a recount away from the White House."

He threw the paper on the table. "Yeah, you're probably right. What a town, huh? What do you think of this commission O'Conor's set up?"

"What commission?"

"You live on this planet or just visiting? The group he's appointed to look into Flanagan's program. You know, whether it had anything to do with the Whitmore killing, whether the cops are running around like the Mongol horde. You didn't see that?"

"I sort of lost interest in the news after Nixon resigned."

"Here." He unfolded the paper and handed me the front page. The inch-high headline, which passed for dignified restraint in the *Clarion*, announced: BLUE MURDER?, followed, in only slightly smaller type, by an explanation: RELUCTANT MAYOR SETS PANEL TO INVESTIGATE CHARGES OF MINORITY MISTREATMENT BY POLICE— OFFERS FLANAGAN STRONG SUPPORT.

A subhead wrapped it up: POLICE COMMISSIONER FLANAGAN UNDER PRESSURE WHILE RIGHTS LEADERS HAIL MOVE; PANEL HEAD KERSHAW PROMISES QUICK BUT THOROUGH INVESTIGATION.

"So? A little diversion for the chattering classes. Flanagan'll come out smelling like a rose." I handed back the paper.

Bucky glowered at the offending story, as though the tabloid itself had risen up and assaulted him. "O'Conor should have told those hyenas baying after Dapper to take a hike, but I guess he probably had to throw them this bone. You know what I think?"

"No, but I bet I will."

"I think this is O'Conor's way of squelching those dildos, once and for all. And do you know why I think that?"

"No, but I bet I will."

"I think our mayor's made sure this thing leaves the loonies speechless." He leaned back, folded his hands across his belly, and smirked like a man who's seen everybody's cards.

"All right, I'll bite—what's that mean?"

"Well, first of all, you see that Eliot Kershaw's heading this freak show?"

"So? He's supposed to be a straight shooter."

"Well, between us, I think the circuits may be starting to short, but, yeah—he's straight. That's why O'Conor wanted him heading it—absolute credibility. But O'Conor's bought a little insurance, case the crazies are too much for the old boy. Lean over." He pushed his nose toward the middle of the table and dropped his voice to a whisper.

"I handle some investments for the Kershaw family trust. I brought some papers by for Kershaw to sign this morning, and who should drop in but Tip Finn, the real-estate developer. Seems Kershaw's firm does his legal work."

"And nobody thought to call me? Bucky, what are you saying?"

"I'm getting there. Anyway, afterward Finn gave me a lift back to the office. Quite a guy, you know? Self-made rich, grew up in Southie, tough as nails. Got a trophy second wife who's been working him into the smart set, except he isn't completely housebroken yet. He thinks appointing Flanagan was the best thing O'Conor's done, and he writes a lot of checks."

"Your kind of man, Buck. Now—"

"Not happy O'Conor gave in and appointed this commission. Major-league pissed off, in fact. Thinks it's divisive and bad for business. Said just when we'd finally gotten people thinking about moving back into town, a bunch of crackpots want to give the asylum back to the lunatics."

"No argument there."

"No, and he let O'Conor know it, too."

"Well, if he bankrolls O'Conor, he'll get a listen."

"Yeah, but Finn's not the kind of guy who's content just being listened to. He's used to getting his way."

"What do you mean, 'getting his way'?"

The whisper grew sibilant. "Like, make sure this panel doesn't get hijacked by the hand-wringers O'Conor has to put on if it isn't going to look like a rubber-stamp for Flanagan."

"How's he going to do that?"

"This is on the Q.T., right?"

"No, Buck—soon as I leave, I'm selling it to *Inside Edition*. Hurry up, will you?"

"Okay, okay." He leaned even closer. "Seems O'Conor's been after Finn to do a showpiece project someplace downtown. You know—City Hall helps line up some HUD money, developer throws in a little, then he takes a bunch of vacant land, puts in condos, few subsidized townhouses, retail, O'Conor trumpets the thing as evidence that *this* Democrat will work with business to revitalize the inner city. O'Conor wants this *real* bad. Finn finally figured things were squared away enough, announced last week he was ready to go."

"So what?"

"I told you Finn is used to getting his way. Fifteen minutes after he heard about this panel, he was on the horn to O'Conor: if he wants this project, to say nothing of Finn's financial backing in the future, the Kershaw Commission'd better give Flanagan a blessing that'd do Billy Graham proud, and quick."

"And O'Conor said?"

"And O'Conor said not to worry, he had had to do something to placate some of his supporters, but he had no doubt Flanagan's administration would come through with flying colors. And Finn, who didn't drop out of high school and make several million dollars letting guys tell him the check's in the mail, said, sorry, he needed a little more comfort than that."

"And he got it?"

"My question exactly. And Mr. Finn's reply was, 'Let's just say Conor's not leaving this to the weak sisters.'"

"Meaning?"

"Meaning O'Conor decided Tip Finn ought to be one of the panel members. One vote already counted, you might say." He leaned back, preened, waved for the waiter.

"Nice business, politics."

"Hey—you think the ranters and ravers O'Conor's gonna have to cast in this sit-com are ready to give Dapper a fair shake? Finn says Reverend James is going to be on it, for Chrissake!"

"That's hardly surprising, Buck—the kid was in his church, and the guy's got a following. You want O'Conor to pack it with the NRA board of directors?"

"What I'm saying is, the antis'll come at this like Stalin at a purge. Finn just adds a little counterweight."

"I suppose. Why is Finn telling you this?"

"Wants me to come in on his new deal. I told him I was a little worried about this Whitmore thing, didn't want to put money into downtown real estate and then have the town go up in flames so nobody wanted to come within twenty miles of it. That opened him up."

"Where's he putting this project?"

"Hah! *That* the man *isn't* telling."

"What's the big secret?"

"You kidding? Any leaks before he's got the land locked up and the price goes out of sight." Bucky leaned back and ruminated. "I knew that, your old buddy Buckster would be out quietly going into the real-estate business, be there waiting when Tip came around. Right now, it's a bunch of vacant lots somewhere; he can have his agents sneak around and grab the land for a song."

He folded his arms, smug smeared all over his face. "I like Dapper's chances a whole lot better now; he may not know how to cover his back, but O'Conor sure does. How you doing?"

I shrugged. "I'm living."

"Any word from . . . ?" He arched his eyebrows.

"Um." I spilled salt into a pile on the table, then tried to get the shaker to stand on edge in it. It fell over. I pushed the salt back together and tried again.

"'Um'? What's 'um'?"

"'Um' is 'I got a letter.' Don't want to talk about it. Damn—I almost had it."

"A letter? Well, what'd she say?"

"Nothing. I don't want to talk about it."

"Nothing? You don't hear from her in what—months?

Then she sends you a letter that says—nothing? Come on, tell ole Uncle Buckster. She wants to get back together?" He leered like a sailor with a lap full of dancer.

"Something like that." The shaker hung for a second, then fell on its side. "They must use crummy salt here."

"Hey, Nase—that's great! I knew she'd come around. When's she get here?"

"It's not that simple."

"Whataya mean, 'It's not that simple'? Rachel's the best thing to happen to you since you met me. You got antsy, fucked it up, now she's ready to give you another shot. You take it, PDQ. End of analysis. QED." He took another pull. When he lowered the stein, a frothy white doughnut ringed his mouth.

"She's talking about marriage, Buck." It had to have something to do with the way the crystals lined up.

"Of course she's talking about marriage. I didn't think she was looking for a pen pal. And you'd better jump at it." Bucky swiped at his lips, then looked around again for the waiter. I had half the salt out of the shaker and it still wouldn't stay put.

"That's a *huge* step. Rachel was right—I probably *am* scared of permanence."

"All men are scared of permanence. It's too much like death, which is the most permanent thing there is, except maybe a congressman. Women like it 'cause they got ovaries."

"Huh? What does . . . never mind. The thing is, another person complicates your life. I want a life without complications." The shaker clattered to the floor. "Fact is, I've even been thinking about getting out of the P.I. business. Too many complications." I blew the salt across the table into Hanrahan's lap. "I can hang a spoon from my nose. Want to see?"

The waiter arrived and slammed down my plate and Bucky's stein.

"Get out? What the hell would you do?"

"I dunno. I kind of like driving a cab; maybe I'll go on hacking. Be an honest working man for once." I slathered dark mustard over the Brats and bit in.

"Working man? Driving a cab? Why not open a worm ranch?"

"Cleared two hundred bucks last week. Over and above the P.I. money."

"Two hundred bucks! You signed up for food stamps yet? You're going to get married, have kids, you've got to make some money."

"Exactly my point. That's a *major* complication."

"What's the problem? You can make a decent buck doing investigations."

"Investigations? Serving as a glorified peeping Tom is more like it. Or how about bait—stake me out, wait to see if something comes to eat me? That's what I've been doing, and now I'm even out of that."

A canny look crept into Bucky's little black eyes. "You don't troll for carp if you want to eat salmon, Nase. You've been fishing in the wrong waters. Now, I've got a—"

I cut him off. "How are Deidre, the kids?"

"Great, great. Moira got into MIT. Listen, I—"

"Hey, that's terrific. She's happy?"

"She's thrilled. Look, the reason I called you is—"

"You're not?"

A big black cloud settled on Bucky's head, chasing away whatever it was he'd been trying to tell me. "Twenty-five K, man—after-tax dollars? Six more kids in the pipeline? Time to start selling blood."

"Buckmaker—my only other contact with new money peddles her ass at conventions; don't tell me you're hurting?"

"Bet she's giving quantity discounts. Business is in the crapper, buddy. The greedy little swine I used to keep in BMWs are just hoping to hang onto the family minivan today. The market hasn't been any fun since all the real players went to jail."

"So you needed to lose weight. Give Moira my congratulations, will you?"

"Give them to her yourself. Come by for dinner. They all ask about you. Now, about this idea of mine—"

"Thanks, Buckeroo. Maybe soon. One of the cab companies is looking for night drivers, so it may be a little tough. Speaking of which"—I glanced at the clock over the bar—"I've really got to be going, want to get one of those jobs."

"Wait a minute, wait a minute." His slab hand shot out and grabbed my windbreaker. "I got something I want to talk to you about. Another job. A good job—your entrée to the big time."

"What kind of job?"

"An investigator's job—what else?"

"Buck, really—I just got fired from one of those, and I think that's it. Now I have to—"

"Just one minute, Nase. Come on."

"All right, all right. One minute." I sat on the edge of the booth, ready to bolt. "But I don't want another P.I. job."

"Yeah, yeah, right. He picked up the paper. "Bet you missed this part." He cleared his throat and read:

The mayor is expected to name the remaining commission members within a day. In a brief appearance on City Hall's steps at noon, the mayor said, "I intend to appoint respected community leaders from a variety of backgrounds and perspectives. They will retain experienced, professional investigators to review the facts dispassionately and report their findings to the commission, which will base its recommendations on those facts.

He looked up from the paper. " 'Experienced, professional investigators'—get it now?"

"Yeah, I get it now. I told you, I'm looking for a midlife career change. All the rage—you ought to try it. Now I'm out of here. Thanks anyway."

"Come on, Nase. Kershaw, Finn, any other sane people O'Conor appoints—they could use some help; good, responsible staff, make sure everything's done up right."

"I meet any detectives like that, I'll tell them they're hiring."

"Kershaw trusts my judgment. I bet he'd leap at the chance, have a guy with your experience working for him."

"You're right, the meat's got to be starting to spoil, he trusts your judgment. And are you just faking *your* senility? I keep telling you, I don't *want* to play detective anymore. Makes driving a cab seem the last word in gracious living."

"This would be different. Upscale, civilized conditions. You'd be working in the open, for the good guys. No heavy lifting. Make a nice paycheck, polish the résumé. Open an office on Beacon Street afterward: 'N. Nichols—discreet inquiries for the carriage trade.' Think of the ink, the exposure."

He gave me his sincere, innocent look. I'd seen it on our old Airedale, over a fresh pile in the middle of the living-room rug. "Okay, I get it: what's in it for you, Buck?"

"In it for me? Why does there have to be something in it for me? I just—"

"Five seconds, I'm out of here."

"Aw, come on—"

"Four. Three . . ."

"All right, all right. I just thought . . . maybe, if you were working for this group, you could sort of . . . let me know how it was going from time to time. Know what I mean?" He gave me a nice look at his big, white choppers, upper and lower.

"No, I don't know what you mean. You mean leak what's

coming out? Why? What kind of scam are you running?"

"Aw, Nase. Just want to know everything's on the up and up." His mouth opened, formed a word, but no sound came out and it snapped shut. He shook his head. "I'm just trying to get you a nice spot of work." Now he sounded wounded.

"Just trying to get me indicted for impeding a public investigation. Forget it."

"Come on, Nase; it isn't like that. Anyway, this city needs Dapper. It doesn't need some inquisition tearing apart the police department so they can put Sister Souljah in charge. You can help make sure that doesn't happen—be doing the Lord's work."

"This city needs an atom bomb attack. You need a high colonic. Good night." I slid out of the booth.

"Nase, come on." He got a panicky expression. "I sort of . . . well, I sort of tried it out this afternoon? How's it going to look, I can't deliver?"

"'Tried it out'? What does that mean, 'tried it out'? What'd you do?"

"Called Kershaw, said I had this friend, lot of experience, could maybe help with this investigation. Got Finn to call, too. Kershaw seemed interested, wanted to meet you for an interview."

"He seem interested in the idea I was going to be your mole?"

"Well, I didn't mention that part."

"I'm gone." I tossed down a ten. "Any change, hang on to it—consider me one of your investors."

"Come on, man—I pitched you pretty good. What am I going to say if—"

"The rosary, meatball. Then your kids drop out of school to work in the mills, and your suicide gets a half inch in the back of the *Weekly Hibernian*. Good night."

"Ahh, come on . . . " Bucky's whine followed me all the way to the door.

The Boston Clarion
Editorial
August 19, 1994

DAPPER HAS 'EM SCARED

The croissant-and-quiche set is howling for the head of
Police Commissioner Dapper Flanagan. The commish's
crime? Simply that in less than two years, he's taken a
dispirited police force, crippled by court rulings and
racial and gender quotas, and given it back its spirit.
This makes the country-club crowd nervous—cops
aren't supposed to feel good about their work, 'cause
they're the "instrument of oppression."

The primary vehicle for rebuilding the department's
morale—and standing in the community, which deter-
mines any police department's morale—has been
Dapper's aggressive campaign against the criminals
who dog the lives of those too poor to escape to the
suburbs and sit behind electric fences, chattering about
the "root causes" of crime. In Mattapan and Roxbury,
Dorchester and Southie, people know the cause of
crime: criminals. They know how to reduce crime, too:
take away the job satisfaction. That's what Dapper's
been doing.

Dap's initiatives have included his reintroduction of
foot patrols in the inner city, and the Blue Tornado
program, sending unmarked cars on roving patrols
through high-crime areas. When they see a deal going
down, no matter how small, they act—fast and hard.
The directive Dapper sent down: there will be no
"minor" drug trafficking, no sanctuaries where the
police won't go, no place where drug dealing will be
treated as business as usual. In other words, the law
will be enforced in poor—and especially black—

neighborhoods, not just in the rich, white enclaves where private security patrols protect the tongue-cluckers from the consequences of the policies they inflict on others.

Dapper Flanagan is a simple man who sees life in simple terms. As he said when he first announced Blue Tornado, "Drugs have victimized a lot more Americans than Hitler ever did, but if we'd fought Hitler the way we fight drugs, we'd all be speaking German. We're in a war—it's time to start fighting back."

While this logic is a little tough for the average professor to follow, it makes sense to normal people, which is why the commissioner's program has been the subject of national attention. It works. Streets that crawled with dealers a year ago are clean now, and the crimes that they breed in their wake like rats bring disease are down as well. Rats on the run can't stop to bite.

The dealers don't like this, don't like having to cower in dark buildings, don't like never being able to breathe easy, and yes, don't like getting their heads broken when they resist—because Dapper made it clear up front that in this war, nothing short of unconditional surrender will do. "They can come in on their feet, or they can come in on their faces—but they're coming in," as Dapper put it.

Naturally, the dealers and their allies—the academics, the ACLU, and the congenitally sensitive—haven't given up without a fight. Almost from the first day Dapper took over, the charges of "police brutality" and "excessive force" have been flying furiously. After all, a good offense is the best defense. Yet after each of these charges has been reviewed through the department's administrative process, not a single one has held up; they've all been the hollow whine of losers who've finally met their match.

Dapper Flanagan thinks it's fine the drug dealers are

unhappy. The people of Roxbury, Dorchester, South Boston, and Charlestown think it's fine the drug dealers are unhappy. Just about anybody who lives where the thugs feed thinks it's fine the drug dealers are unhappy. In fact, we wouldn't be surprised if Blue Tornado and his other programs haven't made Dapper Flanagan—an unknown career policeman when the mayor wisely promoted him from the ranks to the top job—just about the most popular public figure in Boston, at least now that Larry Bird's retired.

This week, following the tragic death of young Purnell Whitmore of Roxbury and reports that a witness had placed a man who may have been a policeman—as yet unproven—at the scene, Mayor O'Conor had a chance to stand up to those eager to seize on any pretext to drive a wedge between the police and minorities by expressing his confidence in the integrity of the police, who are as eager as anybody to run this lead down; by instead appointing the Kershaw Commission to rehash old charges and air new ones, he has bought temporary peace on the left at the price of a grievous blow to public confidence in our safety forces.

Mayor O'Conor—whom we've endorsed in each of his campaigns and whom we'd like to endorse in the next one—had better stop listening to those hand-wringers from Wellesley and Cambridge he sometimes hangs around with. It's one thing to take their money—elections are expensive—but it would be a fatal political error to take their advice. After all, Mister Mayor, we know where we can find a pretty good alternative, if you go soft on us.

Listening, Dap?

chapter 6

"COME ON, NASE—KERSHAW SAID HE'D SEE YOU right away. Let me set it up."

"I told you, no! I don't want another investigator's job, and I especially don't want one with O'Conor's puppet show. I *like* driving a cab."

"How're you going to support Rachel and the kids on a cabbie's pay?"

"'Rachel and the kids'? I haven't even decided if I'm going to write her back, and you've got us breeding? Anyway, you keep hiring me to drive you to Dover, I'll be able to support a harem." The meter's click added another fifty cents to the already impressive total.

"Ahh . . ."

He'd sulked the dozen miles since he'd flagged me down on Atlantic Avenue as I was pulling out of the cab yard. I'd guessed what I was letting myself in for, but he'd sworn his car was dead and he had to get to Tip Finn's party, "a meat market for money," as he'd put it. I hadn't minded as long as we were on the Mass Pike, but he was starting to spoil the *haute* New England landscape, which at incalculable expense retained the pastoral simplicity its current owners' ancestors had fled for the city a century ago.

He started to say something else, so I rolled down the window and let the sweet country air, with its faint esters of horse and ripening hay, whisk his words away until I pulled my head back in. "I've got to charge for waiting time, you know."

"Turn here." He pointed to a pair of field-stone gateposts. "You can wait inside. You might even meet someone useful."

"I don't want to meet anyone useful."

"Okay, meet someone useless—there'll be a lot of them, and you'll have something in common."

I let that pass while I took in the looming white house perched on top of a low hill. Every window was lit, and between the light pouring out into the dark night and the buzz of partygoers, it reminded me of a beehive.

"Quite a little place he's got." The Finn horse farm stood out, even by Dover standards. The last time I'd been this close to anything like it, I'd been on my school trip to Washington and JACK AND JACKIE had been on the mailbox.

"Guy didn't claw his way out of Southie to live in a three-decker in Watertown." We pulled up at the front door and turned the car over to a valet.

I wondered if this was what Finn had fantasized as a poor boy in South Boston, a big white house in the country where the gentry lived, wondered if that's where the restless drive had started. I'd spent my fantasy life planning to be president; somehow the restless drive hadn't followed.

A maid got us through the front hall, and after that, Bucky and I used our sonar to find the bar. Bucky did the blocking, and it wasn't long before bourbon was reminding my throat why mint grew and I could focus on my surroundings.

The bar ran the width of a room slightly smaller than the Boston Garden. It was dotted with round tables circling a small dance floor laid down in the center. A five-piece band beat out bad Motown while a half-dozen middle-aged white couples in assorted pastels demonstrated how racial stereotypes get started.

"Look at my boy working the crowd. Conor's gonna coin money tonight." Bucky killed his scotch and snatched another off a passing tray, then returned to contemplating the throng of men and women surrounding O'Conor's crisp figure at the far end of the room.

The mayor was dispensing wit and charm while a circle of aging groupies marked his every phrase with appreciative nods and titters. Bucky beamed at the sight. "St. Jack Reincarnate, almost ready for prime time. They haven't had one this close to launch since Teddy went on bulk training. Of course, we're talking the attention span of a flea, so Conor'd better take'em for everything he can, while he can."

"You bring such an uplifting view to life, Buckchuck—one of the things I like about you."

"Just call 'em as I see 'em, laddie. And speaking of uplifting views, how about that one?"

This time his look led my eye to a tall woman with stylishly cut raven hair, splashed with a brilliant white streak from her forehead back, who had peeled off from the crowd surrounding the mayor and was working her way, against the flow, toward us. It was slow going because she stopped to talk to just about everybody, and each pause seemed to require a fair amount of kissing and patting and hand-holding. She owned a fine chest, presented in a dress that made sure you knew it.

"Easy, Buck—you've already got a date."

"So does she, fortunately—that's Wanda Pryce-Jones, professor of contemporary culture at Tufts. Spends her third husband's money on trendy lefty causes and prospective fourth husbands. Read about her in *Boston Monthly*."

A waitress passed with a tray of toast rounds capped with lobster meat and caviar and we each snagged a pair. "Not much Yankee understatement here, Buckman." I tongued a fish egg off my lip and sent it tumbling after its siblings as I surveyed the expanse of Rizzo sports jackets and Ungaro pants suits.

"Thank God for that. No, when we bog Irish manage to dig our way out of the muck, we like to let everybody know it. Ah—Tip. Good to see you. The friend I was telling you about, Nason Nichols."

Bucky had turned at the approach of a short, bandy man who carried himself with the neat precision of a cotillion dance master. His hair was coal black with a little silver at the temples, and except for the lines around the eyes, I wouldn't have guessed Finn was closing on seventy. He gave me a quick, hard handshake, mumbled a perfunctory greeting.

"Appreciate your having me."

He looked around the room and didn't seem to have heard, until his right hand made a slight dismissive motion and I decided he was either embarassed by gratitude or the favor was on a level with tipping the carhop a buck.

We were surrounded by a wall of discordant sound, and I had to raise my voice to a near shout: "Nice party."

"Think so?" He snorted. "My wife's idea of a good time. Cost of doing business, way I look at it. Remind the bankers I'm still alive, raise a few bucks for Conor every now and then, and try to keep him from listening to my wife's coupon-clipping friends—never had to meet a payroll in their lives." He stared at the crowd surrounding O'Conor, shook his head. "God, look at them. Couldn't stand that, all those people sucking up to you, putting in their two cents. Don't know how he takes it."

O'Conor didn't look like he was suffering, but I kept it to myself. "I suppose it never hurts to listen."

"The hell it doesn't—listen to jackasses long enough, sooner or later you start braying like one of them."

"You mean this commission he's set up?"

"Damn right. Waste of time, getting people all stirred up. We're not lucky, some idiot will say some damn fool thing and you'll have half of Boston trying to kill the other half. Try raising money then!"

Bucky tried to spread a little comfort: "Well, if he had to set it up, at least he's made sure there're some responsible people on it."

Finn thought about this but kept the sour look ready to go. Eventually he nodded, none too enthusiastically. "Some. Heard a few of the other names, though—Judas priest." He shook his head, cast his drooping eyes over the room. "Most of the people in this room think money's something other people should make so their kind can spend it. Try telling them what kind of an atmosphere you need, you want to create jobs, make money." Finn swirled the liquor in his almost-full glass and dropped his voice. "I'll say this"—his flat rasp dared us to disagree—"it may not sit too well with my wife and her la-la friends, but it'll take a hell of a showing before *I* believe the police department's doing anything wrong; far as I'm concerned, Flanagan's got this town ready to go again, and I made damn sure O'Conor knows it."

An older man who had crept up behind Finn apparently didn't realize he hadn't been invited to share Finn's insights, because he smiled uncertainly as he stepped into the space next to his host. "Don't you think, Tip, you ought to wait and see? This thing with this young man . . . if there was a policeman involved . . . maybe there is something wrong with the department . . ."

Finn gave the man the sour smile. "You know, Harry, you keep eavesdropping and one of these days you're going to overhear one of the young bucks your wife keeps company with behind your back."

The older man blanched and fell back. His mouth worked soundlessly until he backed into the throng and disappeared.

"Goddamn bleeding hearts. Not one of 'em ever met a payroll."

It wasn't an invitation to dialogue, and anyway I'd had all the Finn I could take. I was relieved when he set his drink, hardly touched, on the bar, then turned and slid toward the door.

My "nice meeting you" might have been heard, or it might not have, since I didn't deliver it with a lot of punch. Finn kept his hands in his pockets, but nobody was reaching to shake them anyway. In fact, no one seemed to see him at all. I watched him until he went through the door.

"Sweet guy; lot of soul. If Flanagan is running death squads, there's a recruit." I signaled a bartender for another drink.

Bucky was staring at the doorway where Finn had disappeared. He started to say something, stopped, shook his head slowly. "Wouldn't be hard to dislike the little shit, would it? Ah, well—whatever he uses for a heart's in the right place as far as Dapper's concerned, and that's what matters. Permit me to relieve you of those, my good man." He snatched a bowl of shrimp from a passing waiter and started sucking them into his mouth like a sperm whale in a school of krill.

The stunning woman with the distinctive coiffure was

still working her way in our direction, trailed by a confused-looking man thirty years her senior. As we watched, she stopped, barked briefly, and left him sitting alone before resuming her cruise. "Nice to see two crazy kids in love, too."

"Ah, yes—Professor Pryce-Jones and her consort of the day. Have to catch her new book, *Rap—A People Sings*. Hear it's a treat. And the proceeds go to fund the liberation movement in Sri Lanka. Or maybe it's to save the dappled lousewort? I forget. It's the thought that counts. Ah— Professor Pryce-Jones. Allow me to introduce myself. Bucky Hanrahan."

The raven-haired woman took her time sizing us up. "Of course—you work with . . . Nikki Gruber, at MassPIRG?" She eyed Bucky clinically.

"Close. I'm in investments. Work with Eliot Kershaw, time to time."

"Oh, yes—he's told me *all* about you. I *do* hope you keep his portfolio green." She canted her head fetchingly.

"Wind power, compost, and Brazil nut futures—won't have anything else. Like you to meet a friend of mine, Nason Nichols."

"Mr. Nichols—a pleasure." Her hand squeezed mine while we established eye contact. Hers were brown and huge and said they were interested in absolutely no one but me, at least for my allotted seconds.

"And what do you do, Mr. Nichols?"

"I drive a—"

"Hard bargain. Nase is a . . . security consultant." Bucky looked like a man with Bell's palsy as he signaled to me over her shoulders.

"Oh? What kind of security consulting do you do, Mr. Nichols?"

Bucky looked so stricken I decided to play along. "Well, recently I've been in . . . ah . . . transportation, Wanda."

"DOT or MBTA?"

"C.A.B."

"Really!" The professor squeezed my hand harder. "That's *terribly* interesting. You *must* talk to Conor. He needs to develop a comprehensive mass transportation program, wouldn't you say? It just makes me sick to see all those cars choking the streets every day."

She wore her self-righteousness like a bumper sticker, and it was too inviting a target. "Absolutely. I'm working up a proposal, let you turn that three-car garage of yours into a homeless shelter and get *terrific* tax benefits."

Pryce-Jones played it back silently. Suddenly my hand was my own again. "I see. That's very interesting." The smile stayed in place, but now it looked as though it were done with wires.

Bucky glared at me. "Nase's *main* field isn't transportation at all, Wanda; it's . . . ah . . . police procedures, that sort of thing. He may be working for the Kershaw Commission—if the . . . ah . . . terms can be worked out."

Her eyes roamed my face, gradually losing their wary squint as the smile recovered some warmth. "I'm very interested in your area, Mr. Nichols." She leaned forward and dropped her voice: "Conor won't be announcing it publicly until tomorrow, but I'm going to be one of the panel members."

"Oh? You have an interest in police work?"

"I have an interest in doing something about this . . . this . . . Gestapo that awful man Flanagan runs. This may be our best opportunity."

"I guess I hadn't thought of it that way."

"Don't misunderstand me." Her fingers rested on my forearm for a second. "It's absolutely tragic, of course. Just dreadful. But with the police acting like . . . storm troopers wherever they see people of color, well—something like this was bound to happen, wasn't it?" Fortunately, she didn't wait for an answer. "And that's why I say what happened may not be *all* bad, don't you think, if it leads to a whole new approach to public safety?"

What I thought was how nice it would feel to throw my

drink in her face. What I said was "Perhaps it can serve some larger purpose. I hope so."

"Exactly—you put it so much more succinctly. I'm glad you understand. Conor's been far too tolerant with the man as it is, and I told him so."

"Really? What did he say?"

If she'd been a house cat, she would have licked her paws. "Why, that's when he said I should be on the commission. Of course, Tip's wife and I go way back, too, even if Tip is positively *antediluvian*, and Theo James and I worked together on Stella Crenshaw's campaign, and of course Eliot Kershaw is like a grandfather to me, so it makes perfect sense."

"Perfect."

She leaned over as though sharing her most intimate secret; given her dress, in a way she was. "I think Conor may be finally ready to admit that those . . . *bigots* in South Boston and Charlestown and places like that aren't his *natural* constituency. I mean, if he wants to go *on*, and of course he does."

I tore my gaze away from her chest and offered my warmest smile. "No, he definitely needs a better class of bigots."

Then I laughed, and after a second, she laughed and then Bucky laughed and it was fine. Pryce-Jones looked me over appraisingly. "I'm sure we're going to get along fine, Mason. I *do* hope we'll be working together."

"Nason."

"Of course . . . Nason. Oh—there's Corey Webster; I'm afraid I *must* have a word with him. You will excuse me?"

She bustled toward a lanky man with a bald spot the size of a soup plate capping a lank ponytail, grazing at a table of hors d'oeuvres on the other side of the room. Even from a distance, his chamois work shirt, faded jeans, and Doc Martens stood out against the expensive livery of the other guests.

We watched her beige silk bottom until it disappeared. "Asshole," he hissed. "Finn *told* me she was going to be on the panel. You'll lose the job if you go around baiting people like that."

"People like that are exactly why I'm going to keep on driving a cab. I'd rather work for Madame DeFarge."

"Now maybe you understand what Dapper's up against. Just think about it, okay? Please?"

I started to say no but I couldn't face another round of nagging. "I'll think about it."

"I hope so. I'm going to the bathroom. Try not to get in any fights while I'm gone."

I rested my elbows on the bar and saw that someone had left an open pack of Camels lying unattended. I picked up old Joe, sniffed the earthy aroma, and started to put it back when the voice said, "Go ahead—one won't hurt." I knew it well; it spoke to me whenever I'd had a couple drinks, and it knew I had its number.

Except this time it wasn't cackling and satanic but low and just a little tipsy, because it belonged to a woman standing to my left, a tall, solid-looking woman with a tilted red smile and eyes that didn't look away, holding out a lighter in a slightly wavy hand.

"I'm sorry—I didn't know they were yours." I put the pack back on the bar.

"They weren't—I bummed them off the bartender. I only bum them, and only when I can get these. Better than a patch, huh?" She shook one out, tapped the end against her red nail, missed, tapped again, and then got the thing stoked on the first try.

"Ahh." She leaned against the bar and blew the rich smoke out into the room, then pulled at her drink. The glass came away with a red lip print. "Hard liquor and cigarettes—the only sins left, now that all the others are just life-style choices. Want one? The warning says it's safe this month, assuming you're not pregnant." The voice had a self-mocking tone that went with the lopsided smile, a tone that said, "I'm looking at middle age and not wearing a ring, and so are you, so what the hell."

So what the hell, starting with the smoke. I lit one, took a tentative pull, then a deeper one, and almost instantly felt that rush that'll cross your eyes if you aren't in training. I swayed and grabbed for the bar, got woman instead.

A strong hand took my forearm. "Whoa, Nason—we just met. Here." She handed me her glass and I sipped a little bourbon. It wasn't cut with much and almost put me down again, but then things leveled out, and after a few seconds, I was able to come up for air.

"Thanks. Phew. How'd you know my name?"

"I was standing behind you while you were doing your number on Wanda Pryce-Jones."

"My number?" I tried the smoke again, gingerly, and this time it went down okay.

"Don't play dumb—I loved it. 'It just makes me sick to see all those cars choking the streets every day.'" Her voice was a lot deeper than the professor's, but she got the supercilious drawl right. "Sure—herd all the working stiffs onto cattle wagons, make it easier to get around in the Mercedes."

"Maybe I laid it on a little thick."

"Don't worry about it; she didn't have a clue. Most of them"—she swept her arm in the general direction of the crowd—"only time they'd think you were putting them on is if you said you'd voted for Reagan. Ole Wanda figured you had to be one of us, or you wouldn't be here, and that meant you thought just like she did—about everything. Nobody here but us us, you see? The 'better class of bigot.'" She chortled and a little of her drink sloshed out of the glass. "Whoops."

"Our host fits that picture?" Somehow Finn hadn't struck me as a member of the hive.

"The Tipster? He's an honorary us. He's foursquare

behind Conor, his wife's a true believer, and if he's still a
little . . . unevolved . . . on some issues, as Wanda might
say, that's only because he hasn't completed his training.
They'll forgive him as long as the Mrs. keeps throwing the
parties and he keeps writing the checks."

"What're you?"

"I'm a little drunk. Only way to get through these
things." She thrust out her hand and I took it. It squeezed
hard. "Lynn Daniels, when I'm sober. 'Oh, that Lynn' when
I'm not."

"I meant in the Pryce-Jones scheme of things."

"Where do I fit in?"

"Right."

"Hey, I've paid my dues—worked my tail off in each of
Conor's campaigns. Anyway, if you're a woman lawyer, the
Wandas just *assume* you think like they do. And most of the
time I'm a good girl and don't say things like *girl*, and don't
try to play with their bedmates, so they let me come to their
parties and mostly overlook my occasional lapses."

"Like?"

Her wide mouth twisted, and for a second, it wasn't
offbeat and whimsical, merely hard. "Like when I remind
some of those star-fuckers over there"—the hand with the
glass in it waved dismissively toward the knot surrounding
O'Conor—"that there actually are one or two people in the
Commonwealth who weren't born with trust funds, and
maybe taxing them to death to support graffiti artists or the
Shining Path or whatever it is they're lobbying for today
isn't the smartest thing Conor could do. That's when I'm
'Oh, that Lynn.'"

She got pretty wound up, and the effort to point at
O'Conor's audience put more bourbon on the floor. "Oh,
shit." She looked down at the spot and shook her head.
"That's what I mean. I get carried away. Sorry."

An image from a news broadcast I'd watched in a local
bar swam into mind: a harried, intense woman tearing into

a nattering reporter, lambasting him for a set of particularly
loaded questions, refusing to accept the rules of the game,
ultimately reducing him to stammering incoherence. A last
drag on the Camel gave it form. "Wait a minute—you're the
lawyer who had that case in Brighton, the old Hungarian
couple who wouldn't rent to a black guy."

"Nope." She was still scuffing at the spot on the floor.

"But I'm sure I remember—"

"I represented an old Hungarian couple in Brighton who
wouldn't rent to a guy who had lied on his application,
wasn't working where he'd said or any place else for that
matter, and whose reference turned out to be his parole
officer—who, incidently, was very happy to hear the guy
was thinking of him, since he was three months overdue
for a visit. He also happened to be black, which didn't have
a damn thing to do with it."

"Oh—I didn't remember that part."

"That's because that part didn't get reported. It was a lot
better story that POCAT was going to come over and picket
until the city brought charges against my clients for violat-
ing the fair housing laws."

"Pardon my ignorance, but what the hell is a 'pocat'?"

"Well you might ask. It's the brainchild of a child without
a brain, Corey Webster. He's freeloading somewhere over
there right now." She waved toward the food table. "Never
forgave his parents for being middle class. Got in some
trouble where he was teaching and took up 'community
organization' instead. Had this idea of uniting the ABWs,
called it People of Color Advancing Together, or POCAT."

She read my dazed look and laughed. "Anybody but
white—ABWs. You WEMs are all alike; gotta get with the
program."

"White European males?"

"All right—the man's hip!" She gave my arm a little
punch. "Anyway, people like Wanda and Tip's wife keep
Webster as a pet, now that the Black Panthers are extinct.

The *faux* prole look lets 'em feel like they're close to the *people,* you know, without actually having to get dirty. He's a nuisance, nothing more."

"How'd you get rid of him?"

"I wouldn't waste time with him—I sat down with Theo James and gave him the facts. He tugged Webster's leash and Corey heeled like a good boy. I think Theo was peeved Webster would risk their credibility like that. They don't seem so tight any more."

"Theo James—the minister? Where did he come in?"

"Webster thinks the Rev is God's gift to the nonwhite world; POCAT was just Webster and a bunch of handbills until he latched onto Theo."

"How do you know James?" The conversation was a dizzy ride but fun, kind of like the roller coaster at Revere Beach, and I wanted to keep going.

"Theo? Why, we go back a long way. A few years ago, I represented a Roxbury tenant's group trying to get the city to shut down a notorious drug house; Theo got involved and we found some common ground. Since then we've worked together on a couple of things. I can talk to him."

"I'm surprised—you being a WEF and all."

She laughed. The corners of her eyes wrinkled and the sparkle took years off. "Theo's coming along. I've been working on him, and he's come a long way."

"You could have fooled me. I read something he said about Flanagan and his Blue Tornado raids a few months ago, and he made about as much sense as Louis Farrakhan."

"I won't say it hasn't taken a while." She paused, considered her next words, offered them reflectively. "I think the Whitmore killing brought a lot of things home to Theo."

"And you helped him get there? Then more power to you."

For a few seconds, she looked at a spot somewhere behind me. Finally, she reached over and plucked an errant thread off my shoulder. "Sure—I guess you could say I helped him get there."

"Someone told me he'd heard James sounding sane recently. At a rally right after Whitmore was killed, in fact. I wasn't sure I believed it."

"You can believe it—I was there. The Rev's going to turn around a lot of people." She blew the thread across the bar. "Going to *impress* a lot of people, too—Theo James is going to start reaching a much wider constituency, unless I miss my guess."

"I still figure the mayor put him on this Whitmore investigation as a sop to the professional victims."

"That's probably right, but I'm betting Conor's going to be pleasantly surprised. Theo's said some silly things in the past, but he's come around—witness his speech at that rally. Hell, witness the fact he put me up for the panel." She gave a self-deprecating shrug, as if to say "Don't ask me why."

"All of a sudden everyone I meet is connected." We'd turned around and were resting our arms on the bar, side by side, backs to the room, just two pals having a chat in our own little hideaway, and the nice, warm smell of nicotine and bourbon on her breath was the sweetest perfume I'd inhaled in a long time. I wanted more. "What's *your* constituency?"

She rested her chin in her hand and thought about it. "Hmm—the terminally pissed off?"

"That's everybody in Boston."

"No—ninety percent of Boston is pissed off; the rest is indignant. That's different."

"What's the difference?"

"Pissed off is what you are when you get mugged; indignant is what Wanda Pryce-Jones is when the police mess up the mugger."

"I like it. And let me guess where that brings you out on Flanagan."

She drew herself up. She was a tall woman and didn't have to strain to look me in the eyes: "Right—pissed off. I told James, I told Conor, and I'll tell you: I think this is a kick in the groin to a damn good man and a damn good department. I'll be amazed if the police don't have this guy in custody pronto, and if a cop did do it, I'm betting it's for some crazy reason that has nothing to do with the way Flanagan's running the department."

Her nostrils flared and she looked ready to duke it out on the spot if I didn't like it. I did, and said so, and she unwound a little. "But I also said that I'd come out where the facts lead. I expect to feel the same at the end as I do now, but if I don't, I'll say so. Conor wants a sure vote for Flanagan, he'd better look elsewhere."

"Probably should have a few sure votes for him, since he's appointed at least one person who can't wait to indict. Your friend Wanda, I mean."

"Right. I won't be the other side of that coin. I'll give it a fair look."

"How did O'Conor react to that?"

"He 'wouldn't have it any other way.'" She laughed. "That's bullshit, of course—if he could have, he would have appointed the Dapper Flanagan Fan Club, and finished it in a day. Flanagan's his most popular appointment, and no one knows it better than His Honor."

"I expect that wouldn't have played too well with some of our fellow guests."

"Or the *Hub*. This way's smarter. Wanda and one or two others get to flap their gums and be in Conor's debt forever, there'll be a couple who'd back Flanagan if it turned out he'd killed the kid himself, and the rest of us will call the facts reasonably straight. Which, if they're remotely what I think they are, ought to leave Flanagan sitting pretty and the *Hub* looking someplace else for its Pulitzer."

"Congratulations are probably out of place, but I think he did well to choose you."

"Thank you." Her features sagged and suddenly she looked like a tired woman who'd seen more than most. "It's a résumé opportunity I'd rather hadn't come up."

"Really? Ms. Pryce-Jones thought the kid's timing couldn't have been better."

Her jaw set, drawing the bright slash of lipstick into a scarlet circumflex. "Yeah—I heard. That's Wanda, to a T: what're eggs for, if not omelets? People like her use people like Whitmore like scientists use mice." She pounded back the last of her drink and set the glass hard on the bar. "What a bitch."

She had a great voice, a deep purr that was pure music after the months alone, and I wanted to keep it going. "Come on—other than the fact that she's arrogant, insensitive and morally bankrupt, what have you got against Pryce-Jones?"

She made a disgusted look with her mouth. "She's had life easy, thinks she was born to run other people's lives, and . . . never mind." She turned away and shook her head.

"Come on—it was just getting interesting."

She turned back, blinking. "And men fall all over her, damn it."

She looked down at the floor while I tried to think of a gallant reply. I was too slow, and after a few seconds more than was comfortable, she looked up and forced a brittle little smile and a brittle little chuckle. "But, hey"—she touched my arm again—"what about you? I heard your friend say you might be interested in a job with us?"

"Well, actually I . . ."

"I'd like that. Working with you, I mean. I hope you'll take it." Suddenly her cheeks took on the color of her lipstick. "God, listen to me. I sound like midnight in a singles bar. That's too much booze." She snatched her purse off the bar and extended her hand. "Sorry—I'd better call a cab. I don't think I should drive."

I took the hand and led her toward the door. "Your

carriage is waiting, madam. And by the way—I already fell all over you once tonight—may I try again?"

Halfway home, I remembered Bucky and circled back. His mouth opened when he saw the woman sleeping in the front seat, but he shut it when I told him to line me up with Kershaw in the morning. I listened to the Red Sox and soft snores as we drove back to Boston.

chapter 7

A GREAT BLUE HERON, THAT WAS IT. I'D BEEN sitting in his office for five minutes, making chitchat across the desk, all the while trying to figure out what Kershaw reminded me of, when it came to me: the long, pointed nose; the angular features; the arms that flapped disjointedly; the sudden, darting movements; even the bony knees under the worn, gray trousers—a great blue heron, with its little eyes fixed on a fish. I was the fish, and it made me extremely uncomfortable.

"How d'ye think this ought to come out, then, hmm?" Kershaw peered at me over steepled fingers, his long, loose frame piled into the chair like so many leftover parts. A teacup, of nice export china matching the cup poised precariously on my knee, rested untouched on the desk.

"I'm sorry?" Kershaw's staccato utterances were growing increasingly gnomic.

"Our work. How do you see the end product?" He sat

back in his rocker, eyes never leaving mine. "Assume you've got a notion; most people do." He folded his arms across his chest and rocked, never losing eye contact.

"How it ought to come out?"

"Umm."

I lowered the teacup to the floor and tried the right ankle on the left knee. Yes. I sat back. "No, to be honest I don't think I do. Know how it ought to come out, that is." No, it didn't feel right. I pushed it slowly off, pulled the left ankle up to the right knee. Much better. "Of course, I have my own impressions. Ah, prejudices, you might say."

"Umm?" A tangle of eyebrows, looking like so much steel wool pasted below his forehead, arched inquisitively.

"I'm somewhat . . . skeptical, I suppose. About these charges of—"

Pencil-thin fingers flapped dismissively. "Can't go through life without predispositions. Have you *decided*, man? *That's* the question."

"Well, I assumed that we—that is, you—that is, the commission—wasn't supposed to decide how it was going to come out. Ahead of time, I mean. I mean . . ." If he'd only stop *staring*, just blink once or twice . . .

"Ahh." He stopped rocking, leaned back, and shifted his gaze to the ceiling. I liked that.

"I'm sorry?"

"Harvard."

"Sir?"

"Tells, y'know. Always tells." Suddenly he shot forward, so that the hatchet face was nearer mine by two feet. He peered at me as though daring disagreement.

"I'm . . . sorry?"

"Harvard, man, Harvard. Know you went. Hanrahan said so. Tells. Looked it up. Didn't graduate. Good. Waste of time, graduating. Takes after two years, or not at all."

"Would you mind telling my father?" I forced a smile.

"Tell your father." He coughed. No, it was a chuckle.

"Umm, I daresay fathers're like that. One myself. Very good. Like your answer."

" 'Tell my father'?"

"Not deciding ahead of time. Exactly right. No agenda. Never had an ax to grind in my life; don't mean to start now. Mayor's commitment: complete impartiality. You'll do."

"You mean . . ."

" 'Course. Hanrahan said you were a good man. Tip Finn put in a word, too. Wanted to have this little chat, chance to test the chemistry, some such, hem? Transportation security?"

"Well . . ."

"Solid fellow."

"I'm sorry?"

"Hanrahan. Stupidest thing we ever did."

"I'm sorry?"

"Why, keeping the Irish, other types out. New blood. Need it. Checked with Bingham."

"Bingham?" I groped for the reference, then remembered the colorless drone who headed a Route 128 high-tech I'd done some work for once. "Stanley Bingham? Of Zoltec?"

" 'Course. Other Binghams all dead. No point checking with them." The corners of his lip twitched, almost imperceptably, his right eyelid blinking furiously. I'd never realized that Yankee humor was so easily confused with Alzheimer's, or maybe it was the other way around.

"No. No, there wouldn't be."

"Said you were good. Bit eccentric, but good."

"I'm . . . happy to hear it. Good, I mean."

"Don't scorn eccentric, man. Know about Hughes?"

"Hughes?"

"Dexter Hughes. 'Thirty-nine. Year ahead of me."

"No, sir. I don't think I've had the pleasure."

"Died in 'forty-one. Wouldn't have."

"I . . . guess not."

"Ate nothing but shellfish. Great eccentric."

"Really? That is . . . eccentric."

"What?" He fixed me with the little avian eyes. "Wouldn't join a house at Harvard. Turned 'em down cold. What I meant, eccentric."

"Ah, yes. That's *certainly* . . . eccentric. Isn't it?"

"Square peg, don't you see?"

"Absolutely. Square peg, round . . . hole?"

"Exactly. Tragic, really." He shook his head.

"I guess it would be hard to fit in that way."

Kershaw looked at me blankly.

"Square pegs—in round holes. Never . . . really . . . fit in? No friends . . . an outcast? Kind of . . . tragic? I mean— it would be, wouldn't it?" I wondered if I could be experiencing the early stages of a psychotic break, approaching a descent into madness that would soon find me baying at the moon from a ward at Bridgewater.

The damp puddles of faded blue snapped into alignment. "Good lord, no! Beloved by everybody. Died of ptomaine. Bad oysters. Tragic."

"Oh. That is tragic. Truly . . . tragic."

"Never see his like again."

"I'm sure that's right."

"Well, can't spend all day reminiscing. S'pose I'd better get about, let 'em see the old man's still kicking, eh? Meet the other members, staff, day after tomorrow. Eleven. My office." He left me by the elevator and ambled down the book-lined hallway, head bobbing this way and that, looking for all the world like he was hunting sticks for a nest.

I found a pay phone in the lobby and called Bucky.

"How'd it go?"

"I got the job."

"All right—my man! Whadya think of Kershaw?"

I groped for the words. "How shall I put this? He's . . . ah . . . charmingly vague at times?"

"Think he's low on gas, huh?"

"I think the old boy's running on fumes, Buck-passer."

The Boston Hub
August 20, 1994

EMBATTLED COMMISSIONER BLASTS CITIZEN'S PANEL; FLANAGAN CRITIC NAMED TO GROUP

BOSTON—Police Commissioner Francis X. "Dapper" Flanagan, under fire from minority activists for police initiatives in the inner city, yesterday issued a stinging attack on the independent investigatory group Mayor Conor O'Conor appointed in the wake of the unsolved murder of nineteen-year-old African-American student Purnell Whitmore of Roxbury.

The Kershaw Commission, named for its chairperson, prominent Boston attorney Eliot Kershaw, is Mayor O'Conor's response to demands from community leaders for an independent investigation of a series of incidents involving charges of police brutality, of which the Whitmore slaying is only the most recent.

Whitmore, an honors student at prestigious Yale University, was a rare success story in Roxbury, and reports that a police officer may have been involved in his murder ten days ago led to the mayor's appointment of the Kershaw panel. Sources close to the mayor report that he had hoped to avoid the politically risky move, but that continued pressure finally forced his hand.

The group, composed of eleven men and women representing a cross-section of community interests, holds its first meeting tomorrow. Its report and recommendations are promised within weeks.

Commissioner Flanagan was particularly incensed by the mayor's designation of the Rev. Theophilus James, pastor of Roxbury's African Apostolic Temple of Glory and a frequent police department critic, to serve

on the Kershaw Commission. "This man has cam-
paigned against every effort to drive crime out of the
inner city and has never hesitated to play the race card
to advance his career; the mayor might as well have
appointed Rodney King."

The Rev. James's response to Flanagan's remarks
was "While I have had occasion to question Commissioner Flanagan's initiatives in the past, my abiding
wish now is that God guide the police quickly to the
man who killed Purnell Whitmore. No one is more
eager than I to have this ugly incident behind us, so
that the brave men and women of our safety forces can
enjoy the confidence of all our citizens. I have no
animus toward Commissioner Flanagan, and I pledge
that I can and will review his activities, as well as those
of the police department, with a fair and open mind."

City Hall sources close to the mayor's office said that
they had expected the Rev. James's appointment to
generate opposition in many quarters, owing to his
sharp attacks on the police and Commissioner Flanagan in the past, and expressed relief at his "conciliato-
ry tone."

chapter 8

TWO DAYS LATER, I SAT IN THE VISITORS' GALLERY of the City Hall rotunda, waiting for the mayor to introduce the members of the Kershaw Commission to the public. Several hundred people had jammed in for the unveiling.

Television lights blazed down on the empty dais while functionaries hustled about, placing name cards in front of the eleven empty seats on either side of the lectern, testing the sound system and striking no-nonsense poses whenever the cameras panned their way.

Outside the cordoned-off arena, men and women of various hues milled about, trading embraces, handshakes, and recent histories, while TV news teams vied for the best angles and print reporters, pads in hand, buttonholed only-too-ready representatives of various subsects to press for incisive analysis of the upcoming event.

Most of the people were upscale and decorous, but a knot of twenty or thirty pasty, middle-aged men and women had surrounded a reporter in a corner near me and were trying to outshout each other to make their points, variations on the theme of a placard brandished by one particularly fearsome-looking woman with a face like moldy dough: CODDLE COPS, NOT CROOKS. Their drab overcoats and windbreakers boasting union affiliations set them off at least as much as did their message.

Una Selkirk, the lacquered face of Channel 4's six-o'clock news, moved purposefully through the crowd, trailed by a sweating, bearded man straining under the weight of a camera that perched on his shoulder like a Cyclopean parrot. She stopped a few feet from where I sat, arrested by the mass of a dense, rainbow-colored throng surrounding a handsome, goateed black man in a crisp, charcoal-gray silk suit that fit his heavy frame the way a thousand dollars of hand-tailoring is supposed to make clothes fit. I looked closely and recognized the man I'd seen in the back of the big Lincoln after the Whitmore service— the Reverend Theophilus James.

The brilliant white band of a clerical collar circled his thick neck above a black shirt. A gold crucifix nestled against a torso that could have looked fat but managed to look prosperous instead. His head, six inches above any others in sight, was capped with an immaculate Prince Valiant hairdo that framed the full face before curling over the back of his collar.

Strain as she might, Selkirk was unable to get more than an arm through the tightly packed gathering. "Let me through, please. TV 4 News. Let me through, please. God damn it, let me through! Reverend James! Over here." She waved an arm in the air and her voice, a far cry from the modulated purr she used on the air, mounted in volume until the minister looked away from the person to whom he had been talking and spotted her.

"Una! How are you? Let her in, please, folks." He had a mellifluous, bass voice that cut through the din with ease.

The crowd parted like the Red Sea, long enough for

Selkirk and the cameraman to make their way to the nucleus, and then re-formed around them.

"Let's give them a little room, folks. Una—*wonderful* to see you." The minister enveloped her right hand in both of his and held it.

"It's *always* good to see you, Reverend James. And congratulations on your appointment."

"Thank you, Una, but I'm afraid that it is consecration, not congratulation, that is appropriate." He stared into her eyes, still holding her hand.

"Of course, Reverend." She shifted vocal gears. "Reverend James, so many of our viewers look to you for leadership in times of crisis; I wonder if I could ask you some questions for tonight's broadcast."

"Certainly, Una." His big hands quickly swiped the mane, patting a single, errant lock back into place against the snow-white collar. The cameraman fumbled with a switch and suddenly Reverend James and Selkirk were washed in white light.

At a nod from the cameraman, Selkirk spoke into her microphone. "Thank you, Bill. I'm standing in the rotunda of Boston City Hall with the Reverend Theophilus James, pastor of Roxbury's African Apostolic Temple of Glory and a prominent spokesperson for people of color throughout the area. Good morning, Reverend James." She pointed the microphone at him.

"Good morning, Una." His face was composed, serious. His voice, touched with the barest hint of South, had the easy timbre of a professional speaker. He ignored the camera with the insouciance of a veteran.

"Reverend James, you're here waiting for Mayor O'Conor to officially introduce you and the other newly appointed members of the mayor's emergency committee to investigate charges of systematic police brutality, charges that have long circulated but that the tragic death of Purnell Whitmore have brought to the fore. Can you tell us how the committee plans to proceed?"

"Well, Una, until the committee meets in executive session after Mayor O'Conor's introduction, I can only tell you how I plan to proceed. And that is with good faith and a humble heart at the great challenge that lies before us."

"And will you—"

"Excuse me, Una. And with the hope our work enables us to ensure all the people of Boston that the brave men and women who serve with our safety forces deserve our unqualified respect and support."

A buzz of amens and say it's swept through the crowd of onlookers.

"Reverend, you have been outspoken in your . . . ah . . . criticism of Commissioner Flanagan and his initiatives in the past. No doubt some of our viewers wonder: can this man look at the record impartially, or is his mind made up already?"

She was tossing them in over the center of the plate, big, fat juicy pitches, and James met this one with the meat of his bat. "I did not seek this appointment, Una, precisely because I feared some would question my impartiality. Having reluctantly agreed to serve, at our good mayor's insistence, let me assure anyone who might be listening: I bring charity toward all, malice toward none. I would not bring a spirit to this endeavor that was anything but the spirit by which I would wish to have my life judged."

"I see." Selkirk's paint-by-number face registered confusion, but she soldiered on. "Reverend, this group the mayor has appointed is supposed to look at the whole pattern of police relations with minorities since Commissioner Flanagan took over. But in the meantime, the police have confirmed that a witness says that a white policeman was seen with Purnell Whitmore shortly before he was murdered, and that they appeared to be having an altercation. Many ask: can the police be trusted to find this man? Or will they protect one of their own?" She arched her eyebrows quizzically.

James gave the question a long, sober pause. "When I

heard that a policeman murdered Purnell Whitmore, I confess I had the same concern. Indeed, I felt many of my earlier reservations about this program revived."

Selkirk sniffed blood. "You're saying, then, that in your mind a policeman *is* responsible?"

He looked at her sadly. "If the policeman seen with Purnell didn't do it, why hasn't he come forward? Yes, it would seem one of those to whom we look for protection is instead the one from whom we must be protected."

He clasped his hands at his waist and looked out at the crowd at just the right angle to give the camera his fine profile. "However, we can't judge the whole department by the depravity of one man. I expect the police will do everything in their power to bring this man to justice—and I will make it my business to see that they do."

She kept the mike extended, but Reverend James stood mute until a buzz passed through the crowd. Selkirk looked gratefully over her shoulder. "Well, Reverend—I see the mayor has arrived, so we'll have to excuse you in just a second. But first, I wonder if I could ask just one more question."

If James had been paying more heed to the reporter and less to the crowd, he might have seen the look that said, "Okay—try this one on for size," but he was too busy acknowledging supporters and had dropped his guard.

The TV light was brutal and Selkirk's face looked as though it would last about one more minute before the makeup let go like a Los Angeles mudslide, so she didn't wait for his full attention. "As recently as a month ago, you were quoted as saying—" She pulled a clipping from her pocket. "I want to make sure I get this right: 'Blue Tornado is simply the latest assault in the white war on black people. Only a comprehensive jobs program in the black community will end the scourge of drugs. People with hope won't do dope.' Did I quote you accurately, Reverend?"

She had his full attention now; his eyes were wary. "Umm, yes, I believe so. Of course, in context, I meant—"

"Yet now you seem to be saying that you have an open mind concerning Blue Tornado and, indeed, all of Commissioner Flanagan's . . . ah . . . reforms. How do you respond to those who say that you've changed your tune because Commissioner Flanagan's initiatives are even more popular in the black community than with whites? In other words, Reverend, are you changing your beliefs to fit the popular mood?" She held the stiff smile that takes years of training and a tube of lip liner.

James wasn't about to let on that he hadn't been expecting a breaking ball at batting practice. "I have never worried about the popularity of my beliefs, Una, and I bear the scars to prove it." He smiled briefly. "I've caught more than a few blows from police truncheons for no greater crime than insisting that black Bostonians have the right to live anywhere white Bostonians live. I *was* concerned about many of Commissioner Flanagan's initiatives. But public safety is the most basic civil right, Una—or perhaps you think otherwise?"

James paused, stared benignly at Selkirk while she fingered the mike cable like a string of worry beads. "Why, no, but—"

"Of course. And of course African-Americans share with all Americans a desire to be left in peace to get on with their lives. If, at the end of the investigation, our work confirms that our safety forces have done no more than provide that opportunity, then I will be the first to rejoice."

He once more beamed patiently at her as she tried to digest this, then pointed toward the hubbub where the mayor had entered. "I must be going, Una. As always, a pleasure to talk with you."

"Thank you for sharing your views with us, Reverend James." She gave the crowd he'd pointed to a puzzled look.

"Thank *you*, Una, for helping our voices be heard. And they *shall* be heard!"

The camera swiveled to face Selkirk as Reverend James began to wend his way to the dais, pressing palms and stroking shoulders as he went. His wide body parted the crowd effortlessly.

"Una Selkirk, TV 4 News, at City Hall, where we have just completed an exclusive interview with the Reverend Theophilus James." She reached up, fiddled with an earphone in her right ear, paused, then nodded and stared into the camera. "It *was* a measured statement. Scant wonder that so many Bostonians of all races look to Reverend James for leadership in this unhappy time. Back to you, Bill."

The seats behind the place cards gradually filled with earnest-looking men and women blinking under the glare of the television lights. Reverend James sat impassively, two seats to the right of the lectern, except when a voice from the audience drew a wave from the big right hand, scattering sunbeams in all directions as the spots hit the diamonds on the gold ring. Finn was to his left, arms crossed at his chest, glowering. Wanda Pryce-Jones and Lynn Daniels were seated at opposite ends of the table, chatting quietly with their companions.

Kershaw ascended the dais last, his gaunt, gray frame stepping gingerly, an arthritic heron with sore feet. He bobbed his head at each of the seated panelists, shook hands with the mayor, patted Reverend James on the back, and took his seat. The mayor stood expectantly until the hall grew quiet, then cleared his throat.

"My friends." He paused, touched the papers on the lectern, then resumed, the rhythms of his speech echoing the compassion etched on his face. "We have frequently met here in happier times. We remember here days of gladness, days of light; days when we came together as family, to seek a newer, better world. Today, our family gathers in sorrow, because one of our children is lost to us forever."

He took time to touch the papers again while the sound of muffled sobs made the round of the hall. "There is an empty place in this great hall, an emptiness that touches each of us, and I ask each of you for your prayers, your patience, and your good will, that we may understand and heal."

He looked up, across the lights, and continued. "There can be no gladness—no light—until a mother's cry is answered. Her cry, her tears, are ours. Mrs. Whitmore, I know I speak for every man and woman of good will in this great city of ours when I say we will not rest, we will not falter, and yes,"—his voice swelled—"the sounds of laughter will not be heard in our hearts again until we have brought to justice the person responsible for your son's senseless death."

He waited while throats cleared, noses blew, then resumed in measured words, growing in intensity. "Every untimely death is a tragedy. But Purnell Whitmore's death is a double tragedy. Not only have we lost a young man who had already—in a few, short years—distinguished himself in every endeavor, been a credit to himself, to his school, his church, his community, and most of all, his loving mother; as though that were not enough, many of our citizens believe they see, in the very serious questions that have been raised about the circumstances of Purnell Whitmore's death, confirmation of their worst fears about our safety forces. It is to address the facts and restore public confidence that I have asked Eliot Kershaw to chair a panel of distinguished Bostonians from many walks of life, holding many points of view, to investigate the circumstances of Purnell Whitmore's murder, determine whether there has been any pattern of racial abuse at the hands of the police, and recommend appropriate corrective measures *if the facts warrant.*"

His voice dropped after a pause. "My fellow Bostonians, I do want to emphasize this point: I asked Eliot Kershaw to chair this commission because of his nationwide reputation for fairness and candor. He has my pledge, as I have his, that the facts, and only the facts, will determine the outcome of this inquiry. There will be no rush to judgment, no character assassination, no private political agendas. I

have appointed this commission to lead in a healing process, not a witch hunt."

He paused to search the faces before him with the deep
green eyes. They held momentarily on the upturned face of
a middle-aged woman, who responded with a flush. "So
please understand that I don't imply for a minute, as some
have suggested, that I doubt the integrity, decency, or
professionalism of the vast majority of the almost two
thousand men and women of the Boston Police Department
who daily risk their lives that all of us can live our lives in
peace. Nor have I any reason to question the competence
and good will of Commissioner Flanagan, whose leadership
of the department has earned national recognition. All of
us—"

"Buncha racist pigs!" The voice came from the dark
beyond the island of light, and the "shhs" were quickly
overwhelmed by its echoes: "Cracker bastards!" "Killers!"
"Murderers of black people!"

The mayor held up his hand. "My friends, please—I
understand your feelings. But—"

"It isn't you they're beating on!"

"Don't *need* any more proof!"

"Flanagan's gotta go!"

The TV cameras followed the lights as they swiveled to
find the epicenter of the outbreak. After probing the shad-
owed crowd for a few seconds, they settled on a group of
men and women, black, brown, and white, standing with
raised fists in the middle of the audience. The man I'd seen
at Finn's, Corey Webster, still in a work shirt and jeans,
stood with his back to the rostrum, directing a chant with
metronomic waves of his arms: "Hey, hey, ho, ho, Flanagan's gotta go! Hey, hey, ho, ho, Flana-gan's gotta go! Hey,
hey . . ."

Soon several dozen others had stood and joined the
mindless chorus. Across the room, the people who had
been agitating the reporter about crook-coddling tried to set
up a countermovement, bleating, "We love Dapper! We love

Dapper" while those surrounding them drew away and stared as though they had stumbled into a witches' coven.

O'Conor rapped sharply on the lectern. "Please, friends. May we have order. I understand—" Only a slight tightening of his jaw betrayed his mood.

The woman with the placard broke away from her group to dash across the floor to Webster's cluster. She tried to smash the sign over Webster's bald head, but two men intercepted her and the sign fluttered harmlessly to the floor. She started forward again to cries of "Stop it!" and "Shame," and then one of her own team grabbed her from behind and held her.

She started shrieking: "My Mary can't even walk to school because of you people! Why don't you go back to the jungle!" Gobs of spittle flew out behind the words as she wrestled with her captors.

O'Conor had folded his arms across his chest, and stood staring impassively at the disturbance, apparently prepared to wait it out.

"*Shame!*" It sounded as though God himself had commandeered the microphone. Everyone, even the fishwife, grew still and looked to the dais.

"Shame upon you." Reverend James was standing at the lectern, arms outstretched, his bulk all but hiding O'Conor. Slowly, wearing the scowl of an Old Testament prophet, he lowered his arms and gripped the lectern.

"I am ashamed—ashamed that my people would show such disrespect to our fine mayor, ashamed that they would bespoil this moment with appeals to hatred." He turned to face the Flanagan faction. "Brothers and sisters, your fears are my fears; your pain, my pain. Only Christ could carry the cross alone; we must all labor together if we're to bear this cross. Help us make this young man's death mean something, so we can say of Purnell Whitmore, as we do of our Lord, that he died for all of us." His look softened, and though I was fifty feet away, I felt its warmth.

One by one, the members of both groups cast their eyes

down. "Lord,"—Reverend James spread his arms again and looked up at the ceiling—"Lord, hear these, thy children. Grant them the peace that surpasseth understanding . . ."

Soft murmurs of "Jesus!" and "Amen!" accompanied the sound of people resuming their seats, until all but Webster were sitting, heads bowed, while Reverend James finished.

"Mister Mayor, please continue. There will be no more disturbance." He resumed his seat and looked respectfully up at the mayor. The only sound was the defeated slap of Webster's Doc Martens as they carried him out of the hall.

The rest of the show was anticlimactic. O'Conor, pro that he was, recovered his cadence within a few beats, calling once again for fairness, deliberation, and respect for the hard and dangerous work Boston's thin blue line performed. He was an adroit wordsmith, and by the time he had worked in the obligatory Kennedy quotation and turned to introduce the commission members, murmurs of "Uh-huh" and "he's right" could be heard around the rotunda.

Kershaw stood, gave the mayor an appreciative handshake, added his flat, New England vowels to the mayor's pledge of impartiality and due process, and sat. There was none of the elliptical free-associating that had made our private talk seem like a psychedelic tour of hyperspace. Reverend James closed the proceedings by importuning divine guidance in the task at hand and justice for the evil force that had snatched a young life.

chapter 9

AND THAT, I BELIEVE, IS EVERYBODY? VERY GOOD."
The panel members were seated around a large table in a conference room, Kershaw at the head. The introductions had been brief, since the members already knew each other, as allies or adversaries. Kershaw identified me as an investigator he'd hired after appropriate inquiries and strong recommendations, and if anyone cared, it didn't show. Wanda Pryce-Jones gave me one of those vague "I know I know you, but I think you're one of the *little* people" acknowledgments, which was fine with me. Finn offered a curt nod, then resumed the look of surly impatience he'd worn at City Hall. Only Lynn Daniels mustered a smile, a brief reprise of the one that had brought me along, and it dampened whatever lingering doubts I had.

I accepted a cup of coffee and took a chair against the wall. The panelists engaged in warm-up chatter or eyed each other warily while Kershaw busied himself pulling papers out of an old briefcase as shapeless as a dead cow's udder.

Lynn had called it right—the mayor had appointed an all-party congress, divining the city's fault lines with exquisite accuracy. The factions were so balanced that, while all would *feel* represented, it was a safe bet that at the end of the day, Flanagan would be even more firmly entrenched, O'Conor's hold on the loyalties of the beleaguered would be secure, and the village scolds, as typified by Wanda Pryce-Jones, would be out of ammo.

Kershaw, of course, was supposed to make the whole thing run—keep the factions talking, provide the structure, lend his reputation for straight shooting to the end product. He had national cachet, having appeared on television day after day, years before, as he stood in for a noxious president before a Senate committee baying for blood. He'd become something of a folk hero in the process—even though his client was widely reviled—for the dexterity with which his dry, Yankee ripostes had punctured the flatulent posturing of his interlocutors. Eventually even the dimmest senatorial bulb had realized it was time to cut losses, some obscure constitutional prerogative was saved, and citizen Kershaw returned home, luster burnished, to a career counseling the rich and an endless succession of good works, citizens' committees, dollar-a-year jobs, and honoraria. My only question was whether he still had as much mind as a programmable VCR.

Reverend James's standing was of newer vintage. He'd first caught the public's attention a few years ago, when he'd led a coalition to integrate a white section of Dorchester. It had resulted in some glorious dust-ups, with howling mobs of poor whites descending on the infiltrating columns while gangs of youths—black *and* white—took advantage of the confusion to loot stores and burn cars. It quickly slopped over into an adjacent black neighborhood and, in the end, there were as many outraged black property owners as white, the whites in the targeted area had fled to other parts, and the neighborhood was as segregated as before—only now it was all black. Somehow this had led the media to attach "prominent black spokesman" to James's name as automatically as it mentioned his clerical title and to seek his eloquent sound bites whenever there was an issue affecting anyone darker than a marshmallow. "Don't wanna be Sambo, better be Rambo" was a recent contribution, lauded by *Hub* editorialists as a pithy lesson in black self-esteem. No one had gotten more mileage out of denouncing the police in general and Flanagan in particular. If Lynn Daniels was right, James was a far more fair-minded man than I'd assumed, and his recent performance suggested she might be correct; I counted him a toss-up.

After her remarks at Finn's, I didn't expect any surprises out of Pryce-Jones. Her opinion was as good as written, and to hell with the facts. If things came out as I expected, her faction's anti-Flanagan sniping would be at least temporarily suppressed, while O'Conor would have bought the faction's continued loyalty—a nice finesse.

Lynn Daniels had won my loyalty, although some of that could have been glands. She'd sounded solid, like someone with a mind and not just a set of reflexes, and I took her at her word: a tough sell if anyone planned on railroading a result, either way.

I'm sure I wasn't the only person who'd lifted his eyebrows at the news the mayor had appointed Sowell Endicott to the panel, but it was an inspired choice. Endicott was a black professor of criminology at the University of Massachusetts, a perennial hotbed of ugly racial clashes. When a reporter asked had him how the university should respond to an African-American student organization making some point or another by occupying an administration building, Endicott had replied: "Call Orkin." This attitude, so at odds with academic orthodoxy, coupled with a body of unsentimental work on penology, had won him the enduring emnity of the feverishly compassionate and a reputation for tough-minded objectivity with those members of the community who thought with their minds and not their epidermis.

The rest of the group had ideologies bracketing the possibilities: a strident Irishwoman from South Boston who held a seat on the school board and occasionally vented observations about minority groups that would have seemed congenial to Goebbels; the director of community relations for the Boston Archdiocese, an amiable bridge-builder who turned up on the op-ed pages to explain the wiggle-room in Cardinal Kelleher's Draconian proscriptions; the co-director of an environmental group that regularly importuned the Massachusetts legislature to accord people and unicellular life forms equal claims to the planet; the head of Teamsters local 398, who'd once called Jimmy Hoffa a pansy, beat an indictment every five years or so, and would probably be secretary of labor if Mussolini ever became president; the heir to a shipping fortune, who lavished millions on candidates who agreed that since Prohibition had worked so well with alcohol it ought to be extended to guns; and finally Finn, who'd made it clear that this was a little piece of Kabuki theater that was just another business expense.

All in all, a finely tuned machine: three sure votes for unilateral disarmament, three for the Fourth Reich, and four—Kershaw, Daniels, Endicott, and the archdiocesan— for common sense and a fair hearing. If Lynn Daniels was right, James might be a wild card instead of the throwaway antipolice vote O'Conor probably expected, but that would only pad O'Conor's margin, cementing my conviction that O'Conor was a master tactician.

"S'pose . . ." I looked up as Kershaw cleared his throat. "S'pose we ought to proceed, hem? Set of agreed principles, schedule, that sort of thing?" He had a way of following a question by peering inquisitively over half-glasses perched on the end of his long nose with a look that implied that fate hung on the answer, although it occurred to me he might just be trying to remember the question.

Kershaw started to pass around a sheaf of papers. "Don't mean to presume. Only a talking piece; want everybody—"

The door opened and Kershaw stopped midsentence. Eleven heads swiveled.

"Mr. Kershaw? I am at the right office, aren't I?"

The voice was a woman's, but the body that came through the door was that of a large German shepherd. The woman followed, matching the dog's measured pace, her right hand grasping a metal handle strapped to the dog's back. They stopped just inside the door, the dog immediately sinking to its haunches. "Mr. Kershaw?"

Kershaw tugged his ear in momentary perplexity, and then a light went on. "Ah, Miss Kiernan. How careless of me. Started without you."

The dog stood and escorted the woman toward Kershaw's voice until she stood in front of him. "Won't happen again. I would have been on time,"—she thrust out her hand— "but I'm afraid your building doesn't comply with the laws on access for the handicapped." She cocked a head topped with a mass of tight red curls.

"Oh. I . . ." He pushed his hand hesitantly toward hers.

"No problem. I won't sue you until we get this job done. Good to be here." She pumped his hand, then gave the dog's lead a slight tug and made the rounds of the table as Kershaw introduced the players. At each stop, the dog settled back and waited, a watchful "Don't make me rip your throat out" look lighting its face.

She reached me last. Her hand was dry and strong. "Nichols, huh? Peggy Kiernan. Mr. Kershaw said you'd be here." The red curls stopped just south of my chin.

"I'm afraid I . . ." I looked at Kershaw.

"Oh, my. Yes. Should have explained." He sank into his seat. "Miss Kiernan's our chief investigator. On loan from the district attorney's office. Very talented, from what I hear. We had a little chat yesterday, and I think she'll be a great help." He put elbows on the table and brought his fingertips to his nose. "A great help."

"Hope so, Mr. Kershaw. Look forward to working with all of you." She moved forward until she felt the edge of the chair next to mine, stooped to tap the seat, and sank into it. The dog, tongue lolling, planted himself at her feet.

"Well, as I was saying . . ." Kershaw returned to his agenda.

"Miss anything?" Kiernan's light, clear voice interrupted the funk I was developing at the news that there was a chief investigator and I wasn't it.

"Little bonding, some light sparring. Nothing serious. No assignments. Kershaw was just getting into that." I looked her over, quickly at first and then more deliberately when it sank in that she wasn't going to notice.

"Good thing. These folks are going to need guidance, unless I miss my guess."

"I wouldn't be surprised."

"Nichols, huh? Never heard of you. Know a lot of the private guys. You from out of town?" She was slim, somewhere in her midthirties, with curly red clown hair. Below the dark glasses a round, freckled face stopped short of pretty but would be fun to watch laughing. She didn't wear make-up and looked as though she took a lot of showers.

"Been away a while."

"Kershaw said you were a friend of Tip Finn's?" She had fixed on my voice and faced me while she spoke.

"More like a friend of Tip Finn's friend."

"Said Tip Finn recommended you."

"I suppose he did."

She drew out her lip and looked thoughtful. "Kershaw said you had 'relevant experience.' What would that be?"

"I was a cab driver."

She cocked her head and listened for a second, as though replaying it to see if she'd heard right. "You kidding?"

"Kershaw translates that into something he calls 'transportation security.'"

"You aren't kidding."

"Well, on my résumé I say that I'm a P.I., by way of the military police in Vietnam, but I'd rather think of myself as a cabby with connections."

She laughed softly, showing little, white teeth with a small gap in the top front.

"How about you?"

"How'd I get the job?"

"Right."

"Well, the first reason is that I've got a pretty good reputation as a prosecutor. I've been at it ten years now, and I guess people think I know how to run an investigation. Any prosecutor would kill for a shot like this, and frankly, I've earned it."

"And the second reason?"

"The second reason is the reason why the first reason doesn't matter. The mayor's my uncle."

I stared at her. "You kidding?"

"And you thought you had connections."

As we turned to listen to the deliberations, I thought that O'Conor really was a clever lad; this thing wasn't going any place he hadn't pointed it.

". . . hearings. There's nothing like sunlight on a festering sore. And it's not just blacks, you know. How they treat gays and lesbians should be a major part . . ." The woman from the environmental group was holding forth.

"Jesus Christ—you gotta be kidding." The Teamsters rep shot her the look he'd developed for scabs. "I got a union to run—let's worry about the faggots some other time."

"Ah . . . Ted, wouldn't it be better if we all avoided . . . ah . . . provocative language? After all, we're here to bring people together." The archdiocesan flack's palsied smile oozed good fellowship.

"I couldn't agree more, Daniel. Let's all avoid name-calling. I have no intention of calling Mr. . . . Marcello a cryptofascist, even though he is one. What we . . ."

"*Marciano.*" The Teamsters rep gave her his "How'd you like your knees broken?" glare.

"Whatever. What we *do* have to do is consider the make-up of the department. I'm sure much of what we're seeing simply reflects the aggressive, racist attitudes of any group of white, heterosexual men."

Wanda Pryce-Jones bobbed her expensive hair enthusiastically. "Absolutely. Have any of you looked at the percentage of women who take the entrance examination—"

Lynn Daniels caught my eye, rolled hers, then leaned back and started massaging her temples.

"We're not here, *sweetie*, to worry about whether the police department takes in enough women, or dwarfs, or whatever you're pushing these days." The school board member's bulldog face was set to bite. "We're here to put these *fairy* stories"—she scowled at the shipping heir—"to rest once and for all, so the *men* who put their lives at risk can—"

"Really!" The shipping heir looked around the table for reinforcements as his piping voice declared *his* concern. "We should consider whether they need guns at all. In England, you know . . ."

". . . a time for healing, not hurting. Why, I . . ."

"Perhaps we should . . ."

"I think . . ."

Kiernan leaned over and whispered: "I'll go with the union guy in five rounds. He snarls better than Leba."

"I'll take the school board against the field: her teeth are bigger than the dog's, and I think she's rabid." Our heads were close together, and I liked the clean, just-washed smell of her hair.

Kershaw broke in. "All right, let's everybody settle down. You're all strong-willed, articulate people with legitimate points of view, but—"

"Legitimate points of view! Why, did you hear what

she—" The shipping heir stabbed a shaky finger at the school-board woman.

"That won't be helpful, Blaine." Without raising his voice, Kershaw managed to snap the words as though he'd sent them out on the end of a whip, and the man slowly lowered the offending digit.

Kershaw seemed to pop in and out of focus, and now he was once again the hickory-tough, nimble-witted advocate who had dominated boardrooms, hearing rooms, and courtrooms for five decades. He looked around the table once more, noted the averted eyes and pinched lips, and nodded.

"Good. Now, we are here for one purpose, and only that purpose: to determine whether the Boston Police Department, under Commissioner Flanagan, has systematically deprived minorities of their civil rights. We are not here to pursue our individual criminal justice agendas, however worthy they may be. Are we all agreed on that?" His watery eyes searched the table. Finding no dissenters, he gave a sharp nod. "Good—that's settled, then." He swiveled to face Pryce-Jones. "And do you know, Wanda, the one lesson almost fifty years of public life has taught me?"

"I'm afraid I do not." She'd crossed her arms across her chest and gone into a pout.

"Never miss an opportunity to go to the bathroom. Five minutes? There's coffee for those who want it." He rose slowly, a segment at a time, then loped out the door.

chapter 10

MY DOG HAS A BETTER IDEA HOW TO DO THIS than most of these people." Kiernan held her coffee cupped in both hands and whispered conspiratorily while we waited for the meeting to resume.

"What's your program?"

"When I got tapped for this, I lined up a bunch of paralegals and some law students first thing. We've got to go through the records, see what they show."

"May take a while."

"Not too long. Flanagan's only been in eighteen months. You expect an excess-force complaint about every other day—guys figure that gives them a card to play—but most of the horseshit ones get dropped pretty early. It's the ones that the complainant thinks enough of to stick with through internal review that we got to worry about. See if the process is rigged, that sort of thing. We'd better also look at the cops' own use-of-force reports, see what they show—

any patterns, how they compare with before Flanagan took over."

"Sounds right. Count me in."

"Maybe we can find some better use for you. You'd probably find it pretty slow going after P.I. work."

It had a dismissive ring to it, but the double door to the conference room opened and Kershaw walked in and took his seat at the head of the table before I could get worked up. "Well, shall we resume? A bit more to do, I think." The table filled again.

"For want of a better starting point, would you all please take a look at my outline." Papers rustled, reading glasses were extracted, heads bent.

I glanced over my copy. "Nothing very startling here," I whispered in Kiernan's ear. "Some boilerplate about objectivity and fairness and the need for strict confidentiality until the final report's released." I felt a pang as I thought about Bucky's expectations of me and wondered what that was all about.

"Umm. Anything substantive?"

"Let's see." I flipped to the second page. "Ah, yes—here we are. 'The chief investigator will report to the chairperson daily. Staff, under the direction of the chief investigator, will review such records and conduct such inquiries as it deems appropriate, at all times keeping the chairperson advised of its progress. Upon completion of its review, staff, under the direction of the chief investigator, will prepare a report on its findings, which will be furnished to the commission for its use in preparing its official report and recommendations.'"

She nodded. "Good. Keeps Kershaw in control so we don't have eleven chiefs. The man's been around the track a few times."

I looked up when Kershaw cleared his throat. "Well, let's talk about this. Any questions, comments, that sort of thing? Don't be shy—haven't bitten anyone since I got false teeth."

Appreciative titters. The environmentalist raised her hand. "I don't see anything about hearings—or am I missing something?"

"No, you're quite right, Robin. We won't be holding hearings for some time to come, if at all."

"But aren't we here to shine a light on what's been going on? I mean . . ."

"She *is* missing something—a brain. She wants a media circus." I looked across, but no one seemed to have heard Kiernan's venomous whisper.

"I have to say, Eliot, I think there's something to what Robin says. We can't just spend weeks behind closed doors. The public won't stand for it." It was the archdiocesan representative, wearing a faceful of good intentions.

"He means the *Hub* won't stand for it, having to wait for all those juicy stories." Kiernan barely bothered to lower her voice.

Kershaw shook his head, hard. "No. The mayor made it very clear to me that he doesn't think it is in the best interests of the city to draw this out, and I agree. There is no reason why it should take more than a few weeks for our staff"—he nodded in our direction—"to examine the records and report their findings to us. We can determine the need for further action then. If we had hearings now, with no hard facts, we'd simply be inviting people to strike poses."

"That's what most of them want, of course: to get on television asking 'How many people of color did you beat today?' kind of questions, to impress their friends. Kershaw knows that." Derision oiled Kiernan's monologue.

"Eliot, I have to tell you that I was talking to Corey Webster the other night. The chairman of POCAT?" Pryce-Jones was leaning forward, forearms on the table, and had adopted a patient, humoring teacher tone. "He was threatening to take his people into the streets. Of course I counseled restraint, but I just don't know how long I can control him if we don't appear to be making progress. I think hearings might . . ."

"That's her way of reminding Kershaw and everyone else that she can set Webster's dogs loose, any time she wants." I was starting to like the feel of Kiernan's commentary against my ear, but if she got any louder, she wasn't going to have a lot of friends around the table.

Sowell Endicott, who'd kept his peace during the earlier clamor, chuckled. "Lady, I'm sure if you tell Mr. Webster you'll cut off his allowance if he misbehaves, he'll be a good boy. That is right, isn't it? You fund that bunch of children?"

Pryce-Jones fired a venemous look across the table. "I don't have to tell you who I—"

Kershaw rapped bony knuckles on the table. "Wanda, I'm sure you'll use your considerable influence constructively, as you always do. You tell that fellow you'll hold him personally responsible for any mischief. We're not going to have our schedule dictated by outside threats."

Pryce-Jones slumped back and once more folded her arms protectively across her chest. Her "Yes, Eliot" was barely audible.

"Guy did a pretty good job on that twit." Maybe no one else heard Kiernan's aside, but Endicott turned his head a fraction and either his eye twitched or it was a wink.

"Eliot, with all respect, I really do think we should at least get Commissioner Flanagan in right away. There's a great deal he should answer for that we know about already. Why, just last spring he—"

The environmentalist's mincing indignation was apparently more than Kiernan could bear, because she was suddenly on her feet. "May I speak, please?"

Several people looked vaguely startled, as though they'd forgotten we were there. Without waiting for an answer, Kiernan felt her way to the table next to Kershaw and stood with her arms folded across her chest. The dog padded over and took up station next to her.

"Lady, Dapper Flanagan'll chew your ass to ribbons, you hold hearings now. Remember Ollie North? Ate those senators' lunches. Thought they'd haul him in, make a few speeches about the seperation of powers, nation of laws not of men, all that gas, get some prime time back home? Only he gave a prettier speech than they did, and they didn't have a stopper, 'cause they hadn't done their homework. You like sucking wind?"

The woman paled under her tan. "I *beg* your—"

"Flanagan'll pull the same thing. He shows up—that pretty uniform, all those decorations—what're you gonna say? 'Commissioner Flanagan, isn't it true your men have been picking on black people—and you *let* them?'" Ms. Kiernan did a nice imitation of the woman's plummy vowels.

I heard a choking sound and saw that Sowell Endicott had his hand plastered over his mouth in an only partially successful effort to suppress a snort. Kiernan's target sent a quick dagger his way, sputtered: "Of course not. I'd—"

"He'll think about it long and hard, give the cameras a patient, pained look. And then do you know what he'll say, all nice and slow?"

"I didn't mean to suggest for a minute—"

"'Bet . . . your . . . ass.'"

"What? Now, *really*—"

"Oh, he won't *say* 'Bet your ass.' He'll say, all soft and sincere, '*Ms.* Hoyt'—and he'll get that right, the *Ms.*, draw it out so everybody who doesn't watch PBS gets the joke— '*Ms.* Hoyt, last year I held a boy in my arms—six months on the force—as the last drops of blood poured from the bullet hole through his heart. You weren't there, *Ms.* Hoyt, because you were whale-watching off Nantucket or getting your cellulite sucked out at some fat farm, but *if* you'd been there, you'd have heard him whisper, 'Is the little girl on her way to her first Communion okay? Did I stop that coked-out rapist in time? I did? Then tell the squad not to grieve for me, because I got to do my duty.'"

"Oh, but—"

"'An' when we laid that darlin' lad to rest, *Ms.* Hoyt?'" She had slipped into a gentle brogue, and if she'd broken out with "Danny Boy," I wouldn't have been surprised.

"Y-yes?"

"'That sweet little girl kissed her crucifix and placed it on that young man's cold, white shirt, just before they closed the coffin and lowered it into the welcoming sod.' Should I go on, or do you get the picture?"

The woman's mouth was a perfect ring as she shook dazed eyes from side to side. "No—I mean—"

"Right. You get the picture. And do you know what he'll really be saying?"

"I don't think—"

"He's saying, 'Bet your ass my men've been picking on people of color. They've been kicking white ass, brown ass, yellow ass, and if necessary, purple ass, any Martian tries something in *my* city.' And you know what else?"

The environmentalist, looking more and more like a stroke victim, gave the same, slow head shake, her fingers kneading the skin under her neck as though she were debating whether to pull it over her face.

"A million people in Boston, including ninety percent of the blacks, are going to watch that show and say, 'God bless Commissioner Flanagan.' You want to be known as the woman who single-handedly canonized dear old Dapper?"

The woman seemed to be having trouble getting her lips in synch. Finally she wrenched herself out of her daze. "Now *you* listen—I don't need to put up with—" Her hand clutched at the rope of woven rain-forest bark circling the stringy neck.

"That's what'll happen, lady, we treat this like a photo op. I don't know what the evidence will look like when we're finished, but we'd damn well better know what it looks like before you put Flannagan on the stand, or he'll leave you feeling like you just had open-heart surgery without anesthesia."

"Eliot! I simply will not let her—" The woman's face colored a deep red. The others gaped, goggle-eyed, except Endicott, whose face was pure glee, and Lynn Daniels, who was into serious tick-tack-toe on the legal pad.

"Now, don't get in a state, Robin. Miss Kiernan's a prosecutor, and they tend to be a little . . . blunt. I'm sure she didn't mean anything personal. Let's listen to the young lady for a minute, because she happens to be dead right." Kershaw turned to Kiernan. "What's your proposal, Miss Kiernan? I take it you have one?"

"There's only one way to proceed, Mr. Kershaw."

"Which is?"

"Hard work. Police-type work, the kind of work I know how to do—a thorough, professional investigation. Then you have your hearings, if they seem indicated."

"Why don't you tell us how you'd go about it."

"Look for patterns. Such as, is it disproportionately the same guys coming in all the time with the arrestee in pieces because he 'resisted arrest'; is the perp who can't walk 'cause he 'resisted arrest' disproportionately likely to be black or some other minority? Have the numbers changed since Flanagan took over? And most important, you look at the administrative record, see whether the perp who files an excess-force claim had something to beef about, or if it's just garbage the guy dreams up 'cause it's the best he's got. *That's* the kind of evidence you bang a guy with when he tries to wrap himself in the flag."

The shipping heir, in acute distress, uttered a plaintive wail: "But we already know there's been so much police brutality. Why, we see arrests on television all the time, and sometimes it's . . . simply appallingly violent."

"That's just the point, mister—police work *is* brutal. Lot of times, *please* just won't cut it. You see a fifteen-second clip of a narcotics bust and six cops are stomping on one guy, what the hell's it mean?" Ms. Kiernan looked ready to call the dog in to give the man a taste of police brutality firsthand. She took a deep breath, exhaled, and proceeded in more measured tones. "Nothing. You can't tell anything from that clip, because you weren't there. You don't know if those cops just felt like stomping some citizen, maybe 'cause he's black or Puerto Rican or something else, or if they're stomping him because he showed them something that said they'd better stomp him or he's going to stomp them, or worse."

"Well, how are you ever going to tell which it is, then?" The man wore a 'What did I do to deserve this?' look, and I almost felt sorry for him.

"Patterns, mister, patterns. And they're in the records. Let me get my hands on those excess-force reports, review the administrative records, and I can tell you pretty damn quick whether there are questionable patterns and whether Flanagan's winking at them. I can tell you whether the complaints dismissed after the administrative review should've been or if something's getting buried. Then you have your hearings if it looks like there's something to talk about."

"Exactly right." Kershaw nodded quickly, then tapped his eraser on the table. "Any doubt that's the way to go?" His little eyes circled the room.

"It's the only way to go." Sowell Endicott looked Kiernan over approvingly.

"That's right. Let's get this done." Finn's abrasive rasp, missing up till then, swiveled heads. "Let's cut the crap. Government wants to know if I'm complying with the equal-opportunity employment laws, they look at my records. Let her"—he nodded at Peggy—"look at the damn records, tell us what's what. I don't have time to screw around with a lot of talk. I got a business to run, okay?"

Pryce-Jones stirred briefly, seemed about to gather her resources for a last sally, but looked at Finn and thought better of it. "Well, Tip—I had hoped for more from you." She folded her hands under her chin and sulked like a disgruntled schoolmarm.

"Fine, fine. That's settled, then. Splendid." Kershaw started to gather his papers.

"Just one more thing, Eliot." James's deep voice, silent since the group convened, got instant attention. "The police investigation of the Whitmore killing: we must satisfy ourselves it is proceeding aggressively."

There were a few nods and umms, but Kershaw, looking uncertain, rubbed his sharp chin. "I'm not sure that's within our mandate, is it?"

"With all respect, I can't think of anything that has more bearing on our purpose." James spoke slowly, quietly, forcefully. "Until that man is under arrest, every man in the department is a suspect. I have committed my standing in the African-American community to the proposition that we must wage war on the crime that is decimating us; I can't expect my people to follow unless they have faith that the police are with us in that war, not against us. We must satisfy ourselves that the police are doing everything in their power to bring that man to justice. I—"

Endicott broke in: "Excuse me, Reverend, but you keep saying 'that man.' You mean the person the witness is reported to have seen with Whitmore?"

"Well, of course. The policeman who killed Purnell Whitmore. I want nothing more than to be able to tell Mrs. Whitmore that the police have that man, and I can think of nothing that will encourage confidence in the police faster than knowing that they've been as diligent in apprehending one of their own as they would be if a black man had murdered a white boy."

"Well, actually, Reverend,"—Endicott's tone was gentle—"I assume that what Mrs. Whitmore wants—what we all want—is for the police to catch the person who did it. It's a little soon to decide it was a policeman."

James appeared more disappointed than angry. "Please —this isn't an academic exercise, Mr. Endicott. I knew that boy; I know his mother. He was like a son to me. I'm familiar with your reputation, as I'm sure you are with mine. I tried to leave my biases behind me when I accepted this position. Won't you do the same?"

Endicott kept his voice level. "Not my bias in favor of the truth, Reverend, no. I'd hate to think anything *we* did pressured the police into assuming a policeman did it, to the exclusion of all other possibilities. Probably too much pressure that way already, thanks to the media."

James's restraint dissolved in a rush. "'Other possibilities'! They have a witness who *saw* a policeman push the boy into that alley! If you think that by being an apologist for the police you can—"

I don't know if anyone else noticed Endicott's knuckles whiten as he clenched his fists, but Lynn Daniels intervened before he could reply. "Theo, calm down." She laid a hand on his forearm. "Mr. Endicott is perfectly correct; the last thing any of us want is for the police to jump to conclusions. Mr. Endicott,"—she looked over at him, the restraining hand still resting on James's arm—"you do agree that it's critical for the police to run down the person the witness saw as quickly as possible?"

"Of course. I also assume they're doing everything possible to find him; *they* know they're all under a cloud until he's brought in. If anything, I'm concerned they're so fixated on getting this cop—if it was a cop—that they're passing up other leads."

"But you can appreciate Theo's concern; he has a special responsibility here. He has to be able to assure Mrs. Whitmore everything possible is being done. I think that would calm the whole community." Daniels gave James a sympathetic nod. "We ought to be able to monitor the Whitmore investigation without getting in the way."

Endicott looked skeptical, but then Peggy Kiernan chimed in. "Mr. Nichols here has experience with police procedures. *He* could monitor the investigation. I'm sure he'd be careful."

It made me uncomfortable, all those eyes turning to look at me, and Kiernan's assumption that she could put me on a make-work project rankled. "I've handled police investigations, yes, but—"

"There, then. That's all right, isn't it?" Lynn looked around the table. "Nason—ah . . . Mr. Nichols—could look after that. You'll do that, won't you, Mr. Nichols?"

The others were all looking at me, so I was probably the only one who caught Lynn's smile. I didn't return it. "If Mr. Kershaw agrees that's what I should do."

Kershaw was looking pensively at Kiernan. "Perhaps that's right. You can spare Mr. Nichols, Miss Kiernan?"

"I think so."

Kershaw continued to massage his chin. "I think Theo's right. Hadn't thought of that." Suddenly he nodded decisively. "Certainly." He dropped his hand onto the table: "You do that, Mr. . . . . ah . . . ."

"Nichols."

"That's it. Yes, that'll be splendid."

Lynn turned to James. "Theo, will that take care of it?"

She still had her hand resting on his big forearm.

"I suppose. But Mr. Nichols,"—his eyes bore in on me and I began to understand what people meant about his force—"I'm counting on you. More important, Mrs. Whitmore is counting on you. If the police aren't doing everything they should be to catch the *policeman* who murdered Purnell—" He scowled at Endicott. "If they're off chasing phantoms, you'll let us know right away." It wasn't a question.

Kershaw moved into the silence. "Very good, then. Miss Kiernan, will you and Mr. . . . . ah . . . yes, the two of you prepare an action outline for us to review?" He looked around the table and rubbed his hands together, looking for all the world as though we'd just finished dinner in a private room at Locke-Ober. "That's all taken care of, then. A good morning's work. Yes, just fine." He pushed jerkily back from the table and the others rose with him.

I was waiting for Kiernan when I felt a hand on my shoulder. "May I have a word with you, Mr. Nichols?" Endicott didn't wait for an answer, and I followed him to a far corner.

"You heard my concern. I don't think there's a chance in hell the police would lie down on this, because a cop may be involved—I *do* think they may press so hard to find the guy that witness saw that they could overlook other possibilities. There's too much heat; that's when things get missed. What do you think?" Endicott's mischievous look was long gone.

"I think you're right. Whatever you may think of Flanagan, this isn't Mississippi thirty years ago. The police surfaced this suspect the minute they talked to the witness. They wouldn't have done that if they meant to cover for one of their own. I'm wasting time."

Endicott looked over at Kershaw, who was standing by the door as his guests filed out. "You've got to do as Mr. Kershaw said. But if, in the process, you see other leads . . . ?" He looked at me from under raised eyebrows.

"I'll keep my eyes open. That's all I can do."

Kiernan and the dog arrived before Endicott could add anything. "I've read some of your stuff, Mr. Endicott. Not bad. Not bad at all." Kiernan must have felt the smile that had come across his face at her approach, because suddenly she was wearing a matching model.

"Sowell, please. I appreciate that. Ah, maybe we could discuss it some time?" He was scratching the dog's head when I slipped away and caught up with Lynn Daniels by the door.

She gave me a poke in the ribs and a wink. "Welcome to the diversity circus, Nason. Ain't this gonna be fun?"

"A ball. And thanks for the job assignment. I might as well be counting parking tickets."

Daniels watched James's large back disappear down the hall to the elevators. "I know, but Theo was getting squirrelly; this was the only way to cool him off. I can't blame him, really. This shouldn't take much of your time." She slid a business card into my breast pocket. "Maybe you can report your conclusions to me. Over dinner?" She turned and hurried away before I could answer.

chapter 11

WHAT A BUNCH OF DO-DICKS. YOU REALLY DRIVE a cab?"

"Um-huh. You really the mayor's niece?"

"Think those doofuses let me talk to them like that, I weren't?" The light changed, but the dog didn't move until it had checked both directions.

"Got a point. Impressed me."

"Can't stand all that talk. Got a job, do it." The dog stopped at the Union Oyster House. "In here." I followed her through the door.

"Hey, Peg!" Two men at the bar broke off their conversation when they caught sight of us.

"Howya doin', Tommy?"

Others looked up, chimed in. "Hear Vasquez caught ten and ten."

"Sullivan really cite Ruhling?"

"Reversible says it's com-ing ba-ack."

She laughed derisively. "His hair'll come back first."

I let her lead the way, or rather I took the only option she gave me. The place was crowded with Government Center types on their lunch break, but everyone gave the dog a wide berth and we followed a straight line to a corner table.

I slid in. "Reversible?"

"Howard Ruhling. Little maggot, works for the defender's office. Says, 'Yer Hon-or, that ruling's reversible' so often he caught the handle 'Reversible Ruhling.' He's oh and six with me, as of yesterday." She ran her hand across the table, touched a bowl, fished out an oyster cracker, and popped it in her mouth.

"Ernie Axner, Peg. Gotta talk to ya." An oily, fat man plopped into the seat next to her and dropped a Samsonite case on the table. The knot on his tie was three inches below his throat, draped with a spray of gray hairs that lay over it like Spanish moss.

"Not now, Ernie. Can't you see I'm busy?"

The fat man noticed me long enough to mutter, "Hey, pal," then pulled his hand away before I had to touch it.

"I need a break with the Simpson kid, Peg. Lemme plead to simple, do the auto concurrent?" He snatched a handful of the crackers and started flinging them in like he was shooting baskets, pig eyes fastened on her face.

She snorted. "Lady's ear showed up at the ER—what?— an hour after the rest of her, guy's gonna plead to simple? You're talking aggravated, *with* specs. You want Christmas early, I'll toss in the auto. Now, get lost, okay?"

He fed in more crackers, not looking, a good three inches through open air. Celtics needed a slow white guy, replace Bird, they could do worse. "Peg, sweetheart, he pleads to that, kid's looking at Walpole—"

"Kid's been looking at Walpole since he was born. Congratulations—just passed the entrance exam, full scholarship. Now, bug off, Ernie. I gotta get my appetite back."

The fat man pushed away from the table with a groan. "He's a nice-lookin' kid, Peg. They'll—"

"He'll have an active social life, Ernie. Lot more active than that lady. Have a happy day."

He popped another cracker, muttered "shit," and gathered up the case. "How about he pleads, you put in a good word, maybe get a little slack on the sentence?" He blotted his lips with his necktie.

"How about you talk to Leba, see if you understand her any better than you do me?"

"Aw, Peg." He backed away.

I watched his sweat-stained back recede. "Nice meeting your friends like this. They all so personable?"

"Ernie the attorney? He's one of the better ones, actually, if you can prefer one bottom-feeder over another. Talk to the real slime in my office, front of witnesses. Least Ernie's not a co-conspirator."

A waitress who was going to look bored at Armageddon demanded Kiernan's order.

"Chowder and crabcakes."

"Yours?"

"Crabcakes. No chowder. Makes me sorrier than ever I didn't go to law school. Now, why don't you fill me in on the program. You seem to have it all figured out."

"Sure." She ran a hand through her mop of curly red hair. "Like the man said: you check out the Whitmore investigation, make sure it's on the up and up."

"You have any doubt about that? Think the department's so far gone they got some guy the whole city's howling for tucked away in Flanagan's basement?"

"Doesn't matter what I think. Gotta be done, and you're the man."

"Look, Ms. Kiernan—"

"Peg, or Peggy."

"Okay, Peggy—you could have told them it's a crock, like Endicott said."

"You heard James—think he was going to let it go?"

"Maybe not, but—"

"Look, Nichols—"

"Nason, or Nase."

"Whatever. I lined up my team before I knew you were joining the party. You think I should have told James we'd put a paralegal on his project? You've got the background, you were the logical guy. Sorry, but there it is."

Her reasoning was too good, and sulking in front of a blind person is a lonely sport. "It won't take long, you know. They're screwing around, it's going to be obvious."

"Maybe so, but you'd better do it right. You know, who's on it, how many, what instructions. What kinda procedure, see what I mean?"

"I know what you mean. I've been through it."

"Good. So you know the drill: who've they interviewed, they cutting any corners, would you have done anything they haven't done. Twenty-twenty hindsight. You've been there."

"Yeah. I hated it."

"So now you get to dish it. *Carpe diem.*"

"And if they're doing it right?"

"Then that's what we report."

A hand descended on my shoulder. "Nason Nichols, chauffeur to the stars. And in such good company, too. Bernie Lawson, Peg. How you doing?"

"Hi, Bernie. You know this guy?"

"Known this guy since he pulled me out of a love hotel in Saigon 'bout three minutes before Charlie turned it into a deep-fat fryer." He lowered himself into the seat the fat man had vacated. "You out of the cab business, Nase?"

"I guess so. For the time being."

Lawson looked at her, then back at me. "You two working together?"

I nodded across the table. "I think I'm working *for* her."

"You're involved with this Kershaw thing?"

"Thought I'd fill the time while the cab got a face lift."

He gave Kiernan a sad look. "Heard you'd signed on with them, Peg. True?"

"Gospel, Bernie." She gave him that chipper smile I'd seen in the meeting, the one that said, "And you can stick it if you don't like it."

"Why, Peg? What you wanna be lining up with those cheeseheads for? They out to tear the heart out of the department."

He looked at her with basset eyes until she felt it and the smile faded into a thin, compressed line.

"We're out to investigate some pretty serious charges, Lieutenant. Anything wrong with that?"

"Lady, it's tough out there—you know that. Some punk pumped up on PCP, think he comes along 'cause you say 'please'? You get guys out there, every night, only way you get their attention long enough to read their rights, crack 'em one across the chops. Most of us, we're just trying to survive out there."

"Then there's nothing to worry about, is there?"

"If I thought it was going to be a fair investigation, no."

"It'll be a fair investigation, Lieutenant." Her tone said the argument was over.

Bernie started a staring contest I knew he couldn't win, so I broke into it. "Off the record, Bernie, anybody we ought to take a look at? You know, guys who get a kick out of bouncing people around?"

"Look, we got nineteen hundred cops on the force, Nase. Bound to be some bad ones. But like I told you the other night, Dapper's laid down the law, and he means it. Anybody gets out of line, it sure as hell isn't because he's winking at it. You know that, Peg." He sounded surprised he had to spell it out.

Peggy was relentless. "He's the one who's keeping the bad ones around, isn't he?"

Lawson twisted in his seat, looked at Peggy as though wondering who she was. "It's not as easy as all that, and you know it. Guys get seniority, cover their backsides.

Commissioner can't just say, 'Hey, Smith, I hear you're a bad ass; you're gone.' People have to file complaints, and Dapper's got to be able to make a case. None of the complaints that have come through under his watch have stood up."

"Then there shouldn't be any problem if we review them, huh?"

"No, but—"

"I've got an idea, Lieutenant: why don't you tell us who the bad ones are, so we can zero in on their records? Save a lot of time."

Peggy's la-di-da tone seemed calculated to get under Bernie's skin, and I could feel the effort he was making to control himself. "Peg, you know I can't do that. Hell, you're one of—"

" 'One of us,' Lieutenant? That the way you think it goes? Old Peg Kiernan, hard-ass DA, always ready to cut some slack for her friends on the force?"

"Peg, will you cut it out? I meant—"

"Or maybe you meant, Peg Kiernan's O'Conor's niece; gonna go easy on old Dap. Not gonna rough up her uncle's buddy, make 'em both look bad."

Lawson's face hardened. "I was going to say one of the ones I thought we could trust."

"Oh? Well, then, why don't you trust *me*? Tell us who *you* think the bad asses are, Lieutenant. Tell us what they've done, who we should call in. Give us a statement—in writing. Help *us* make a case." The smile turned into a crease.

Lawson looked from her to me, then down at the table. He slowly unclenched his fists. "Peg, I can't do that. I . . . I'm . . ."

"Yes, Lieutenant?"

He spoke softly, pain just behind the words. "Peg, I'm the third most senior black officer on the force. When I joined, weren't twenty of us. Now there're a couple hundred. I've spent twenty years to get to the point where I'm accepted for what I am, which is a damn good cop. The younger black cops look up to me, and I can help them along because the white cops trust me. I couldn't jeopardize that; I just couldn't . . ." His voice trailed off. "I'm sorry."

"You know about these guys, but you can't talk about them?"

"Peg, all I said was there're a few bad apples. Dapper's getting them out as fast as he can, and they don't have a damn thing to do with any of the programs Dapper's put in. He sure as hell isn't letting the department run wild."

"But you won't tell us who they are?"

"I'm sorry, Peg."

"Great. So you cover for them and tell me we shouldn't be looking over your shoulder. Tell it to Mrs. Whitmore, Lieutenant."

The chair clattered against the floor when Lawson jerked to his feet. "If you were a man—if you weren't—" He stopped himself, bit off the sentence.

"'One of us,' Lieutenant?" The smile was frozen on.

"Forget it." He whirled and left.

I watched his straight, tense body shove through the herd of laughing, preening citizens from the easy side of the street upstaging each other with tales of their little triumphs, until I could see it no longer and looked back at Kiernan. A freckle on her cheek was magnified by the crystalline drop she'd missed when she swiped her hand under her dark glasses.

"Pretty tough on Bernie, don't you think?"

"Think I should have told him not to worry, Peg Kiernan's not about to let anything happen to upset her uncle's applecart? That'd be a good thing to get around headquarters, huh?"

I watched the tear lose its mooring, start to work its way down the white skin. "Sure. Guess you're right. Sorry."

The waitress plopped a cup of chowder in front of her. I wondered if she'd snag the tear before it made it to the bottom.

"Just because I'm a prosecutor, they think anything the cops do, that's gotta be okay with me."

"That must be it." She might not, with me looking.

"Think I'm Irish, name like Kiernan, I'm one of them."

"They do think that way. I wouldn't doubt it." The chowder looked good; little chunks of clam floating on the top, yellow globules of butter beading on the milk.

"They all stick together, you know. You just saw that."

"Yep—even made Bernie an honorary member of the Ancient Order Of Hibernians." Lot of places make it too thick, put potatoes in, but the Oyster House keeps it simple, just milk and butter and clams, a little paprika.

"Thinks 'cause he's black he gets a special dispensation, isn't accountable." A second tear followed the curve of her cheek to nestle up against the first.

"A real affirmative-action candidate, old Bernie." Salt—yeah, a little salt's a must.

"And Dapper Flanagan—anything old Dap does, hey, gotta close ranks, stick together, stand up for Dapper. Guy may be a . . . a . . . Neanderthal, but what the hell, stick up for your own."

"Hundred years ago, Bernie would've been fronting for Simon Legree. You got him figured, all right." Could just come right out, ask for some.

"Well, let me tell you something, Nichols—"

"Nase. Or Nason." My napkin slipped to the floor and I bent over for it.

"Huh? Oh, yeah. Anyway, nobody puts Peggy Kiernan in a slot. *Nobody.*"

The tears were gone when I sat back up. Damn, she was quick. "Obviously not. You going to eat that chowder? Probably cool enough now."

"Think just because Flanagan's one of my uncle's biggest assets, I'm gonna bend over backward to protect his butt."

"Nah, they wouldn't think that. Now, if you really don't want it, I'll take it."

"Well, I told my uncle he could find another fish if he

thought I'd risk *my* reputation on a rigged investigation. Gonna play this one straight or not at all."

Her voice had gradually risen until people at the adjoining tables had suspended their forks midway to their mouths while they listened. She picked up an oyster cracker and took a tiny nibble. When she resumed speaking, her voice was little more than a whisper. "Of course, we both know how he *expects* it to come out, don't we?"

"Not hard to figure. You're saving it for the dog, maybe?"

"Well, you don't have to worry about it. I know what I'm doing."

"Not a worry in the world. Not sure dogs like clams, though."

"You see, I owe my uncle a lot. More than I could ever repay."

"Speaks well for you, you feel that way. Maybe it's the pepper—never knew a dog that could stand pepper."

"I was his ward, you know?"

"No, can't say I did. I suppose we could give her some on a spoon, check it out that way."

"My parents died when I was twelve. He took me in, took care of me. Raised me like I was his own." She was far away, a little wistful smile on her lips, her hand dropping below the table to fondle the dog. She leaned across the table. "So he knows he can count on me to do the right thing. He doesn't have a thing to worry about, see?"

"Hey, that's terrific. *Now will you please eat that chowder or give it to me?*"

She snapped back. "Huh? Are you nuts? Get your own chowder. Now, you all straight on your end of things?" She found the spoon and went to work.

After a few, silent moments she laid the spoon on the table. "That wasn't bad. You should have had some." She wiped her mouth and grinned. "We're gonna do this right. Yes, sir. You take care of your side of it, and I'll make sure we bring this out just right. Yeah, we're gonna have some fun."

We worked through the crabcakes. I thought about the odd woman on the other side of the table and wondered if the next few weeks would be fun.

There was a little bit of unfinished business I meant to attend to before I'd feel comfortable devoting all my time to the Kershaw Commission, and after I left Peggy, I decided it was as good a time as any to take care of it. It was time to play hardball with the Quark.

I didn't expect to find Wilkins at home, of course, any more than the savants at MIT expect to turn their eyes on a piece of fermium and find lots of little neutrinos cooing "Choose me, fuse me; I'm your nubile Nobel baby." We work for a living.

A deli on Brighton Avenue sold me the equipment I needed. I loaded it in the tool kit and walked around to the back of the apartment house with the "I got business here" stride that's half the game. Up the fire escape and open the can of sardines. Smash the windowpane. "Psst—here, Bootsie. Dinner. Lovely, stinky *poisson.*"

Soon I was back in my lair, pen in hand: "*Found, Allston area: gray cat, white paws, answers to name of Bootsie. Looks tender; will find out if cat not claimed within forty-eight hours. Principals only.*"

I looked over the text, added my phone number, called it in to the *Hub* classified department. When I hung up, it was with the certainty that at last, the Quark had met his match. I had but to wait.

chapter 12

BUCKY WATCHED THE CUE BALL ROLL TOWARD the pocket. "Damn. Rack 'em up."

"Can I play?"

I looked down. Padraic Hanrahan, ten, was standing behind me, sawed-off cue in hand.

"Beat it, punk—this is a man's game." Bucky popped the balls in the rack, squared it, lifted it off.

"Aw, come on, Dad—you're just afraid I'll beat you. You don't mind, do you, Uncle Nase?"

"Hell, no—I need some competition."

"Okay, Dad?" He was already chalking the stick.

"Okay, kid—don't say I didn't warn you. You break."

"Hey, I got an idea: let's bet on it!"

"Don't be silly, Paddy; it'd be taking candy from a baby."

"I thought this was a man's game. Here." He pulled a mangled dollar out of his pocket and slapped it on the rim of the table.

Bucky looked at the dollar, then at his son, then back again to the dollar. "Might as well pass it over now, sucker." He covered the dollar and I tossed on mine.

"So I was right, huh? O'Conor has it wired?" He polished off the quarter inch of Bushmill's in the bottom of his glass, then picked up his cue.

I thought about it. "Well, he sure put together Noah's ark. Some of them should be certified—but yeah, four or five will give the record a fair look, and they'll line up with the reflexive police-lovers, make a credible majority. I'd say this one's a lock."

"I told you O'Conor's no dummy. Tell me about the niece." He smacked the cue against his leg, nodded his head in admiration. "His niece—awesome move."

"Smart lady, all right. Tough. Knows how to do it."

"Knows how to make sure nobody gets any wrong ideas, huh?"

I lined up my shot. "Oh, she'd know how to do that, all right."

"Whaddya mean, 'she'd know how to'? That's what she's there for, isn't it?"

"Good a guess as any."

"'Good a guess as any'? I want good a guess as any, I'd be over at the parish house, playing bingo. What's that mean?"

"I'm saying . . . nothing. Nothing, okay? Didn't mean to get you all stirred up."

"Well, don't *do* that. I don't need angst."

"Sorry." I put the six hard down the rail.

"Uncle Nase! You shot my ball." We were playing cut-throat, and Padraic was anxiously counting his remaining balls.

"It's a dog-eat-dog world, Paddy." I lined up a tricky two-cushion on the twelve, Bucky's ball. Just a little left of center, not too hard . . .

"Freshen your glass?" Bucky brought the bottle down hard on the table.

The stick jerked and the cue ball kissed the twelve like

maiden aunts meeting at a funeral, then rolled resignedly into a side pocket. "Damn it, Buck!"

"Sorry, sorry. Just trying to be hospitable." He spotted the cue, chalked, then bent over the table and pumped a couple of times.

"Here, Dad." Padraic rattled the ice in his father's glass.

Padraic's ten shot into a corner pocket. "Thank you, son." Bucky took the glass, drained it, and set it down. "The sound of whiskey never disturbed a Hanrahan."

He sank my three, then missed. "Closing in, boys, closing in. Might as well quit now."

"Want to double up?" Padraic peered at his father from the corner of his eye.

"Never throw good money after bad, boy—haven't I taught you that?"

"And that's why you won't double up, Dad? You'd be throwing good money after bad?" He looked up at his father.

"Okay, kid, it's bankruptcy court for you. Put it up."

"Thanks, Dad." He stood on his tiptoes, tongue curling out of his mouth while he sighted down the stick.

"What's your role in all this?"

I sipped my drink. "I bird-dog the Whitmore investigation."

"You know as well as I do the cops are going all out. If you knew Dapper the way I know Dapper . . ."

"Set it to music, Buck. I'm stuck with this." I explained the origin of my assignment.

"Well, I told you you wouldn't have to break a sweat. Any idea when this carnival's over?"

"Few weeks, anyway."

"Can't you be more specific? Like, when the report will issue?"

"Why?"

"Why?"

"Yeah, why? Why do you want to know when the report's coming out? And don't give me that crap about 'just want to make sure everything's on the up and up.' You've got something going, and I want to know what it is."

"Well . . . ah . . . I . . ."

"Cut the bullshit. You want to know, tell me."

"Ah, Jeez. It's just a little business deal I got going. Like to be done before anything comes out, case things get a little riled up for a while. You know how it is."

"No, I don't. What kind of business deal?"

"A little real-estate deal. Talking to Finn gave me the idea. But I don't want to be in the middle of something, have meatballs like Webster stirring things up because they don't like the outcome. Like to have a little warning, that report's coming out."

"You're crazy."

"I knew you'd come through."

"Hey, Dad?" Padraic poked his father in the stomach with the tip of his cue. "Were those striped balls all yours?"

We looked at the table. "Why, you little hustler—I'll break your thumbs."

Bucky cornered him at the dinner table, but the steaming salmon distracted him. After grace, Pegeen, the fifteen-year-old, started explaining why she was waiting for the female condom to come on the market before she did anything.

Bucky interrupted. "Fortunately, darlin', you'll be three years in the convent before that becomes a temptation." He turned to me, ignoring her "Aw, Dad." "So the way it's set up, everything goes through the boss lady?"

"She reports our findings to Kershaw and the others, sure."

"O'Conor's niece gets to decide what they see? Perfect, absolutely perfect. She won't run anything by them the wackos can twist around."

I put the day through reruns. "Yeah . . . it could work that way."

"Of course it's going to work that way. This is a play, O'Conor's the playwright, and the playwright is *supposed* to make it come out the way he wants. O'Conor's doing it like a master, and thank God for that."

I pushed Bucky's knife out from under my nose. "Maybe you're right about what O'Conor wants, but . . ."

"But what?"

"I don't know, Buck. But if O'Conor's got this whole thing scripted, then he's written some funny lines for this woman—Kiernan. She's making some funny noises."

" 'Funny noises'? Don't give me 'funny noises,' Nase. What're you saying?"

I filled him in on lunch and the encounter with Bernie Lawson.

When I finished, his chest heaved with relief. "Like she said, she doesn't want it to look hinky when you've done anointing Dapper. You say she had half the restaurant listening? Great touch."

Then something slipped into place, something that had eluded me that morning. "But you know, she said something strange." I replayed the sound track, heard it again.

"What?"

"Something about Flanagan." I had it almost back, and then it slipped away again.

"My man, you're addled. Too much whiskey."

"No, really." It started to jell. "Sure—that's it."

"What's it?"

"It was during lunch; she said Flanagan was a Neanderthal."

"Deirdre, get the stomach pump. Nase is suffering from acute alcohol poisoning. Come to think of it, grab me another stout instead; I'll join him. . . . What in hell's so strange about that? He *is* a Neanderthal. Wish we had a few more of them."

"But there's a reason that sticks in my mind. The other night at Amrhein's: that toady, Dave, in the back room? That's what he called Flanagan—don't you remember?— when Flanagan went out of the room to take the call about the Whitmore case. He said it to O'Conor."

"What're you trying to say, Nase?"

I thought about it. "I don't know. Maybe nothing. But isn't it odd two people would pick that word, a couple days apart?"

"Maybe your boss hangs out with that jerk, heard him call Flanagan that?"

I thought about it, shrugged. "Sure. Maybe. As good a guess as any."

Deirdre brought the bottle of beer and plopped it down in front of Bucky. He rested his hand on her hip while he poured with the other. "I'm going to hear that a lot, aren't I—'as good a guess as any'?"

"Would you prefer 'it feels right'?"

He kneaded Deirdre's flank. "Yeah—'it feels right.' It sure does."

She slapped his hand away with a laugh. I laughed, too, and felt lonely.

chapter 13

THE NEXT MORNING, I TOOK THE MBTA OVER TO
Government Center and walked to the Area A police
station. Since a cop had been put at the scene of the
Whitmore murder, Internal Affairs would be handling the
investigation. I found it on the third floor, and a secretary
connected me with a Captain Cooper, the officer in charge
of the investigation. He was a short man, with a lot of
years in. A tic tugged at the right side of his face when he
spoke.

"Nichols, huh? And why the hell should I tell you
anything about the investigation?"

"I'm with the Kershaw Commission." I showed him the
piece of paper with the mayor's signature on it. "It's just
part of my job, Captain."

He read it carefully, then said, "Wait here." He walked
back into an office and closed the door. Through the glass, I
could see his silhouette on the phone. After a few minutes,

he came back and threw the paper on the desk. "So you're one of the hotshots out to get Dapper, huh?"

"Like I said, I'm just doing a job, Captain. I'm not out to get anybody. Now, can I see the Whitmore file?"

He glared across the desk. His tic had accelerated. "Think you can do better'n us, huh? I got men on it 'round the clock. You're gonna show us up?"

"How many times I got to say I'm just doing what I'm told, same as you? Now do I get that file, or do I make my own phone call?"

"Guys like you make me sick." He turned with a jerk and went back into the office. When he came back, he was carrying a gusset folder. He slid it across the desk. "Chief's office says we gotta play along. You read it here. Millie,"— the secretary turned in her swivel chair—"watch this guy. Anything comes out of the file, goes back in the file, hear? You"—he jabbed a forefinger at me—"just stay outta my investigation, see? Find you messing things up, sticking your nose where it doesn't belong, I'll squash you like a bug, mayor or no mayor." He went back into the office and slammed the door.

I pulled up a chair and unsnapped the elastic around the file. "High-strung guy, your captain."

Millie had turned her chair around and sat facing me, cheeks vibrating with disapproval. "He's a fine man. They're all fine men here. I think it's a disgrace." She folded her hands in her lap and prepared to watch as long as it took.

The gusset held two manilla folders: one contained forensic and autopsy reports; the second, Form 26's— witness statements and the investigating officers' notes.

The forensics included numerous photographs of the body and of the crime scene, the alley in which the body had been found. It had been stuffed in a Dumpster tucked away in an alcove past a dogleg; it might have been weeks before it was found, had an old man looking for aluminum cans not looked in the day after Whitmore disappeared.

The alley was a shortcut between the Whitmore house and James's church, which Whitmore had been heading for. A schematic attached to one of the crime-scene reports showed that it formed a narrow canyon between the houses and apartment buildings on either side until, halfway between the entrance closest to the Whitmore residence and the exit next to the church, it broke into an opening surrounded by apartment buildings. The open space was just large enough to hold a basketball court. The alley ran alongside one end of the court before plunging back into the tight space between buildings that ended when the alley emerged alongside the church driveway, paralleling it to the street.

According to area residents, it wasn't unusual for Purnell to take the alley to the church, often stopping at the playground to shoot baskets or play in a pick-up game before the light gave out. The Dumpster that had held Whitmore's body was in the section of the alley before the playground, sandwiched between two apartment buildings and hidden by the dogleg.

I pulled the photos of the body back and made myself study them. The pictures were not unlike those I'd had to take in Vietnam, but unless you're a ghoul, you never get used to them. A body doesn't belong in garbage; we aren't garbage. A body sprawled on the sidewalk has a dignity that had been denied Purnell Whitmore, and the clinical police photos hit with sickening force, the more so for their absolute lack of art.

Though the body lay on a bed of refuse, the clothing looked crisp and clean: a button-down, blue Oxford-cloth shirt under a light-blue windbreaker; khaki pants, dark-blue belt, no socks, brown penny loafer. The other loafer had been flung in after, so that it lay cradled in the crook of the boy's arm. The composition had an improbable, new-wave energy, like some twisted satire of a Benetton ad.

The prints of the face were ghastly. I'd seen pictures of Whitmore in the papers; he was a fine-looking young man, face close enough to adolescence to tell us what the child had looked like, near enough adult to say something about the man he was becoming. And now he would not become that man, and the police pictures of the back of his head told us why: the deformation of a skull that had taken blows hard enough to drive bone fragments deep into the brain. Lifeless eyes stared in horror or astonishment at this thing they were not meant to see for another sixty years, and which no man should meet the way Purnell Whitmore had.

The autopsy report came next, confirming what the pictures had already told me: Whitmore had died of massive internal injuries to the brain. Using the nuanced ambiguity of his breed, the coroner went on to opine that "the pattern of cranial compression, taken with the exterior laceration of the scalp, the presence of subcutaneous, sabulous granules in the scalp and contusions anterior and posterior to the clavicles, is not inconsistent with a force delivered through the shoulders, repeatedly directing the victim's skull against a granulated, lithoidal surface."

In English, someone had gripped Purnell Whitmore by the shoulders and systematically beaten his head to a pulp against a brick wall.

Several pages of medical jargon and lab reports added little beyond the conclusion that Whitmore had been killed some time between seven-thirty and nine-thirty at night. There were no foreign tissue samples under his nails, no interesting bits of hair or dust, nothing to tie him to the last person to see him alive.

Additional bureaucratic forms detailed the meager contents of Whitmore's pockets: keychain and housekeys; comb; wallet with ninety dollars in ones, fives, and a single ten. Bernie Lawson had that right: robbery hadn't been the motive.

I pushed the crime scene and autopsy records aside and thought about the picture they presented. A nineteen-year-old boy—young man, really—had been grasped from the front and slammed against a wall until he died. Five-ten, one hundred and eighty pounds. A stand-out running back, three-year starter in basketball, talented outfielder. Muscular, fit. No signs of struggle in the alley or on the body, beyond that noted. Whoever had taken the boy down had caught him by surprise, stunned or killed him quickly; there were no marks on his knuckles, no sign of blows, given or taken. Things didn't have the feel of an argument that turned into a fight. Someone he hadn't been wary of had taken him when he wasn't on guard, delivered the first, disabling blow before he could react.

The Form 26 reports in the second folder confirmed Captain Cooper's claim that the department was pursuing the investigation aggressively: the latest report had been filed less than twelve hours before, and by none other than my old pal, Hal Hairston.

I hadn't realized that Hal had transferred to Internal Affairs; I'd always assumed that if he ever had anything to do with IA, it would have been when they came to arrest him for one of the hundred little scams he ran. Hal wasn't a bad guy, and I'd done him the greatest favor of his life when I'd taken Brenda Schneider, the woman who was to become my wife and, none too soon, my ex-wife, away from him. Having someone on the case with that kind of debt to me was a plus.

The reports were spindled chronologically. I flipped to the back and added to what I knew from the newspapers, occasionally taking notes.

Whitmore had told his mother he was going to a Boston Pops young people's concert on the Storrow Drive esplanade with his church fellowship class. He'd left his house at six-thirty, more than enough time to get to the church and catch the bus that was scheduled to leave at seven-thirty. He never appeared, but no-shows weren't unusual, and nobody took much note of it except a girl in the class, Shawna Moore, who'd started to cry when it came time for the bus to leave. She told the fellowship class leader, who was also the bus driver, that she'd been expecting Whitmore and she'd hoped they'd walk home together afterward. The driver, Benjamin Crews, told the police he had simply assumed Whitmore had forgotten about the outing or had found something else he'd preferred doing. Whitmore hadn't attended many of the fellowship classes, and Crews hadn't attached any significance to his failure to appear this time.

A Blue Tornado squad, acting on reports of drug activity in the neighborhood, had moved in at seven-twenty-five, when three unmarked cars had descended on an ostensibly abandoned house two blocks from the alley. Twelve to fifteen black males and females had been intercepted in or around the house. Several fled and were pursued by officers on foot. Eventually, eight were taken into custody after being found in possession of what were subsequently confirmed to be controlled substances. The police had moved out of the area at approximately eight-forty-five.

Mrs. Whitmore became concerned when Purnell wasn't home by eleven-thirty. She called Crews at home; that's when she found out he'd never appeared. Frantic, she'd called the homes of some of the kids in the neighborhood; none of them had seen him. Her 911 call had come in at five after midnight.

Press criticism of the police had really gotten rolling when Mrs. Whitmore had told reporters about her call and her efforts to get the police to look for Purnell, but as far as I could tell from the transcript of the call and the dispatcher's record, they'd done about what you'd expect: the particulars had been noted, she'd been assured that the local patrol would keep an eye open for the boy, and a sympathetic officer had told her that it wasn't all that unusual for a nineteen-year-old boy not to come home right on time. Somehow various editorialists had translated this into POLICE TURN DEAF EAR TO MOTHER'S PLEA and raised the specter of racism, but I didn't see what else should have been done.

The two-man patrol on duty in the area *had* been

notified to keep an eye out, but it wouldn't have made any difference; Whitmore was already dead when they got the call.

The first—and so far only—lead had come when the police began questioning people in the neighborhood. Sheer doggedness had led them to a Mrs. Eulilie Hastings, an elderly widow whose account of her observations the night of the killing had shifted the whole focus of the investigation.

As her story unfolded, Mrs. Hastings had gone out on the porch of her apartment, the second level of a three-decker across the street and twenty feet down from the entrance to the alley, to pull in her laundry. She was sure she'd gone out at seven-twenty-five because her favorite TV show came on at seven-thirty and she'd wanted to get the laundry in before it started.

Mrs. Hastings's time estimate had to be about right because she'd heard shouts and sirens from the Blue Tornado action start just as she went out on the porch, but these were Roxbury's standard background music and she didn't pay it much mind; she'd only looked down at the street to be ready to duck if people came by shooting.

It was getting dark and kids had broken the street light again, but it wasn't so dark that when Mrs. Hastings looked down at the otherwise deserted street she couldn't make out two figures in front of the alley. One was a little larger than the other. She thought the large one was in a dark suit, the smaller one in a bright-colored shirt or jacket. It looked like they were shaking hands when she first noticed them.

She thought nothing of it until she saw one of them make a sudden movement and the other appeared to fall back. Then the first, larger figure seemed to push the second one into the alley. As the smaller figure stumbled into the alley, he turned, and Mrs. Hastings saw the large, white Y on the back of his jacket.

Curious, Mrs. Hastings kept looking while she folded sheets. After what she estimated to have been no more than five minutes, a single figure re-emerged. It turned and started to walk down the street. When the figure was roughly across the street from her, a passing car caught it in its headlights: it was a white man, the dark suit was a police uniform, and she could clearly see a night stick. He was still walking when she went inside.

Mrs. Hastings had been questioned repeatedly, and her story had neither expanded nor changed: she hadn't seen the man's car if he had one, she'd only seen his white left cheek and had no idea what he looked like, and she hadn't heard a sound. She hadn't thought anything of it when the other figure hadn't re-emerged from the alley; people passed through all the time. When pressed to say why she was sure it was a policeman she'd seen and couldn't have been someone wearing a similar uniform, such as a private security guard, Mrs. Hastings had made the sensible observation that she hadn't realized private security guards carried night sticks or, indeed, that they were to be found in her neighborhood at all.

It was at this point that Homicide had decided that either a policeman or someone dressed as one had some questions to answer. Following department rules, the chief's office had been notified and Internal Affairs took over the investigation.

Although Internal Affairs had been on the case for only a little over a week, they had generated an impressive number of witness interviews.

The first order of business, of course, had been the six officers on the Blue Tornado sweep. They had been questioned, cross-questioned, questioned again. The two who'd pursued suspects on foot had been grilled for hours, accounting for every second; if they'd blown their noses, it was in the reports. Their best witnesses were the two men and a woman they'd run down and the squad cars they'd called in; there wasn't an unaccounted-for minute.

The tenants in the buildings within several blocks of the alley had been systematically interviewed, many of them

for the second time, following Mrs. Hastings's report; one
family had even been traced to the small town in Arkansas
where they'd gone to visit relatives the day after the
murder. The reports were all the same: negative. No one
except Mrs. Hastings had seen Whitmore on the street; no
one else had seen a policeman.

They'd grilled the patrol assigned to that part of Roxbury
the night of the killing, the squad that had gotten the call to
look out for the boy. One of them, a Sergeant Pfeiffer, was a
fifteen-year veteran; his partner was a third-year patrolman
named Ritchie. They'd been questioned seperately, twice
each, and there were no inconsistencies in their stories.
They hadn't been within six blocks of the alley all night; a
kitchen fire, a domestic quarrel, and a D&D had taken up all
of the time during which Whitmore was killed. Witnesses
confirmed their presence at each scene. Pfeiffer and Ritchie
were acquainted with Whitmore enough to recognize him
and hadn't seen him the night he was killed, though they'd
kept their eyes open for him after they drew the squawk.
Neither officer had been out of the sight of the other for
more than a few minutes the entire evening.

The IA investigators hadn't stopped there: they were
systematically calling in patrols from surrounding districts,
questioning them. It was taking time, but so far, nothing.

I tucked away my notebook and wished I had a cigarette
to shove in my mouth instead of a Certs. Millie had started
on the *Star*, but even the story about the Peruvian woman
who gave birth to a llama didn't keep her from looking at
me sharply every minute or so. I caught her eye, threw her a
wink, and was rewarded with a sniff. It was the most fun
I'd had all morning.

While I hadn't learned much about the Whitmore case, I
had learned one thing. Either the police department was
engaged in a cover-up that made Watergate look like a kid
fibbing about missing cookies, or it was doing everything
that could reasonably be expected, the cops weren't protecting their own or ignoring the murder of a minority

group member, and Endicott's concern was legitimate—the investigation was directed so intensely at locating the missing policeman that it hadn't gotten around to the more basic, talk-to-everyone-who-had-seen-Purnell-Whitmore-in-the-last-five-years approach that police with no promising leads pursue. If a cop *hadn't* done it, there was going to be a lot of ground to cover.

I swallowed the mint and stood up. "Tell me, Millie— that is your name, Millie, isn't it?"

She nodded, warily.

"Then tell me: are you, Captain Cooper, Hal Hairston, Sergeant Pfeiffer and Officer Ritchie, Commissioner Flanagan, Chief Denihan, and at least several dozen other cops up to your asses in a homicide and a conspiracy to conceal same?"

Her mouth dropped. "You're out of your mind, mister."

"I was afraid you'd say that. Okay, you're in the clear. 'Bye."

chapter 14

I RAN INTO HAIRSTON IN THE LOBBY OUTSIDE THE elevator. I hadn't seen him in over a year, but he'd aged ten. His eyes were sunk deeply into their sockets, and he blinked constantly while he talked. His smile was more like a rictus, and even that collapsed when I told him why I was there.

"Come in here." He led the way into the men's room and peered under the doors of the stalls, then turned on a tap. "Go in there and shut the door." He waved his head at a stall.

"Most guys I meet this way at least offer to buy me a drink first."

"That's funny. Captain Cooper sees me talking to you, I'm collecting change from parking meters the next twenty years. Anything to do with your witch hunt is poison around here."

"Flanagan was supposed to send down orders for the department to cooperate."

"He did. Some of the guys figure suicide's outside their job description."

I walked into the stall and pushed the door to. "I don't see what you've got to be worried about. From the file, it looks like you're doing everything anyone could expect."

"I'm coming off a sixteen-hour shift, my friend. My third this week." He worked his hands under the water. "Orders are, pull out all stops on this one; anyone thinks this guy's getting rhythm because he's a cop'd better think again. No, sir—we're out to get this guy, and we will."

"So what's the problem? We'll tell 'em you're doing your job; you get the guy or you don't, not the department's fault. End of story."

"It doesn't matter what you tell them. They're out for blood. The Whitmore thing is just an excuse."

"I'm coming out of here. I feel like a pervert, and if you scrub any longer you aren't going to have any fingerprints left."

"Huh?" He looked down at his hands. "Oh, yeah. Maybe they can use me on one of the death squads—leave no traces. Coming?"

We didn't speak until we got on the elevator. "Just mark my words, Nase—that bunch of butt-sockets you're working for isn't going to listen to anything you've got to say."

"You guys are paranoid. Not saying I blame you, but you've got more friends than enemies. The department'll get a fair shake."

"Hah!" We shuddered to a stop at the first floor. Hal put his fingers to his lips as the door opened. "Just remember, Nase—I don't know you, okay?"

"My pal."

Peggy Kiernan was waiting in front of the door as it slid into the wall. The dog and a frizzy-haired young woman carrying a briefcase were standing with her. Hairston stepped past them and disappeared without a word.

"Hello, Nichols. Let's go back up." The three of them stepped on and the frizzy-haired young woman pushed the button for the second floor.

"How'd you do that?" The dog nosed the seat of my pants.

"Do what?"

"Know it was me." I was glad when the dog was satisfied and turned eyes front.

"When you lose your sight, the other senses compensate. I smelled you."

"Smelled me?" I inhaled. "You can recognize people by their smell?"

"Hmm." The door opened and we stepped off. "This way." She started purposefully down a grim green hallway. "In your case, breath mints and"—she turned and sniffed my cheek—"bay rum. Cheap bay rum. Everybody has a unique smell. I never forget one."

"I'm impressed."

"You're gullible."

"What do you mean?"

"I heard you talking to that guy just before he got off."

"And my unique smell?"

"You get so I can smell you coming, believe me, I'll let you know."

We walked into a large, open room crammed with battered metal desks. A dozen men and women, half uniforms, half plainclothes, were pounding on typewriters, talking on the phone, or gathered in little groups drinking coffee. As soon as they saw us, the drone died like a record player in a power failure.

Peggy strode forward as though she owned the place. I had to hustle to keep up; the young woman with the briefcase trailed behind. "Do you see a door marked Dead Storage? Supposed to be up here."

"To your right." I stepped past her, walked up to the door, and pushed it open.

"Hey—you can't go in there! That's off limits." A middle-aged man with a pot belly and a shoulder holster over his shirt got up from his desk and stood staring at us.

"To you—not to me. It's our war room for the duration. Let's go." The dog nosed into the room, Peggy right with him.

The man rushed over, pushed past me, and thrust his chin an inch away from Peggy's. "War room! Who the hell—"

"Peggy Kiernan. From the Kershaw Commission. This is my associate, Mr. Nichols, my reader, Ms. Randall, and my dog, Leba—who will check you for hernias if you're not out of my face in five seconds."

The man held his pose until the dog growled, then backed away. "Sorry. I . . . didn't know who you were. They told me you'd be moving in here."

Peggy cocked her head. "You'd be . . . ?"

"Captain McDaniel—acting commander of the vice squad."

"Ah, yes—Captain McDaniel. You handled the Mercer bust—what?—six, seven years ago?"

That stopped him while he thought. "Right, but how did you—"

"My case. You fucked up the search so bad I almost had to *nolo* him."

"You're full of shit. He pled to two counts."

"Right—because his lawyer knew even less about the fourth amendment than you did, if that's possible."

"I guess that was back when you were still interested in putting guys like that away, hadn't jumped on the political bandwagon."

"I'm still interested in putting guys like that away, Captain—that's why we're here."

His face grew deep red. "Now, look—"

"No, *you* look. I'm going to be using this office for the next couple of weeks. I'm going to have a lot of records brought in here, and we're going to be busy. You don't get in

our way, we'll all get along just fine. You do, and the mayor
will land on you like a ton of bricks, to say nothing of the
press. Understood?"

Before he could answer, we were interrupted by a female
officer with a perplexed look. "Captain, excuse me, but
there are some men here with handcarts. They say they're
supposed to unload them in here?"

Peggy answered for him. "Ah, that'll be the computers.
Laura, show them where to set them up. They said there'd
be some tables. Now, Captain, as you can see, we've got a
lot of work to do, and not a lot of time to do it. So much as
I'd like to keep on chatting, I'm afraid you'll have to excuse
us now."

He puffed up as though he were going to explode, then
pushed by me and left.

Flecks of dust hung in the narrow paths of light admitted
by the yellowed venetian blinds. The smell was attic, the
decor U.S. Army, the year 1940. Rows of battered olive-
green file cabinets lined the walls, separated by rickety
tables and folding chairs. Peggy asked to be shown to a
convenient perch and I led her to an old wooden desk at the
far end of the cavernous space. Someone found a light
switch, and a weak, incandescent wash revealed the room
in all its institutional horror.

Peggy drew her fingertips across the dust that coated the
desk top. "Well, isn't this homey. Sit, Leba." The dog looked
around, decided it was okay, and sank to the floor distaste-
fully. The frizzy-haired girl handed Peggy the briefcase and
waited expectantly, rather like the dog.

"Laura, this is Mr. Nichols. Laura Randall, my reader."

I took the girl's limp hand. "Laura, why don't you call
down to Central Records, find out when they're going to get
those files up here. Have a seat, Nichols."

Peggy felt her way around the desk and found the chair.
"Useful morning?"

I pulled up a chair. "Oh, yeah. I checked the wrapper,

and it's obvious—they took the kid in, sweated him until he owned to running the East Coast branch of the Symbionese Liberation Army, then dumped the body during a skinhead outing."

"Nothing, huh?"

"Look, Ms. Kiernan—"

"Peggy, okay?"

"If we can scrap 'Nichols,' once and for all? We've been working on that."

She laughed. "Okay. Hang around these guys too much. No more Nichols."

"Good. Anyway, this whole thing is wrong."

"Meaning?"

"Meaning it were your kid, this is what you'd want them to be doing. Meaning they're going whole hog, looking for this cop. The premise is wrong."

"What premise?" She folded her hands under her chin and assumed the attitude of a patient tutor.

"That the cops can't be trusted to work this thing, find the cop who did it. If one did."

"You've got a better candidate?"

"No. They've got to find the cop, if there was a cop. If there was a cop, and he was with the kid just before he bought it, the cop's as good a bet as any. My point is, I went through the file, and I can't imagine what else they could do to find him."

"If they want to."

"Hey—I'm not Bernie Lawson; you don't have to prove your objectivity to me."

"Humor me. How can you be sure they're doing everything they can to get this guy?"

"It's obvious."

"If it's so obvious, Nichols—"

"There you go again."

"Okay. If it's so obvious, *Nason*,"—she dragged it out—"how come they haven't come up with this cop?"

"Because he doesn't want to be come up with. Because all we got is a guy in a uniform that some old lady, across the street, in bad light, *thinks* was a police uniform. Because it could've been some guy in a costume. Because police work isn't easy. There are probably other reasons, but those'll do for now."

"Yeah. There could be other reasons—like they don't want to find him, or like they know who it is and are covering for him. They hit the costume shops, see if any cop outfits been rented?"

"No, but—"

"Think they would've, white kid been killed?"

"Oh, for God's sake. There are four guys, working double shifts. It takes time."

"Maybe there should be eight guys. How many would they have assigned, it'd been a white kid?"

"White kid, poor family, nobody to bring heat, pull guys off other cases that also need doing? Two, and you know it. There are half a dozen open homicides out there right now, none of them getting this kind of attention."

"They could pull guys from burglary, other details, they wanted to."

"They put the whole force on, you'd be saying how come they don't have the National Guard in. Nobody wins lawyer word games."

"Wrong—lawyers do. I'm a lawyer."

"Look, Peggy. Be reasonable. There are other people who need cops out there. You know that. What's your point? If we're supposed to be checking an investigation, then take my word: either at least two dozen cops have coopered up the file or it's a straight investigation."

"So what do you suggest?"

"I'll check out a few of the reports, make sure they're for real—which they are—interview some of the investigating team, and then we tell Kershaw the police are taking this Whitmore thing seriously, and all I do is get in the way."

"Okay."

She threw as good an off-speed pitch as I'd seen in a while. "Okay? You mean you agree?"

"Sure. You tell me it's straight, why should I doubt you? Easy enough to confirm. Figured it was anyway."

"You figured it was anyway! Then why the hell—"

"Sure—Sowell called it right. I know that."

" 'Sowell?' "

"Um. Endicott. Smart guy."

I ignored her goony little grin. "Then why were you busting my . . . chops like that?"

"One or two of our bosses can actually ask an intelligent question. I wanted to hear what the answers were going to be."

"Okay. Fair enough. And then I move over to your side of it?"

"Up to Kershaw. Okay—Nason?"

"Right, chief. Now I know how the Job Corps works." I stood and saluted, then felt foolish. I said, "See you," and felt even more foolish.

"Not if I see you first!" She had great timing, just enough delay before letting the laugh go. "God, I love that line. Works every time." She was still chuckling as I went out the door.

chapter 15

ROXBURY IS NOT A PRETTY PART OF TOWN. IT'S kind of shoved up under the downtown, hard against the expressway, north of the suburbs. It's poor and black and squalid, and if it's not as large as its counterparts in New York and Chicago and Los Angeles, it's block for block the peer of any of them for dirt, despair, and messy deaths.

There's a McDonald's and a Burger King at the intersection of Martin Luther King and Washington, in the heart of Roxbury, that the locals have taken to calling "McDeath" and "Murder King" because the dealers like to drive by and take out the competition while it's grazing. It's a testament to the drawing power of plastic food that both places were doing good business when I pulled through the square looking for Rodman Street. The alley where Purnell Whitmore was found ran off Rodman.

I missed it the first time but caught it on the rerun, and I turned down it. The alley was two blocks down. I found a hydrant and pulled into the space.

I got out of the car and looked around. The street was lined with frame triple-deckers, broken bottles, old tires. The only brick building was the apartment house next to the alley. Its windows were boarded, the front door padlocked. Scorch marks blackened the window frames of the top story. A hole gaped in the roof where a fire had vented. Swirls of spray paint turned the ground-floor walls into a gallery of abstract expressionism. I went down the alley running alongside.

A few feet in, a stairwell, littered with broken glass, old pop cans, and newspapers, led to a metal door into the basement of the apartment house. I went down the stairs and pushed on the door; it gave a little, then caught and wouldn't open further. I climbed back up the steps, and as my eyes reached ground level, they spotted a small, plastic vial a few feet away.

I rolled it around in my fingers, then held it up to the light. A few flecks of gray powder clung to the sides. I looked around and spotted a few more, scattered under broken bottles and old candy wrappers. Glass splinters showed where others had been trampled underfoot.

The Dumpster, which must have been left when the apartment house was condemned, was just around the dogleg turn. The lid was up and the crew that had searched the trash for clues had left most of it on the ground. I peered in, but except for a few pieces of orange peel and an egg carton, Whitmore's bier was empty.

I strolled on, down the alley to the playground Whitmore hadn't reached. The gangs had decorated the walls like dogs staking out territory by peeing on hydrants. Here an X-Man had proclaimed his dominance, there a Gangsta had answered the challenge, and so on until the alleyway opened onto a quarter acre of cracked asphalt and weeds.

A group of teen-age boys were playing half-court basketball, shooting at a netless hoop on a battered backboard.

Occasional "yo's" punctuated the hard chorus of panting and foot slaps, but most of the talking was done by body movements that the Boston Ballet couldn't match. I marveled at the grace and energy, then fingered the vial in my pocket. They had a lot more grace and energy than I had ever had, but too many of them wouldn't in a few years. I tossed the vial on the ground and went on.

Past the playground, dilapidated three-deckers and once-proud apartment buildings backed up to the alley, half a block of decay that ended when the alley came out on the street. For the last thirty feet, the right side of the alley ran parallel to the parking lot behind Reverend James's church and the driveway leading into it. A broken-down fence separated the alley from the church lot, but it was more openings than fence, and I stepped through and walked around to the front.

It was a handsome old relic, the once-red brick gone to near black from years of city air. The sign out front proclaimed the African Apostolic Temple of Glory, The Reverend Theophilus James, Pastor, but faded markings over the door indicated that an earlier generation of congregants had conducted their services in Hebrew.

I backtracked and turned the corner to the rear of the building, where a set of steps ran down to a basement door. A card over a button next to the door said RECTORY—PLEASE RING.

It occurred to me that if James was in, he could call Mrs. Whitmore and prepare her for my visit. It wasn't one I wanted to make, but there was no way to duck it, and I preferred not to make it cold. I had rung the buzzer and was waiting when a car pulled up behind me and a man got out and walked over.

Corey Webster was a more solid piece of work than he looked from a distance, lean and stringy but with ropy muscles ridging the long arms that looked like they really could swing a pick. The cut-off sleeves of the thermal undershirt he wore in spite of the heat highlighted the biceps nicely, and the sweat-stained armpits gave the outfit an earthy authenticity.

"I rang. I don't think anyone's in."

I stepped aside, as much to escape the rank odor as out of courtesy, since Webster's almost imperceptible nod hadn't invited that.

He pressed the button hard, paused, muttered something, then pressed it again, holding it down as though determined to push it through the doorframe. The glass in the door window reflected the sheen of perspiration gleaming on his bald head.

I'd turned to go when his hand grabbed my upper arm. "Hold it, buddy—where's James?"

"I'm not his keeper, and I'm not your buddy. Now let go of my arm."

His eyes, bloodshot and twitchy, focused on my face. "Wait a minute—you were at Finn's the other night. I saw you talking to that Daniels woman. You're working with her, aren't you?"

I tried to snatch my arm away, but his grip, hard enough to hurt, held it tight as he leaned into my face. "He got that crap from her, I know he did. All that Tom shit he's laying out now. Well, you'd better believe—"

"I'm not asking again." I looked down at his hand, still clenching my arm.

His eyes followed mine and he dropped his hand with a grunt, but only so he could jab my chest with a long forefinger. "Let me tell you, man—"

"Please don't do that."

"—she isn't turning James into her Oreo. I—"

"Corey?"

"—don't know what—"

"Corey?"

"—that bitch has been giving him, but—"

I slapped his hand away and slammed mine up under his chin, cupping it hard. "I know it's hopelessly bourgeois of me, but you've got to do something about your dental hygiene. Marx had better breath than you, and he ate shit."

Playground rules dictated that he come back with "So's your mother," and then we could go at it, but it was too hot and I didn't feel like playing, so after we'd played eye hockey for a couple of seconds, I dropped my hand and started up the steps.

I'd reached the top when something that felt like a stun gun went off against my back, narrowly missing a kidney and knocking me face first to the asphalt. I looked back over my shoulder just in time to see Webster drawing back his heavy, black boot for a kick. He took slow, deliberate aim. "Gonna teach you to stay out of my business, man." As the foot started forward, I rolled to my right, and the boot glanced off my left knee.

I started to push to my feet, but the knee froze and I collapsed again. All I could do was draw myself into a ball and wait. Then there was the sound of meat being tenderized, followed by an animal yelp. After a few seconds I realized it hadn't come from me and I uncoiled and struggled to my feet.

Webster had his hands pressed to the small of his back, gasping painfully as he kneaded the flesh. A short, solid-looking black man stood in front of him, warily brandishing a shovel.

Webster tried to straighten himself, and the man cocked the shovel. "Don't know what this is all about, but it isn't going to happen here."

Although the man had to be in his sixties, he didn't look like an easy mark. Webster took a couple of seconds to calculate the odds and then reached the sane decision.

I staggered to my feet and stepped aside to let him take stiff little half-steps to his car, a battered Jeep wagon with a diagonal pair of red and green stripes over the chalked, black finish of the passenger door. A round, green escutcheon on the door enclosed a crossed pair of human arms, one black, one brown, above the legend NO JUSTICE, NO PEACE. POCAT in red letters capped the works.

He turned and glared at us from the far side of the car. "Don't think this is over, man."

He popped the clutch and almost stalled the car, but he still managed to draw a little rubber on the way out. I looked at the bizarre beast until it disappeared, then turned to my rescuer.

"I'm grateful to you, mister. I was about to catch a pretty good stomping."

The man passed a hand over his stubby gray hair. "I was fixing to patch up some brickwork when I came around the corner and saw him punch you in the back. Good thing I had this with me." He shook the shovel, then tossed it onto a wheelbarrow loaded with concrete. "Want me to call the police?"

"I don't think so. They've got bigger things to worry about."

"Afraid that's right. Somebody ought to do something about that fellow, though. Don't like him coming around here."

"You know him?"

"I recognize him. Been around the church a lot this last year. Pastor's got to deal with all types, but that one's bad news."

"My name's Nason Nichols. Is Reverend James in?"

"No, sir. Just me—Ben Crews. Bookkeeper, maintenance man, and lead baritone."

I stepped forward and shook the man's leathery hand. The knee ached and I was going to have a sore back, but nothing seemed seriously damaged. "I believe you also teach the fellowship classes and drive the bus, Mr. Crews?"

"That I do. How'd you know, if you don't mind my asking?"

"I read the police reports. I'm an investigator with the Kershaw Commission—the group the mayor appointed after Purnell Whitmore was murdered?"

"Yes, sir—I know about that. Hope they find the son of a bitch did that, find him soon. That was a fine boy."

"That's what I understand. They're working hard on it."

"Young men like that in pretty short supply around here, Mr. Nichols."

"Young men like that are in pretty short supply any-place."

He nodded, slowly. "A lot of fine young men died in Korea, but at least that was for something. This kind of killing . . ." He shook his head. "No sense to it."

"No, there isn't." I thanked him again and gingerly retraced my steps up the alley.

By the time I took out my notes and found Mrs. Hastings's address, I'd decided my pride had taken a worse beating than my body, thanks to Mr. Crews. I didn't need to take a note to remind myself Corey Webster owed me one.

Whoever owned the house where Mrs. Hastings lived had made an effort, laying on paint within the memory of man and setting off the tiny patch of bare earth in the front with a border of old tires, cut in half and painted white. Three tomato plants, heavy with almost ripe fruit, sagged against cantilevered wooden stakes. I pushed the second of a stack of three doorbells by a side door.

"Who's there?"

"Mrs. Hastings?" I went back to the front yard. An old woman in a black wig and a flower-print dress was leaning over the porch rail on the second floor.

"Yes?"

"My name's Nichols. I'm a detective looking into the Whitmore case. Wondered if I could talk to you for a few moments."

"Ah already told everything ah know."

"I know, but if we could just go over it again? It won't take a minute."

"Ah reckon so. Come around to the side, Ah'll let you in." Mrs. Hastings pushed away from the railing. In a moment I heard locks opening, chains sliding. "Yessah. Y'all come on in."

She was a large woman, and she wheezed heavily as she mounted the stairs. She was wearing slippers, and she set each foot down slowly before putting her weight on it. "Just fixin' to have some tea. You'll join me?"

"Thank you. If it's not too much trouble?"

"No trouble at all." She scuffed slowly back to the kitchen.

"Mind if I look at your porch?"

"You go right ahead."

I walked out onto the porch and looked right. The entrance to the alley was well within sight. In near dark, though, better eyes than mine would have had trouble spotting features. It was no surprise the old woman hadn't gotten a good look at the man with Whitmore.

"Here's your tea." Mrs. Hastings set a tray on the table in the living room, and I took a last look at the street and stepped back in.

"Don' feel good out there, thinkin' about what happened." She passed me a cup.

"No—it doesn't."

"He was a fine boy, from what Ah hear. Musta killed his mama to lose him, 'specially like that." She shook her old head, then lowered herself into a chair. "Well, what can Ah tell you?"

I pulled out my notes. "I'm just trying to make sure the police didn't overlook anything."

"Aren't you the police?"

"No, ma'am. I'm working for the Kershaw Commission? The group the mayor appointed to look into this, and to see if the police have been mistreating . . . minorities?"

Mrs. Hastings shook her head again. "Never heard about that, but if it'll help catch whoever did that terrible thing, Ah'm all for it."

"Well, we hope we can help. Could you just run through

what you remember seeing that night? From the time you went to your porch?"

I followed my notes as she talked, hoping I'd hear something new, but I didn't. The police had asked all the questions I could think of, and Mrs. Hastings either had the answers or, more often than not, didn't have them.

"An' tha's all Ah can say, mister." She looked down, smoothed the dress over her legs, and shook her head. The too-stiff acrylic hair caught the light from her window, so that her skin seemed even older and more lifeless than it was. "Wish there was more, Ah really do. Some more tea?"

"No, ma'am, but thank you. We appreciate your time."

"No trouble at all. Ah jus' wish Ah'd thought to call the police when Ah saw that man push that boy back in there. But he *was* the police." Her voice held wonder at the illogic of it.

"Yes, ma'am—you couldn't have known."

"Way the boy come out an' shook hands with him, Ah 'magined they knew each other."

I stopped my hand halfway to my jacket pocket and flipped the notebook open again. "How do you mean, Mrs. Hastings, 'the way the boy came out and shook hands with him'? I thought they were standing outside the alley when you went out on the porch."

"Why, time Ah got settled, they was. They was standin' right in front of the alley, seemed to be talkin', an' then that man pushed the boy back in the alley an' Ah couldn' see them no more, least till the man come out alone."

"But you saw the boy come out of the alley first? Before he shook hands with the man?"

She set her cup down carefully and looked up at the ceiling. "Umm, uh! Ah don' know, mister." Her lips tightened as she concentrated. "Seem like Ah did." She looked away again, then down at the floor. She wagged her head and looked up. "Ah do believe Ah did. The boy come out an' right away see the man; they shake hands. Tha's why Ah figured they knew each other."

"But you didn't tell the police you saw the boy come out of the alley first, did you?"

She thought for a minute. "Can't rightly say. Might not have remembered. Jus' one of those things you got in your eye, know what Ah mean? Come back to me now." Her face fell and she frowned. "Hope Ah didn' mess nothin' up for the police."

"I'm sure you didn't. I'll mention it to them, but it probably doesn't mean anything."

She shuffled to the door. "Ah hope you catch that man, bring some peace to that poor woman."

"Yes, ma'am—I do, too."

Her hand paused on the uppermost lock. "Did you say you was also 'vestigatin' whether the police was mistreatin' . . . 'minorities'?"

"Well, yes, ma'am—we're checking to see if there's been a . . . pattern of . . . police brutality. The possibility that the Whitmore boy was killed by a policeman got it started, but it goes beyond that."

"You say 'minorities,' you mean colored folk?" There was a sharp glint in her old eyes.

"Well, yes, I guess so. Mostly . . . black people."

"Uh-huh. Thought so." She nodded her head, then turned the nods into shakes as she twisted the top lock open. "Thought tha's what you meant. Uh—um." She fumbled with the deadbolt and I reached over to help her.

"Don't you think we should be looking at that, Mrs. Hastings?" I turned back as she held the door open for me.

"No matter to me, mister. Whatever y'all wanna do, tha's fine with me. You take care, now." She kept her eyes downcast.

"Thank you very much. I appreciate all your help." I turned and started down the stairs.

"You welcome." She paused, then resumed uncertainly. "Only . . . mister?"

I stopped a few steps down and looked back. Worry creased the old woman's face. "Yes?"

"Hope you won't be scarin' all the police away, all this talk of them mistreatin' folks. I cain't hardly get out to the store down to the corner no more, gangs an' addicts so bad. Ain' the police beatin' up folks, shootin' um, takin' their money. Like to see more policemen, tell the truth. Most folks roun' here would. Yes, sir—wish they was a lot more police 'round about." Agitation caused her mouth to work around poorly fitting false teeth as though she were chewing a cud.

Anger welled up in her. "And if they been crackin' a few heads, why, they a few can use some crackin'. Yes, sir. It's a hard thing to say, but tha's the way Ah feel—Ah surely do." She nodded decisively, then disappeared behind the door. The locks clicked and the chains rattled as Mrs. Hastings retreated into her fortress. She wouldn't have heard me even if I'd had anything to add.

chapter 16

NOW IT WAS TIME FOR THE STOP I DIDN'T WANT to make, but I couldn't think of anything else to do, so I walked the short blocks to the Whitmore apartment. I moved as slowly as I had the day I'd called on a young widow to tell her I'd known her husband in Vietnam, but all too soon I was pushing another doorbell on the side of another faded three-decker.

The face that appeared in the glass panel of the door was younger than Mrs. Hastings's had been, too worn to call pretty but fresh enough to tell me where Purnell Whitmore had gotten his clean good looks. It was a face left with only an echo of life, though.

"You aren't from the press, are you?" Her speech through the two inches the burglar chain allowed was slow, low, and tired—terribly tired. "I can't talk to the press any-more."

"No, ma'am. I'm an investigator with the Kershaw Commission?" She nodded in answer to my inflection.

"Name of Nichols. Nason Nichols." I pulled out the letter confirming my appointment and handed it through the crack.

"I'm looking into the circumstances of your son's death, Mrs. Whitmore. I'm sorry, but I hope it will help us catch the man who did it. May I ask you a few questions?" I said it fast, faster than I'd intended, but it came out easier that way.

"You're trying to see if a policeman did this, aren't you?" She handed the letter back.

I nodded. "Yes, ma'am. And to make sure he's caught if he did. May I come in?"

"I know about that. Reverend James told me about it. Just a second, please." The door shut, the chain slid back, then she ushered me in.

The living room was small, but neat and spotless. Mrs. Whitmore showed me to a couch against a wall lined with books, then took a seat in an armchair on the other side of the coffee table. From where I sat, looking over her shoulder, I could see a row of trophies lining the mantel over the fireplace. Each was topped with the bronze figure of a young athlete.

Mrs. Whitmore caught the direction of my look and a slow half-smile lit her face for a second, then faded like a movie run in reverse. "Some of Purnell's awards. He was a marvelous athlete. Since he was a little boy, any game, he could play it."

"I heard that."

"Must have got it from his daddy—didn't get it from me." She shook her head, the half-smile reappearing briefly.

"Yes, ma'am. His father was a good athlete?"

"I guess you could say he was a good runner, Mr. Nichols." She gave a sour little laugh.

"Track?"

"Ran off when I was seventeen—six months' pregnant with Purnell."

"Oh. That must have been tough."

"Mister, lots of the children around here are born to silly girls like I was, thought a few minutes on a couch was love. The tough part was raising that baby so he wouldn't make the same kind of mistake, or worse."

"I understand."

"No, you don't. But I had a lot of joy, too. God blessed me with joyful memories. That helps some. Now, I know you have questions to ask, Mr. Nichols. I'll answer them as best I can." She smoothed her dark skirt over her knees and waited.

"Thank you. I'll try to be brief."

"No, sir. Don't you try to be brief—you be thorough. Purnell deserves that. Don't you worry about me. I got—*I've* got—all the time in the world. All I've got." She set her jaw and locked her eyes on mine. The vulnerability of the mortally wounded receded and I heard the strong woman who'd devoted nineteen years to bringing a fatherless boy to the edge of escape.

"Of course." I pulled out the pad and pencil. "I'm going to have to ask you things the police may have already asked you."

"I understand." Her face settled into a kind of calm and her eyes grew distant, as though she were putting herself into a trance.

"That night—what time did Purnell leave?"

"Six-thirty. I remember, because we got to talking, over dinner, and he'd taken a shower when he got home and wasn't wearing his watch. All of a sudden he said, 'What time is it, Mama?' and I told him, and he went running off. He was always running, always had something to do. Ran off so fast he forgot his watch, which he never did. That was the reason I thought he was late that night. Just got caught up in something, didn't know what time it was—'cause he never gave me cause to worry."

"Did he say why he was in such a hurry?"

"He was going to a church outing, had to catch the bus."

"But the bus wasn't leaving until seven-thirty."

"He liked to stop on the way to play basketball. Did it all the time."

"I see. You know Purnell was seen talking to a policeman the night . . . it happened? That's why we're involved?"

"Mr. Nichols, 'it' didn't 'happen.' People mean to be kind, talking around it like that, but they make it sound like some accident on the other side of the world. There was no accident. My son was murdered. Beaten to death by someone who wanted him dead. And yes, I know about the policeman."

"I'm sorry. You're right. I won't do that again. Did your son know any policemen? Was he friends with any, I mean?"

She thought a second, shook her head. "The police asked me that. Not that I know. I don't remember him mentioning any policemen. Is there any reason to think he might have?"

"Only that the woman who saw him said that Purnell shook hands with the policeman when they met. That doesn't sound like they were strangers."

"Oh—of course. I wasn't thinking. But no, I don't remember Purnell talking about being friends with a policeman."

"Maybe not friends, then. Had he met any . . . professionally?"

"You mean, had Purnell been in trouble, gotten picked up by the police?" She said it matter-of-factly.

"Yes, ma'am. I know he didn't have a record, but sometimes kids get picked up and let go without any record being made. I'm sorry to have to ask."

"Don't be. It's a sensible question. But the answer is no. At least I never knew about any trouble like that, and Purnell and I were very close. I would have known."

"How about his friends? Who did he hang around with? Any kids who might have some ideas about this?"

"Well, Mr. Nichols, Purnell didn't have a lot of time to 'hang around.' I saw to that. When he was home, he kept his days pretty full, between school and sports, his job and all. Nights, too, what with homework and the church. This last year he was gone, of course. Gone to college." A little wonder crept in as she said the word, thought what it meant, what she'd thought it meant, but she pulled herself back. "Fact is, he had less and less in common with the boys around here, the farther he went. Thank God." She nodded decisively.

"But he must have known some of the young people in the neighborhood—the kids he shot baskets with, for instance. You say he liked to do that?"

She turned inward and a little smile mirrored the memories she saw. "Lordy, yes—he *loved* basketball. Of all his sports, I think he loved basketball best. He was all-city his last year in high school, you know."

"I did know. I'm sorry I never saw him play. He must have been awfully good."

"I went to all his games." She drifted away to an arena where only happy memories played. "My son, and all those people would be calling: 'Two more, Whit-more; two more, Whit-more.' He'd get the ball, dribble past those poor white boys like they were nailed to the floor, and jump." Her eyes rose to the ceiling, watching it happen. "Jump so high I sometimes thought he'd come down with a star in his hands, walk over to me, and say, 'Here, Mama—look what I brought you.' "

If I had had it in my power, I would have left her in that never-again place forever, but she brought herself back, much too soon—although it would always be much too soon. "I'm sorry. You were asking me about boys in the neighborhood, and here I am going on about . . . nothing."

"No, ma'am, certainly not nothing. But if there are some friends around here I could talk to . . ."

"Of course. Let me think." She arched her hands and tapped the forefingers together. "Well, he used to play sometimes with a boy named Lucas. Lucas . . . Jeffries. Family lives over on Solomon. Used to come over all the time. But he's in jail, last I heard. Then there was one named Lionel. He got shot dead last Christmas. There was a boy named Culbert Hamkins, but I hear he died, too. Another one was named . . . Mouse." Her mouth drew up in disgust. "I never knew his real name. But I don't think I've seen him in over a year. Young men can change awful fast around here, Mr. Nichols. The streets just eat them up. Drugs, gangs, liquor. Something finds them."

"Yes, ma'am. You mentioned your son had a job. What did he do?"

"He was a stockboy in a dress shop downtown. Had a fancy French name—Jack's, I think it was, on Newberry Street. Worked after school, weekends, and vacations. Since he was sixteen. Started in again when he got home from New Haven in June."

"Probably not a place to meet a policeman."

"Most likely not." Her voice cracked. "He saved almost every cent he earned. Every week he'd come home, give me the money he'd earned, I'd put it in the bank. Right up till he was killed—except when he bought me that."

She pointed to a stereo set standing in the corner. Pride displaced the pain in her voice. "For my birthday last month."

"It's a beauty."

"It was so extravagant, I was going to make him take it back. Then he said 'Mama, I wanted to do something for you, after all you've done for me. I want you to have this, and I guess I can spend my money any way I want. You don't let me spend it on my favorite girl, I guess I'll just have to spend it on some other girls.' And his eyes were so twinkly and his smile so big that I just couldn't help myself."

"I'm sure that was the right thing to do."

"He bought me a big stack of tapes, too. Opera music. I'd heard it only on the radio before. Purnell said he heard me singing along, thought I'd like it. I surely did."

"It's a beautiful gift."

"I just can't stand to play them now."

"I understand."

"Reverend James says the pain will pass, peace will come. He says prayer will help."

"I'm sure he's right."

"He's a good man, and he's been a comfort to me, but what would help the most is to catch the man who did this."

"We will."

"I believe you will, and I'll ask God to help you."

There aren't words, no matter how badly we want them, and so I mumbled: "Well, I can't think of anything else now. Thank you so much for your time."

"No, thank you for yours."

I'd started for the door when Mrs. Whitmore touched my sleeve. "Would you let me show you the rest of Purnell's awards?"

I stopped myself from looking at my watch. "Of course." I followed her down the hall to a closed door.

"This is his bedroom. *Was* his bedroom." She stood aside so I could step in.

It was a boy's room, a successful, normal boy's room. The desk held a neat row of schoolbooks, pads of paper and pencils, a small radio in the corner. A desktop calendar with a local funeral home's name on it was crammed with appointments. The top of the dresser held a bottle of aftershave and the little knickknacks that wind up on the tops of dressers. A Boston Latin letter jacket hung over the bedpost; a Yale pennant had a place of honor over the headboard. Nike shoes were propelling Michael Jordan into orbit on a poster over the dresser.

Much of the remaining wall space was occupied by tokens of the accomplishments Purnell Whitmore had crammed into a short life: church awards, honor-roll acknowledgments, a National Merit Scholarship certificate, best orator in a regional debating tournament. The letter from Yale that began "Congratulations. You have been admitted to the Class of . . ." was taped to the center of the mirror above the desk.

"I kept this for him. For me, really, 'cause he wasn't half so proud as I was." Mrs. Whitmore was holding a scrapbook with a yellow cover.

"Would you let me see it?"

A grateful warmth came into her eyes. "Of course." She settled onto the bed and opened the book. "Come sit here." She patted the bed next to her and opened the book as though it were the Holy Scriptures.

She turned the pages slowly, caressing memories as she pressed recalcitrant corners back into place. News clippings reporting feats of sporting prowess curled under yellowing Scotch tape. Mrs. Whitmore pointed to the first one. "Just look at this." Her finger traced the line of type at the top while I scanned the clip from the old *Record American*: Whitmore, P. had won the local punt, pass, and kick competition, eight- to ten-year-old category. I looked at the date; he'd been seven.

"Remarkable."

"Yes, sir. He was. He surely was." She slowly turned the pages as the headlines grew bigger, the adjectives more lavish: WHITMORE LEADS TIGERS TO BEST RECORD SINCE '58; WHITMORE FOUR FOR FOUR AS TIGERS SWEEP; WHITMORE THRILLS LATIN FANS IN GRIDIRON DEBUT; LATIN SINKS B & N ON CLUTCH WHITMORE FREE THROW; WHITMORE DUNK AT BUZZER CLINCHES REC LEAGUE TITLE; YALE FROSH CRUSH CORNELL BEHIND WHITMORE RUSHING.

And then there were no more clippings, and wouldn't be, and her hand rested lifelessly on the blank, gray page. It was still there when I left the room.

chapter 17

I COULDN'T BLAME THE POLICE FOR PUTTING ALL their manpower on the angle Mrs. Hastings had given them; it smelled like a winner. But as Endicott had anticipated, it meant they hadn't gotten around to many of the people they probably would have talked to if they hadn't caught her lead—the kids he'd shot baskets with, the friends, the employer. As long as I had the time, I figured I'd accept Endicott's invitation, see if being useful felt the way I vaguely remembered.

Shawna Moore, the girl who'd waited for Whitmore on the church bus, had huge, doelike eyes that would have been beautiful if they hadn't been swollen with the cold that had kept her inside on a beautiful day. We sat in her living room while she kept one watery eye on a baby brother who made periodic, wobbly dashes for freedom.

"How long had you known Purnell?"

She started to answer but stopped and wiped her eyes

and sniffled. "Not so long. He was in my Bible study group two years ago, but I hardly spoke to him. He was so . . . grown-up, you know? I was just a kid then." She wiped her eyes again and it wasn't the cold.

"I'm sorry. I know this is hard for you. Would you rather I'd come back?"

She shook her head. "It's all right. My mama says I've got to get over it. It's just so . . . hard, sometimes, when I . . . remember. She doesn't understand how hard it is."

"She may have forgotten. We do that as we get older. When did you and Purnell become friendly?"

She smiled shyly behind the tissues. "Last summer. There was a fellowship picnic, and we got to talking, and I guess he decided . . . maybe I wasn't such a kid anymore. That was in June, and he asked me if he could walk me home, and after that I saw him every time there was a meeting. He'd walk me home most times."

"Did he ever say anything about anyplace where he might have met a policeman? Any trouble he might have had, for instance?"

"Trouble—Purnell? No, sir! Purnell wouldn't have gotten in any trouble—he had *dreams*. Purnell was going to *be* somebody. Not like the other boys around here. That was a fine college he was going to, wasn't it? Jeremiah—you get back here!"

The toddler cast a covetous eye on the doorway but sank reluctantly to the floor. "Yes, it is."

"He said he was going to learn how to make money there, that that was where the rich white kids went. That's true, isn't it?"

"A lot of rich white people send their children to Yale, yes."

"We talked about that, what it would be like to be rich. Live in a big house, in a pretty place. We . . ."

She stopped and looked down at the tissue. "You won't tell my parents, will you? They're very . . . old-fashioned."

"I won't tell."

"We talked about getting married someday. When he finished at that college. We talked about the pretty house and the places we'd go and the children we'd have." She dropped her head into her hands. I watched her thin shoulders shake until I found them in my arms and felt the warm tears on the side of my neck. The little boy sat on the floor, hitting a block with a tiny plastic hammer, while the little girl sat on the couch and cried until the tears ran out and there were no more.

"Feel better?"

She wiped her eyes with the back of her hand. "I feel so stupid. I'm sorry."

"It's natural you should feel sad. Natural to cry."

"I thought it was all done."

"It hasn't been very long, Shawna. Give it time."

"No—I mean I thought I'd gotten over it earlier this summer. When I realized Purnell's dreams had changed, and I . . . I wasn't in them anymore."

Then she was in my arms again, and I was rubbing the back of her head, wondering why so much weight should fall on such a small frame, and why I had none of the phrases that could cure pain.

Finally she pulled away, sniffed, blew her nose, smiled ruefully. "He was so . . . different when he got back. Like he was . . . angry all the time."

"Angry about what?"

She shook her head. "I don't know! I didn't understand. When he came home this summer, it was like he didn't have any time for me. I saw him less and less. Sometimes he'd come to the fellowship classes and leave before they were over. Other times, I'd see him hanging around outside afterward, and he'd . . . avoid me. That's when I knew it was . . . over."

"But you expected him the night he was killed. You told Mr. Crews you thought he was coming and had hoped to walk home with him."

The big eyes blinked and teared but she kept herself

together and nodded, slowly. "You promise you won't say anything to my parents?"

"Promise."

"Will you watch my brother for a minute?"

She ducked out of the room and returned with a small blue box in her hand. She passed it over wordlessly and I opened it. A thin silver bracelet set with a single sapphire gleamed up at me.

"It's beautiful. Purnell gave it to you?"

"Yes, sir. Two days before he . . . died. I came out of the house and he was waiting for me. He just pushed it in my hand and walked off before I could say anything."

I looked at the box. Shreve, Crump & Low doesn't carry trash. "It's a lovely bracelet."

"That's why I thought maybe . . . it was going to be the way it had been before. I thought it meant he'd come to the concert and we'd . . . talk again. About us, you know? That's why I wore my best dress." Her voice quavered and her hand stole to her eyes.

I stood up and gave her back the bracelet. "I think you were right. I think you were still part of his dream."

She looked down at the box, turned it in her hands. "I'll never know, will I?"

"We never know for sure how we fit in someone else's dream." I bent over and kissed her hair. "But if you tell your parents what you've told me, they may remember how hard it is to lose one."

There was too much day left to knock off quite yet, so I found a phone booth with a set of Yellow Pages and checked Clothing. "Jack's" didn't make it, nor did "Jacques," but scanning from the beginning finally produced Couture Avec Jacques on Newberry Street. I'd just have time to drop by and then catch the full glory of Boston rush hour on the way home.

The shop was a bastion of high fashion squeezed into a narrow brownstone near the intersection of Newberry and

Clarendon. A short, brown-haired young woman with a boyish haircut was tilting a hat on a stand when I came in, consternation drawing her carmine lips into a thin line.

"I can't seem to get it to stay at the right angle." She cocked her head and stared at it, a tangle of exotic feathers and bits of leather that could have been roadkill were it not for the price.

"Maybe if you shoot it again it'll stop moving."

She giggled, a nice sound. "I'm sorry. May I show you something?"

"You already have. If I promise not to call the Audubon Society, would you be willing to give me some information?"

"Sure, I'll try—even if you do call them." She lowered her voice to a whisper. "They're from turkeys and geese. They dye them to look like that. Jake lets people think they're smuggled in from Central America. He says everybody wants to be the last person to wear an endangered species. Or is it specie?"

"Jake? As in Couture Avec Jacques?"

Another giggle and a shrug. "Think 'Schmata By Levine' would make it on Newberry Street?"

"Good point. My name's Nichols, incidently—Nason Nichols."

"Hallie Frankel. What can I tell you?"

"You had a stockboy working here, Purnell Whitmore? The young man who was murdered?"

Her head nodded up and down, slowly. "You're a policeman?" She looked me over as though I were one of their mannequins.

"Private. I work for the Kershaw Commission, the citizen's group looking into possible police misconduct. You know about that?" I started to tug out my credentials.

"That's all right. I read about it in the papers. I'll tell you what I can. It's terrible, what happened to that young man."

"Yes, it is. How long have you worked here?"

She thought a second. "Let's see, now. I started here right

after Memorial Day, so that would be"—she screwed up the lips, stared at the ceiling, and went through her fingers—"eleven weeks?"

"Just about. So you got to know Whitmore pretty well?"

"Well, no, not really." The brown bob danced when she shook her head.

"But he was working here when you were. He started right after he got back from college."

She nodded. "That's true. What I meant was, I didn't get to know him very well because we overlapped only a little while."

"How can that be? His mother said he was working here right up until he was killed."

"What?" The young woman's clown mouth pulled a frown. "That's not right. I was here the day he was fired, and that had to have been in"—she tapped a forefinger against her chin—"June; mid-June, I think." She nodded decisively. "I could probably find the exact day in our records, if you like?"

"I don't think that's necessary just yet. You say he was fired?"

"Right. Not long after he started, I heard Jake complaining to Purnell because he wasn't showing up, or was showing up late. After that, he came in when he was supposed to for a few days and then, one day, he didn't come in again. We were doing inventory and I could tell, like, Jake wasn't happy, you know? The next day he *did* show up, but late, and Jake really lit into him. I could hear him yelling, even though I was up here and his office is in the basement. And then Purnell said something, I couldn't hear what, and Jake was yelling some more, and then the cellar door slammed and Purnell came walking through here, fast. He didn't see me at first, and as he went by one of the dummies, he knocked it over—just reached out and knocked it over, on purpose. And then he saw me, and he got all embarassed, and he went back and picked it up and mumbled something—an apology, I think. And he said, "See you," and walked out, and that was the last time I ever saw him."

"Did Jake tell you what the yelling was about?"

"He just said he'd had to let Purnell go; he wasn't dependable. Said college had spoiled him, thought he was too good to work here. So you see, I never had a chance to get to know him very well, although he was always real polite to me. Polite and helpful, when he showed up."

I pocketed the notebook and pen. "Thank you, Ms. Frankel. You've been a big help."

"I've never known anyone who was . . . murdered before. Was he . . . in some kind of trouble?"

"I'm afraid it's a pretty rough world where he lived; I don't know about any trouble, just bad luck."

"Oh. I . . . I'm glad, I guess. I mean, it's terrible the way he was killed, but I'm glad it wasn't because he was . . . up to something bad. He was always a real gentleman with me. When he got fired, and then that other policeman came around asking about him, why, I thought maybe—"

"The other policeman?"

"Well, I guess you're not technically a policeman. This man was. He had, like, a uniform and a badge and all that stuff. Asked me some questions about Purnell, and it got me wondering if everything was okay with him. So then when I read he'd been killed, why, I—"

"You mean this policeman came around *before* Whitmore was killed?"

"Why, yes." She used the ceiling and her fingers again. "Probably six, maybe seven weeks ago. Early July, I think. In the afternoon—around three, maybe?"

"Was anyone else in the shop?"

"No. I was alone. Jake had gone to New York, and there weren't any customers."

"Was it a Boston police uniform?"

"I . . . think so, but they all look alike, don't they?"

"Did he give his name?"

Her front teeth scraped the red off her lower lip while she thought. "Why, I don't believe he did. He came in, said he was sorry to bother me, but he was looking for a young man named Purnell Whitmore, and had he come in yet. I said he didn't work here anymore, and told him what had happened. He seemed kinda . . . concerned, like. Then he thanked me and left."

"He should have been wearing a nameplate. Did you see that?"

"I'm sorry; I just don't remember."

"Do you happen to remember the badge number?"

"I'm sorry—I never looked. Why do you—" Her hand flew to her mouth and her eyes bulged. "A . . . policeman—the papers said a policeman was seen with him. You don't suppose . . ."

"It's a possibility. We're exploring every lead. Can you tell me what this man looked like?"

I took as complete a description as she could give me, but it was maddeningly vague: hair sort of light brownish; height about the same as mine, only maybe a little taller, but maybe not; age somewhere between twenty-five and thirty-five; and so on. I had real doubts she'd be able to make a positive ID.

"I guess I spend too much time concentrating on what people are wearing and not on the people. I wish I could be more help."

"What you've told me may help a lot."

"I'm sorry. I just never made the connection, or I would have called the police." The young woman looked devastated.

"That's understandable—it was a while ago."

As soon as I left, I called Hairston, who was out. I said I'd call back and pulled out Lynn Daniels's business card.

Her secretary put me right through, and Lynn's obvious pleasure told me that my nervousness had been wasted. Unfortunately, so was the dinner invitation, because she had a meeting with James.

"Break it. Call up and tell him you decided Corey Webster was more your type."

"Ugh! Whatever made you think of him?"

"It'll keep. Can't you slip the James meeting?"

"Damn it—that's not fair. I've been hoping for weeks that a nice man would call me up and ask me out, and he picks the one night I absolutely can't."

"No chance, huh?"

"Not tonight, Nase. I'm sorry. Theo called this morning and insisted I come by right after work to help him plan this anticrime campaign he announced the other night. I just can't let him down."

"Can't he plan a war by himself?"

"Believe me, you wouldn't want him to. It took him a *long* time to understand who the enemy is; I want to be there to make sure he doesn't backslide. It's bridge-building time, and I don't want him blowing them up instead."

"Attack at dawn, huh?"

"You bet. We're going to show this town what Theo can do when he's not marginalizing himself with a lot of old grievances and stale rhetoric. I'm really turned on by it."

The current of her excitement flowed over the wires and I acknowledged defeat as gracefully as I knew how. "Well, you know where this leaves me for dinner?"

"Where?"

"Wanda Pryce-Jones."

"I hope you get herpes. But if you survive the experience, can we make it another night—soon?"

I promised, meaning it, and then got through to Bucky, who thought that squash, steam, and drinks at the Harvard Club sounded like a great idea. I didn't have the heart to tell him he hadn't been in the starting line-up.

chapter 18

OW! WATCH IT!" BUCKY LOOKED DOWN AT THE strawberry on the back of his thigh where my shot had smacked him.

"Sorry. If you'd clear out the tee so I could take a shot, that wouldn't happen." Bucky played squash as a contact sport. If I didn't hit him from time to time, I might as well stay off the court. "Nine–five."

"A gentleman wouldn't take that point."

"A gentleman wouldn't play with you." Out of the corner of my eye, I saw that Bucky's attention was wandering again, so I served, suddenly, a hard shot right at him. He barely got his racquet up in time to keep the ball out of his teeth.

"You prick—I wasn't ready!"

"Will you get in the game? What's eating you, anyway?"

"You read the *Hub* this morning?"

"I haven't had any use for the *Hub* since Brenda walked out with the cat."

"That clown Webster said POCAT was going to give the system 'one last chance' and then they'd 'seek justice in the streets.'"

"They're blowhards. It's all talk. James was their big gun, and he's finished with them."

"It's easy enough for you to be blasé about it—you get burned out, and they've done you a favor." He scowled, served to my backhand. We traded rails three or four times, and then Bucky mishit and the ball came off the side wall and hung in the middle of the court, an easy put-away. I was just about to stroke it when he smacked his racquet hard against the backwall. I jerked, and the ball hit the tin with an ugly clang.

"Don't do that!"

"Sorry—got too close to the wall." He whirled and his racquet flew up, but I was expecting it and had him hopelessly out of position in two shots. "Ten–six and counting, Buckster." He was breathing hard.

He inched his way to the front corner and picked up a towel. "Grip's a little wet. Wouldn't want it to slip. Could do a lot of damage, flies outta my hand and hits somebody. Heh, heh." He wiped the handle slowly, then walked back at a speed that could have been measured in geological time.

"You feel like playing, or do you want to forfeit?"

"Forfeit—to you? Serve."

He concentrated on the game, and five minutes later I was spent. He has surprising quickness for a big man, and unless I hit my shots perfectly, he'd pick them off every time. My serves weren't deep enough, and he was returning them as low rails that hugged the wall and died. He was up fourteen–eleven when I put one in the middle of the court and he backed me into a corner with his big butt while he got his shot set. " 'Bye-'bye." He dinked it an inch over the tin and I didn't even try.

"Like that forfeit, buddy?"

We kept playing, but Bucky's mind got farther and farther from the little white room, and more and more points came my way simply because he wasn't there. Finally, I got him out of position, drove the ball past him, and his lunging shot off the backwall caromed back into his face with a smack that I could feel.

"Shit!" He smashed his racquet against the wall, and a hundred dollars' worth of graphite made a splintering sound.

"Damn it." He pressed his hand to his nose, looked at the ruined racquet.

"You all right?"

"Sorry—I shouldn't have done that."

"It's okay. Bad day?"

"It's just . . . never mind. Lot on my mind. Sorry."

"Let's get some steam, restore our fluid levels. I'm whipped." I'd rather share a cell with Jeffrey Dahmer than a squash court with an enraged Hanrahan.

We cooked for a while in the steam room while I amused him with my Corey Webster encounter, then repaired to the bar and martinis.

"Feeling better?"

"Much. The thought of you dancing with Webster has restored my soul. These don't hurt any, either."

"He's a mean little bastard. Not so little, come to think of it." I rubbed my knee, still sore from its encounter with Webster's boot. "I don't think he's wired right."

"Ought to be wired up to about ten thousand volts. What's your take on the Whitmore thing?"

"This stays with you?"

"Sure."

I filled him in on what I'd learned at the dress shop.

He let out a long, silent whistle when I finished. "Kid gets fired, doesn't tell his mother? Nothing strange about that. The cop coming to the dress shop, though—wow. You think it was the same guy who was with him the night he was killed?"

"Doesn't have to be, but I'm going on the assumption it was, or it gets too weird."

"But that means this cop was *hunting* for the kid. Jesus— that's sick."

"I know. At least you could understand what happened if some cop lost it in a bust, but that's not my take on it."

"Going to be a big disappointment to the *Hub* if some wacko did it—hard to tag Dapper for that. How do you figure it went down?"

"Look at the physical evidence. This wasn't an arrest that got out of hand. There's no sign of a fight, no bruises on the face, no torn nails or swollen knuckles. The kid hadn't been worked over with a night stick. He was a prime athlete, had to be strong as a horse. Anybody did this in a struggle, there'd be some sign of it."

"Then what was it?"

"Someone who could take Whitmore when he wasn't expecting it. Somebody talking to him, then"—I brought my hands up and suddenly smacked them against Bucky's shoulders, so that he almost fell off the barstool— "slammed him into a wall, like that—pow! Dazed him, and then he finished the job."

He pulled himself erect and nodded. "The old lady said the cop and Whitmore acted like they knew each other."

"True. And that's consistent with the cop's coming looking for Whitmore at the dress shop. They were friends, or at least acquaintances."

Bucky fished an olive out of his glass and sucked on it reflectively. "Something wrong here, Nase."

"You could say that."

"No." He shook his head. "I don't mean the cop's cruising around looking for the kid. I mean"—he signaled the bartender—"something else. Something doesn't fit. Shit."

"It's just—"

"That's it!" He slammed his hand on the polished wood of the bar. "They met like friends, right? But then the cop shoved the kid into the alley. That's *not* friendly, huh?"

"You mean, he pushes the kid into the alley. Whitmore's going to be startled—"

"—angry, wary, whatever." Bucky's fist swallowed the fresh glass. "If the cop goes for him right away, think Whitmore's going to be standing there, back to the wall, loose enough the cop can suddenly slam his head into it? As you point out, this was an athletic kid, and his guard's going to be up, guy's just grabbed him that way."

I thought about it. "Okay—so they talk a little, Whitmore relaxes, and then it happens."

Bucky gave me a disgusted look. "Oh, sure. He whomps the kid against the wall, and then for good measure gives him half a dozen more, drags the body around until he finds a convenient Dumpster, tosses it in, picks up a shoe, wipes it—no prints, right?—and tosses *it* in, then walks out, cool as a cucumber, no more than five minutes later?"

"It could've worked that way."

"Maybe. Sure. But the timing's pretty tight in any case. *Really* tight if the cop had to first talk nice to Whitmore after shoving him into the alley. That's *two* things you've got to wonder about, if the cop did it."

"Or maybe the cop didn't do the kid. Great."

"Just a thought. You were feeling bored—keep it in mind. What's your next move?"

"I'll tell Hairston and the boss lady about the cop looking for Whitmore before he was killed. Hal'll interview the sales clerk, see if she can pick him out of a face book or do a drawing, but it's a reach. I probably ought to talk to Mrs. Whitmore again, see if she has any idea what her son was doing when he was supposedly working at the shop, but I hate the idea."

"He was probably just goofing off."

"The money, Buck—where'd he get the money for the bracelet and the stereo, if he wasn't working at the shop?"

"His savings?"

"Maybe, but Mrs. Whitmore said she kept them. That's one of the things I've got to ask her about. After that, I don't know."

"Speaking of after that, what about Rachel?"

I didn't want to think about that, about the crinkly letter back in my apartment, unanswered, especially not so soon after calling Lynn. "Don't start."

"If you want my opinion—"

"I don't."

"If you want my opinion . . ."

I brought up the Sox's pitching woes, but even that diverted him for only a second. He was still yammering at me as I washed down the last peanut with the last drop of gin and headed home.

I checked my answering machine: no Quark. Could he have missed my missive? Perhaps the man had more taste than I'd anticipated and refused to read the *Hub*. Was my catnapping going to leave me in permanent possession of a rather unfriendly, malodorous feline that clearly wished me ill? I looked at the beast, and instantly, it darted under my sofa, so that all I could see were its murderous, beady little eyes, staring at me. Wondering, no doubt, how my flesh would taste.

"Believe me, Bootsie," I assured it, "I'm as eager to have Daddy call as you are. You see, I dislike you. No—I detest you."

It answered with a hiss.

I put on Strauss's *Four Last Songs*, threw half a chicken in the oven, poured a glass of wine, and went to the drawer and pulled the letter out. I sank into the chair but didn't open the letter, just tapped it on the back of my wrist.

After a few minutes, Kiri Te Kanawa's pliant voice and the chardonnay worked their chemistry on the fragile little thing that is my conscience, and I got up and found a pen and paper. When I sat down with the chicken and some salad an hour later, the floor was littered with paper balls.

chapter 19

THE WAR-ROOM DOOR WAS CLOSED WHEN I ARrived just after nine, a hand-lettered sign advising that unauthorized visitors were not welcome. A shiny new lock backed up the message.

It was a relief to shut the door behind me and close out the baleful stares that had followed me through the squad room, even though the heat thrown off by ten people, four computers, and a dog had produced an atmosphere that was well on its way to being the same puke-green color as the walls.

Somehow Peggy had managed to retain her scrubbed look, although Laura Randall and the young men and women pawing through boxes of records or pounding on computers appeared to be in various stages of meltdown. A portable radio snarled some atonal rock bleat. My entrance hardly drew a glance.

"Whew. You may not be able to smell me coming, but

your crew's going to be announcing itself from a long way away." I plopped into a chair across from Peggy's desk.

She was pounding away at a braillewriter but stopped to take a sniff. "Hello, Nason. Yeah, it is getting pretty ripe. I thought conditions were rough over in the DA's office, but this place should be condemned. How's it going?"

I filled her in on my activities and took the attaboy as my due.

"Well—not a bad piece of work. Not bad at all. And you just a cabbie."

There's no point in looking modest in front of a blind person, so I didn't work at it. "Cops would have got there eventually."

"Sure. Little off the reservation, though, weren't you? Thought all you were going to do was look over the cops' shoulders."

"You got a problem with it?"

"Hell, no. You want to freelance in your spare time, be my guest. Just don't get in anybody's way, and stay on top of the police investigation. I talked to Kershaw, and it's like I thought—he wants you to stay with it until the case is solved. I got the impression it's a concession to James."

I looked around the grim room. "Yeah, maybe that's not such a bad idea. How's your work coming?"

She hit some keys on the braillewriter and a printer on the desk next to it started to cough out lines of type. "Doing an assignment sheet, show Kershaw how we're proceeding."

I craned my neck and was surprised to see that the printer was spitting out normal letters. "Hey, that's something. I didn't know that you could do that." It sounded patronizing as soon as it was halfway out.

"It's either this or get the dog to learn shorthand. Goes the other way, too. See this?"

She handed me a sheet of paper covered with little raised bumps. "That's a copy of a page from one of the files on an excessive-force complaint. The kids feed the file into a scanner, the machine spits this out. Pretty neat, huh?"

"Amazing." Where had I been during the technological revolution? I still couldn't keep my microwave going.

Peggy was on a roll. "Take a look at something else." She called her assistant. "Laura, can you show Mr. Nichols one of the coding forms?"

The young woman scurried over with a paper in her hand and sat down next to me, all eagerness and moist, glowing purpose: "We've gone back to 'ninety, so we can tell if there're any changes in the number and type of force incidents since Commissioner Flanagan took over." She pointed over her shoulder at the worker bees poring over the files they were pulling out of cardboard banker's boxes. Every few seconds, they'd make a pencil mark on a piece of paper. "That's what they're looking at."

Laura slid the form over to me. "We fill one of these out for each 304 report." The department jargon, so newly learned, raced off her tongue as if she were a twenty-year veteran.

Department rule 304, governing the use of nonlethal force, requires a written report after each arrest in which a suspect is struck or physically subdued. The reports are furnished to the arresting officer's commander, with a copy to Internal Affairs. Any report indicating possible noncompliance with department policy may lead to an investigation and disciplinary action; the results of any investigation are furnished to the commissioner for final action. It's all set out in printed rules, and every member of the force knows the rules. It's up to the brass—ultimately, the commissioner—to make sure they're followed.

The coding sheet listed numbered categories: date of incident, cause of arrest, badge numbers of officers involved, disposition, arrestee's race, officer's race, location of arrest, reason for using force, type of force used, whether the arrestee was injured, whether an allegation of excessive force was filed, administrative action taken—if any, and written comments. Laura explained the significance of each, in a voice barely able to conceal her excitement at being at the heart of things when she was so young.

"See, the reporting officer's race isn't in the 304 report, so we get that out of the personnel files. And then we'll input all this information into the database on the computers, and we'll be able to cross-reference and tell right away if there've been more force used in arrests since Flanagan was appointed, and like who the officers are who are involved, and if it's white officers beating up, like, African-Americans, and whether complaints have been filed." She looked at me, wide eyed. "Isn't it incredible?"

"Close to a miracle." The young woman beamed, immune to irony.

"Thanks, Laura. Why don't you check on the others now." Peggy turned to me as Laura trotted off. "Somehow I sense you're not as overwhelmed as Laura."

"It looks neat, but the 304's aren't going to tell you much by themselves. You'd hardly expect the arresting officer to file one saying he'd bounced some guy down the steps because he didn't like his color. What about arrestee complaints? How're you checking those out?"

"My—you *do* know your police procedures, don't you?" She felt across the desk until her hand closed on a stack of papers. "Take a look at these."

They were covered with rows of raised dots, as meaningless to me as if she'd handed me the Rosetta Stone. "Braille, huh? What's on them?"

"The complaint files. Laura feeds the originals into that optical scanner, they get converted by the computer, and that printer spits them out."

"Amazing. So you'll know how the excess-force complaints have been handled?"

"Every damn one since Flanagan took over, from filing to final disposition. Then I'll write up my analysis of them."

"How can you tell if the administrative review was straight?"

"I've got ten years in as a prosecutor. I may be blind, but I can smell bullshit. Any questions, we can get witnesses in."

"If *you* decide there're any questions."

"I'm the one. Like they say—'justice is blind.'" The grin was back, only this was the mocking little one I didn't like. I didn't need any more of it. I groaned as I pushed myself to my feet.

"Where you off to?"

"Looking for another merit badge."

"Hey, Nase."

I turned back. "Swing by after work. We can compare notes. I may even buy you a drink."

"Yes, sir."

chapter 20

EVEN ROXBURY WAS LOOKING ITS BEST. IT WAS A late summer morning charged with promise, moving toward eighty, and the only cloud in sight was the one I saw as I thought about seeing Mrs. Whitmore again. I decided to put that off as long as I could.

A fat terrier on the end of a piece of clothesline tugged an old man past the entrance to the alley. He tipped his cap and I regretted I wasn't wearing one so I could have reciprocated. His soft "mornin'" stayed with me while I looked over the scene.

Mrs. Hastings had told the police she'd seen the policeman talking to Whitmore outside the entrance to the alley, but she'd told me that she remembered seeing Whitmore step out of the alley first. If he'd headed down the alley to get to the church, why had he come back out? Maybe he had forgotten something; maybe he'd just changed his mind and decided not to go. And maybe he'd done whatever had taken him down the alley and was on his way somewhere else. I started down the narrow byway.

A few feet in, a gust tumbled a can into the cellarwell of the abandoned apartment house, where it came to rest against the door. The adjacent buildings held it in shadow, and as the sound faded, I noticed a hair-thin halo of light at the foot of the cellar steps.

The door was no more giving than it had been the last time, but I leaned into it until the latch pulled out of the rotten jamb and I stepped in. A rat scrambled to escape my menace, and then it was quiet.

At first I thought it was light from outside that let me see the hallway leading toward the front of the building, but as my eyes adjusted, I realized there was as much light in front of me as behind, light coming from the end of a hallway that ran to the front of the building. I pulled my revolver and started toward it.

The hall dead-ended in a stairway. Someone had dangled a lightbulb over the railing overhead, and in the weak light, I could see pools of urine, sticky on the steps, and miss most of them. I started up, then ran my fingers across a tread. It was dirty, but not coated with dust. There had been recent foot traffic.

The trail of excretion and cigarette butts stopped outside a gunmetal-gray door on the second landing. I listened but couldn't hear anything on the other side of it, so I turned the knob slowly, the gun ready, and pushed. The door swung open easily.

The room inside was unoccupied but hadn't been for long, because cigarette smoke hung in the already-stifling air, if you could call it air. The floor was littered with empty vials like the one I'd found outside, trailing away from a burn-scarred table set with a broken crack pipe, a couple of candle stubs, and a coffee can overflowing with butts. There were a few chairs and a mattress on the floor that looked like it had been used to blot up human body fluids. A single bulb hung from a cord that snaked across the ceiling and out a crack between a board and the window.

The gaunt, gray man in a sleeveless undershirt who stepped out of the dark doorway from the back room was even more surprised than I was. Bulging veins criss-crossed his skinny forearms; a dark, keloid scar in the shape of a lightening bolt stood out against his right bicep, below a crudely tattooed cross.

"Wha' the fuck?" He whipped a knife out of his pocket, far quicker than I would have expected. It made a sharp little snapping sound as the blade flicked open. His eyes blinked rapidly but his hand was steady.

"Exactly." I showed him the gun. "Little mistake. This isn't the model suite, is it?"

He shambled toward me, the waist-high knife screaming for attention. "Gonna stick you, mofo." His eyes were as red as a feral animal's.

"Guns *trump* knives, meatball—or don't you know the rules?"

"Motherfucker!" He kicked in his afterburner and covered half the space between us before I decided that anything less than a bazooka wasn't going to get his attention. I stepped aside and laid the gun hard against the side of his head as his momentum carried him by. He dropped to one knee but kept swiping the air with the hand that wasn't clapped over his bloody eye.

"I *told* you guns trump knives." I stepped past him, and as he tried to stagger to his feet, I whacked the back of his head hard enough so that he went down and stayed down. The knife had dropped by his side and I kicked it across the room, then walked into the room he'd come out of.

A single window opened onto a light well, and after my eyes adjusted, I could make out a filthy cot and a sagging dresser. I tugged open the drawers, but they were empty, so

I flipped the mattress, then dragged the cot away from the wall and spotted the floorboard my host had left askew when he'd last gone to his cache. I pulled out a shoebox and opened it.

There were maybe fifteen of the little vials, each with its load of rock, and a greasy wad of bills in a rubber band. I did a quick count and estimated five hundred dollars, give or take. A sandwich bag held a few large nuggets for inventory. A small scale completed the kit, except for a small bundle of glassine packets that I almost missed. I pulled it out and poured the contents of one of them onto my palm. I touched my tongue to the white crystals and was rewarded with the alkaline taste of cocaine. My man was ready to service the upmarket, should it come calling. I tossed the stuff on the floor and stepped back into the front room.

He had managed to get to his hands and knees but seemed satisfied to watch the pool of blood forming below his chin. He wasn't looking particularly frisky, but I kept my gun on him until I was out the door.

Even the alley air smelled good after the urinal I'd been in. I took in deep lungfuls while keeping an eye on the cellar steps. If the dealer came up them, I was definitely going to shoot him, but I didn't think he would. He'd take some of that nice painkiller, and when he woke up again, he'd have a whole new vision to share with his customers.

The presence of an active crack house on the route Purnell Whitmore would have taken to get to the playground contributed a whole new possibility: Whitmore could have encountered the wrong customer at the wrong time. Someone with the need working on him might have seen a nicely dressed young man as financing waiting to happen.

But would he have methodically flattened his skull,

stuffed the body in the Dumpster, bothered to toss in the shoe or, most particularly, left ninety dollars in the wallet? No way. Whoever killed Purnell Whitmore wasn't after a dream state. I took a last look at death's door and was glad to leave it behind.

chapter 21

THE BOYS WERE OUT ALREADY—LARGE BOYS, wiry boys, boys who understood the geometry of a spheroid off a plane as Euclid never had, boys who had something to teach Newton about gravity. Their raucous calls reverberated past me as I stepped back into the sunlight and stood watching the game.

A small, darting figure, a short youth in a torn T-shirt, looked over at me from a crowd gathered at the foul line of the near basket. He gave me a thumbs-up, grinned, then held up his hand, posted down against a boy a foot taller, broke right, took a pass. He had a shot, faked it, left a tall boy hanging in midair, dished off, and screened for his teammate's easy layup. The big kid he'd been guarding turned for the rebound, watched the ball sink, then delivered an elbow to the short kid's face, calmly and deliberately.

"Cocksucker!" The small boy clapped his hand to his

nose, started for the other boy, let his teammates hold him back. "Shit." He staggered off the court while the game went on and I walked over to him.

"Asshole." He wiped his nose on the bottom of his shirt. "Believe that shit?"

"You okay?"

"It's nothing, man." He gave me an earnest, street-tough look that collapsed in a half-laugh, half-whimper. His eyes teared and he brushed the back of his hand over them. "Hurt like hell, tell the truth. Motherfucker can't play worth jackshit. Only way he can deal with me. Had refs, asshole'd foul out first quarter."

"You had him faked out of his jock. Ought to tell one of your bigger teammates"—I pointed to a tall, pudgy boy at least as large as the kid who'd thrown the elbow—"get under that guy the next time you get him jumping for a rebound. Let him know you've got guys who'll look after you. Might be better than a ref."

He spat. "That dude's too much out for hisself, know what I mean? Won't pass off, look out for other guys, like you say. Gonna hurt my chances, I come out with this nosebleed?"

"Hurt your chances?"

"'Cause I can take it, Jack—be back in, soon as this bleedin' stop. Put in twenty more over that asshole—just you watch. Put me in with refs, like you guys got, nobody gonna stay with me."

"I think you have me confused with somebody else."

He looked me up and down. "You ain' scoutin'? Why you here, ain't it?"

"Afraid not."

He appraised me again, sniffled, wiped his arm across his nose. "Shee-it. You the *man!* Damn! Here I thought you was one of them scouts."

"Sorry. But I'm not a cop, either. I'm a private detective, working for the city. Looking into this thing with Purnell

Whitmore—the young man who was murdered. Did you know him?"

"You flackin' me? You really a detective?"

"You got it." I showed him my license.

"Damn—never met no detective. You got a piece?"

"Sure."

"What you carry?"

"A thirty-eight."

"Shit, that ain't no weapon. Ought to get a Glock, Cobray, righteous iron like that."

"When I start dealing, I will. Did you know Purnell?"

The excitement faded, replaced by a wary look. "Sure, man, I knew Purnell."

"He could have come through here the night he was killed. Were you here that night?"

His eyelids dropped. "Maybe."

I reached into my pocket and pulled out a ten. My hand closed over it just ahead of his. "Were you here that night?"

"I was hangin' around, yeah, but I didn't see Purnell. Hadn' seen him in a while."

"What time were you here?"

He thought a minute. "Got here 'round seven, left when it got too dark—maybe eight-thirty, little after. Woulda left sooner, only this seem like a good place to be at the time."

"How's that?"

"Shee-it, man—they was a raid that night; we wasn' goin' noplace till the cops cleared out."

"It must have been pretty dark. Could he have come through without you seeing him? Say around seven-thirty, a little after?"

"Coulda happened, I suppose."

"Did you see *anybody* come by during that time?"

He scratched his head. "They was one guy—least I think it was a guy."

"Why do you think it was a guy?"

"Built like a guy an' walked like a guy."

"Where?"

" 'Long the alley there."

"Where were you?"

"Over there, around the basket." He pointed toward the far end of the playground, a good fifty feet from the mouth of the alley. "We was shootin' around when I saw this guy walkin' 'long the alley, other end of the court there. Walkin' real slow, close up against the buildings." He gestured over his shoulder with a thumb. "Couldn' hardly make him out. I figured maybe he was gettin' away from the cops."

"He was walking in the direction of the church?"

"Not like he was in any hurry to get there, but yeah— that direction."

"Could you see what he was wearing—what color his clothes were, for instance?"

"Nope—too dark down at that end."

"Were his clothes light or dark?"

He gave it some thought. "I dunno—light, maybe? Seems I could see his shape against the building, anyway."

"Could it have been Purnell?"

A veil dropped over his face. "What reason would Purnell have for wantin' to get away from the cops?"

"None that I know of, but could it have been him?"

He shrugged his shoulders. "Coulda been. Coulda been anybody. You 'bout done, mister? I gotta get back in."

"Few more. Was this person you saw Purnell's size?"

"Close enough, I guess."

"What time was it when you saw this person come through?"

"I dunno. Little while before we left."

"Around eight?"

"Earlier. Quarter of, maybe."

"When was the last time Purnell had been down here?"

"Tell you, told that other guy: Purnell moved outta here when he went off to that college; dude was hangin' else-wheres."

"What other guy?"

A canny glint came into the young man's eyes. "I don't

want no trouble with the cops; maybe you got your ten bucks' worth, mister."

"I got twenty here, and there won't be any trouble. What other guy?"

"Man came around here, couple weeks ago, lookin' for Purnell. Just like you, only he say he was scoutin'. Reason I figured you was."

"He give his name?"

"Nope. Just ast had Purnell been playin' ball, had we seen him."

"What'd you tell him?"

"I *tole* you, man—see the dude around, time to time, but not down here."

"Where had you seen him?"

"Shee-it, mister—around, okay? Seen him on the street sometimes, sometimes hangin' 'round the church back there—wherever."

"Did this man say why he was looking for Purnell?"

"Yeah. Said he wanted to talk to him about playin' some ball."

"Was he in uniform?"

"Nope."

"How'd you know he was a cop?"

"Said so. Said he was scoutin' for the rec league, wanted to see Purnell."

"Rec league?"

"Recreation department, man. Runs sports programs for us ghet-to kids. Keep us *clean*, see?"

Something knocked for attention but I told it to wait. "What did this guy look like?"

He looked me up and down. " 'Bout like you."

"My size?"

"Maybe a little bigger all 'round."

"Can you give me any more than that—hair color, eyes, that sort of thing?"

An impish grin spread across his face. "Sorry, mister.

Fact is, you white guys all look, like, pretty much the same to me, see what I mean?"

"Sure. Thanks for your help." I passed over the money.

He swiped his nose and looked at the back of his hand. One of the other boys called out, "Hey, Mouse—you comin'?" and waved his arm.

"One more question . . . Mouse?"

He stopped and turned back. "Yo?"

"Do you have any idea why Purnell stopped coming around? Stopped playing ball, I mean?"

His features arranged themselves in a lifeless neutrality. "No idea, mister."

"You were a friend of his once—Mrs. Whitmore told me. It might help us find out who killed him, if we knew what he'd been doing."

"Purnell's dead, man; don't matter now what he was doin'. All I know." He turned and sprinted back to the others.

chapter 22

"I'M SORRY TO BOTHER YOU AGAIN, BUT I'VE learned something and wondered if it would mean anything to you."

She pushed her hair back and tucked the edges of her housecoat together. "Have you found . . . ?"

"No, ma'am. But I may have some leads. May I come in?"

"Please." She led me back to the living room. "What have you found out?"

"The scrapbook you showed me? I think Purnell may have played for a team in the summer recreation league."

"I believe he did. Last summer. Let's look again, if you think it may be important."

She led me back to Purnell's bedroom and pulled out the book. I flipped the pages until I found the entry I'd gone by the last time: WHITMORE DUNK AT BUZZER CLINCHES REC LEAGUE TITLE.

"There it is." I tapped the entry. "I think maybe an off-duty policeman might have been helping out."

She shook her head. "I don't know about that. But there's a picture of his team over there." She pointed to the wall by the closet and the eight-by-ten photo in the dime-store frame. I got up and peered at the legend on the bottom: ROXBURY JETS, RECREATION DEPARTMENT SUMMER LEAGUE CHAMPS. Ten boys, lined up on a patch of asphalt, lithe and cocky. Purnell Whitmore stood in the center of the first row, holding a plaque at waist level. Two boys knelt in front of him, holding a pair of basketballs like a heraldic device. The only white faces in the picture were those of two of the four men in T-shirts standing at the ends of the rows, muscular and serious.

"Do you know the names of any of these men?"

"No, sir. I never heard Purnell mention them. You think they're policemen?"

"I believe at least one of them might be."

"Can you find their names?"

"No question about it—there'll be a record. It won't take much time."

"And one of those men might be . . ." Her voice trailed off.

"It's possible. Worth looking at. Only possible, though."

She turned and stared at the white faces, from one to the other and back, as though trying to detect the emanation of evil. Then her hand jerked forward and she lifted the picture from the wall. "I don't want it up there."

"I understand. May I have it? I promise to give it back."

"You take it—you use it to find the man who killed Purnell." She thrust it at me.

"I'll do my best." I took the picture. "This may help—I can't say."

"I'll pray for that."

We walked back to the front hall. "There is something else. I . . ." I was trying to frame it when the doorbell buzzed a reprieve.

"So many neighbors meaning to help. I'm sorry."

"That's all right. I'll wait." I stepped into the living room while she answered the door.

"Why, Reverend James!"

"Good morning, Sister Rose. I was in the neighborhood and thought I would come by to see how you're getting along. Mrs. Warren dropped off this casserole for you."

"That's good of you, Pastor, and bless her. I was just talking to Mr. Nichols. He's helping with the investigation." She led him into the living room.

"Hello, Reverend." He'd traded in the dark suit I'd seen him in before for a three-piece, white-linen number over a black shirt and the clerical collar. He was sporting a crucifix only a tad smaller than the original, but on his broad chest, it looked almost demure.

He nodded in my direction. "I'd hoped this would be over by now, Mr. Nichols. Are the police making any progress?"

Mrs. Whitmore set the casserole on the coffee table. "Mr. Nichols thinks he may have identified the policeman. The policeman who was seen with Purnell."

James's face brightened. "That's wonderful news, Mr. Nichols. Wonderful. Have they arrested him?"

"I don't even have a name yet. And I don't know if he had anything to do with Purnell's"—I remembered Mrs. Whitmore's directive—"murder, either. It's nothing more than a lead."

"Of course he was responsible. Why wouldn't this man have come forward if he weren't?"

"I don't know, Reverend; that's a good question. But I do know he was looking for Purnell for some weeks before he was killed. It had nothing to do with the street sweep."

"Looking for Purnell?" Mrs. Whitmore's voice had dropped to a whisper.

"Yes, ma'am. This policeman wanted to talk to Purnell. He knew him from someplace, maybe the basketball program, and he was asking people who knew him where he was. He was at the playground asking about him, and before that at the dress shop."

She stared up at me. "At the dress shop?"

"Mrs. Whitmore, Purnell wasn't working at the dress shop this summer; he was fired after just a few days. He hadn't been playing basketball the nights you thought he was, and he seems to have come into quite a lot of money."

"But he told me—"

"He lied to you, Mrs. Whitmore."

"No! He wouldn't. He never . . ." Her hand cupped her mouth as though she were going to be sick.

"I need to know, Mrs. Whitmore. What was he doing? Do you have any idea?"

"Oh, my God—what are you saying?" She had her eyes clenched shut, blocking out the picture I'd painted.

"I'm not saying anything, Mrs. Whitmore, I'm asking. Have you any—"

James's hand clamped on my elbow and turned me so I faced him. His eyes searched mine. "Please, Mr. Nichols. I'm sure you think this is necessary, but for God's sake, hasn't the poor woman suffered enough? What difference can it make what the boy was doing?" His voice softened. "Find out who this man was so the police can bring him in. Help them do their job, so Mrs. Whitmore can find some peace."

I started to turn back to Mrs. Whitmore, but James tightened his hold. His deep eyes bore into mine. "I said leave it, Mr. Nichols. You've done what I asked, and I'm grateful to you." He held his grip until I nodded.

Mrs. Whitmore sat huddled on the chair, her hands pressed into her chest. I stepped over to her and touched her shoulder. It quivered under my hand. "I'm sorry. I shouldn't have told you like this. If you think of anything, will you call me? It might be important." I dropped a card on the coffee table and let myself out.

chapter 23

I STARED AT THE INSCRIPTIONS ON THE WALL NEXT to the pay phone while the harried clerk tried to find Hal. Vito made Renée beg, Al put horses to shame, and Roger had an endowment only slightly smaller than Harvard's. It got me wondering if I'd stated my case forcefully enough in the letter I'd finally dropped in the slot. Perhaps "Dear Rachel—I've grown in ways you can't imagine since last I saw you" would have intrigued her more than the awkward uncertainties that survived the night.

A hoarse "Hal Hairston" brought me back and I filled him in quickly.

"Terrific—we've got a stalker. A cop stalking the kid. Wish I owned shares in the newspapers."

"You ought to be able to run down the guys in the basketball league easy enough."

"Yeah. Bring that picture in pronto, okay?"

"One hour. What do you make of Whitmore?"

"Hey, man, do what you want with that, but you want my advice: leave it alone. You start asking questions about the kid, *this* kid, you'd better have a good flak jacket. Anyway, what's it got to do with anything, few holes in his life?"

"You'll make chief yet. Later."

chapter 24

THE PLAZA BAR WAS QUIET, DARK, AND MERCI-
fully cool. "Ahh—that's good." Peggy wiped her lips and
pressed the frosted glass against her cheek. "Jesus, that
room's an oven. They ought to be giving us a tropical-duty
allowance. You're lucky to be out and about."

I thought about my day and tried to decide if I felt lucky.
No. "It may get a little hotter soon." I brought her up to date.

"Wow. You *have* gotten out in front of the cops."

"I caught some breaks is all."

"You made some breaks. You know, Nichols—oops"—
she held up her palm—"Nase. *Nase,* dammit. There—I've
got it. You know, Nase, I had you figured wrong. Real
wrong. Sorry about that."

I didn't like the sound of that and had started to ask her
what she meant when she raised her glass in a toast.
"Here's looking at you, kid." She giggled and I shrugged

and clicked glasses instead, although it wasn't the funniest line I'd ever heard.

"Thanks, I guess. Anyway, they'll have the guys in the picture in no time. If one of them's a cop, bingo. Question him, maybe a lineup with Mrs. Hastings. If he did it, we stand a pretty good chance of knowing within a day or two. That leaves your end of it. How's it going?"

"It's going. The kids are good. Enthusiastic. We'll get through it pretty quick."

"What's it looking like so far?"

"I have no idea. The kids are still inputting data, and all I'm doing is drilling excess-force complaint files into my fingertips."

"Some of our employers aren't going to care *what* you come up with, you know; their minds are made up."

"The knee-jerkers? Sure, but they're preaching to the converted anyway. Most people won't pay any attention to them; they're too predictable."

"Want to compare scorecards?"

"You show me yours, I show you mine, so to speak?"

"The dog will tell you I'm blushing."

She reached out cold fingers and touched my cheek. "Damn—I believe you *are* blushing. Sorry. I told you I hung around with cops too much, and DAs aren't much better. Okay—let's start with the ones who would crucify Flanagan if we produced affidavits from the twelve apostles that he was the second coming of Christ. I make Pryce-Jones . . ."

"Easy."

She held up her hand and ticked them off on her fingers. "The fruity guy . . ."

"A lay-down."

"And the tree-hugger makes three."

"Who?"

"The ecofreak, what's-her-name."

"Ah, yes—old what's-her-name. Perfect score."

"What about James?" she asked.

"A week ago, I would have sworn he'd be the first to put the knife in; now, I'm not so sure. I call him a toss-up."

"I'll go with that. This anticrime program he just came out with makes Dapper sound like a weenie. Kind of surprising." She rattled her ice cubes and popped one in her mouth. "So let's have another drink and then you give me your list of the ones who'd stand behind Dap if we proved he was Hitler in hiding."

I flagged down a waitress and started. "The Teamsters guy, Marciano—Marcello—whatever it is."

" 'Jus' remember I know which way yer kids walk to school, lady.' Yeah. Next?"

"The one that looks like your dog." I felt myself flush for the second time. "Oh—sorry."

"It's okay, but you may have trouble with Leba. The school board, right?"

"Right."

"That it?"

"Oh, yeah—Finn. Put him at the top of the Flanagan column."

She fished around in her old-fashioned and pulled out the orange slice. She stopped it halfway to her mouth, started to say something, shook her head, and nipped a piece of orange instead. She waited until she'd swallowed and her tongue had snaked a tidbit off the corner of her mouth. "Got him all penciled in, do you?"

"That's where he's supposed to be, isn't it?"

"I suppose people think so." She assumed the school-marmish, we-know-what-we-know voice that put my teeth on edge.

" 'Think so'?" I dropped my voice until the surrounding din closed in around us: "Come on, Peg—I know all about it."

She dropped the rind on the table and pulled out the cherry. "Know about what?"

"The deal with your uncle. The reason Finn's on."

The bright red cherry dangled from its stem, midway between glass and hand. "What deal with my uncle?"

"The real-estate deal. Finn's project. Don't worry about it; it isn't going any farther. But we both know what's expected from Finn, and I'm sure he'll perform like a champ, so you don't have to play dumb, and you don't have to talk like I'm dumb."

All the play had left her voice, and her ivory skin had turned bone-white. "How do you know about it?"

"My friend's in it with Finn; he got it from him."

"The guy who recommended you to Kershaw?"

"Exactly."

A long ten-count passed, and then she bit off the cherry and chewed it slowly. "I might have guessed."

"What do you mean, you 'might have guessed'?"

She smiled, a bright, not terribly convincing effort. "Nothing. Anyway, glad to have you in the club." Once again, she hoisted her glass in my direction, then took a hard pull.

I didn't try to match it. "So anyway, we put Finn in the Flanagan column, right? I mean, that's the whole point, isn't it?"

"Okay—now I get you." She gave a wry shrug. "Absolutely. Everyone knows Tip's a Flanagan fan."

"How did you hear about it?"

"Finn's deal with my uncle?"

We were both whispering, a little pocket of intimacy in the eye of the bar's hubbub. "Right."

"I am O'Conor's niece, you know. Think he's going to keep me in the dark?" She chuckled softly. "Hey—there's a new one."

"Yeah." I hoped she wouldn't use it often. "So it'll work out fine." The conversation had taken a peculiar turn, but we seemed back on track. "Another drink?"

" 'Fraid not—got a dinner date. Better be going." She flipped out a ten. "Give me a ring tomorrow, let me know how you're doing."

I watched the two of them wend their way out, wondering whether I'd miss the company. I decided I wouldn't—she was too off center—but if I had another drink, I was going to be asking the harpist to play "We'll Meet Again," and if I didn't I was going home to leftover chicken and Vanna White. I chose a third option.

The Boston Clarion
Editorial
August 22, 1994

A GIFTED PREACHER GETS RELIGION

Some may not have heard it yet, but recently, Boston has been getting some sound advice about crime and social policy from an unexpected quarter. Roxbury's Rev. Theophilus James, long the local African-American representative of the "blame anyone but the criminal" viewpoint so popular among the city's cultural elite, has had an epiphany, it appears, and today no one in Boston is talking more sensibly about the cures for the crime epidemic that makes life a daily struggle for those unable to hide out in secluded suburban retreats.

"Criminals cause crime," says the Rev. James, voicing a thought that is revolutionary in the salons where, we suspect, the Rev. James will no longer be as welcome as he was in the days not long past when his impressive oratorical skills served the reigning orthodoxy with such statements as "White racism causes black criminals."

From the pulpit and in the press, the Rev. James's thundering words have begun to give voice to those in the African-American community too long without a champion. To those who still claim that poverty causes crime—insulting the great majority of poor people, who work hard and live honestly—the Rev. James replies, "Criminals don't need jobs; they have the only jobs they want—crime. They need jail." And he adds, "We need more police and fewer social workers." To those whose reflexive invocation of race has long seduced his community, the Rev. James offers a blunt rebuff: "Culture, not color, will determine success. We must nurture old virtues, not old grievances."

Yesterday, the Rev. James offered a well-conceived program for a communitywide war on crime, long on specifics and devoid of the usual calls for new social entitlements and racial quotas. It is prefaced by a demand that society at all levels must begin drawing sharp moral lines: "We need a culture that is as quick to condemn today's criminal as it is yesterday's bigot."

Nobody was more critical of the Rev. James than we, in the days when he sounded like a parody of a Harvard professor. We said he was ill-using his abundant talents and ill-serving his people, and he was. Today, however, he has become a voice of sanity, and his people are all those, of every race and creed, who reject the false gods of racial politics and moral laxity. We welcome his leadership and salute his crusade.

chapter 25

LYNN DANIELS HAD A NICE WAY OF DISMISSING small things with a tone. "Are we breaking the rules?"

"Your dining with the help? Probably. I won't tell if you don't." The waiter handed us menus, then uncorked a bottle of wine.

"Let's really break them, then. How's the investigation going?"

"It all comes to you eventually anyway." I tasted the wine and decided it had been a good choice. Calling Lynn had been one, too. To every thing there is a season, and all that. What if Rachel had changed her mind? We weren't engaged. Hell, we hadn't even seen each other in six months. I started from the beginning and finished as the waiter reappeared, and if he thought I was a quasi-adulterer, he didn't let on.

The worried look that settled on Lynn as I described my

encounter with Webster chased the last little worm of conscience. "He didn't hurt you, did he?"

"Webster? Nothing permanent, but I'm glad the handyman came along when he did, or I'd probably be singing the *Internationale*—in falsetto. That's one crazy guy."

"Maybe he was high on something."

"I hear *Das Kapital* will do that to you."

She chuckled, a nice, throaty sound. "Just a thought. The rumor is that he got in some drug trouble a while ago—that's why he got fired from his teaching job. I don't know. I do know it's a damn good thing Theo's split with him."

"Webster seems to hold you responsible for that."

She seemed momentarily distracted by the idea, then nodded. "I suppose I am, in a way. God knows I spent enough time trying to get Theo to realize he wasn't going anywhere with all that racial crap. Thank heavens he finally got it."

"In the nick of time, I'd say. He could have raised all kinds of hell if he'd used the Whitmore thing to fan those flames. You told me he was coming around, but I had my doubts."

"Come to trust me, have you?"

She clasped her hands under her chin and batted her eyes expectantly, and I had to laugh. "All I know is, the James who's sounding like a cross between Clarence Thomas and Cotton Mather sure isn't the James who once talked like Flanagan was responsible for everything from sickle cell anemia to drive-by shootings."

Her eyes lit up like little sparklers as she switched speeds. "What do you think of the new model?"

"The one I heard when O'Conor was introducing all of you? Not bad."

"'Not bad' my foot." She scooched in her seat as excitement grew on her. "He's good, Nase—damn good. Get him off the race angle, get him talking about stuff the uptown crowd sneers at—*that's* going to raise all kinds of hell. It's like Nixon going to China."

"And you just wound him up and turned him loose, eh?"

I'd meant it as a joke, but she played with it for a few seconds as she swirled her glass, shiny brown hair licking her neck in synch with the circling wine. Finally she shrugged, as though inner terms had been reached, and let a half-smile form over the rim of her glass. "Sure, that's me—Theo James's Svengali." The smile faded, but not the hard little light behind her eyes. "And why not? Better me than Webster or the Pryce-Jones crowd. You heard what they liked from him; think that was doing anybody any good?"

The waiter broke in to take our orders, and when we'd given them, Lynn picked up her glass again. "Anyhow, great work. They'll have that cop in custody soon. Maybe they already do."

We touched glasses. The Café Budapest had been a good choice, too, or maybe Lynn just made it seem as though the candlelight was particularly soft and warm, the flowers especially fresh. "Cheers. They may have—I'll find out tomorrow. That should lighten the air."

"Will it ever. I know Theo will be relieved. He's risked a lot of capital being a peacemaker; we might have lost him if he'd gotten the idea the police were screwing around with this guy."

"That was never a risk; the risk is they've been so set on the cop, they've let other things go."

" 'Other things'? What do you mean?"

"What if the cop didn't kill Whitmore, Lynn? We have to consider that possibility."

She pondered it while she topped up our glasses. "Any reason to think he didn't?"

I gave her the thoughts Bucky had run by me, then added the fact I'd gotten from the young man called Mouse.

When I finished she gave me a wry look. "Pretty thin, I'd say. *Somebody* walking past the playground after the cop had been with Whitmore, and *maybe* the cop didn't have time? I think I like the cop best."

"So do I, but this guy coming through the playground should be checked out. That's the kind of thing that may slip through the cracks."

Lynn was intrigued. "How would you check that out?"

"The person the kid saw was walking toward the church. Maybe someone there that night saw whoever it was; that could clear it up."

"But if anyone had seen the Whitmore boy around the church, surely they would have come forward by now?"

"Sure. All I'm saying is that *if* somebody came walking out of the alley, approaching the church, around seven-forty-five, seven-fifty, and we can find out who it was, it settles something. Otherwise, there's at least the possibility that it *was* Whitmore who came through the playground then, which means he was still alive when the cop left him."

I could see the gears whirring behind her eyes. "But then who killed him?"

"Exactly. Could have been someone farther down the alley. Someone he knew, maybe. They stopped to talk, he wasn't expecting trouble, and then . . . you know. Then the guy ducked into one of the buildings alongside the alley or maybe even walked out by the church."

It was her turn to look skeptical. "That's a real long shot. I think you just like playing detective."

"It *is* a long shot. God willing, the cop's in custody and spilling his guts right now. But if he isn't, I think I'll drop by the church tomorrow, see if James saw anybody who might have been our guy."

Lynn's eyebrows furrowed. "Around seven-forty-five?"

"Probably a little later—why?"

"I can save you that visit. Theo couldn't have seen anyone around the church then."

"How do you know?"

"Because I was with him in the church basement."

"*That's* when you were with him—the night Whitmore was killed?"

"Right. That's the night we got together to talk about my clients, the old Hungarian couple. Down in his office."

"Do you remember what time you got there?"

"Let's see." She stared off into space, her lips reflecting a silent computation. "About seven-thirty." She nodded decisively. "Right—it was just seven-thirty. I remember because I stopped off to get a sandwich and I was afraid I was going to be late, but I made it on the nose."

"I don't suppose you heard anything—footsteps, anything like that?"

"Uh-uh. Theo's office is way down in the bowels of the building, and there're no windows. We wouldn't have been able to hear anybody outside."

"How long were you with him?"

"Let me think." She tapped her chin as she reflected. "A good three hours. Sure—at least that. I left about . . . ten-forty-five, eleven o'clock." She traced the times on the tablecloth with her fork.

"How could you stand it?"

"Hmm?"

"That's a long time to spend with anyone, much less James."

"Tell me about it." She replaced the fork, smoothed the tablecloth, rearranged the salt and pepper, leaned back, and admired her work. "I thought it would go on forever."

"You missed a crumb. Anyway, you're right—James won't be any help. Was there anyone else around when you arrived—someone who might have seen this person?"

She stared at the wall as she reflected. "Well, Webster had been there, but . . ." She shook her head. "No. I was trying to think if he might have still been around when I got there, but I definitely didn't see him. That's a sight I don't forget easily, worse luck . . . especially after that night."

"Why especially after that night?"

"Because when I arrived, Theo was all worked up over some garbage Webster had been laying on him about the police. It took forever just to get him to focus on my problem. It wasn't any picnic."

"Oh, well. Sorry to bring it up."

"That's okay—it worked out fine in the end. We took care of my clients' problem, Theo realized Corey Webster had been full of shit on that, and that gave me my opening to work on him on a lot of the things he's addressing now. So it was worth it."

"You've put a lot of energy into Reverend James, Lynn. What do you get out of it?"

Before she could answer, our plates of smoked salmon arrived. After the waiter had ground pepper over them, Lynn looked down at hers appreciatively. "That looks delicious, doesn't it?"

"It does."

"But before they'd take our order, we had to get a table, right? We could have stood outside with our noses pressed against the window, but they wouldn't have served us, would they?"

"I must have had too much wine, Lynn—you're losing me."

"I mean I've spent too much of my life with my nose pressed against the window, watching other people place their orders. That's what Theo gets me."

"A plate of smoked salmon?"

"No, silly man—a place at the table."

chapter 26

WHEN I GOT TO THE POLICE STATION THE NEXT morning, the halls were teeming with people changing shifts, some in a hurry to start another crime-filled day, others in an equal hurry to get home and spend a few hours forgetting what they'd just spent a night seeing. Hairston was one of the truly damned, rolling off one shift and starting the next. He looked like an autopsy candidate, and I told him so when I finally caught up with him outside IA.

"Can't happen soon enough. Only way I'm gonna get out." He snatched the cup of coffee I'd picked up on the way in, flipped off the lid, started slurping it as we loped down the hall.

"Bad night, huh?"

"It was all set to be hell anyway, then you called and really put it over the top."

"Any help?"

"Between me and you, right? You haven't heard this?"

"Yeah, sure." One of us was pressing for a heart attack and the other wasn't going to have enough wind left for mouth-to-mouth. "Just slow down, okay?"

"Here." He pulled me into an empty office and shut the door, panting hard. He pulled out a crushed pack of Marlboros and shook one free. "Want one?"

"Thanks anyway. My health insurance lapsed. What's up?"

A cloud enveloped my head. "We got the guy."

"The cop?"

His tone changed. "Yeah. Patrolman named Hurley, on the force seven, eight years. Gonna talk to him now, down the hall. Which, by the way, is why I gotta go."

"Wait! How do you know it's him?"

"Well, for starters, there's a little thing called police work. What we do, when we're not busy oppressing the poor. Kind that takes time, something the press can't seem to get. Questioned over three hundred cops since the kid was found. Yesterday we got one, seemed kinda nervous. From over in Area D, Back Bay, nowhere near Roxbury. Finally, she admits her partner'd talked her into waiting in a diner at Kenmore Square while he took the squad car, night the kid was killed. Said he needed to see someone confidential. She's a rookie, doesn't know shit, figured what the hell, he's getting some on the side, something like that. Says okay. He's gone about an hour—plenty of time. And the time works."

"But can you put him with the kid that night?"

"Don't know yet. That's why we're gonna talk to him. But I'll tell you where we *can* put him." If Hairston had suddenly coughed yellow feathers, he couldn't have looked more like the cat that ate the canary.

"Where?"

"At the kid's rec-league basketball games, that's where." He pulled out a copy of the photo I'd gotten from Mrs. Whitmore and tapped it.

I glanced at the image under his finger. "Hurley, huh?"

"Yep. That was a great lead, Nase. You shoulda been a cop, except then you woulda got the credit instead of me."

"Nah, I'm too honest to be a cop." I looked at the earnest young face under a flat-top haircut, the muscular torso so squared away and proud. "Let me sit in on the interrogation."

Hal threw his butt onto the floor and ground it out. "Hah! I should walk in there with Alan Dershowitz, I'd be more popular."

"Not in the room, then. In the observation room."

"Nase, my guys'll kill me, they see you hanging around."

"That was a great tip I gave you, Hal. Now it's payoff time."

"Aw, shit. Okay, but if anyone catches you, you sneaked in on your own."

"Deal."

Hal cracked the door and peered out. "Okay, let's go." We scurried through the depressing corridors until Hal stopped in front of an opaque glass door and unlocked it. "Okay—in there. Don't move around, don't smoke, don't breathe." He walked over to a tape recorder and pushed a button. "Lock the door and wait for me to come get you."

"No wonder they call this the hospitality suite. Thanks, buddy."

I settled into one of the four wooden chairs barely visible in the light coming through the one-way glass window set in the wall. On the other side of the window two men I didn't know, one black and one white, were sitting at a gray metal table. They were in shirt sleeves, ties askew, the bags under their eyes matching Hal's. The black detective, a large, older man with hair going gray, was smoking a cigar. The short white detective picked at a callus on his palm, flinging minute bits of dead skin on the floor. I could hear his heavy breathing over the speaker on the wall above the window.

There was the sound of a door opening and Hurley appeared stage right, followed by Hairston. Hurley stopped a few feet from the table and swayed from foot to foot. The black detective looked at him incuriously, through hooded eyes. The white one kept working on his hand, not turning around.

"Hurley, huh?" The black man blew out smoke.

Hurley couldn't decide what to do with his hands, which moved from his belt to his pants pockets to a crossed position on his chest, and then started over. They must have called him in from off duty, because he was wearing a T-shirt, faded jeans, and the shadow of a day's beard. The sandy flat-top gave him a retro fifties look. "Yes, sir."

"I'm Bosworth. That's Stein." He pointed across the table but Stein didn't look up. "Internal Affairs. Mind if we ask you a few questions?"

"No, sir."

"This is being taped. Any objections?"

"No, sir." He'd moved his hands up under his armpits and seemed to have locked them in. His face was pale and shiny under the stiff glare.

"Have a seat, John. Be a lot more comfortable." Hairston had walked up behind him and quietly moved a straight-backed chair into place, so that when he applied light pressure to Hurley's shoulders, he sat immediately. The chair was a good three feet from the table, leaving Hurley looking isolated and vulnerable.

"Uh—thank you."

"Sure. How about some coffee? A smoke?" Hairston left a hand resting on the young man's broad shoulder.

"No, thank you. I don't think so, sir."

"Hal. Call me Hal." He patted the shoulder, then retreated to a chair against the wall, almost directly behind Hurley. "You change your mind, just let me know."

Hurley was still looking around for his new pal Hal when Stein said, "Why'd you kill the Whitmore kid?" He hadn't looked up or turned to face Hurley, and his voice was so low I could barely hear him.

Hurley heard him clearly enough, though, because he

shook his head like a fighter trying to recover from a hard shot to the chin. Before he could force out a sound, Bosworth said, in a ho-hum tone, "We got a positive make by an eyewitness."

Stein sat up and slowly swiveled to look at Hurley. He ran his eyes over him, up and down, as though memorizing the parts. "Described you to a T. Picked you out of the face book like you was best friends."

"Man, I'm tired and wanna go home." Bosworth took a deep pull on the cigar. "Don't let's have to waste time with a lineup." He shook his head as though that was the stupidest thought imaginable.

"I—I didn't. I don't know what . . ." The two men at the table stared at him. Hurley turned almost completely around, but Hal was pretending to read a magazine and didn't look up. "Listen, you've got to believe me. I . . . I didn't. I mean, I don't . . . please!"

Bosworth shook his head, sighed. "Why don't you tell us about it. Got all the time in the world."

Hurley held his eyes as long as he could, then dropped his face into his hands. "I didn't kill him! I swear I didn't. You've got to—"

"Come on, Owen—let's book this asshole. We've got enough without listening to his bullshit." Stein bit off a hangnail and spat it on the floor.

"Yeah, maybe you're—"

Hal looked up. "Come on, guys, give the man a break. Let him tell his side of it; that's only fair." By the time Hurley looked around, Hal's nose was back in the magazine.

"Yeah, maybe you're right." Bosworth heaved a great sigh. "Okay, Hurley, what's your story? Why'd you leave your post that night?"

Hurley had a face that reflected every underlying neural impulse, so it was as easy to read as a comic book. It was painful to watch him construct an answer, even more painful to hear its halting delivery: "My wife."

"What about your wife?"

"She called. I had to go home."

"So you went home that night?"

"Yes." He bobbed his head. "The baby was sick."

"She call the station?"

"Yes. No—I called her."

"Thought you said she called."

"I meant . . . I don't remember."

Stein burst out of his torpor, shot to his feet, circled around behind Hurley in three quick strides. "Jee-sus. I can't believe this shit." He suddenly rested both hands hard on the back of the chair and Hurley's shoulders jumped. "Listen—give me fifteen minutes alone with this creep; I'll give you a signed confession."

"Ease off, Mike. No point calling the guy a liar. Have the dispatcher send a car around, pick up his wife—she'll confirm your story, that'll be that, right?" Bosworth smiled at Hurley as Stein started for the door.

"No!" Hurley's panicked shout stopped Stein halfway across the floor. "Leave her alone. Leave her alone, or I'll—"

"Or you'll kill me, tough guy?" Stein took little shuffling steps back to Hurley and stood behind him, leaning over so that his mouth was inches from his ear. "Got so you like it, have you?"

"Okay, Mike—cool it. Let the guy talk, like Hairston says. What's the story, Hurley? Where'd you really go that night?"

Stein pushed away from Hurley. "Yeah, yeah. Makes me sick." He slid into his chair. "Okay, sonny—we'll try it their way. Then it's *my* turn." He started picking at his hand again.

"Am . . . am I under arrest?" Hurley's voice cracked.

"Hell no, boy. You can walk out of here this minute, you want to." Bosworth sounded offended by the suggestion.

"Yeah—go out and get yourself some smart lawyer, Hurley. You're gonna need one."

"Didn't know you had anything to hide, that's all." Deep

disappointment registered on Bosworth's rubbery face. "Figured you'd be willing to talk to us, not come in here with a dumb story like that, drag your wife into it."

"Call my cousin Lenny, you want a smart Jewish lawyer," said Stein.

"All the other cops, they *wanted* to help us find the guy who did this." Now Bosworth sounded hurt.

Stein spoke without looking up from his hand: "Old lady's always hacking at me: 'Why can't you be a lawyer like your cousin Lenny?'"

"That's why your partner told us about you being off post that night. Just trying to do the right thing."

"Be great, next time, tell her, 'Lenny's so fucking smart, how come the Hurley creep's getting butt-banged by every blood in Walpole, next fifty years?'" Stein's smirk was a thing of beauty.

Hurley looked like a man who had stumbled into a madhouse and couldn't find the way out. "I . . . I do want to cooperate. I know I shouldn't have . . . shouldn't have . . ."

"Yes, son . . . what shouldn't you have done?" Bosworth gave Hurley a nod.

"I . . . I . . . I did leave my post. But, but . . ."

"There you go. Now we're getting somewhere. Yes, sir." Bosworth pulled a box of Rum Crooks out of his pocket and lit one off the stub of the first. "Why don't you tell us why? The real reason?"

Hurley's hands started roving again. "I . . . I . . ."

"Let's begin at the beginning, okay? You knew the kid, right?"

"I don't . . . I can't . . ." Hurley was a terrible liar; his stammering marked the slow construction of the falsehood as indelibly as if he were copying it from a manual.

"Come on, John—you knew the Whitmore kid. We know that." Bosworth pulled a folded copy of the basketball-league picture from his pocket and held it up. "That's you; that's the kid." He tossed the picture on the table.

"Nice-looking kid. Nice body. See him in the shower,

locker room? Maybe you got a little thing for him, huh? Had
a little fun, he wanted money or he'd tell the old lady, you
killed him?" Stein's leer sent little shivers across my back.

Hurley shot out of his seat and stood, hands clenched,
glaring down at Stein. "Damn you! He wasn't . . ."

Hal bounced to his feet and rested a hand on Hurley's
shoulder. "Hold on, John. Don't blame you for getting hot,
but hold on. Stein,"—Hal spoke through clenched teeth—
"you've got no call to talk like that. John's had a clean
record, and if he went off post to see Whitmore, I'm sure he
had a good reason. Now, why don't you just shut your sick
mouth and let the man talk?" Hal's glare was worth an
Academy Award nomination. "Sorry about that, John. Go
ahead." Gentle pressure eased Hurley back into the chair.

Stein scowled at Hal, who turned toward the mirror and
winked before resuming his place against the wall.

"He wasn't what, son?" Bosworth spoke gently.

"He wasn't . . . like that."

"Purnell Whitmore?"

"Yes."

"You knew him from the basketball league?"

"Yes, sir. I knew him."

"And you stayed in touch with him?"

"No, sir."

"You went looking for him around town, didn't you?"

"Looking for him?"

"Come on, Hurley—you know what I mean. The dress
shop, the playground—they can ID you. Already identified
you from your photo." Bosworth lied with the fluency of
long practice.

"I . . . I went there. To those places. Yes, sir."

"To find Whitmore."

"Yes, sir."

"And you found him."

"No, sir. I . . . I mean . . ."

"Well, you saw him the night he was killed, didn't you?"

A good minute went by with no answer, Hurley just

staring at the wall above Bosworth's head. His eyes finally dropped to Bosworth's face. "Yes, sir. Yes, I did. I saw him that night."

"That's why you left your post—to see him."

"Yes, sir."

"To see Whitmore."

"Yes, sir."

"Had you arranged the meeting?"

"No, sir."

"You just hoped you'd run into him?"

"Well, I knew where he lived. I thought I might run into him."

"But you didn't go to his house."

Hurley began to twist in his seat. His large pink hands were thrust between his knees, one massaging the other without letup. "No, sir."

"Most likely place to find him."

"Yes, sir." The right hand stole up the left wrist, began tweezing the fine hairs on the arm.

"More likely than a dress shop or the playground."

Hurley stared straight ahead, not making eye contact, mouth working soundlessly.

"Unless you didn't want anyone to know you were looking for him."

"No—I mean, yes, but . . ."

Stein, head bent and staring at the floor, made a disgusted snort.

"Why were you looking for him?"

Hurley resumed his examination of the wall. After a long silence, he rasped, "I just wanted to talk to him, that's all." His tongue circled his lips.

"What about?"

Hurley's mouth started to move, stopped, started again. "Nothing in particular. Just say hello, see how he was doing. Nothing . . . particular."

"Five minutes, guys—that's all I want, five minutes alone with him." Stein's forearm cradled his head on the table.

"It's the truth!" Hurley's eyes bulged, and he looked like a caricature of a frightened rabbit, but it was grotesque on that big, open face. He swiped at his lips and wiped his palm on his shirt.

"Let me see if I get this. I'm really trying to follow, son, but it's tough." Bosworth leaned back and scratched his head. "You worked with the Whitmore boy last summer. You go almost a year without seeing or talking to him, then you decide you want to talk to him about nothing in particular, chase him around Boston, leave your post to find him, don't call his house or go there, run into him outside an alley, push him back into it, and walk out alone several minutes later. That about it?"

"I know it sounds—"

"That about it, I said?"

"Yes! That's what happened."

"So why'd you kill him?" Bosworth sounded no more than idly curious.

Hurley bolted out of his seat as though he already felt the current boiling his innards. "I didn't kill him! How many times do I have to tell you? I didn't kill him!"

He stepped toward the table, his hands held out supplicatively, but staggered backward into the chair at Stein's snarled warning. "I . . . didn't . . . kill him. Please?" His voice trailed off like a man no longer sure and looking to Bosworth for confirmation.

Bosworth's shrug said he wouldn't haggle fine points. "Okay, okay—so you didn't mean to kill him. Why'd you beat him up?"

"I didn't, I tell you. I didn't touch him." His head sunk back into his hands.

The big man looked disappointed. "Come on, boy— eyewitness saw you push him back there into that alley. That right?"

"No! Yes. I don't remember." His voice trailed off. Defeat seemed to overtake him in waves, overwhelming the patches of defiance. Now he settled his face in his hands, until he remembered where he was, forced himself to look at Bosworth.

Bosworth pursed his lips thoughtfully. "You don't remember if you pushed him into the alley."

"No, sir."

"So if a witness says she saw you do it, you can't say she's wrong."

"No, sir." The chin lifted a fraction more, a little whisper of dignity creeping into the voice.

Bosworth knocked some ashes on the floor. "We know Purnell never came out. He made you mad, didn't he?"

"All right—yes! He said something that made me mad, and I may have pushed him back into the alley. But that's all. I just wanted to talk to him. I didn't hit him, I didn't hurt him, I didn't kill him!"

"Big guy like you, wouldn't need to mean to. Got a little carried away, lost your temper, maybe he hit his head on the wall. Not your fault at all. That the way it happened?"

Hurley clenched his eyes shut. "No! No, no, no! That's not what happened."

"Done it myself, back when I worked the streets. Some punk dissed you once too often, something would just like to snap. Next day, you wake up, punk's in the hospital, wife's asking you how come there's blood on your shirt. That the way it happened, son—little blackout?"

"No! I'm telling you, I didn't hurt him." His hands had moved down to the seat of the chair, clutching at it as though it were all that held him earthbound, and he swayed forward and back, almost rhythmically. "I didn't hurt him. He was fine when I left. He was fine when I left. He was fine . . ."

"So what went down?" Bosworth drew on the cigar, exhaled. Nothing came out. He took it out of his mouth and looked at the tip, shook his head. He pulled out a Zippo and fired it again.

"What . . . went down? What do you mean?"

"Jesus Christ, man—you say you're a cop?" Stein's disgust was no longer feigned.

"You mean, what . . . happened?"

Stein massaged his temples. "God help us. Yeah—'what happened'?" Tell us the story you're gonna tell my cousin Lenny. I got a right to laugh, too."

"I told you. I found Purnell. I . . . wanted to know how he was doing. I'd worked with him in the basketball program. I liked him. We talked for a few minutes, and I left. That's all. That's all that happened!" He thrust out his chin and for a second looked again like the proud young kid in the photo.

It didn't last. "Why'd you push him back in the alley? What'd he say, made you mad?"

Hurley sagged. "He . . ."

"Yeah?"

"Never mind. It doesn't matter." His hands wrapped around his forearms, and he seemed to be trying to pull his head down into his chest cavity.

"'Doesn't matter'? Kid's dead, head beat in like a rotten tomato, you say it doesn't matter what you were doing with him? You trying an insanity defense?" Stein was staring at him as though Hurley had started speaking in tongues, and even Hal's mouth hung open.

"I mean, why we went back there."

"Gonna matter plenty to you, boy." Bosworth knocked an inch of ash off against the table. "Gonna matter plenty. Listen,"—he took a deep breath and his voice softened— "all we want is to close the books on this. Like Hairston says, you've got a good record, been a good cop. Anybody can fuck up. Give us something we can go with, couple answers, we can shut the fucking papers up, everything will cool down. Get a good lawyer—not Stein's shyster cousin— a good lawyer. PBA will help—talk about stress, how the kid jumped you, what the hell. We'll go to bat for you. But you gotta tell us what went down, we're gonna help you. Now, one more time: why'd you do him? Come on, son—

you'll feel better." Bosworth rested his big forearms on the table and looked at Hurley as though he *were* his son.

"I didn't kill him." All the indignation was gone, all the insistence; Hurley sounded like a middle-age Catholic reciting the rosary.

"Then what did you talk about? Why won't you tell us?"

"I . . . can't. I *can't* tell you. Please, God, I can't tell you. Don't ask me again—please, don't ask me again." The plea had a keening quality to it.

Bosworth rolled the sodden tip of the cigar from one side of his mouth to the other, then back to the center. "I see. Okay. O-kay. That's how it is." He pushed himself upright. "Be back in a minute." Hurley had his face back in his hands and didn't catch the look that passed between the three men. Bosworth was almost out the door when Stein rose to join him.

Hurley's heaving gasps were the only sound I heard until Hal picked up his chair, walked over, and sat down beside him. His arm reached around the broad back and gave it a squeeze. "Guess that was your wife who answered the phone when I called, huh?"

"Nora?" Hurley wiped his eyes with the back of his hand and forced his breathing under control.

"That's her name, Nora?"

"Y-yes, sir."

"Pretty name. She sounded nice. Sweet. That's impor- tant."

Hurley nodded. "She is. Nora's . . . gentle. She won't be able to handle this." He shuddered and Hal grabbed his shoulders again.

"Heard the baby, too. How old is it?"

"Six months."

"Cute age. A boy?"

"Um-huh. John-John."

"Terrible thing, lose a child."

"Oh, God—don't!"

"It's okay, it's okay." Hal's hand cupped the back of Hurley's neck. "When I saw Mrs. Whitmore—well, that boy, he was all she had. I dunno, maybe Owen—guy who just left—he came on a little hard, but he lost a little girl last year, broke him up pretty bad." He stopped, looked at the man under his arm.

Hurley just rolled his shoulders, his chest making great heaving motions.

"Stein—well, between you and me, Stein's just a shit, know what I mean? Sick bastard. Around here, Stein caught on fire, guys wouldn't piss on him to put it out. Anyway, I wouldn't blame you, don't feel like talking to them."

"No—it's not that . . ."

"Here. Lemme give you my phone number. My home number, too. Anything you want to talk about, just gimme a call. Anytime." Hairston scribbled on a card and pushed it into Hurley's hand. "You don't want me telling them, that's okay. It'll be just between you and me."

Hurley looked down at his fist. He started to unfold his fingers, but Hal gently cupped them back around the card. "Just you and me. Okay?"

"But I can't—"

"It's okay, John. Listen—get that lawyer. Get the best one you can afford."

"But I didn't—"

"Some of these guys work wonders. Cooperate, cut a deal, have you out sooner than you think. That Nora, she'll stand by you, don't you worry. I could tell."

"I didn't—"

Hairston stood. "You call now, you hear? Anytime." He put his hand on Hurley's head, quickly, then removed it at the sound of the door opening. Hurley was still looking at his hand as Hairston, standing behind him, met Bosworth's and Stein's looks and shook his head.

"Okay, Hurley—you can go now." Bosworth lumbered

over and picked up the personnel file, then shoved it under his arm. Stein started flipping through the magazine Hal had been reading. "I said you can go."

Hurley looked around as though it were a trick, made no effort to stand.

"Come on, son—we gotta be going, can't leave you here."

"I—I can go?"

"I told you: you're not under arrest—yet."

"Don't be making any travel plans, though." Stein looked back over his shoulder. "Fact, I wouldn't be making any plans at all, I was you. Not for quite a few years." He resumed reading.

"Yes . . . sir." Hurley rose like an old man, holding on to the seat with one hand until he could test his legs, old man's legs. "Yes . . . sir." He shambled toward the door Hal held open.

"And Hurley . . . ?"

Bosworth's call stopped him. "Yes, sir?"

"You're on administrative leave until further notice, understand?"

"Yes, sir." Even his voice was old.

I heard Hal push the door shut, and then he joined the others at the table. They sank into their chairs like boxers coming off ten hard rounds. "Ever hear one like that?" Stein sounded genuinely stunned, the stage sneer gone. "DA's gonna come in his suit, hears that story."

"Craziest thing I ever heard." Bosworth pulled his cigar stump three inches into his mouth, pushed it out again. "Like shooting fish in a barrel."

Hal scratched his chin. "Be nice if we had a motive."

"Come on, Hal—I wasn't kidding about the homo angle; works perfect."

"I dunno—wouldn't have figured Hurley for that."

"Shit, who can tell, nowadays? You're probably queer."

"Wendy wishes. Ah, hell—let the DA dream up a motive. Why should we do all the work?"

"Hurley tells that story, jury'll probably tag him for global warming just for good measure." Bosworth pawed at his head.

"Think we should of tried the 'Okay, Stein, he's all yours' routine?"

Stein and Bosworth thought a second. "Nah." Stein shook his head. "He wasn't gonna tell us what went down even if I *coulda* used a rubber hose. He was scared shitless anyhow and didn't say nothing."

"I think that's right. Must be something *real* bad, guy don't even make a stab at a story. You told him to call you, he gets religion?" Bosworth looked at his watch.

"Oh, yeah. Told him how you'd lost a kid, weren't really a bad guy. I dunno—maybe he'll call." Hal sounded dubious.

"Lost a kid? Couple months ago, it was my wife died. Next day, guy sends me flowers—Herrmann, guy from auto squad, in for receiving? Where do you get this shit?"

"Makes 'em feel sorry for you. Love me, feel sorry for you, hate Stein. Learned it in a course."

They all stood. Stein looked put-upon. "How come I always gotta be the prick?"

Bosworth swung a big arm across Stein's shoulders. "Because, my man, it's the role you were born to play. Come on, I'll buy you a cup of coffee. Hal, you coming?"

"Had enough coffee. Time to give some back. I'll catch up on you guys, start on the report." They walked out of the room.

Hal pulled out a cigarette, looked at it like he'd never seen one before. A flame lit the room for a second, then the gloom closed in again.

"Not bad, Hal. Those *Miami Vice* reruns are helping your technique."

"Oh, man." He settled in next to me and stretched his legs. "Wendy says we should move to New Hampshire, sell mustard. Maybe we oughta. Stomach can't take too much more of this."

"What do you make of it?"

"Who the hell knows. Some kind of shakedown, maybe, went wrong?"

"Shakedown? What would this guy shake him down for?"

"Tickets to the Yale–Harvard game? Like I say—who the hell knows, who the hell cares. He walks into the alley with the kid, walks out without him, next thing the kid's a stiff and the guy won't say what he was doing with him? Come on. My mother could try the case."

"So he's going to be charged?"

"Does a fat baby fart? This guy's history."

"When?"

"Probably question him again, all the good it'll do, process the papers—tomorrow, day after latest."

"Pretty good work, Hal."

"Yeah, I guess."

"What's the matter? You don't like the guy for this?"

"It ain't up to me. See any better candidates around?"

"But . . . ?"

"You gonna go running to your boss?"

"Between us. But . . . ?"

He took a deep drag, exhaled through his nose. "But why won't the asshole give us a story?"

"Yeah, that is weird, isn't it?"

"Guy offs somebody, you question him, he gives you a story. Isn't that right?" Hal's voice turned plaintive.

" 'I wasn't there, and if I was there, I didn't do it, and if I did do it, it was self-defense, and if it wasn't self-defense, I was insane, and if I wasn't insane, my parents abused me, so it's not my fault.' "

"Right, right—like that." Hal nodded energetically.

"Kind of an unwritten rule, you might say."

"Gives us something to go on, something to tear apart, little bit at a time."

"Anybody should know that, it's a cop."

"You don't just sit there, say, 'I didn't do it, but I won't tell you what went down.'" Now Hal sounded hurt, as though they'd been playing cards and he'd caught Hurley cheating.

"Think the other guys feel the same way?"

"Now I *know* you're crazy."

"Not going to talk with them about it, huh?"

"Tell the chief, 'Cancel the press conference; guy can't be guilty—he's got no story'? Lucky if I spend the next ten years at the impoundment lot."

"Little momentum built up against this guy, huh?"

"How about the MBTA coming down on a cockroach?"

"Well, it probably fits."

"Yeah. Probably."

"Guy just isn't smart enough to think up a good story."

"Yeah, that's probably it. I gotta go." He flipped the butt on the floor, ground a heel on it, then flicked it under the chair.

"Good job, Hal."

"Yeah. Ain't it great?" He peered out the door for a second, and then he was gone.

chapter 27

So my job was done. I wandered back to headquarters, braved the veiled scowls of the squad room, took the pungent impact of the fetid atmosphere in the war room. Peggy's acolyte, Laura, broke off from the group gathered over a computer at the far end. "Peggy isn't in, Mr. Nichols; she had to meet with Mr. Kershaw. She shouldn't be long, if you want to wait."

"I will, thanks. How's it going?"

"Really well. Do you want to see?"

It would have taken a harder heart than mine to deny the puppy eagerness, though a cup of coffee and the sports section were closer to my needs. She led me back to the computer, very much the watch captain as she introduced me to Rick and Sue and Steffi and the others, then commandeered the pilot's chair in front of the console. "We don't have everything in the database yet, but we're starting to get results. Look."

Tip of tongue peeking out, eyes squinched, nose close enough to screen to serve as a pointer, uncertain fingers tapping Delphic instructions: "Se 4 by 2, all-for-all." She pushed a key and sat back while little lights flashed and the machine made digestion noises. "That tells it to search the name field, and to find the names from 1990, the first year we're entering. We're keying in all the 304 reports, but this asks for only the ones that were followed by an excess-force complaint."

"I see." It made perfect sense, sort of.

"Se = 137 entries." A cursor pulsed beneath the message on the screen, begging to be needed. Laura tapped more keys: "D by 2."

A young man standing behind me said, "That tells it to show the search results in chron order. Earliest first."

"Ah." I nodded knowingly, wondering where I'd been the last ten years, whether it was too late to trade in the English I'd grown up with for this stripped-down, leaner model.

In seconds, the screen filled with words, some of which I could even read:

R. 00001. Cunningham, Arthur P. Pt. 1/C. R: C. BN 167037. Rep. Dt. 90/01/12. NLF. DOA same. Area B. Comp Wt. AT. R: A/A. Charge XF. Admin Hrg. DWP. See 3674.

"Impressive, all right." It made as much sense as the chart at the opthamologist's.

"It says—see . . ."—Laura bounced in the chair as her finger traced the hieroglyphs on the screen—"this is record number one. A patrolman first class named Cunningham, of the Caucasian race, badge number 167037, reported using nonlethal force in an arrest on January 12, 1990. It was in Area B, and—"

"Wait, Laura—the report was filed January 12, 1990. The

arrest was the same date. That's what that means." The young man behind me pointed at the screen.

"Mr. Nichols understands that." She sniffed, went on: "Anyway, the arrested person—arrestee, we call them—he filed an excess-force charge. There were no other complainants, or it would say so."

"Then, this means"—she peered at the "R: A/A"—"resisting arrest?"

A chorus of jeers. "Noo, dummy—that means the complainant was an African-American!"

"Oh . . . yes." The young woman mottled. "Anyway, there was an administrative hearing scheduled, but the charges were dismissed for want of prosecution. Peggy says that means the perp didn't follow through. And this"—she pointed to the last entry—"is the file number. Peggy looks at those." She looked flustered. "Reads them, I mean, after we feed them through the scanner and they're translated into braille."

She slumped back in the chair and exhaled. "Isn't it . . . incredible?"

One of her cohorts squawked: "Laura, you've missed the whole point."

Another chimed in: "See, Mr. . . . Nicklaus, it's like this. You—"

"Nichols. It's Mr. Nichols, Kenny. It is, isn't it, sir? But you have to see. Laura, let me." A fat youth wearing a plastic pocket protector stuffed with pens came close to sitting in the young woman's lap before she surrendered to her survival instincts and abandoned the chair.

He wasted no more time than it took to crack his knuckles before hitting the keyboard with a dismissive chord that blasted the evidence of Laura's efforts into the digital netherworld. Then, memory purged of every wasted byte, he caressed the keys as though summoning *Eine Kleine Nächtmusik*.

His technique was that of the practiced lover dallying with a long-time mistress. Exhibiting a mastery of tempi worthy of a Horowitz, his sausage fingers stroked the beige console into squeaks of cyborgic orgasm, data ejaculating onto the screen faster than the eye could absorb it.

After a short minute, the young man rested his hands on the edge of the desk, the bliss of a job well done suffusing the overstuffed face. "There." The screen relaxed in iridescent, postcoital complaisance, its message succinct: Cunningham, Patrolman First Class Arthur P., had No Further Entries.

The young people stared, looked uneasy. "Well, see, that's maybe not the best example." The fat boy flexed his fingers, touched a key. "Watch what happens when we ask for all the entries after Blue Tornado started."

He ran off new arpeggios, daring riffs, transcendent chords. In seconds, we had a new screenful, as meaningless to me as if he'd thrust the Chinese alphabet under my nose, but transporting his teammates into a higher plane of feeling.

"Ah."

"See?"

"How're they going to explain *that*, Mr. Nichols?"

If they had to ask me, they were indeed in trouble. "Maybe you'd better help me, Laura—I'm not sure I know what they're going to be explaining. In fact, I'm not even sure who 'they' are."

Several of them stole looks at me, "what manner of man is this" looks, rather as I would have looked at someone who peered behind a television to see how the tiny people got in, but they were nice kids, and none of them guffawed or became openly derisive. "Why, this shows that the number of excessive-force complaints is way up since Blue Tornado started."

"Complaints by people arrested in street sweeps!"

"African-Americans!"

"And the accused arresting officers have been overwhelmingly white!"

The clamor died with "the people rest" finality. The people stared at me, ready for the jury verdict.

"Awesome. Truly amazing, gang."

Laura beamed. "Well, there's a lot more data to input, but we think it's pretty clear."

"And Peggy—what does Peggy think?"

"Why, she thinks the same. At least . . . I *think* she does. I mean . . . that's what the data show."

"I see." I stared at the screen, but it didn't mean a lot more than it had the first time. "I wonder, though."

"What's that, Mr. Nichols?"

"Well, if Blue Tornado means the police are arresting people who didn't get arrested before, which I thought was the whole idea, you'd expect more use-of-force reports, wouldn't you? I mean, even if force wasn't being used any more than before?"

She let this stew, then nodded uncertainly.

"And if there are more use-of-force incidents, you would expect more *claims* of excessive force, even if the police didn't change their methods at all, and even if the *percentage* of arrestees asserting claims didn't go up, or even went down a bit?"

"Why, no—why should that be?"

"Sure—for any given number of arrests effected with force, we know you're going to get a certain number of excessive-force claims; if the police don't use force any more frequently than before, but the *number* of arrests goes up, the number of complaints will probably go up, too."

"Oh! I . . . guess so."

"And if most of the arrestees in the neighborhoods where the street sweeps are taking place are black, most of the people filing excessive-force charges are going to be black, aren't they?"

Laura's face said she was having trouble with this new puzzle, but she finally let the piece fall into place. "Uh-huh."

"And if most of the police force, like most of Boston, is

white, you'd expect most of the officers charged with excessive force to be white, wouldn't you?"

Laura's thin lips tightened into a truculent line, locked against further self-impeachment, until one of the bystanders answered for her: "He's right, Laura. That makes sense."

"So you see, Laura, the Blue Tornado sweeps were bound to produce at least the *appearance* of an increase in the number of black detainees claiming to be the victims of excessive force at the hands of white cops. That *alone* doesn't prove anything about the attitudes or methods of the department under Commissioner Flanagan."

Laura's blotchy forehead furrowed. "But then what—"

"You've got a lot of nice numbers here—but are you sure they mean anything? Or maybe they just mean anything anyone wants them to mean."

"Gosh, I . . ." Uncertain eyes darted to the screen, looking for an answer in the cryptic numbers. "I don't know. Like, are you saying . . ."

Laura's chin quivered, and I was afraid she was going to cry. Her platoon stared dumbly at the monitor, as though willing it to supply the rebuttal. When it came, it was from the other direction.

"It's fine, Laura—we'll work all that out."

Relief flooded the girl's face as Peggy stepped into our midst. "Mr. Nichols is just playing devil's advocate. You guys keep plugging in the data, and we'll worry about interpreting it when we're done. I was just with Mr. Kershaw, and he's very eager for us to finish."

"Sure, Peggy." Laura was only too eager to return to the island of certainty in the little whirring box. "Come on, guys, back to work. 'Bye, Mr. Nichols."

"'Bye." I followed Peggy back to her desk at the other end of the room and sat down.

"Really, Nason. I would have thought picking on children was beneath you." She opened her briefcase, pulled out a brown envelope, slid it into the desk drawer.

"Maybe I went at it a little too hard, but those kids are

probably a pretty good proxy for the way our bosses are going to read that stuff."

"Those kids are a hell of a lot swifter than some of our bosses."

"Um. They seem to have decided that data paints a pretty bad picture of Flanagan's regime."

"I get that impression." She gave me a tight little smile.

"All the commission will know, from this data, is that since Flannagan took over, the incidents of force are way up and the excessive-force charges are way up?"

"That's what they'll get from the data, okay." Whatever friendliness had been in her voice when she first came in had been displaced by a cool lack of intonation.

"The way it's been set up almost forces that conclusion, if you don't know the right questions to ask."

"And what questions are those?"

"Like I was saying to those kids: if the police are getting down on street crime more than they did before, you'd expect the number of excessive-force complaints to be up, simply because there're more arrests, hence more use of force—right?"

"You and I know that, sure."

"You and I also know those charges can be valid, or they can be a lawyer's way of trying to play *Let's Make a Deal* when he doesn't have anything else. The relevant question is whether they stand up any better than they did before Flanagan took over."

"That's the relevant question, all right."

"Well, what's the answer? Any increase in valid beefs since Blue Tornado and the other stuff he's been doing?"

She folded her arms across her chest, her speech growing even more abrupt: "We talking for real?"

"Of course I mean for real. What's the answer?"

"Well, then, the answer is no. I've got some to go, but so far most of the complaints are garbage, like they always have been, and the ones that aren't have been dealt with strictly by the book. He's been hell on guys who got out of line, matter of fact. Already bounced half a dozen he inherited."

I felt a weight lift. "The commission hears that, it pretty well puts Flannagan in the clear."

"Right."

"But that won't be in the database, right?"

"Well, that really isn't the sort of thing that goes into a database, is it?" The tight smile returned.

"The only thing that I know goes into a database are my credit records. I take it you'll be handling this with the commission, make sure they get what they need to understand the data?"

"I'll do what I'm here to do, Nichols. You don't have to worry about me."

The conversation had been strangely chilly, a continuation of the mood that had fallen upon her the night before, but when she broke in on my pout, it was in a marginally warmer vein: "And speaking of doing our jobs, what have you done to advance the ball today, besides coming around and getting my team all stirred up?"

I savored the moment. "They got the guy."

"Huh? The guy who did Whitmore?"

"Sure looks like it." I filled her in on Hurley.

"Won't say why he wanted to find Whitmore, huh? Means it's gotta be dirty, wouldn't you say?"

"Except then you'd expect he *would* have a story."

"Yeah, maybe." She thought about it, tossed her head. "Yeah, that is funny. Hell, maybe he's just too dumb to come up with anything. It isn't easy to come up with an innocent explanation for leaving your post to get together with a kid who's found dead the next day. This sounds like the kind of lay-down my boss will snatch. You still think the cops did an okay job looking for this guy?"

"Absolutely."

"You came up with the link between Whitmore and Hurley."

"IA found the guy without any help from me."

"You gave 'em the picture; that kept Hurley from denying he knew Whitmore. You say the eyewitness couldn't give a positive make. Guy could have bluffed it out, no picture."

"This guy couldn't bluff a two-year-old. He was going to cave, whether they had the picture or not."

Peggy threw up her hands. "Okay, okay—never heard a guy so unwilling to take credit. Write it up; that's the way we'll report it."

She called Laura over. "Laura takes shorthand. Dictate it to her, she'll type it up, and we'll give it to Kershaw."

She turned and looked at me again—at least that was the way I thought of it. "You know, Nichols, you're a funny guy. I can't quite figure out . . ." Her voice trailed off, and I was left nursing yet another of her backhanded compliments.

I spent the rest of the morning and a while after lunch reviewing my notes, dictating my thoughts, and editing drafts until I was comfortable with the results and felt I could defend them comfortably against any critics. I left the final mark-up with Laura, told her I'd be back for it later, and headed off to find a private phone and report to my other client.

Bucky was out, so I left word to call and rang my answering machine and bade it disgorge its contents. A bond salesman—had I reviewed my portfolio recently? My mother—I should stay out of the woods; *Reader's Digest* said Lyme disease was everywhere. And then—bingo!

A soft, halting voice, androgynous in its sibilance: "This is Norman Wilkins. Your ad says you have my cat, Bootsie. I miss her dreadfully. Won't you please call so I can come get her? I'll be happy to pay a reward. My number is 539-3939. Please call soon."

Oh, yes; this was indeed proving to be a stellar day. He answered on the first ring.

"Mr. Wilkins?"

"Who are you?" He had a bland, mashed-potatoes voice, not a hard edge in it.

"Never mind that. I have the feline. You want her back. I'm ready to trade."

"How much do you want?"

"Not how much, Mr. Wilkins; who. I want you."

There was a long pause. "What do you mean?"

"I mean you will show up in person to get Bootsie. You will give me a signed receipt, and I will give you Bootsie."

"I don't understand. Why do you want a receipt for Bootsie?"

"I don't want a receipt for Bootsie, Mr. Wilkins—I want a receipt for the divorce papers I'm going to hand you before I hand you Bootsie."

He let this stew for half a minute. "I thought so. I thought you might be one of those men. You didn't find Bootsie—you *stole* her. That isn't fair; you should be ashamed."

"Mr. Wilkins, I'm not *one* of those men—I'm the king: the orneriest, wiliest, most ruthless process server in the entire Bay State, if not the world. And if you don't meet me outside the newsstand at Harvard Square at five-thirty tonight and give me that receipt, I'm turning Bootsie over to a man named Lum Fat down in Chinatown, and she'll show up on column A. Sweet and sour tabby, Mr. Wilkins."

"You wouldn't!"

"Don't try me, Mr. Wilkins. I lost all human feelings years ago. Five-thirty; be there." I hung up and headed home.

chapter 28

I WAS STILL EXULTING IN TRIUMPHS PAST AND future when I walked into my apartment. The Judas cat came out to greet me, and I realized I'd actually miss her, and her master as well. Maybe even the whole, rotten business, come to think of it, which I would have, if the phone hadn't rung.

"Ah, Buckrum—and how's my favorite titan of finance this fine day?"

"Depends. How's your gig going?"

I told him.

"Hey—that is great. Congratulations. What about the other part of it—the Blue Tornado investigation?"

"I don't have much to do with that. Lot of wasted energy, I suspect." I described the morning's database demonstration.

"Mush, huh?"

"Sure seems likely."

"Smart, turning it into a number-crunching exercise; niece is the only one who knows the record, she tells 'em what it says, the loonies aren't gonna have a lot of ammo. Kind of curious when they'll be done, though."

"Few more days."

"You don't know exactly, huh?"

"Christ, if it's that important to know exactly when it'll be wrapped up, call Kershaw and ask him. Tell him you want to go over his portfolio or something."

"One jump ahead of you, as always. I called him this morning; his office said he's out of town."

"Well, then, you'll just have to wait."

"Kind of critical to my, ah . . . business dealings."

"I don't even want to know. Sorry I . . ." Suddenly the morning came back. The girl, Laura: *Peggy's out; she had to meet with Mr. Kershaw.* And then Peggy, returning: *I just met with Mr. Kershaw; he's very eager to finish.* "Buckster?"

"Yeah?"

"What time did you call Kershaw's office?"

"Around ten, ten-thirty. Why?"

"And his office said he was out of town?"

"Right—at the family manse in Maine. Taking a long weekend."

"Peggy Kiernan told me this morning that she'd just come from a meeting with Kershaw."

I listened while gears ground this into small bits. "Come on! You misunderstood her. She said she'd *talked* to him, right? Like on the phone?"

I thought about it. "Wrong. She told her assistant she was going to meet with him, then came back and told us all she'd just met with him. Could he have canceled his plans, come back early?"

"His secretary said she knew he was in Maine because he'd just called in from Blue Hill."

"Then Kiernan lied about where she was."

"What the hell for?"

"Must have been because she didn't want to say where she *had* been."

"Where *had* she been?"

"Beats me."

"Maybe she went out for a drink, didn't want anyone to know. That's as good a guess as any, as you would say."

"At eleven o'clock in the morning? Not even close to as good a guess as any."

"What is, then?"

"I don't have one. But there's been something strange about her right from the get-go, and now this."

"What do you mean, 'strange'?"

"I mean I can't figure out where she's coming from. Sometimes she sounds like you'd expect, career prosecutor, O'Conor's niece and all; other times . . . I don't know. Like she's got her own program."

"What would that be?"

"I haven't a clue."

"Maybe she's got her period."

"I knew you'd figure it out. And now I've got to go, see a man about a cat."

"Wait a minute! You can't just—"

"'Bye."

Bootsie had grown attached to the place; didn't feel like hopping in the shopping bag. It took many enticements, lots of dangled treats, and it was too close to five-thirty before I had the hissing beast tucked away, tied off, and on her way to a family reunion.

The time and location had been a mistake, I saw it at once: the newsstand at the exit of the Harvard Square MBTA stop was a hive of people swapping places, Boston workers home to Cambridge, Cambridge workers home to Boston, a huge mess, easy to miss my man, and Bootsie, unhappy camper, snarling and clawing to see what was what.

Thousands of people, each one needing to go through me to buy a paper, read about that ax murder on the way home, see what the market had done, check the latest lottery results. Bump me one way, then the other—"Sorry," "Excuse me," "Would you pu-leeze," no dignity in it at all— hard to focus on the lie, Peggy's lie, much less the other things that didn't fit, especially when the damned cat's head would worm its way out of the bag, look around, and fix me with that malevolent stare, have to push it back down, pray the animal rights freaks wouldn't notice, fall upon my bipedal animal body, rend it limb from limb.

Look at my watch: five-thirty-two. If Wilkins called the bluff, I owned the cat; would we be able to re-establish a trusting relationship? And what of my relationship with Peggy? "Say, I was wondering—where were you this morning when you weren't with Kershaw? And why do you oscillate between conviviality and contempt? And most particularly, why can't I decide what you really think about this exercise?"

Rippp. No, Bootsie! Back in bag. Tuck in the paw, clench the tear. What is happening? Why is this woman clutching at me, slipping to the ground? God almighty, she's having a heart attack; don't just stand there, do something, someone. Can't you see the old crone's going to die? Sweet Jesus, it's getting as bad as Sodom-on-Hudson; they're just stepping around her. Oh, lord, he stepped over her. Am I the only one who knows CPR. I don't want to any more than any of you, but you do have to live with yourself—oh, God, somebody call for help.

It wasn't nearly as horrible as I'd expected; the color came back right away and the breath was better than I remembered in a lot of women half her age. "Call an ambulance, damn it!" They looked down at me, distressed, sheep eyes: don't want to miss that train, have to wait another seven minutes; she looks all right—it can't be serious, but maybe he's attacking her—you hear about these things; what do you think?

"Somebody call an ambulance, I said!" I remembered you were supposed to unfasten their collar, reached for it, stopped to listen to the strangled words whispered in my ear: "Let's go someplace private, we're gonna get down and dirty."

I looked over where I'd dropped the bag: no bag. I spotted a fat rear end disappearing down the subway steps, a furry head peering back next to it, and struggled to rise. Strong arms held me to the ground: "Sonny, I haven't been kissed like that since his daddy passed. Don't let's quit now."

chapter 29

SOMEWHERE IN THIS CRUEL CITY, THE QUARK cavorted, my erstwhile triumph ashes. Was that disdain I detected in the Wursthaus waitress who slung me stew and a stein of lager? Had she witnessed my humiliation, hooted with the others as the suddenly sprightly object of my ministrations sprang to her feet and dashed down the subway steps, pausing only to pinch my cheek? I should have ordered fricasee of crow and a flagon of bitter gall.

I searched for consolation, found it in the Whitmore case developments, then felt it slip away as I gave the day a harder look than I'd allowed so far.

Hurley was a prosecutor's dream: Central Casting's pick for the perfect solution to a hideous problem, "Case Closed" written across his chest. A man at the right place, at the right time, with the wrong story.

Or rather, with no story, which was the rub: it's the rare man who holds his tongue when speech can hardly hurt.

Hurley's silence would only embolden an ambitious prosecutor with an outraged community at his back, and might
well leave a jury thinking murder one made a nice match,
but it left me with the nagging worry that not only had I lost
the right man when the Quark outwitted me, I'd helped
deliver the wrong man when I'd furnished the lead tying
Hurley to Whitmore.

And then there was the enigmatic Kiernan, sheparding
the other side of the investigation, the one that was supposed to mollify the loony left but conclude with an official
blessing for a resurgent sense of social order. What lay
behind *her* mercurial shifts, odd ellipses, apparent lie? I
replayed our conversation about her group's work, heard
again the hostility, the evasiveness, the lack of enthusiasm
with which she'd offered the assurances I sought.

By coffee, I reached the conclusion that there was
nothing I could do on that front but wait and see, but I
could throw a sop to my conscience by flagging my concern
that Hurley might, just might, deserve more deliberation
than a justice system under extreme pressure to produce a
quick resolution to a nasty situation was ready to afford.

The old sergeant at the front door barely had the energy
to glance at my pass; the few people I passed in the halls
paid me as much attention as they would the janitor; the
squad room was between shifts and empty. The opaque
glass in the war-room door was dark, the door locked. I
cursed because I'd wasted a trip, then remembered Laura
had given me a key. After a little twisting and jiggling, it
turned, and I stepped into the deserted room and fumbled
around the wall until I found the light switch. It bathed the
room in the yellow gloom that was all the old incandescent
hanging lamps offered.

I blinked a couple of times until my eyes adjusted, and
then I saw the manila folder, with my name in big, block
letters, lying on Peggy's desk. I flipped it open and glanced
at the report, then took it to the far end of the room, near
the computers, where the light was brightest.

First page, fine. Second, fine. Third: "Conclusions." The place to put in my doubts about Hurley, while plugging the fine job Hal and his team had done. I sat down and started to compose an insert, for all the good it was likely to do Hurley.

I looked around, startled, not expecting noise, realized it was the phone ringing on Peggy's desk. I let it go, and it stopped after half a dozen rings. I turned back to my addendum: "While this investigator is satisfied that the department's effort to identify and apprehend the perpetrator has been vigorous and comprehensive, meeting or exceeding all reasonable professional standards, this is not to say"—I went back, underlined the *not*—"that this investigator is"—too pompous, starting to sound like a lawyer; crossed out *this investigator is* in both places, inserted *I am*—"satisfied that the police have in fact identified the perpetrator. In their understandable desire to apprehend the perpetrator of this vicious homicide"—I stopped, wondered whether you caught bureaucratese from something in the air, whether it could be viral, for instance. When the ringing started again, I crossed the floor to the phone, grateful for the break.

"Hello?"

There was too long a silence, and I was starting to hang up when a low voice said, "What number is this?"

I read off the number on the dial. "Who—" And then I was talking to the dial tone. I replaced the receiver and looked at my watch, then slid into the desk chair, wondering why the voice had been so familiar, deciding it was because even in the space of a few words, it was soothing, mellifluous, warm. An asset to its owner. A distinctive, commanding voice. The best political voice in America— the voice of Conor O'Conor. Who hadn't identified himself, hadn't asked to speak to his niece, hadn't taken even a few seconds for the reflexive stroking of a voter.

I was getting awfully tired of questions, and then I remembered the desk drawer, the envelope Peggy had shoved in it after her meeting with "Kershaw," and decided there was at least one I might be able to answer right away.

It was an old, prison-built wooden desk, the drawer worn and loose. Peggy had locked it before she left, but while my lock-picking skills are nil, this didn't take any, just a little patience and some penknife work and then it was open. I pulled out the envelope, lifted the metal tabs, and slid out the typed report, but it was too dark to read it where I sat, so I shut the drawer and crossed back to the cone of light at the far end of the room.

I had just sat down when I heard a key scratching in the door lock. I froze as the door swung open and Peggy and the dog stepped into the room. She stood just inside, said, "Laura?", and waited. After a few seconds, she felt her way to her desk and sat down, while I stared, hardly breathing.

I thought she'd come for the report, but she didn't go for the drawer. She reached for the phone, felt the raised bumps on the buttons, dialed a number.

She spoke so quietly that at first I didn't realize someone had answered, but as my hearing adjusted to her low tones, I was able to pick up most of her end.

"I gave him the draft this morning, the one I worked up. He loved it."

Pause, then: "He was going to meet with Finn later, go over it again, but Tip'll do what's expected. My uncle's a great judge of character. He buys only the best." She laughed, the mean little sound that she'd used with me.

Another pause. Peggy tapped the desk with a pencil while she listened, the flat drumbeat keeping nice time with my heart. Then: "Oh, yeah. The plan's the same— Flanagan's out. Dead. His own mother wouldn't keep him on, she read this thing."

She switched the phone to the other ear, waited, nodding. "Um, right—Finn'll sell it in Southie, Dorchester, places like that: 'You know Dapper Flanagan had no bigger boost-er; I thought the whole thing was a crock, same as you all did, but Judas Priest—when you see the facts, they're clear as day—disgrace to the whole city,' etcetera, etcetera. They may not like it, but they'll trust Tip. They won't turn on my uncle if Tip says he didn't have any choice."

She rubbed under the glasses while the dog looked at me. It cocked its head, swiveled it slowly one way, then the other, started to rise. "Sit, Leba."

It made a small whine deep in its throat, hesitated, then sank back to the floor, panting in the warm room. "Right. He'll wait a few months, when nobody will make the connection. Um-huh—the whole Seaside project. Umm . . . right, right. City'll take all of it. Above market? You bet. That's the whole idea. Finn makes out like a bandit."

There was a much longer silence, then: "Don't worry— it'll be clear enough. We got him." A hard, ugly smile cut across her face. "We got him good."

More silence. "Um. Well, we do what we have to do. I owe this one to my uncle."

A head nod. "Thank you—I appreciate that. Yes, I will. Good night, Mr. Kershaw."

She didn't get up right away, just sat, staring at me, and then she cocked her head at the same angle as the dog, and the two of them remained like that for several seconds, as though the thudding of my heart, which I could hear so clearly, was audible across the room. And then she stood abruptly, smiled at me, a real smile this time, genuine and joyous, accompanied the dog to the door, and left.

I waited until I was sure she was gone for good before exhaling. My pulse was racing, and I made myself count to fifty before I pulled out the report and started to read.

chapter 30

"SON OF A BITCH."

"Three sons of bitches. Who knows—maybe more. And one bitch. Two, if you count the dog, but I'm not sure she's in on it."

"This report—it'll hold up?" Bucky slapped it against his knee.

"Easy—I have to put that back. Yeah, it'll hold up. The way they've got that database cooked, they could prove anything. Like this"—I flipped through it, found a passage: "The incidence of excessive-force complaints has increased more than two hundred percent since Blue Tornado became operative; file analysis of those complaints shows systematic disregard for—*and in many instances affirmative steps to conceal*—well-documented instances of misconduct during Blue Tornado actions."

"Nase, I can't believe this."

"Believe it. You've got Kershaw, whose word is gold, and

Finn, who's assumed to be a rock-ribbed Flanagan man, on board with this thing. Three others are dying to ace Flanagan and the department. Whoever's left—Endicott, Daniels, the others—what're they going to do? They'll assume the data are right; what conclusions can they reach? They aren't going to read all the files, see if they support this."

"They *can't* just make it up and hope to get away with it." Bucky sloshed another inch of Bushmill's in his glass, then topped up mine. We'd gone to his basement to escape the sounds of young Hanrahans; the muffled thuds and shrieks overhead sounded like the last days in the Führer's bunker.

"I told you—she'll give them a print-out that backs this up. It's cooked so it *has* to. Those law students, the paralegals—that's their take from it."

"God, this is awful."

"And the soft part, how the complaints since Flanagan took over hold up—who's going to argue with her? She's the only person who's read 'em all, she's an experienced prosecutor, and if anything, people will have expected her to be on Flanagan's side. God knows we thought her uncle was."

"But someone else can read them, prove that they don't show what she says." Bucky was driving the tip of a pocket knife into the worn arm of his chair, grunting savagely at each thrust.

"Who—Flanagan? Who's going to believe him? Anyway, it isn't like a true/false test; you could argue till doomsday about what this stuff means. If he wants to fight it, it'll be all tied up in court. He'll be collecting Social Security by the time he gets anyone to take a second look, and who'll care? It'll be like some guy who gets his conviction reversed after he's served five years."

"But she *told* you he was in the clear—you can tell the commission what she said to you."

"Sure—and she'll deny it. Just like she'll deny she had the conversation I heard her have with Kershaw, assuming I was crazy enough to admit breaking into her desk, then eavesdropping on her. Add a bunch of kids who would testify that I wasn't ready to accept anything negative about Flanagan, I'd be lucky to stay out of Bridgewater."

"But O'Conor *needs* Flanagan—we heard him say so."

"No, we didn't. We heard him listen to a bunch of guys squabbling about Flanagan. We took away what we wanted to take away."

"Oh, Jesus." He rubbed his head until his hair stood out like Brillo. "Sweet, suffering Jesus."

"Easy, Buck—this isn't the end of the world. I mean, this shouldn't happen, but it isn't the first time a decent guy gets stabbed in the back by a politician."

"You don't understand: I'm ruined. I own the largest slum clearance project in New England."

I had the glass almost to my mouth, gaped at his ashen face, set it down. "What the hell are you talking about?"

He cast his eyes down at the floor, refused to meet mine: "I didn't want you to know."

"Know what?"

"I was afraid you wouldn't go along."

"This has got to be *bad*. What have you done?"

"Remember the other night, we met at Wirth's?"

"Yeah?"

"I was maybe not as . . . forthcoming . . . as I might have been."

"In other words, you lied to me?"

"No!" He started tugging little tufts of wadding out of the chair, rolling them into balls and flinging them on the floor. "I just . . . left a little out, maybe . . . altered the emphasis of a few things."

"Level with me, Hanrahan."

"Let me tell you about Finn first; maybe you'll understand." He threw back his drink, then poured another, the first time I'd ever seen him spill whiskey.

"This guy, you ordered a boxcar load of bastards, they delivered only Finn?—you wouldn't feel cheated. Guy's swindled, screwed, diddled, or otherwise violated just about every person he ever dealt with, starting with the dear parents he's honoring with that community center in Southie—took their life savings for his first project, never paid it back."

He stopped to take a drink, then continued: "Few years ago, things were booming, guy I knew gave up a good real-estate job to go to work for Finn. I told him he was nuts, but Finn promised him the earth, the moon, and the stars. Guy figured he'd learn a lot, get rich, get out. What he didn't figure was that Finn would use him to get to a couple of big corporate tenants, sign them up for one of his projects, then throw him out without so much as a thank-you. Laughed at the employment agreement, and when this guy sued, Finn made up a bunch of bullshit about catching the guy doing something shady. Had some toadies testify, phonied up some purchase orders. My guy loses the lawsuit, loses his house, the summer place on the Cape. Moved to Waltham, started drinking, had a few flopshit jobs, and lost them, too. He couldn't take it, Nase—packed up, left his family, hit the road. May be dead now, for all I know. Shattered his family. Nice, huh?"

"Rotten."

"Guy was my brother-in-law."

"Oh, lord."

"Yep. A bright, decent guy, with a great future, and his only mistake was trusting someone who sees people as something to use. I dunno, maybe he was weak, didn't have enough strength, but maybe he wouldn't ever have had to find out, he hadn't run into Finn. I mean, how many of us do have the strength to survive that kind of thing, huh? Most of the people who'd handle that okay are probably the kind of people who'd do it to somebody else. Anyway, he made a mistake, and he paid for it, and my sister's paid for it, and her kids are paying for it."

He poured us both another round, his hand steady again. "Now, the mistake the Finns of this world sometimes make is they fuck so many people, they can't keep track. So they run into a big, friendly guy like me, laughs a lot, made a few bucks, they just see another pigeon, guy they can use, throw away when they're done. Like my brother-in-law. That was Finn's big mistake." His face twisted. "At least I thought it was."

"What did you do, Buck?"

"Listen to this." The spasm passed. "You're gonna *love* this play." He set the bottle down, leaned over, rubbed his hands together.

"Finn is hocked past his eyeballs. Lot of other developers, they either cratered when the bubble burst a few years ago, or they had the good sense to see it was coming and got out in time. Not Finn. He just kept going, hopping from one shaky deal to another, none of the lenders wanting to be the one to pull the plug and bring the whole heap crashing down.

"I had heard these rumors, see, so when I ran into Finn at Kershaw's office and he gives me this sales pitch for his new project on the way home, I decide to do a little checking. Asshole treated me like I was there to be plucked, and I played along, begged the fucker for the chance to come in so he'd really open up to me."

"You don't mean you gave him money?"

"Are you kidding? But I told him I was dying to, just needed time to raise it."

"This an example of stuff left out, or is this a shift in emphasis?"

"See? I knew you wouldn't understand. Anyhow, the Seaside Complex down by the harbor he put up last year, thing you heard Kiernan talking about? Soon as Finn lets me off, I go down to the Seaside leasing office, tell them I'm looking for twenty thousand feet, what've they got? Well, we dance around a little, and by the time I'm done, they'll give me a cash rebate, building allowance, and a blow job. All on the Q.T., of course: 'Wouldn't want the other tenants to know we'd let you drive such a bargain, Mr. Smith'—

like he *had* a lot of tenants. I'd sign a lease at thirty bucks a foot, but by the time all the sweeteners come back, I'd be paying an effective rate less than half that."

"Why would he do that?"

"Because the rumors are right—Seaside's gotta be *hemorrhaging* dollars, and the only way he keeps it from being foreclosed, and him with it, is by raising money for this *new* deal, then bleeding it to keep Seaside afloat. To do that, he's gotta show some security, and signed leases look like money in the bank, someone's dumb enough not to look behind them and see if they're worth a shit—and someone always is."

"So he's borrowing on worthless Seaside leases to raise money to build a new project, which he'll bleed to meet payments on Seaside? How do you stop?"

"*Ka-boom!* That's how. So you don't—you just keep running. Anyway, he showed me the numbers on this project he's doing now. He's hyped the revenues, made every optimistic projection he could, and it only just works, if he's going to siphon enough off to meet payments on Seaside. There's no margin—none."

He leaned closer, licked his lips. "You know how I said Finn was worried about the location of this new project getting out before he acquires the land, because he doesn't want to get held up? This project comes in at a dime more than he's budgeted, he's going to be dipping into his own pocket to make it up. Well, he's gonna get held up, *big time.*" Bushy eyebrows arched, danced across the top of a grin that wasn't funny.

"But he wouldn't say where the project's going. How could you beat him to the land?"

"Ah, yes. Remember I told you I thought maybe Kershaw was slipping a tad? Well, reason I thought that was that when I dropped by his office, he had the paperwork for the project spread out all over his desk, and he left it there when he went to get Finn in the reception area, including a nice, big site map, laid it out clear as day."

"And you just couldn't help noticing."

"Well, anybody else but Finn, I would have just forgotten all about it, but yeah—when he started pitching me on the way to my office, I knew just where he was going to be buying."

"And you beat him to it."

"Oh, yes—I did. I did indeed. Started as soon as the asshole gave me his song and dance, told me about this deal. Chump Hanrahan, glad to have the opportunity to throw in his lot with the great developer, no threat at all. I set up a little dummy company, buried it so far back in the bowels of the Bahamas it'd take a sigmoidoscope to find out who's behind it. And guess who owns this little corporate polyp?"

"Your brother-in-law."

He leaned back, grinned appreciatively. "Well—give young Nichols a shiny gold star. Yeah—and my sister, and the kids. He ever surfaces, be there for him. If not, well, the kids will know their dad left a mark."

"I know I quake in your presence. What I don't know is if you're a saint or the most thoroughly evil person on earth, Buckster. And now tell me why were you so eager to get me working for the commission?"

"I suppose you won't buy 'I just wanted to help out a friend'?"

"No chance."

"I was afraid you'd take that attitude. Okay, I thought it would be handy to know how much time I had to dicker with the landowners. I believed Finn when he said he was going to hold off until this commission got done and came out the way he said he wanted, so I figured you could keep me posted on the progress, and as long as I knew when the commission was going to wrap up, I wouldn't get caught short." His face fell. "Picked up the last parcel today."

"You did lie to me."

"Not a bit. I told you I wanted to know how it was going 'cause I had a real-estate deal cooking. Absolutely true."

"You also told me you didn't know where Finn's project was going."

"Nope. What I said was, 'Finn wouldn't say, and if I knew, I'd be out buying.' And he wouldn't, and I was. Remember—I was educated by Jesuits."

He topped up the drinks again. "Anyway, Plato Frio Partnership, Ltd. owns every damn tenement, warehouse, and vacant lot Tip Finn wants for River Place, as Mr. Finn proposes to call his latest scam."

"Plato Frio?"

"'Cold Plate'—as in 'Revenge is a dish best eaten cold.' Nice touch, huh? It's the poetry in the Celtic soul."

"You amaze me."

"I amaze myself. Yeah, way I had it figured, Finn doesn't do this deal, he's through—the whole house of cards collapses. And to do the deal, he's going to pay through the nose to buy the land—from me. Well, from old Plato Frio, to be technical. Chapter 11 if he doesn't do it, bye-bye big house in Dover if he does. Not bad, huh?"

"Only O'Conor's turning Seaside into a gold mine for Finn by having the city lease it."

"At stratospheric rents. Which means if I try to squeeze the bastard, he just walks away from the new project. Gives the investors back their money, and I just put every cent I own into the wreckage of industrial America."

"What are you going to do?"

"What you're always telling me to do."

"What's that?"

"Commit suicide."

chapter

I LEFT, AFTER SECURING BUCKY'S PROMISE TO defer self-immolation until I saw if there was any way to salvage the situation. I hadn't had as much to drink as he had, but I'd had enough, and it was close enough to midnight that the ideas weren't threatening to swamp me. In fact, I had only one, and I wasn't sure it was worth anything.

Lynn Daniels was my first hope, but she had an unlisted number and five minutes of pleading and artful lies failed to move the implacable information operator. I tried my fallback candidate and got lucky.

Sowell Endicott lived off Memorial Drive, and while he was obviously a little taken aback by my call, he was gracious enough after I reminded him who I was and told him it was important that I saw him right away. The traffic was light and I made it to his place in fifteen minutes. He had a pot of coffee ready when I arrived.

"So—what seems to be the trouble?" We were seated in his small living room, and if he was put out by my visit, he didn't let on. We sipped coffee while he let me get into it at my own pace. He got up once, to refill our cups, but otherwise took it in without a word. I had no way of telling whether I was making any sense.

I finished the second cup and my story at the same time, and glanced at my watch; I'd been going for almost an hour, organizing on the fly, not always terribly coherent, even to my own ears. I set the cup on the coffee table and waited.

He stared at me over the lip of his cup. "That's some story, Mr. Nichols."

"I know."

"All you got is that report, which you admit stealing."

"And Kiernan's call to Kershaw."

"Which, if you're right, they'd deny."

"I know. Look, I know this is hard to believe."

"I don't think you'd want to try selling it around town, no."

He kept staring, and I had to fight the urge to look away, shuffle my feet, shove my hands under my legs. "What do you think?"

He didn't say anything, just stared at me and shook his head. I was about to try something else, argue, anything, but then his answer came, slowly and quietly at first and then in a series of increasingly loud noises that started in his nose and worked their way down until his entire body was engaged. They were great, explosive noises that in another context would have been impossible not to join, because they were guffaws—deep, compelling ones, that wracked his whole body, so that he was clutching his sides and barely staying on the couch.

I felt my face reddening, my temperature rising. "Okay— I guess I know what you think. Thanks for your . . ."

He raised his hand, took a shaky sip of coffee. "I'm sorry. It's just—"Another spasm caught him and he turned his head just in time to put the coffee on the floor instead of on me.

"Oh, my." He wiped his mouth with the back of his arm. "Sorry."

"I guess it's a funny story. I'd take it on the road, except as you say, it doesn't hold up too well. I'll just hit the road instead." I stood up and offered my hand.

"No, no." He rose and took it, gave it a firm shake. "I *am* sorry. That was rude. It's only that . . ." He bit his lip and shook his head. "No. Look—I appreciate your coming to me. Let me think on this, okay? I will, I promise. It'll be all right. I'll get back to you."

"Sure."

He let me out and locked the door. I was sure I heard another explosion before I stepped onto the elevator.

The station house was even quieter than it had been a few hours before, and I could have been invisible for all the attention I got from the old sergeant at the door. I put the report back in the drawer, twisted the lock back into place, and left for home, or what passed for one.

The Boston Hub
August 24, 1994

KERSHAW COMMISSION REPORT FLAYS
FLANAGAN, DEMANDS REMOVAL;
MAYOR SUSPENDS COMMISSIONER
PENDING REVIEW

BREAK IN WHITMORE SLAYING TOO LITTLE,
TOO LATE FOR EMBATTLED COMMISSIONER?

BOSTON—In an emotional appearance at City Hall early yesterday morning, following the unauthorized release of the Kershaw Commission staff's draft report to the commission, Boston Mayor Conor O'Conor announced that he had suspended Police Commissioner Francis X. "Dapper" Flanagan, pending formal commission action. Deputy Commissioner Timothy Moriarty will serve as acting commissioner until Flanagan's status is clarified.

"I am deeply saddened by the need to take this action," O'Connor said. "In view of the serious charges contained in the staff's report, however regrettable its premature release, I feel I have no alternative, and have therefore placed Commissioner Flanagan on administrative leave, effective immediately. The people of Boston deserve no less."

The mayor acknowledged that he was particularly disturbed by the staff's conclusion that not only has the department's controversial "Blue Tornado" drug interdiction effort resulted in a dramatic increase in apparently well-founded charges of police misconduct toward minorities, but that Commissioner Flannagan had actively suppressed internal department investigations of those charges. "While I have of course been aware of charges that this department initiative encouraged unacceptable behavior toward minorities, it had certainly never occurred to me that Commissioner Flanagan was anything less than zealous in investigating those charges. I accepted his repeated assurances that they were properly handled. Perhaps, in my eagerness to see an end to the dreadful scourge of drugs that plagues our neighborhoods, I was too trusting. If so, I accept full responsibility."

In a dramatic conclusion to his appearance, Mayor O'Conor announced that police had identified a suspect in the savage beating death of Purnell Whitmore, the young man found slain in an alley in Roxbury two weeks ago. The suspect, police Patrolman John F. Hurley of Mattapan, was placed on administrative leave yesterday. Sources within the district attorney's office announced their intention to begin grand jury proceedings immediately, and they expect an indictment shortly. It was an eyewitness report that a policeman had been the last person seen with Whitmore that caused the mayor to convene the Kershaw Commission, since the slaying occurred during a Blue Tornado raid. The staff report does not indicate whether Hurley was involved in the raid, but a knowledgeable source claims that he was.

(Excerpts from the staff report, which summarizes its review of allegations of systematic minority mistreatment in Blue Tornado actions, appear on page B-12. A related editorial appears on page A-2.

chapter 32

WE PARKED AS CLOSE TO FLANAGAN'S AS WE could, walking the remaining half block to the small frame house, indistinguishable from the others crowding the sidewalk on both sides of the street. Neither of us were that eager to arrive. We stopped and looked back down the hill.

"Lived in the same house, all his life. Lotta Townies used to do that—born here, grow up here, marry a Townie, go to work in the navy yard, get planted over by St. Mary's. I was a kid, I knew people who'd never been to downtown Boston. Now the navy yard's a bunch of half-a-million-dollar condos, yuppies have bought up all the houses, and Townies can't afford to stay. Shame."

A slim, gray-haired woman with a broad smile answered the door. "Mr. Hanrahan—I'm so glad to see you. I just took a pie out of the oven. Do you think you and your friend could be persuaded to have some?"

"Does the pope polka? What else would we have come for?" He grabbed her, did a waltz turn, spun her under his arm to face me. "I danced with this woman at her wedding, Nase; twenty-five years later, she still calls me Mr. Hanrahan. Nason Nichols, *Mrs.* Flanagan." Bucky drew a deep breath. "Ah, and you're in for a treat—just smell that pie."

"Maybe a snort to go with it, then." The large body of Dapper Flanagan filled the doorway of the tiny hall. "Come in and sit a spell. Kathleen, do you think you might show these gentlemen into the parlor while I get the bottle?"

"Yes, Francis." She led us into a small parlor, all knickknacks and overstuffed chairs. A wedding photo of a dark-haired Kathleen and a somewhat thinner Dapper, awkward in a dark suit, held pride of place over the mantle, next to the statue of the Virgin.

"How's Dapper getting along, Kathleen?"

Her smile faded. "Oh, he pretends it doesn't bother him, but I know how deeply he's hurt. The idea that he'd cover up wrongdoing! The police department is his whole life; he'd never dishonor it, Mr. Nichols."

"I'm sure he wouldn't, ma'am."

"I *told* him not to take that job, *told* him he'd be surrounded by snakes. And that Conor O'Conor, he's the—"

"Kathleen, where's my damn pipe? You're always hiding my—"

"Yes, dear." She rolled her eyes. "I've got to get him out of the house—he's as grouchy as a bear with a sore paw. Coming, Francis." She scurried out.

Flanagan came in a minute later, carrying a tray laden with a bottle of Four Roses, three plates of blueberry pie, and three glasses.

Smoke circled Flanagan's head as he poured. "See you found your pipe, Dap."

The end of Flanagan's crooked nose twitched. "Umpf. It was in my coat pocket. Don't know how it got there."

"Kathleen probably hid it there. They'll do that, you

know. Deidre specializes in my car keys, or sometimes my glasses. Almost every morning. They use the coat pocket a lot. Funny we never catch on."

The angles of Flanagan's face rearranged themselves into a grin and he hoisted his glass. "God love 'em—if it weren't for Kathleen, I don't think I could find my face. Well, it's good of you to come by. Going crazy, sitting here, trying to get this mix-up straightened out, while Moriarity's got the whole force paralyzed. Nobody knows whether to shit or wind his watch."

"I'm not sure it's a mix-up, Dap."

"What're you saying, Hanrahan—that I did those things?"

"Of course not. But—"

"Sure it's a mix-up—some damn-fool, wet-behind-the-ear bureaucrats need somebody to take 'em by the hand and show 'em what's what. Doing a terrible disservice to Conor, worst part of it." He thrust out his jaw, daring us to argue.

Bucky looked at me. "Dap, I think you'd better listen to—"

"I've got a call in to him, and when we have a sit-down, I mean to tell him, point blank: he's getting some bad advice, making him look silly."

"Did you talk to him?"

Flanagan's ruddy face reddened. "He was busy."

"Sure," Bucky said. "I'll bet he was."

"He was tied up, damn it." His thin, flat voice rose. "Got bounced around to that Dave prick, asked me could he be of service. I said if I ever needed a new asshole, I'd be sure to call him."

"Tact was always your strong suit, Dap."

"If I could talk to Conor, we'd get this straightened out quick. Somebody's—"

"Somebody's mislaid your brains, Francis Flanagan, and you won't be finding them in your coat pocket." Kathleen Flanagan stepped into the room, rested her hands on her hips, shot flames out of her eyes. "It's about time you realized that that sniveling little worm has the knife out for you, and you'll be in little pieces before long if you don't come out of your funk and take him on!"

"Now, Kathleen, don't get all—"

"Don't you 'now, Kathleen' me—there'll be just one Christian martyr in this house, and He's over there." She pointed to a crucifix on the wall. "And if these fine men won't tell you, I will: Conor O'Conor's behind this whole thing."

"Ah, you're talking like a crazy woman. Why would he—"

"Because you're ten times the man he is, or ever will be, and he knows it. He's scared to death of you, him and those la-di-da folk he runs around with. Looking at you sulking around here, though, I don't know why he would be." She sniffed and turned on her heel.

"Ah . . . " Flanagan waved his hand dismissively, confusion and hurt written across his face.

"Listen to her, Dap." Bucky's voice was soft but insistent. "She's telling you the truth."

"Ah, come on—Conor didn't want this. He put me in. You heard what he said: he had to suspend me; he didn't want to. He knows only what those idiots tell him. As soon as—"

Bucky looked at me. "I think you'd better hear what Nase has to say, Dap." He reached over and topped up Flanagan's glass, but the man didn't reach for it, not once, as I laid it out.

He held his pose, almost statuesque, for a few seconds after I finished, big fingers interlaced, a slight tapping of thumb on thumb all that suggested flesh, not stone.

"I see." He sat up. "I see. Kathleen was right, then."

"I'm afraid so."

"Damn. She's *always* right; married twenty-four years, and she's been right every time. Think I'd learn."

"Twenty-five, you forgetful old fool." She stepped back into the room with a pot of coffee, set it on the table, stood rubbing his neck. "And if you learned, what would you need me for, hmm?"

He reached up, engulfed her hand. "There is that, toots."

"I'll get the cups." She withdrew her hand, touched his hair, slipped away.

"It's time for the news; I'd better watch." He lumbered over to the set in the corner and turned it on.

The picture swam into focus, a spa ad offering us firmer thighs in thirty days, then faded into the Channel 4 newsroom, where the anchor couple readied themselves at their desk. The soundtrack pulsed with *You Are There* urgency while Barbie nodded animatedly to someone off camera. Ken made earnest, last-minute edits to mock script. Then a pause, a final pencil flourish, slap the edges of the papers together, track back, take in the map of the world, close, head shot, and, together, the Look: "Don't think we take it lightly, telling one million Bostonians what to think."

The male anchor opened his mouth and poured out flawless baritone syrup: "Good evening. Many Hub residents, expecting an arrest in the murder of young Purnell Whitmore, the Roxbury youth brutally beaten to death two weeks ago, have reacted with *outrage* to reports that Patrolman John Hurley, reportedly seen struggling with Whitmore immediately before the killing, has been placed on administrative leave but allowed to remain at liberty." He turned to the comely co-anchor: "Observers say, Connie, that the situation is more explosive than any time in recent memory."

The camera closed on Connie, who gave us deep concern as she stared into the camera. "Contributing to the tension was today's announcement by local civil rights activist Corey Webster, who pledged to lead People of Color Advancing Together in a picket line outside Patrolman Hurley's house until Officer Hurley is behind bars. For that story, we take you to TV 4's Una Selkirk, in Mattapan." She pursed her lips and looked into our eyes until she dissolved.

Selkirk swam into view, poised in front of a small, single-family house. Gawkers at her side, attracted by the magnetic field of television, gaped. "Thank you, Connie, Barry. I'm standing in front of the home of Patrolman John Hurley on Tanglewood Road in Mattapan, where, in a few minutes, POCAT is expected. There is a *palpable* air of tension in this normally quiet neighborhood, Connie. While we wait, I'd like to get the reaction of the neighbors to today's developments. Let me ask this family." She turned to a couple standing with two large, teen-age boys. "I wonder if you'd tell our viewers how you feel about the prospect of picketers in your neighborhood."

The man nervously pushed chewing gun from one side of his mouth to the other. "Huh?"

"Our information is that POCAT is bringing a contingent here to picket; will Mattapan welcome them?"

"Down here? Tonight?"

"That's what we've been told. We're waiting for them now."

He chewed the gum furiously, blinking under the bright lights, and scratched his armpit.

"Well, maybe we could ask the younger generation. How do you youngsters react to all this excitement?" She switched the microphone to the two boys. The one wearing a Mohawk and a gold earring mumbled something.

"I'm sorry? I didn't catch that."

"I said if them agitators come down here, gonna get their asses kicked."

His mother, a pot-bellied woman in a Baby Inside T-shirt, clouted him on the head. "Don't you be talking like that. I didn't raise you to talk that way."

"Jesus, ma—that hurts." He clapped a hand to his ear. "Whatcha wanna—"

"Go on. Go on home now, you hear?" She raised her

hand and the boys slunk away, casting backward glances. The one with the sore ear flipped a finger.

"Wait—here comes somebody."

The camera turned to take a shot up the street where a young woman, pushing a baby in a stroller, slowed her walk as she came into focus. She walked hesitantly toward the house, her expression going from puzzled to worried to horrified as she approached. The harsh lights took the contrasts out of her face, so that by the time she tried to step past Selkirk, stopping when the microphone blocked her way, we could have been watching a refugee interview in Bosnia. "Ex . . . excuse me, may I get past? Please." She had a tiny, frightened voice. She tried to push the stroller through the gate, but Selkirk insinuated a leg. "One minute, ma'am—just a minute! Do you live here?" Selkirk was in heat.

"Yes, yes—this is my house. What are you doing here? Please let me by; I've got to get my baby—"

"Mrs. Hurley, just a few questions, please." She moved her body around so that the only way Mrs. Hurley was going to get past was by running her over with the stroller. "Would you tell our viewers how you respond to the charges that have been leveled against your husband? That he murdered Purnell Whitmore, I mean?"

The look on the young woman's thin face was pure deer in the headlights. "Oh, no. Please, you've got to let me . . . " A spotlight homed in on her and she raised her hands to block it. The baby began to cry. "Please, please . . ."

"Judas priest! It's enough to make you sick." Flanagan was standing, glaring at the television. "They've no right . . ."

Back on the screen, the front door of the little house opened and the man I'd seen in the interrogation room stood for a second before letting out a shout more beast than man, then charging. Selkirk held her ground until he was halfway down the walk, then backed toward the camera. She held the microphone extended at arm's length as she stutter-stepped backward, as though it were a crucifix and Hurley a vampire.

"Officer Hurley, would you care to . . . your side of the—"

"Get out of here, you animals! Get out of here, or I'll . . . " He swept his sobbing wife into his arms, then herded her and the stroller up the walk. The door slammed and Selkirk resumed her position by the gate. "Well, Connie, Barry—as you can see, a very disturbed man. Clearly, feelings are running high and no one can rule out the possibility . . . Wait—I think I see . . . yes! I believe the protesters are arriving. Can we get a shot . . ."

The camera swiveled toward the other end of the street as a yellow school bus, then another, pulled up. The door of the first one opened and the figure of Corey Webster appeared. He stood in the doorway, rock solid, gave a full face, stern but serene, then a profile, then slowly dismounted, right fist raised, trailed by a stream of bodies, some white, more black. Many looked like suburban members of the Order of the Fevered Brow, but several of the younger black men wore camouflage pants, sleepy looks, and gang colors.

Catcalls began to richochet between the new arrivals and the thickening crowd of neighbors. A woman with a bullhorn began to bark instructions to the people descending from the buses, waving them into a line. It transformed her nasal shouts into sharp, crackling barks: "Stay on the sidewalk, stay on the sidewalk." A man with an armful of placards handed them to the marchers as they filed past.

"Don't let them provoke you." She turned the bullhorn toward the crowd of stunned onlookers: "We have a right to be here. This is a public throughfare. We have a right to be here. Join us. Demand justice. Join us."

The marchers paraded perhaps fifty feet down the street, turned, retraced their steps. They threaded by the crowd of locals, which was swelling before our eyes as people blocks away were drawn by the blare of the bullhorn.

Selkirk stood before the throng looking as though it had turned out in her honor. "Barry, this is extraordinary. As you can see, dozens of men and women, ordinary citizens, have arrived to exercise their right to assemble and make their feelings known, and more are coming as we speak. There is a palpable feeling of excitement, but it certainly appears as though the organizers of this protest want it to be peaceful."

Back in the studio, Connie pressed her hand against her ear. "Right, Una. Una, can you get a few words with Mr. Webster?"

When the picture cut back to Berman, the marchers had a line circling the front of the Hurleys' house. They began to chant: "No justice, no peace; no justice, no peace; no justice . . ."

Webster paraded in their midst, arms linked with a man and a woman. He had added a denim jacket to his wardrobe. A large red escutcheon on the back bore the crossed pair of bare forearms, one black and one brown, over large black letters: POCAT. A red bandanna worn as a headband completed the outfit.

Selkirk scurried over to him, dropped into step. "Mr. Webster, would you care to say a few words to our viewers? What do you hope to accomplish here?"

They reached the turnaround point and reversed direction. "Of course, Una. We are witnessing for justice. We will stay here until justice is done."

"And by that, you mean . . . ?"

"Until Purnell Whitmore's killer is in jail."

"And you believe that person is . . . " They did another about-face.

"If a black man had been the last person seen with a white youth later found murdered, where would he be?" Webster dropped his companions' arms and stepped out of line.

Relief swept across Selkirk's face. "So you are saying—"

"Hey, get outta here!"

The camera followed Selkirk's and Webster's eyes to the sound of the shout, then settled on two men in front of a video store a house away from the Hurleys'. "Come on, man—you're blocking people who want to come in."

A cadaverous man with the crazed eyes of the true believer reached for the other man's cheek. "You are my brother—I love you."

"I ain't your brother, bud, and you're messin' with my business. Now get the hell outta the way."

Selkirk broke off marching and gestured to a cameraman, then composed her face. "Unfortunately, Barry, Connie, it appears that an altercation may be developing. We're going to see if we can find out what's happening."

A camera zoomed in on the group in front of the video store, jerkily at first, then steadying. It picked up a technician poking a boom mike over the heads of some onlookers.

"I want to help you."

"You wanna help me, get outta my neighborhood, let me do some business." The store owner pushed the other man, who stepped back, then immediately resumed his position, hands at his side, a loopy, beatific smile on his face.

"Pray with me."

"Come on, man—gimme a break." He pushed the man again, harder. A little girl with a tape in her hand, trying to step between them to go into the store, was knocked backward as the thin man bobbed back. The tape fell on the sidewalk.

"Now look what you've—"

The little girl's father grabbed the thin man by the neck. "Why, you . . ."

A big, gray-haired woman in a sweatshirt that said DON'T ASSUME I'M STRAIGHT on the front and DON'T ASSUME I'M NOT on the back stepped in and tried to separate the two: "Violence isn't the way," she cried, as she gave the father a forearm shiver that staggered him. The little girl started to cry.

An old man ran up behind the gray-haired woman and punched her in the back. "Why don't you people go back where you came from!"

An onlooker yelled, "Yeah—get the hell outta here!"

A half-dozen others stepped forward and started pushing at the big woman and the thin man. Several marchers broke ranks, surrounded the group, and resumed their chant: "No justice, no peace. No justice, no . . ."

The picture cut back to Selkirk, who had traded in the look of sober resolve for one of stoic despair. "Regrettably, what began as a peaceful demonstration is deteriorating before our eyes into a potentially ugly situation. Barry?"

Back in the studio, Barry shook his head. "It is not a pretty picture, Connie. Let's hope that it doesn't get out of hand." Connie's face told us that this was her fervent wish, too, and Barry then dished us back to Selkirk, after first promising that TV 4 would continue its live coverage of the developing story in Mattapan even if it meant pre-empting regular evening programming.

An abrupt cut brought us back to the video store. The little girl's father took advantage of his adversary's momentary distraction to escalate from shove to punch in the nose. The blow, nicely conceived but poorly executed, missed the man by a wide margin, but caught the sweatshirted woman just above the ear, sending her reeling into her compatriots, scattering them like billiard balls. They began shrieking as though they had come under fire, and several of them fell upon the local and began to pummel and kick him. The woman clambered to her feet, shook herself twice, and dove upon the mélange, by all appearances unconcerned where her blows landed—as long as they did land. Within seconds, the screen was filled with a melee that could have been Wrestlemania with a John Cage sound track.

"Where are the police, damn it? If those TV people knew about this, the department had to." Flanagan hadn't resumed his seat, and now he stood behind me, pounding his huge right fist into his left palm. "They should have been on this from the start. It's getting out of hand. Damn it. Damn it."

Selkirk was in pig's heaven, Edward R. Murrow on a London rooftop at the height of the Blitz. Visions of Pulitzers danced in her eyes as she poked her ubiquitous wand first in one face, then another, extracting garbled sound bites and then returning to Webster, who was standing with arms folded and eyes blazing, very much above the fray, for color commentary.

"Mr. Webster, what do you say to local residents who are complaining that your group is disturbing the peace?"

"I say, Una, that I was arrested at lunch counters in Mississippi for disturbing the peace. I was arrested at Pease Air Force Base for disturbing the peace. People who refuse to accept injustice disturb the false peace of oppression. I am prepared to be arrested for disturbing the peace to-night."

"Does that mean you expect arrests?"

"We are prepared—"

We didn't learn what Webster was prepared for, because he was interrupted by the sound of shattering glass. When the cameraman located its source, one of the young bloods in a fatigue jacket and do-rag was picking a videotape out of the shards that had been the video store's window. He glanced at it, shoved it in his pocket, and was rummaging for another when a woman darted out of the store and brought a two-by-four down across the do-rag, sending its wearer pitching face first into the rubble.

"That's enough. Let's go."

Bucky and I looked up. We'd both been so preoccupied by the maelstrom developing in front of us that we hadn't realized Flanagan had slipped out and gotten his coat.

I glanced back at the television. It had returned to command central, where the handsome young couple struck just the right look of worldly empathy. "After a brief break, we will stay with this rapidly developing story. And now to this." The screen dissolved to a perky kid who loved his mom because she knew how to warm frozen pizza.

"Moriarty and O'Conor may be ready to let this town burn down, but I'm not. Are you coming with me?"

"Right. Coming, Buck?"

"Oh, boy. Let's go."

A worried-looking Kathleen Flanagan had a kiss for her husband and a pat for Bucky and me as we piled out the front door. "Remember, Francis—you're not twenty-one anymore." She stood in the doorway, wiping her hands on a dishtowel as we climbed into Flanagan's Plymouth.

"You'll find out how old I am when I get home, my girl!" She was still standing on the stoop as the car shot forward.

chapter 33

YOU CAN TAKE FORTY MINUTES TO GET FROM Charlestown to Mattapan, more if you're unlucky. We made it in a shade over fifteen, with only one near-death experience at an intersection on Blue Hill Avenue. Bucky was humming "Rising of the Moon" and the adrenal glands had my pulse rate red-lining before we were across the Charles. Flanagan seemed unaffected, barely touching the horn, threading through impossible openings in the traffic, slowing as needed at intersections, all emotion back in his parlor.

We had just passed Franklin Park and turned onto Morton when we overtook two black-and-whites and an unmarked Plymouth. Although their lights were flashing and they were moving fast, their sirens were off.

"About fuckin' time. Shouldn't be running silent, though." Flanagan followed the squad cars down Tanglewood, joining a parade of cars and a rainbow display of pedestrians, flooding into the area from every direction.

Flanagan spun the wheel, skidding the car into an angle across the street, blocking any more thrill-seekers from coming through. He reached into the glove compartment, slipped a slapstick into his pocket, and jumped out.

Bucky and I caught up to him as he shouted to a uniformed officer in one of the black-and-whites to get the other end of the street blocked off. Another uniform told us that Bernie Lawson was the officer in charge. We found him standing next to the Plymouth, talking into the radio handset as his eyes roamed the scene. He threw it onto the seat as we approached, a disgusted look giving way to relief as he recognized us.

"Man, am I glad to see you, Commissioner. Even you don't look too bad, Nase. Like your present company better than last time. Look where it got us." He swept an arm at the mob proceeding a few yards away, as oblivious as if we were school-crossing guards.

"How many men you got, Bernie?" Flanagan didn't seem much more aware of the chaos behind him than with us.

"Five, including me. Enough to cause trouble, not enough to stop it. We need twenty more, full riot gear, we don't want this getting wet." He had to shout to make himself heard.

"Right. Dispatcher say when they'd arrive?"

"They won't."

"What do you mean, 'they won't?' Isn't that who you were talking to?"

"Yes, sir. They won't send backup—said word came down from Moriarty . . . er . . . Acting Commissioner Moriarty, not to overload the situation. 'No police provocation,' way it came down. Had to push pretty hard just to get clearance to come over at all. Wasn't even supposed to use sirens." He kept his face impassive.

"Provocation? They have any idea what's going on here?"

"Folks 'exercising their assembly rights,' way I heard it."

"Jesus Christ!" Flanagan strode over to the Plymouth and grabbed the handset. "This is Dapper Flanagan—patch me through to Moriarty's office. And damn quick."

After a few seconds, the radio squawked. Flanagan registered incredulity, anger, contempt. "Well, you keep trying. You find him, you tell him he'd damn well better get his ass down here. Now get me Chief Denihan, pronto."

He snarled over his shoulder: "Commissioner Moriarty is at a fund-raiser for the mayor and doesn't want to be disturbed."

He turned back. "Hello, Denihan? Flanagan here. I'm down here at this thing in Mattapan. Yeah—there. I don't know if anyone's told you, but—" He stopped. "Listen, God damn it, I don't care what that limp-dick suck-butt said. You get every available man down here *now*, before this thing spreads and we need the National Guard. Or I'll see that you're held *personally* responsible!" He flung the handset back into the car. "Jesus."

"Are they sending more men, Commissioner?"

"I don't know. Denihan's a good man, but he's under orders from Moriarty to keep the police presence 'nonintrusive.' We're just going to have to do what we can with what we've got." He stood, hands on hips, studying the battlefield.

The TV 4 spotlights had been augmented by other teams, so the center of the scene looked like it had been filmed in infrared. The action had spread from the front of the Hurley house a hundred yards in either direction, widening as we watched.

A huge, amorphous hive of people screamed and grappled in a writhing, multicellular mass that resembled a giant version of something you don't want your doctor to find in x-rays of your lungs. Every few seconds, the mass would seem to be about to metastasize, forming momentary, amoeboid pods quickly resorbed into the blob. A shirtless young man with blood running from nose or lips would shoot from the welter like pus from a boil, stagger aimlessly for a few seconds, plunge back in, and be reabsorbed.

Dozens of people, eschewing active combat, paraded in front of the cameras, mugging and shouting. One young man ran up, a woman's torn blouse hoisted triumphantly over his head, thrust his grinning mug into a lens, and worked his lips like a fish before trotting off. No one took the slightest notice of us.

Looters were running into and out of the video store and a candy shop across the street. Windowless cars, some of them crazily askew across the treed lawns, surrendered their radios to tire-iron assault. The small fences that had marked the boundary between lots and sidewalk had been flattened on both sides of the street. A young white man was uprooting a bird feeder in a front yard while an old black woman, wheezing asthmatically, tried to pull him away.

Una Selkirk had retreated to the safety of the TV truck, where she continued to offer animated comment on the situation. Webster and three of his followers had moved to the center of the street and sunk to their knees in an attitude of prayer, although Webster kept looking over in Selkirk's direction. The cheerleader was screaming, "We shall resist, we shall resist" into the bullhorn, well away from the hand-to-hand action.

"Okay, Sergeant—get that damn bullhorn away from that woman; she's just stirring things up. Have a couple men meet me over at that TV truck. On the double."

Flanagan arrived at the broadcasting truck at the same time as the two bluecoats. He grabbed a technician. "Get those cameras out of here—you're going to have every thug in Boston down here!" He turned to the patrolmen. "Swivel those lights around to shine on the crowd."

Selkirk ran up as they moved to comply. "What are you

doing? You can't do that. We have a first-amendment right . . ." She grabbed a patrolman and tried to pull him off the spotlight stand. He looked back at Flanagan.

"There's no amendment says you get to cause a riot so you get a story. You've got five seconds to get in that truck and stay there, or I'll cuff you to it."

Selkirk started fulminating into the microphone. "Well, Connie, Barry, you and millions of our viewers just heard the former police commissioner trample on the Constitution. It's obvious that he doesn't want the public to know . . ." She stopped, fiddled with her earphone, looked angrily at the truck.

The technician leaned out the window and pointed at Bucky, who was folding his pocketknife. "He cut the mike cable—you're off the air."

She threw down the microphone. "God damn it, you'll hear about this. We'll sue . . ." She leaped on Bucky with a shriek and began pounding at his chest.

Flanagan turned to the patrolman: "May I borrow your cuffs, son?" He snapped one on her right wrist, then hauled her off Bucky and carried her, kicking and screaming, over to the truck and pushed her in. He snapped the other cuff on the technician's wrist. She was flailing at him with her free hand when Flanagan slammed the door.

"Bernie—what ordnance do we have?"

"Sidearms and the riot guns. But we can't—"

"Of course not. What about nonlethal?"

"Couple tear gas launchers. Not enough to control this."

"Just enough to send a couple hundred maniacs rampaging through the area, picking up mass on the way. No, we've got to fracture the crowd here, and we'd better do it fast, before somebody starts shooting. The cars have highway flares, don't they?"

"Sure."

Flanagan turned to one of the uniforms. "Get them and the tear gas—quick!"

The officer sent to grab the bullhorn came running up with it. A set of angry, red scratches lined his cheek.

"Lawson, detail two men to take one of the squad cars and the undercover car out quietly. Have them pull around the corner and wait with their lights out until I give them the word over my radio. Then they should put on all the lights, hit the sirens, and lay as much rubber as they can. There haven't been any sirens yet and they won't be expecting them so close. Come in like there're a dozen cars. We drop the gas just behind the rioters, between them and the cars. If we're lucky, they'll break. For Christ's sake, tell them not to run anyone over. Soon as they start moving, the cars move with 'em. Keep 'em going, don't let 'em stop and think. You"—he turned to the man who'd brought the bullhorn—"take the other squad car. Follow the other two, but wait exactly one minute *after* they hit the switches before you start up. Whatever happens, you keep going, around the block and back again, until I radio you to stop."

There was a loud shriek closer than the others, and we all looked around as a man with no shirt came staggering by, his hand held against the side of his face, blood dribbling from his elbow onto the ground. Another man was in close pursuit, a baseball bat held over his head. "Gonna kill you, you black ape!"

Lawson stepped out, grabbed the bat, brought it around into the pursuer's gut. He sank to his knees, making sucking sounds. "We better hurry, Commissioner—gonna have someone dead soon, we don't already."

"Right." The man sent for the ordnance came rushing up, his arms cradling flares and gas launchers. "Okay—the rest of you take the flares. When we launch the gas, throw the flares wherever you see a knot of people, then come in after them. I'm hoping they won't stop to find out what they are. You—" He put his hand on the youngest man's shoulder. The patrolman couldn't have been more than a few years out of high school, and his face was white with fear. Flanagan glanced at his nameplate. "Garson. Rookie, huh?"

"Yes, sir." He was swallowing hard.

"Got a few butterflies, have you?"

"No, sir. I mean . . . I guess so. I . . . I—"

"Me, too. Get 'em every time. You'll be fine. Soon as you hear the sirens, pull those TV lights, see? Get them off any way you have to, but not before then, okay? And all of you—I want these people running, hear? Use force if you have to get 'em going, but nothing heavy. We're not out for arrests. We start mixing it up with 'em, we'll go down. Okay—go!"

Lawson gave hurried instructions to two of his men, then sent them running for the cars as Flanagan hoisted the bullhorn. "Now hear this." His voice overwhelmed the shouts and sounds of destruction, and the din dropped perceptibly. Dozens of heads swiveled to locate the source of this new development and were immediately blinded by the wall of light. The people on the edge of the throng threw up their arms to shield their faces. Movement slowed across the mass.

"Now hear this: this is the police. You are in breach of the peace. Disperse immediately. I repeat—disperse immediately, or tear gas will be used. If you came on one of the buses, get on it now and you will be allowed to leave. If you live in the neighborhood, return to your homes immediately. You have fifteen seconds. One. Two. Three . . ."

A few people began to slink away, but in ones and twos, too few and too slowly. Others, seeking disengagement, were assaulted from behind as soon as they tried to leave. Some broke away and headed for the buses, but most of the swarm, secure in its mass, wasn't persuaded.

The animal soul of the crowd, reviving, started to refocus its hostility. Within seconds, the low drone that had greeted the threat initially was overtaken by shouts, derisive catcalls. Flanagan was up to "eight" when the first stones landed at our feet, "ten" when one bounced off his face, "thirteen" when the inching movement toward us began. I was standing next to him and could hardly hear his "fifteen" over the grunting thing pressing toward us, much less the command into the hand-held radio that followed.

I heard the sirens, though, and the scream of overrevved engines and protesting rubber, just before the picture disappeared as the halogen lights went off.

There was a soft "whump, whump" as the gas charges arced through the air, caught in midflight by the bank of flashing headlights racing down from the far end of the street. "Throw the flares and spread out," Flanagan shouted.

The cars came bearing down as I pulled the cap off a flare, struck it on the end, and let fly. Screams joined the banshee wail of the sirens as red smoke began billowing out of the heart of the throng. After a few seconds, we were rewarded with a man's voice: "It's choking me! Jesus, I can't breathe!"

"Keep 'em coming!" Flanagan pitched another flare, and the rest of us followed. My eyes started to tear as the faint breeze carried gas across the street. Then the third car added its howl to the first two and a dozen people who'd started up the street turned back and dashed past us. "Christ, there're more of them," someone yelled from the thick of the mob.

Others took up the cry, and then a blind panic convulsed the crowd like a physical thing, and men and women who had been locked in mortal embrace were climbing over each other in their eagerness to be gone. People broke, ran, scattered. The first two cars, moving cautiously but revving their engines, sounded like the start of an Indy car race as they herded stragglers off the street. The third wove through, slowed, found the core of the mob, and inched into it, parting it like tall grass, then accelerated away to circle for its return.

Tear gas and flare smoke swirled in a red devil's brew in the wake of the cars, too little light falling from overhead to pierce the haze, so that the remaining figures were more spectral than real. "Okay, let's go in and move 'em on." The flickering light bounced crazily off the flat planes of Flanagan's hard face as he stepped forward.

I fumbled my way into the swirling cloud until I met something solid and gave it a shove. I was choking a little but not so much I couldn't yell: "Dogs! They let the dogs loose. Let me out of here!" The solid thing cried, "Dogs! Jesus, I scared a dogs!" and then wasn't there anymore, so I kept it up, swatting and shoving and howling about dogs, until I emerged on the other side. A couple of kids, no more than twelve, were crouching behind a tree. "You better get out of here, mister—they got dogs." Then they scampered away behind a house.

I was standing on the lawn, pulling in air, when a young man in a sleeveless BORN TO KILL sweatshirt, six feet, two hundred pounds, burst out of the smoke with a case of cigarettes on his shoulder. His foot caught the curb and he sprawled in front of me. "Mother of God, one of 'em's tearing at me!" He scrambled to his feet and tore off down the street, the cigarettes lying in the gutter.

There were still a few shouts and thumps drifting out of the lifting pall, but a small knot of POCAT imports, two men and two women, was all that was left on the sidewalk in front of the Hurley house as first Bernie Lawson, then Flanagan and Bucky, came over and stood beside me.

The wail of the sirens formed a backdrop to the sudden silence. "Why don't you radio the cars, Bernie, tell them to keep on the lookout for stragglers." Flanagan pulled out a handkerchief and dabbed at a cut under his eye as he looked over the street. One patrolman was helping a man to his feet, while the rookie poked a dazed dawdler with his stick until he lurched over to a bus and struggled aboard.

Flanagan was breathing hard. "Kathleen's going to give me what for, I think." He looked down at the spot of blood on his handkerchief. "Let's go get those four out of here, see if anyone needs first aid." We followed him to the quartet in front of the Hurleys'.

The POCAT holdouts were sitting, heads bowed, arms

linked. Webster was nowhere to be seen. "Okay, folks, let's go." Flanagan towered over them, his voice firm but quiet.

They made no move to leave. Flanagan's voice softened fractionally. "We don't want to have to move you—don't make us."

The four sat in mute defiance, looks of imminent martyrdom on their faces. Flanagan heaved an exasperated sigh. "Okay, you're going to be moved." He beckoned to us. "Lend a hand, will you?"

The four of us each grabbed one of them. Their arms went rigid, but the effort to cling together collapsed almost immediately when Bernie applied pressure to his man's ulnar nerve. The man screamed, "You've crippled me, you've crippled me," and was still howling as Bernie dragged him over to the first bus and pitched him in. The rest of us followed with our cargoes.

"Okay, driver—out of here. Now!" The bus pulled out with a wheeze and, as it disappeared down the road, we saw the dark figure of a man, standing on the lawn where the bus had been parked. The red bandanna covered the fringe of hair, so that he looked like a skinhead. He stared at us, then slowly raised his arm, a finger pointing at Flanagan. "You'll pay for this, you bastard! This is the last time you'll terrorize people. We will—"

A middle-aged black man waving a piece of pipe charged across the lawn behind Webster. Flanagan stepped forward to intercept him, but I was closer and grabbed him while he was still a few feet from his target. "Whoa! Hold it!" I wrestled the pipe out of his hands and flung it on the ground, then took his defeated weight as the fight went out of him.

"Look at my store. Look what they did to my store." He waved at the looted candy shop. "Everything I got was in that store. Look what they—"

Webster looked at the man with disdain. "You ought to be thinking about your brothers and sisters and their pain, not your dirty money."

The man in my arms started to struggle again, and I desperately wanted to hand him the pipe and let him go, but weakness got the better of me.

Webster, seeing the man safely restrained, turned to Flanagan: "And you, you fascist pig—you'll be sorry for this."

Webster turned and was walking with measured steps to the remaining bus, his right fist upraised, when a young black man with an arrow shaved into the side of his head leaned out a window. "Hey, dude, where's the green?"

The call was taken up by half a dozen others, as windows the length of the bus went flying up. "Yeah, man—s'posed get ten bucks, came down here." "Where's the bread, Fred?" "Kick yo' ass, don' get my money."

Webster looked quickly at us, then back at the bus. "I don't know what . . ." He swiveled toward the TV van, but Flanagan blocked his way.

"You came on the bus, you go home on the bus."

"I intend to talk to Una—"

"Besides, I think your followers need you." He took Webster's upper arm and started to guide him toward the bus, but Webster's resistance was anything but passive. His free hand caught Flanagan a roundhouse clip on the ear that staggered him. Then Flanagan's hand moved in a blur, there was a sudden muffled thump followed by a scream, and Webster would have collapsed if Flanagan hadn't caught him. He pushed the slapstick back into his pocket and shoved the unresisting Webster onto the bus to a chorus of cheers: "Hey, man—nice work!" "You see that old dude take him down?" "Where's the dough, bro?"

Flanagan waved the bus out. We watched it disappear down the street. Lawson turned to Flanagan. "Guess his trick knee went out, Commissioner."

Flanagan smiled, then shook his head. "Thanks, Bernie, but you report it the way it happened. All you men, you did a good piece of work. Good job, Garson—got those lights just right. Hope we can work together again." He patted the young officer on the shoulder.

"Thank you, Dapper . . . I mean, sir. Sorry, sir."

"Dapper's fine, son."

"Hey! Get me out of here—please!"

We looked at the TV 4 truck. The technician was waving desperately. "Get her off me. You gotta get her off me."

We walked over and looked in. Selkirk was flailing at the door, her eyes pinpricks of malice. Every time she clawed at the handle, the arm of the man cuffed to her seemed to grow another inch. "Please, officer—lemme ride back with those dogs!" He was still pleading when I left the others and headed toward the Hurley bungalow.

chapter 34

I SLIPPED AROUND TO THE BACK OF THE LITTLE house and tapped on the kitchen door. Nothing happened, so I tapped harder, and then I heard tentative footsteps crossing linoleum, saw a shadow behind the curtain masking the window. "Who is it?"

It was a woman's voice, frightened, and then a larger shadow appeared behind the first, pushed it aside. "Get out of here. Get out of here, or I'll—"

I recognized Hurley's voice. "My name's Nichols. I work for the Kershaw Commission. I'd like to talk to you."

"I don't want to talk to you. Get away from my house or—"

"Don't, John! What are you doing?" The woman's voice moved toward panic. "Put that away!" A baby made whimpering sounds.

"Go away, Nora—it's one of them. I'll—"

"Put that down! Put that gun down, John."

"Nora . . ."

"Your wife's right, Hurley. Put the gun away. I want to talk to you. I may be able to help. Will you let me in?"

Words buzzed, the baby blubbered, the lock clicked, and the door opened slowly. I stepped in.

"What do you want?" Hurley held the gun pointing toward the floor.

He looked bigger close up, bigger yet with the thirty-eight in his hand. A worn-looking young woman in a housecoat stood behind him, patting the back of the baby lying on her shoulder.

"I want to talk to you about Purnell Whitmore."

He brought the gun up, waved it at me. "No way! My lawyer told me—"

"Your lawyer told you not to talk to anyone, and he's right, in ordinary circumstances. In ordinary circumstances, in a few months, your lawyer would tell you about the deal he'd cut: there was an argument, Whitmore provoked you, tempers flared, you didn't mean to hurt him. If he's a good lawyer, it'd be a good deal; you'd plead to manslaughter, be out in a couple of years."

The woman stifled her gasp by pressing her lips against the child's head. "Except these aren't ordinary circumstances. You're white, and you're a policeman, and you're accused of killing a black kid—a black kid with a spotless record. You're on too many agendas to cut a good deal. I see you doing murder time—ten, fifteen years, John. Maybe more."

"Oh, yeah? Well, how about I didn't do it, huh? You can take your 'good deal' and—" He was all bravado and pose, kid's values in a man's body, who remembered a world where Mom and Dad took your word and who couldn't understand where it went.

"I didn't *say* you did it. I said I saw what's going to happen—doesn't have anything to do with whether you did it."

"But that can't be right. It isn't . . . " The steam went out and he seemed to shrink as he realized how foolish he sounded.

"No, it's not. Want to talk about the real world?"

"But what . . . ?" The gun arm dropped to his side.

"Let's sit down." There was an enameled kitchen table, and I pulled up a chair and pointed to two more. "I think you should."

He looked at me, down at the gun, back at me. The gun was more weight than he could carry and he let it slip to the counter. He didn't so much sit as slide into the chair at the table. Mrs. Hurley picked up a bottle and helped the baby find the nipple. It was making contented gurgling sounds when she lowered herself into a chair near her husband.

"John-John?"

She looked down at him, smoothed the thin, silky hair, smiled a tired, proud smile over the baby's head. "John Junior, really." She transferred the smile to her husband, reached for his hand, clung to it.

Hurley squeezed back. "How do you know his name?"

"I was listening when they questioned you."

He dropped his wife's hand and started to push to his feet. "Is this—"

"No trick, John. Sit down."

He stayed frozen, half up, half down, until his wife took his hand again and tugged him. "Let's listen to what the man has to say. Please?" She pressed him toward the chair.

He collapsed into it like a man who'd lost his bones. "What difference does it make?"

"It makes a difference to me; it makes a difference to John-John." She turned to me. "Mr. Nichols, my husband didn't kill that boy; my husband never hurt anyone. He never should have become a policeman."

"Nora . . ."

"I'm not convinced he killed the boy. I wouldn't be here if I were."

"Then . . . John's going to be all right?"

"No, he's not—not unless he gets smart fast. I meant what I said: your husband is going down for this, unless we find out who *did* do it. If he didn't." I turned to Hurley. "It's time to stop playing, John—you're going down, unless you start talking right now."

He drew himself up, all big, stubborn, overgrown child. "You say you heard them question me, then you know what happened. What I said, that's the truth."

"Right, right. You wanted to talk to Purnell Whitmore, hunted him over half of Boston, and when you finally found him, you shoved him into an alley and came out a couple minutes later. And he turns up dead in a garbage bin the next day. Mrs. Hurley, say good-bye to your husband tonight; you won't be seeing that much more of him." I pushed back from the table.

"My lawyer told how you'd do this, working on my wife, pretending you want to help me. Well, you get out of—"

"Stop! It's got to stop. Mr. Nichols, John isn't telling the truth. At least not all of it. He—"

"Nora!"

"No! Our baby's going to have a father. He needs a father, John, not a saint. You tell Mr. Nichols, or I will."

"It's a trick, Nora! He's working for them. He's just trying to get me to talk. Well, I won't. I—"

A six-year-old stamping his foot and saying, "I won't!" may be cute the first time; it quickly grows tedious. "Grow up, Hurley. Geraldo Rivera may want to trick you into talking, but the police sure don't. Whatever your story is, it can't put you any deeper in it than you are right now."

Mrs. Hurley saw it even if he didn't, and it was more out of pity for her than concern for him that I added. "I think I know part of it, John, if that helps."

"You . . . know?"

"Purnell Whitmore was dealing drugs, wasn't he? You went to talk to him about that?"

"I don't know what . . ." He looked at his wife. She hiked

the baby back over her shoulder, bounced him, nodded her head once, twice. He splayed his hands across the table, watched his fingers, swallowed. "How did you know?"

"He stopped playing ball, stopped showing up at his job, lied about what he was doing, yet had serious money coming in. What are the alternatives, where he lived? How'd you get onto it?"

He ran his hands through his hair, the stubble springing back like well-mown grass. "His mother, she shouldn't—"

Mrs. Hurley grabbed his forearm, clenched it until the flesh went white. "Do you think I don't know how his mother feels, John? Feel *my* heart; see if you know what she feels." She pulled his hand to her, pressed it against her breast. "Do you feel it? Do you think any mother wouldn't? Do you think you can give her back her son, if you give up yours? If you don't care about me, care about him."

"Nora, don't!" He broke, sobbed, let her gather his head after his hand until the two of them, baby and man-child, were huddled against her.

She cradled them both, rocking gently, hands patting, soothing her boys. Then she kissed the top of his head and ever so gently pushed him upright. "Tell the man, John. Tell him what you told me."

It took him a few seconds to pull himself together, seconds of sniffles and silly pride finding someplace to go. Then he looked at them, wiped his eyes, gathered himself.

"He was a great kid. I coached him in basketball camp last summer." He shook his head, wiped his hand across his nose. "*I* coached *him!* What a joke. Look at me—big, clumsy guy, played a little football in college, thought I'd sign up for the recreation department's summer league, help some kids. Figured I was pretty squared away, seen a little life, going to show these kids how it's done. And right away, I meet this kid, he's not only a better athlete than I ever dreamed of being, he's smarter, more squared away, going to have the life I hoped my kids would have. This kid . . ." He looked away, started to go away.

"I know, at least I think I do. I've learned a lot about him."

He swallowed, brought himself back. "He was a special person. Just a very, very special person. He had this way of relating. It was as though *I* was the kid from the wrong side of the tracks and *he* was the one helping me. 'That's okay, John,' he'd say, 'we'll work on those moves to your right. Got to watch that food you white people eat, though—getting a little porky.' Then he'd laugh, and I'd laugh, and we'd start talking about things that had nothing to do with basketball."

The baby started to gurgle and whimper, and John's wife rocked forward and back in her chair a few times until the baby noises stopped. Then she nodded to her husband, urged him on with the soft, sweet smile.

"We'd get a Coke, sit down behind the bleachers, and talk. Religion, race, politics—sometimes girls, though neither one of us knew much about that." He glanced uncertainly at his wife, drew a reassuring smile in response.

"I'd mention something that interested me, and he'd say, 'You ought to read such-and-such—I learned a lot from it.' I remember I came home one night, a little late 'cause we'd sat around shooting the breeze after practice, and I said to Nora, 'Hon, you won't believe this, but Johnny Hurley, a big mick from Malden, thinks this black kid from the ghetto is one of the most interesting people he's ever met.' Remember, Nora?"

She nodded and patted his hand and he went on. "John-John wasn't born then, but I guess I thought, *This is the kind of boy I want: smarter than me, a better jock than me, more successful than I'll ever be.* You want that, don't you?"

He stopped and exhaled and I was pretty sure it was the longest speech he'd ever made. "I would." I thought about it. "I do."

"Sure." He took a deep breath and ran his hand back over the flat-top: "Anyway, the season ended, and he went off to Yale, down in New Haven. He wrote me a couple of letters, you know? About his courses and these kids he was meeting and how rich they were and all the things they had—cars and TVs and lots of clothes. I kinda got the impression it was rough for him. It would've been for me, I know that."

He had turned in on himself, imagining a place that might as well have been on Mars for all he knew of it. "Then what happened, John?"

"Then? Oh, yes. I guess the last letter was around January, February. I'm not much of a writer, I'm afraid, and what with the baby coming and all, I kind of lost touch. Then one day early this summer, I was down at headquarters, on Berkeley Street, and when I got done, I decided to go over to Newberry Street, see all those fancy shops I'd heard Nora talk about. Thought maybe I could get her birthday present there. Anyway, I was walking down the street, and I saw this sign, Jack's, something like that. It was a ladies' clothes shop, and I remembered Purnell mentioned he'd worked there. So I thought, what the hell, he'd be back from college, and maybe he was working there for the summer, so I'd pop in and surprise him, you know?"

"Sure."

"You heard the interrogation, you know how those guys tried to say maybe I had some . . . something . . ." He colored. "You know. Anyway, it was nothing like that—I just had an . . . an impulse, okay? Thought maybe he'd get a kick, I walk in in uniform. You know: 'Okay, Whitmore—you're coming with me.' Give him a little razzing, that sort of thing. There's nothing wrong with that, is there?"

Mrs. Hurley was looking at her husband with a look we all want, nodding in time to his phrases, and he didn't need my blessing. "So I ask this girl, works there, if Purnell's around, and she tells me he was fired a couple weeks before."

He stopped, got up slowly, went to the refrigerator. "Will you have a beer, Mr. Nichols? Nora?" He passed them to us, opened one for himself, continued. "Didn't seem like him, somehow, but I figured probably he was provoked, so I'd wait till he came out for basketball. See, he'd promised me he'd come around, be like an assistant coach. Younger kids, they really looked up to him, and he could talk to them like none of us could. But then practice started and he didn't show. Couple kids, played with him last summer, said they'd seen him around earlier in the summer, but didn't know where he was, whether he was coming out or not."

He took a pull on the can, shook his head. "Maybe I should have gone to his mother then, but I didn't know her, and I guess I didn't want Purnell getting annoyed with me, bothering his mother." He paused to find the right words. "I guess I was a little . . . intimidated by him. Anyway, Purnell was such a"—he searched for a word again—"together kid, I never figured there was anything really wrong. Fact is, I guess I was more . . . hurt, he hadn't even let me know he wouldn't be helping. I told myself I was going to look him up, give him a little talking-to—you know, about responsibility, remembering old friends, all that. Maybe I was even a little glad, in a way, he'd screwed up a little—there was still something I could teach him?"

It was so artless it could only be the truth, but that wasn't going to be enough when cross-examination time arrived. "So you went prowling around his neighborhood, looking for him?"

I said it softly, but he lurched back, as though I'd hit him. "Why, no—not 'prowling.' I just . . . yeah, I guess you could call it that. They will, won't they? That's what you mean?"

"Right. How often?"

"Just a couple times, after I went off duty."

"Stopped kids, asked them if they'd seen Purnell?"

"Sure. Why—what are they saying?"

"Nothing, yet, but you can bet they'll turn up a couple of those kids, and it'll sound like you were stalking him for weeks."

Mrs. Hurley blanched and bit her lip, but I kept on. "And

then you talked to a kid at the playground, and he told you what Whitmore was up to?"

"In so many words? No. Big white guy, might as well have a badge tattooed on his forehead, looking for a neighborhood kid? No, once they understood I wasn't there to make trouble, they just joshed me, gave me the business. But one of them, a nice kid, he could see I was concerned. After the others got bored and went away, he stayed behind for a minute. He said I should forget it, should give him a tryout; Purnell wouldn't be playing basketball anymore, he was too busy making money."

He looked down at the top of the beer can, wiped the foam with his thumbs. "I'm pretty . . . naive, Mr. Nichols. That's the word, isn't it? Someone who doesn't know what's going on? I thought he meant Purnell had another job, and I asked him where he was working; I wanted to drop in on him.

"The kid must have thought I was joking, because he said something like 'Drop in on him where he's working? I bet you do.' He thought it was funny as hell. I didn't get it. Can you believe it? I'm so dumb I still didn't get it. 'Sure, want to say hi.'

"And he said, '*High*'s the word, you find Purnell,' and at first I *still* didn't get it, and then I did. 'You mean he's involved with drugs?' I must have sounded like the biggest fool he'd ever heard. I guess maybe I am."

His wife reached over and rested her hand on his knee. The baby turned his head and smiled, or maybe it was a burp. "What did the kid say?"

"He said, 'You sayin' it, dude, not me.' And he must have been a decent kid, because he turned back to me and said if I caught up with Purnell, I should tell him to cool it. 'Man's got a ticket out, tell him not to blow it' was what he said."

"What'd you do then?"

"I asked the boy where I could find Purnell. He said he was staying with his mother as far as he knew, and I said no, I didn't want to see him there, was there someplace else

I could find him. The kid said he didn't want it coming back on him, but he'd seen Purnell hanging around his church a lot of nights. I asked him if there was anyplace else, someplace maybe not so public, and he said Purnell came down the alley behind the playground most evenings. He said I might see him coming out if I waited."

"Tell me about the night you caught up with him."

He finished the beer, collapsed the can as easily as if it had been a paper cup, and set it on the table. "I was awful upset after talking to that boy. It made me almost sick, his throwing away his future like that. I thought about calling on his mother, telling her what I'd learned, but he'd told me about how hard she'd worked to get him ahead. I didn't want to do that, at least until I had a chance to confront him, find out if it was true. God, if only . . ." He lowered his fist to the table, raised it, let it fall. The flattened can danced a few turns, then died.

"Anyway, the next day, I heard some of the guys talking in the locker room; there was going to be a Blue Tornado sweep through Purnell's neighborhood. They were saying there'd been a lot of drug activity reported there, there'd likely be some action. You know how guys talk, they're a little nervous?"

"Yes."

He nodded. "So these guys, they're talking about how they're going to do this, going to do that, not going to wind up like some guy who came back with his face half off." He caught his wife's wince, hurried on. "Doesn't mean much, just guys trying to talk themselves up, way we used to before a football game. Scared to death, mostly. It's a scary job. At least, I'm scared a lot."

"Scared the hell out of me."

"Sure—you know. Anyway, I started thinking about it, you know? What that boy had told me about Purnell? Like what if he was one of the people they'd run into, dealing drugs? What if it turned ugly, things got rough? Even if it didn't, what if he was brought in to the station, his mother had to come down?" He shook his head, caressed the baby with a look. "I can't imagine that, how much that would hurt." He stopped, pointed to my beer. "Another? Nora?"

We shook him off and he went on, his voice tired, beaten. "It ate at me. We went on patrol, my partner and me, and I kept listening to the radio, worrying, until I couldn't take it anymore. I pulled rank, dropped her at a coffee shop, told her to stay put while I ran home. She looked at me like I was crazy, so I told her there was a little problem at home. She's a good kid, didn't squawk anymore. I guess I *was* crazy, huh?"

"Home's the only place you don't seem to have a problem; maybe you're more lucky than crazy."

"Lucky." He said it the way he'd said *naïve*, a foreign word he wasn't sure how to pronounce. Then he looked at his wife, the baby. "You're right. I'm lucky."

He smiled, the first one I'd seen on him, but it didn't last. "Anyway, I grabbed a cab back to the station, got my car, and drove over and found the alley. I went on a little way and waited, a couple blocks from where the raid was going down."

"Go on."

"Well, I was watching the rear-view mirror, and I looked away for a minute, and when I checked again, I thought I saw someone just turning into the alley. I figured it could be him, so I got out and walked back, 'cause I didn't want to miss him." His eyes went away, seeing him again.

"What happened then?"

"I got to the entrance to the alley and looked down it, but at first I couldn't see anybody and thought my eyes had maybe been playing tricks on me, you know? Then I saw movement, but I couldn't tell if it was Purnell. The light was bad and he was—I don't know—twenty or thirty feet down the alley by then. So I stepped in a little ways and looked closer and thought I saw a big Y on the back of the person's jacket, so I called out, kind of quiet, 'Hey, Purnell—Purnell

Whitmore—is that you?' And he kind of started, but then he turned around and came out."

"Tell me about your meeting—everything you can remember."

"He was surprised to see me. Shocked, I guess, and kind of . . . uneasy. We shook hands, said 'Hi.' I could tell he wondered what I was doing there, said he was glad to see me, but not like he meant it. Acted nervous as a cat. I guess I wasn't much better. Then he said he couldn't stay, had to get going, had to meet someone. He was jumpy, had a weird smile, kept looking in the direction of all the action."

"All the action?"

"It was about seven-twenty-five, seven-thirty when I ran into him. Just about the time I saw him, the street sweep hit a couple blocks away. You could hear it loud as all get-out—sirens, people yelling, all that."

"Go on."

"I told him I'd been looking for him, hoped he'd come back and help me coach, and he said he'd gotten kind of busy, didn't have too much time for basketball. Then he said he had to go, couldn't hang around; someone was waiting for him.

"And I got a little hot, said I'd asked for him at work, seemed like he didn't have too much time for *it*, either.

"Then *he* got hot, said what business did I have, coming after him. And I said I cared about him, kind of enjoyed watching his life develop, wanted to keep in touch. And he said"—he grew embarrassed—"maybe I should think more about my own life; being a cop making a shitty living didn't look like I knew so much about it, playing ball with kids and driving a ten-year-old car, and he hadn't busted his ass to go to college to wind up like that.

"It hurt, I guess, and so I said at least I wasn't selling drugs, and then I asked him, right out, was he going to meet his drug dealer. And he said, 'None of your fucking business what I'm doing,' and turned to leave.

"It made me angry, real angry, and I grabbed at him. Then I heard a siren—it sounded like it might be coming right past us—and I guess I shoved him back in the alley. Those IA guys said someone saw me push him, so I guess I did. I don't remember, except then we were back in the alley."

"What happened in the alley?"

"I hauled him back a ways, far enough so a squad car wouldn't see us, and told him what I'd heard."

He leaned back, clasped his hands over the big biceps that stretched the T-shirt, looked at the ceiling. "He didn't want to hear it, tried to pull away; told me to get out of his face, all that stuff, but I really put it to him. I guess we were in there for only a few minutes, but I remember I told him what I'd thought when I got to know him, how I was . . . jealous of him, maybe, the chances he had, reminded him what he'd told me about his mother and what she'd done for him. And all the while there were sirens coming down; we could hear shouts, people yelling. I remember really putting my face in his, saying, 'You hear that? You want that? Do that to your mother?'

" 'You leave my mother out of this,' he said, and I could see it really bothered him to think of her finding out."

"Did you hit him, hurt him in any way?"

He squeezed his eyes shut, pinched his lips. "No, sir. No, I didn't. I know what Officer Bosworth said, about blackouts, but I know that didn't happen. What happened was, we were back there, and I remembered what he'd said about meeting somebody, so I thought he might be carrying and I patted him down. I felt something, in his pocket, and I pulled out a bunch of little plastic envelopes with white powder in them."

"White powder—not little gray rocks?"

"Uh-uh. Not crack. More like white sand."

"Cocaine?"

"Probably. Could've been meth, angel dust, something else, I suppose. Anyway, I tore off the tops, emptied the packets on the ground, then kicked the stuff every which way. I guess I went a little bit crazy, but I didn't hurt him, I swear it."

"John couldn't hurt anybody, Mr. Nichols—not like that." Mrs. Hurley's eyes willed me to believe.

"What did Purnell do?"

"Well, he tried to grab the stuff back when I first took it, but then he just sort of sagged against the wall. I'm a lot bigger than he was, and up close, he couldn't do much with me. I remember he had his eyes shut, like he couldn't watch."

"Did Purnell say anything?"

Hurley pressed his lips, shook his head.

"Nothing?"

"No!"

"That's not true! John, tell him what you said he said. Tell him, or I will."

"Don't, Nora!"

"I know it hurts, but you didn't do it—it's not your fault!"

"It is!" The man folded into a fetal position, the last words more like a baby's whimper than speech.

"What did he say, Mrs. Hurley? It's better if I know."

"He said, 'Don't. That doesn't belong to me—he's waiting for it.' Isn't that right, John? Isn't that what you told me?"

He had his eyes covered with his big, left palm and gasped a little as he nodded.

"Did he say who he meant?"

"No. No . . . sir."

"Did you ask him?"

"Yes."

"What did he say?"

"I said, 'Who's this for? Whose is it?' And he just stood there, sort of slumped against the wall, shaking his head back and forth with his eyes closed until I gave up."

"What happened then?"

Hurley gradually uncurled himself, regained some of his composure. "After I'd kicked that stuff all over, I told him he had to give me his word he'd quit. That if he didn't promise, or if I heard he'd started again, I was telling his mother. At first it was like he hadn't heard me—he just kept shaking his head—so I said, 'Do you hear me? I swear I'll tell her, you ever do this again.' And then he started to cry."

"Did he say anything?"

"Not at first—he just cried. Then he said I mustn't, it would kill her. And I said that the only way she wasn't going to find out was if he gave me his promise—and kept it. And he said if he stopped, would I tell her, and I said I wouldn't. I gave my word, you see?"

"I understand. Did he promise?"

"He did then. He said, 'I'll stop. I swear I'll stop; just don't tell her.' "

"Did you believe him?"

"I wasn't sure. I wanted to, didn't want to do that to her. He kept saying, over and over: 'It'd kill my mama; it'd kill my mama.' "

"Did you say anything else to him?"

"Yes." He stopped, bit his lip.

"What?"

"I wanted to be sure, you see—sure that he'd quit?" He looked at me supplicatively, hoping I'd bless in advance whatever he'd done.

"I understand. What did you do?"

"I told him he had to come in and tell me where he'd been getting the stuff. Where he'd been buying it, and where he'd been selling it. I told him I'd protect his identity, but that we had to know. That if I didn't see him within two days, I was going to his mother."

"What did he say?"

"Nothing. He didn't say anything, so I told him again, and finally he nodded."

"Did he say anything else—*anything?*"

"Nothing new. He just kept sobbing and saying I shouldn't tell her. Over and over, he just kept saying that.

He must have loved her an awful lot. I think maybe he
hadn't stopped to think what it would do to her until then."

"What happened then?"

"I left him there and went back to my car."

"How long were you with him all together?"

"Maybe four, five minutes—not long."

"What was he doing when you left?"

His head dropped. "He'd sort of slid to the ground, real
slow, and just sat there, crying, wiping his eyes, trying to
pull himself together. I looked back and that's the way he
was—just sitting there."

"Why didn't you tell this to the IA team?"

"I couldn't. I gave my word, don't you see? He gave his,
and I gave mine. I can't break my promise."

Anger welled up in Mrs. Hurley. "You gave *me* your word
first: 'Till death do us part.' Are you going to keep *that*
promise?" He dropped his eyes rather than meet hers.

"It might help Mrs. Whitmore some, to know her son
meant so much to you." I stood up. "Listen to your wife,
Hurley, and come clean—unless you want *your* son to grow
up fatherless."

Mrs. Hurley grasped at it like a drowning woman. "You
mean, Mr. Nichols, if John says what he just told you, he'll
be all right?"

"I wish I could say yes, but I doubt it. It's nothing but your
husband's word, at this point. There's no better candidate."

"Will you help us?" She clutched at my forearm. "We'd
pay you."

"I can't—I have a conflict of interest."

"Please?"

I eased her fingers off my arm as gently as I could. "Let
me see if I can think of something. I'll get back to you if I
do." I turned back to Hurley. "Meantime, tell your lawyer
what you told me. Maybe he'll see something."

I looked back as I let myself out. The baby peered at me
over its mother's shoulder. She was holding Hurley against
her chest with her free arm, rocking him.

The squad cars had pulled back in and the uniforms were sitting in them with the doors open and the engines idling, having a smoke. Flanagan was standing by his car talking to Lawson. A few people were murmuring on the lawns or picking up debris, and one old man was sitting on the curb, mumbling to himself while tears ran down his face and dropped silently into the gutter. The street looked like a war zone and nobody gave any sign of having missed me. I ignored Bucky's arched eyebrows and bummed a cigarette, then walked over to the old man and handed it to him. He took it wordlessly, then went on crying.

The Boston Hub
August 25, 1994

OUSTED OFFICIAL CRUSHES DEMONSTRATION

MAYOR "OUTRAGED" AT UNAUTHORIZED ACTION, VOWS LEGAL SANCTIONS

BOSTON—Suspended Police Commissioner Francis Flanagan, acting without authority and in direct opposition to City Hall policy, yesterday led a police assault on demonstrators protesting the failure of authorities to arrest John Hurley, the Boston policeman suspected of involvement in the slaying of Roxbury teenager Purnell Whitmore.

The demonstrators, members of a local civil rights group called POCAT (People of Color Advancing Together), were picketing outside Hurley's Mattapan residence when Flanagan and several police officers ordered them to disperse. Upon their refusal, the police, aided by dogs and tear gas, fell upon the demonstrators, injuring several. They also assaulted media representatives covering the demonstration, apparently hoping to avoid identification.

The mayor, after meeting with POCAT's Corey Webster and other civil-rights leaders, promised swift reprisals against Flanagan and the renegade officers. In a statement released late last night, Mayor Connor O'Conor vowed: "This was a cowardly, unprovoked attack on Boston citizens exercising their right to assemble peacefully and speak freely. I have directed the district attorney's office to institute criminal proceedings against the men involved, particularly Francis Flanagan."

chapter 35

THE BAR WAS DARK AND MERCIFULLY COOL, which was why I'd been able to inveigle Hariston into meeting me. He picked at the label on his beer bottle while I ran him through it. "Hal, the old lady corroborates him. She told me the kid came *out* of the alley to meet Hurley. He couldn't have gotten that from the papers—they reported her original story, that they met on the street in *front* of the alley."

"The guy's a cop. Coulda heard it around the station house." He pressed the beer bottle against his forehead. "Jesus, must be a hundred eight back there. That mustard shop in the White Mountains is looking better and better."

"I told only you. Did you tell anyone?"

"Fuck, no."

"Well, then, he's telling the truth."

"Okay, okay—he's telling the truth about that. Big deal. Under oath, he'll probably give the right name, too."

"The cellophane envelopes of cocaine, Hal—I *saw* some in the crack house. Whitmore was taking them to the crack house."

"Nase, Hurley's lawyer wants to dirty the kid. Of *course* Hurley's gonna say he was carrying; couple weeks, he'll say the kid was the key man in the Colombian cartel and Hurley should get a medal."

"Cocaine, Hal—not rock. Crystal cocaine's the high-priced spread, not a street drug in Roxbury. Why would Hurley come up with that detail, he was making it up?"

"His lawyer probably just had a snootful himself; it was the first thing that popped into his mind."

"Hal, if Hurley was just trying to trash the kid's image, he wouldn't *need* to have him carrying coke—he'd just say the kid was holding crack."

Hairston pulled a face. "The kid was a stockboy. Just hypothetically, mind you, why's he gonna be holding coke? Like you say—that's an uptown high."

"Because that dealer had a customer with expensive tastes and the budget to satisfy them. I told you, I saw coke in the guy's stash."

"Yeah, and I think you've been tooting it ever since."

"Don't you see? The dealer killed him, Hal. Whitmore was a stockboy, on his way back to the crack house— probably just dropped off a load at the street market the raid broke up and was coming back for seconds. Maybe he picked up the coke on the street, I don't know. But when Whitmore went back without that coke, the guy thought the kid had ripped him off, was going to sell the stuff and keep the money."

"Would you mind not talking so loud?" Hal looked around the bar. "Even in this town, there're limits on how nuts you can be in public places."

"Hal, the kid was dealing, no doubt about it. When he said, 'He's waiting for it,' he meant his dealer. The crack house was right there—I may even have seen the guy who did it."

"That neighborhood, *any place* is right outside a crack house. And you said yourself, this wasn't a drug killing."

"Not a user taking someone off to steal his watch, no—but a dealer who thinks the help's been stealing the inventory? Bet on it. What else could that mean, someone was waiting for it?"

"*Hurley's* your source for that. You say he's got a lawyer; that's like hiring a scriptwriter. Want to know how this line fits in, see the movie."

He drained his beer. "You gotta buy me another, want me to risk my career listening to this."

I signaled the bartender. "What's wrong with my scenario?"

"What's wrong with it? For starters, the kid had a spotless record. You want me to believe he was dealing drugs?"

"Everybody has a spotless record until they get caught doing something wrong. And look at Whitmore's behavior the last few months: gets fired from his job, still has plenty of money, stops playing basketball with his friends. And one of them *said* Whitmore was into drugs."

"You never got fired from a job? So he gave up playground basketball, bought his mother a record player, a bracelet for some girl, that makes him a drug dealer? And all you got is Hurley's word some kid said Whitmore was into drugs, just like all you got is Hurley's word the kid said someone was waiting for it. Nase, all you got is Hurley's word the kid was carrying."

"You admitted you didn't like Hurley for this."

"I said it bothered me, he didn't have a story. Now he's got one. Maybe not a hundred percent there yet, but a few more visits with his lawyer and he'll be all ready for prime time. And aren't you leaving out one other thing?"

"What's that?"

"Even if I proved Whitmore was the main man from Medellin, so what? After I'm all done dirtying the kid's reputation, what have I got?"

"An alternative to Hurley."

"Great—that's all we need. We solve so many homicides, it's time to blow off a perfectly good perp so I can keep this file open?"

"Hal, Hurley isn't—"

"Nase, my good friend, there isn't enough beer in the world to get me to so much as *hint* this kid was into drugs, or that there is any doubt at all that Hurley is the man who did him. That little fracas you witnessed yesterday will look like a tea party compared to what'd come down on the man dumb enough to raise questions about the Whitmore kid. And that includes you."

"So Hurley goes away for the next fifteen years?"

"That's up to the jury. I'm not going to feel guilty about it, one way or the other. And if you want to feel guilty about something, I suggest you forget about your role in nailing Hurley and concentrate on what this group you're playing with has done to Flanagan and the department. To the whole damn town, come to think of it."

He set down his glass. "Gotta go. We're having a cross burning down at the station, and then we're gonna beat up a few blacks and Hispanics before that dildo Webster takes over as commissioner and stops all the fun. See ya."

After he left, I tried to see how hard it was to balance coins on their edges. Nickels were easy, pennies a challenge, but dimes were hopeless. The bar was too pitted, my fingers too clumsy, and I was doing the thing my teachers were always on me for, thinking about something else, instead of the task before me.

I thought about that grim room in the derelict apartment building, remembered the murderous man in the sleeveless T-shirt, imagined Whitmore's heart pounding as he went to report his loss. Had he discharged his promise to Hurley? Told the man he was getting out? In his fear, had he blurted out that a cop knew all about his business? That the cop was his friend, someone he'd liked to talk to, was going to talk to again in forty-eight hours?

Ah! I'd found a place on the tabletop just that much

flatter and now the shiny new dime looked like it would stand up forever. Little differences make all the difference. A few steps had made all the difference for Purnell Whitmore: just another few steps and Whitmore would have disappeared into the crack-house basement, Hurley wouldn't have seen him, and Whitmore would be alive today. Such a little thing, those few feet to the steps, to make such a big difference.

I bumped the table and the dime fell over. My teachers were right: you can't do a good job when your mind isn't on your work. I picked up the dime and ran back to put it to better use.

Nobody answered at first, but I didn't think they'd be out, and after ten rings, persistence paid off. "Hurley? Nason Nichols. No—I'm afraid not. But I want you to think hard—how far down the alley was Whitmore when you first saw him?"

A few seconds went by. "I'm pretty sure it was at least twenty feet, maybe thirty. It probably took me half a minute from the time I saw him in the mirror till I got back there, and I had to cover at least that much distance. Yeah—I'd say closer to thirty. Why?"

"There's a stairwell for the apartment house there, opens on the alley. Was he past that?"

Another wait. "I'm sorry, I don't remember a stairwell. I probably didn't . . . wait a minute. Sure—before the alley turns?"

"Right."

"Yeah, okay. I remember now, 'cause we passed the steps when we ducked into the alley. What was your question?"

"Was Whitmore past the stairwell when you first spotted him?"

No hesitation this time. "Yes, he was—he was just at the turn. That's why I couldn't make him out at first."

"And he was walking away from you—down the alley?"

"Yes, sir. May I ask what this is all about?"

"That stairwell leads into a crack house. But Whitmore had passed it when you saw him, so he wasn't going back to the crack house."

"But where was he going, then? Remember, he said—"

"I remember. Thanks. This may help."

chapter 36

"MR. NICHOLS, WHY DO YOU WANT TO ASK ME more about Purnell? The police have the man who killed Purnell."

"May I sit down?"

She hesitated, until her graciousness took over, then she stepped back from the door. "Please." She took a chair across from me. "They do have the man, don't they?"

"They think so."

"Then . . ."

"They have a man who will go to jail for a long time for killing Purnell, Mrs. Whitmore. And he should, if he did it."

"But you don't think he did." It was a statement, not a question.

"I have my doubts; some things don't fit. There were other ways Purnell could have been killed that night."

"Reverend James told me the police might try to protect their own. I thought, since they caught the man—"

"The police are convinced a policeman did it, and they're going to see to it he's convicted for it. I'm not a policeman, and I'm not trying to protect a man because he's a policeman. I don't want an innocent man to be punished, or a guilty man to escape punishment. Will you help me make sure they don't have the wrong man?"

"I want the man who murdered him punished. How can I help?"

"First, I have to tell you something I wish you didn't have to know. This isn't going to be easy for you."

"Mister, easy isn't something I know a lot about. Does it have something to do with what you told me the other day?"

"I'm afraid so. Mrs. Whitmore, there's reason to think Purnell was involved in selling drugs. I think that's why he was killed. I need to find out about that."

She didn't react as I'd expected; only the way she clutched the cushion showed me she'd heard. Her head sank slowly. I let it ride, and when she finally spoke, it wasn't anything I'd expected. "I knew it."

"You knew?"

She answered by getting to her feet and walking over to a cabinet. She came back with a small brown booklet and a black plastic box with a belt clip and handed them to me. "I was going through his things the other day, after you and Reverend James left. I found these in the back of his closet. I was afraid it meant he'd been up to something with drugs."

She pointed to the beeper. "People called him with that, didn't they—for drugs?"

"Probably." I turned it over and flipped the switch. "You said he was in such a hurry he forgot his watch that night. He must have forgotten this, too, or he didn't think he needed it. It has a switch, so it wouldn't go off if he was someplace where someone could hear it; that's why you hadn't heard it."

"And this . . ."—she flicked her finger at the bank book, hating to touch it—"this is drug money, isn't it?"

It was an Old Bay passbook for a branch near Copley Square, in Purnell's name. He'd opened it in June, a week after he'd gotten back from New Haven. I flipped through the entries—a hundred, two hundred at a time, some days more, deposits sometimes no more than a few days apart. I found the withdrawals for the stereo and the bracelet, but even with those, the balance was almost three thousand dollars.

"Yes, ma'am, I think so."

She put her shoulders back, lifted her chin. "I knew there was something wrong. Not drugs, maybe, but something. Purnell wasn't himself. He drew away from me, and it hurt. I knew, the way he acted when he brought home that stereo—like he was trying to . . . impress me. I thought of calling that dress shop, but I didn't because . . . because I couldn't stand the thought of his lying to me. If I had . . ."

She turned her head away, and when she turned back her eyes were dry.

"What happened to Purnell, Mr. Nichols?"

"The night Purnell was murdered, he was delivering drugs. I think that's why he left here an hour before he had to be at the church to get the bus. I'm guessing, but I think he went to a crack house, picked up some drugs, and took them to the place that was raided. Then he came back, and I think he was on his way to his last delivery when he ran into a policeman who had been looking for him—looking for him because he cared about him and had heard rumors. He was worried about him, Mrs. Whitmore, wanted to stop him before something bad happened."

"The policeman in the picture—the one they caught?"

"Yes, ma'am. Officer Hurley. He wanted Purnell's promise he'd stop."

"Did he say he would?"

"Yes. When he left Hurley, he meant to quit. He promised he would. Officer Hurley believed him."

Her jaw clenched. "I'm glad. How did Mr. Hurley know Purnell, Mr. Nichols?"

I told her how they'd met, and what Purnell had meant to Hurley, what Purnell must have been to have had that effect on Hurley.

"Why didn't Mr. Hurley tell the police what you've told me?"

"Purnell couldn't stand the idea of your finding out. That's why he said he'd stop. Hurley promised Purnell that if Purnell gave it up, he wouldn't tell you. He wanted to keep that promise. He believed in your son. I think he loved him."

"Bless him. Does he have children?"

"Yes, ma'am—a baby boy."

"I'll pray for him. Takes a lot of prayer, Mr. Nichols, raising a child."

"Purnell loved you, Mrs. Whitmore. At the end, he knew what was right, and he wanted to do right."

Her eyes teared, but behind the tears, there was pride. She smiled, her lips pressed hard together. "I'm glad. I'm glad he had right in his heart at the end."

"I think Purnell kept his promise, Mrs. Whitmore. After Hurley left him, I think he waited a few minutes, and then he went wherever he'd been going when Hurley stopped him. Then he told the person he'd been bringing the drugs to that he was giving up the drug business. Maybe he said a policeman knew what he had been doing. Maybe the person got angry, maybe he panicked at the thought that Purnell could tell on him, but either way, I think that person killed him."

"How can you find that person? I want to help."

"May I look through Purnell's room? There may be something else that will help."

I followed her back. She sat on the bed while I searched the room, starting with the closet. I moved on to the dresser, then asked her to move while I pulled the bed out.

"What are you looking for, Mr. Nichols?"

"I don't know—something that might have indicated who his customers were, where he was going that night. A notebook, an appointment book, something like that."

"I don't remember him carrying anything like that. Let me get you some coffee while you look."

There were lots of notebooks and pads in the desk, but none of them had anything of interest, and I had given up and was sitting at the desk when she returned with the coffee and set it next to my elbow.

"Mrs. Whitmore—wasn't there a desk calendar here the last time?"

"Why, yes. I threw it away the other day. Couldn't stand seeing it, coming from the funeral home and just . . . stopping where it did. You don't suppose . . . ?"

Trash collection in Roxbury isn't good; bluebottles and yellow-jackets droned over the battered can that had a while to fester before pick-up day. I pushed aside a bag of garbage and pulled out the stiff, folded calendar.

Back in the house, we spread it on the coffee table. The Pops concert outing was penciled in: seven-thirty. Shawna Moore could know he'd meant to come. And that meant that Purnell's cocaine drop-off was probably somewhere between the crack house and the church.

I looked back over the entries for August, then sorted through the sheets and saw that he'd kept the previous months, slipping them to the back of the stack in turn. The months he'd been at college were blank, but June and July had numerous markings.

"Purnell went to the church a lot, didn't he? I understand he was seen there often." There were two or three entries a week, some marked "FC", which I took to mean fellowship class, others just "church."

"Oh, yes. Reverend James said he had a vocation. I had hopes he might enter the ministry some day."

I pulled out the bank book and scanned it again, then

compared it to the calendar. I pulled out my own notebook and jotted down some dates.

"What do you see, Mr. Nichols?"

"I'm not sure I see anything, but some days Purnell deposited only fifty or a hundred dollars in this account? Well, most times, the evening before, he'd been to the church."

"But he'd always spent a lot of time with the church. I brought him up that way."

"The night he was killed, he had packages of cocaine in his pocket when Hurley stopped him. He was due at the church to catch the bus, and he told Hurley someone was waiting for it. A little while later, someone saw a person walking toward the church—it might have been Purnell."

"Then you think someone at the church . . ."

"It's possible."

"But who . . ."

"I don't know, but I've got an idea."

chapter 37

I'D BEEN LUCKY: THE WOMAN IN THE BOSTON Business College registration office had told me that Ben Crews had ten minutes before his Introductory Accounting class started. I'd fought my way up the crowded stairway and found him putting up pictures under a caption on a bulletin board at the back of his classroom: CAREERS IN ACCOUNTING.

He stepped back and looked at the display, then swapped two of the pictures and stepped back again. Satisfied, he nodded and offered his hand. "You're looking better than you did the other day at the church, Mr. Nichols."

"Lot better than I would if you hadn't come along when you did."

"Don't like to see a man jump someone from the back, the way that fellow jumped you. Man's got a beef, ought to be man enough to handle it face to face. 'Course, a real man ought to be able to walk away from it altogether. Turn the other cheek, the good book says. What can I do for you?"

"I'm still following up on the Whitmore murder—hoped you might be able to answer a few more questions."

"Why? I thought they had the man."

"They have a policeman they think did it. Now I'm trying to make sure there are no loose ends."

"Well, I'll tell you what I know." He pointed to a couple of desk chairs. "Let's take the weight off. I walked from one end of Korea to the other and back again; feet've never been the same." He sank into a seat with a relieved sigh.

"You're at the church quite a bit?"

"At least two or three times a week, and Sundays of course. Married a church-going woman, and when I got out of the service, I figured maybe it was time I made up for some of the foolishness I'd gotten into over the years. Been teaching kids and helping with odd jobs ever since. The church has come to mean a lot to me."

"Did you know the Whitmore boy very well?"

"Yes, sir. Saw him grow up from a tadpole. That was a fine young man; like to see the man responsible pay for it."

"He was in your fellowship classes?"

"Yes, sir."

"You said you're at the church two or three times a week. You have classes that often?"

"No, sir. During the summer, just the fellowship classes for the older kids, Tuesday nights. The other times I go by and try to keep the books in order, do a little maintenance."

"Any particular time?"

"Nights, mostly. Church isn't air conditioned—gets fearful hot days."

"I understand Purnell Whitmore didn't attend your classes too regularly this summer."

"Active young man, home from college—I can understand that."

"I'm not saying there was anything wrong with it, Mr.

Crews, just that from what I've learned, Purnell wasn't in class very often. Is that right?"

"Yes, sir, that's so. I'd been looking forward to his help with the younger kids, but he came to class only a couple times this summer and left early at that. Rather shoot the breeze outside than sit inside on a nice summer night, I guess. Can't say I blame him."

"Not at all. Is that what he did—hang around outside a lot?"

"I don't know about a lot; I'd see him there from time to time. There's a pop machine in the basement. Young folks get a cold drink, sit out back of the church and talk, maybe smoke. Not a lot of safe places they can do that in Roxbury. No harm to it, except maybe the smoking, and everybody's a damn fool when he's young."

"But Whitmore had signed up for the Pops concert the night he was killed?"

"That's right. Quite a few signed up who didn't come to classes too regularly."

"You didn't see him at all that night?"

"No, sir. I held the bus as long as I could, but when he wasn't there by seven-forty, we had to go; little Shawna Moore was pretty upset about it. But the other kids were getting antsy and the concert started at eight. We were late as it was."

"I thought the bus left at seven-thirty?"

"Supposed to, but Shawna asked if I wouldn't hold up, so I did—long as I could."

"The nights you're there—are there other people around?"

"In the summer?"

"Yes, sir."

"Well, Tuesday and Thursday nights, it's pretty busy—classes for the kids, the ladies have a tea, and there's men's and women's Bible study. Otherwise, in the summer it's usually pretty quiet during the week. Oftentimes, there won't be a car in the lot—except the reverend's, of course.

It's usually there. And his visitors' cars, when he has visitors."

"Get many of those?"

"Yes, sir. Reverend James is quite active in the community, you know. Always meeting with people. A lot of them come by after work."

"Any of them come around regularly?"

"This summer, you mean?"

"Right."

Crews reflected. "There's a Dr. Bradley, lady works at the drug rehabilitation clinic. Reverend James does counseling with them, and she's been in quite a bit."

"Anyone else you can recall?"

He pursed his lips. "Well, there's that fellow tangled with you the other day, but I don't know his name."

"Corey Webster?"

"Like I say, I don't know his name, but he's been around quite a bit."

"How often have you seen him, would you guess?"

"This summer?"

"Yes, sir."

"Didn't always see him. Lot of times I'd just see his Jeep when I'd pull in, figure he was with Reverend James or out back jabbering at the kids."

"That crazy-looking car?"

His face broke out in a broad grin. "That's the one. Damndest looking thing I ever saw, and I've seen a lot of beat-up Jeeps."

"You say he spent a lot of time with the kids?"

"A fair amount, I guess."

"Did you ever see him with Purnell Whitmore?"

He leaned back and twiddled his thumbs while he looked at the ceiling. "I did, come to think of it. Saw them talking by his Jeep one night, oh"—he looked back up at the ceiling—"maybe a month ago. 'Course, if he ran into Purnell out back of the church, I wouldn't have known."

"How often do you think you may have seen him or his car there this summer?"

"All the time. Ask me, too often." He stared at me as though challenging me to report him for insubordination.

"You said you didn't think too much of him. What did you mean?"

He glanced up at the clock. "Kids'll be coming in in a minute. 'Kids'—huh." He chuckled. "Lot of 'em your age. Most of them have worked all day—minimum-wage jobs, a lot of them, and they're tired. But they want to get ahead, and some of them will. People like that fellow you're talking about do a lot more harm than good, telling folks they've been cheated, ought to have it handed to 'em by politicians or get it in the streets, shouldn't have to work for it. Bunch of bull. Glad Pastor James seems to have reached the same conclusion. Haven't seen that junk heap around since that day you were there."

"Did you ever talk to Webster?"

"Don't know if I'd call it talk. Ran into him one night coming out of the church. Would have thought I was his long-lost brother until he saw the VFW pin in my lapel. Then he started giving me all this guff about white militarism. Went completely haywire."

"Haywire?"

"Yelling, waving his arms, not making a lot of sense. Something about black men like me selling out to the white man for an army paycheck. I told him the army was the best thing that ever happened to me and ought to happen to more wild kids like I was. Then the damn fool tried to shove some leaflet in my pocket and tore my jacket."

"What did you do?"

"Introduced my shoe to the seat of his pants. My wife said it wasn't Christian." Crews laughed, a deep, rumbling noise. "I told her I was just helping him turn the other cheek."

I laughing with him, enjoying the image. When I stopped,

I said, "He met with Reverend James the night Whitmore was killed. Did you see him that night?"

He pursed his lips and squinted. "Not him, but that car, come to think of it. Saw his Jeep when I arrived."

"What time was that?"

"Umm—say seven o'clock or so. I walked over after dinner, wanted to fix a leaky faucet before we left. Reverend James's car was there, and that heap."

"Any other cars there?"

He thought about it, then shook his head. "No, sir. Just the Lincoln and the Jeep."

"Where was the bus parked?"

"In the lot, between the two cars."

"Was Webster's Jeep there when the bus left?"

"No, sir."

"You're sure?"

"Pastor James's car was all that was there."

We looked up as people started filing into the classroom, first in ones and twos, and then in bunches. "Well, Mr. Nichols, if there's nothing more, I've got to make accounting interesting for the next two hours."

A lot of them did look tired, but they pepped up as Crews tossed out a little banter. When I left, he was lining them up in rows, debits on one side, credits on the other. The poor woman who was supposed to be equity got in the wrong line and drew KP.

chapter 38

A BUZZ PASSED THROUGH THE THRONG CROWD-ing the City Hall rotunda, and I craned to see what was causing it. The message Endicott had left on my answering machine had said only that I'd want to attend the four-o'clock news conference the mayor had called. I'd had to take it on faith, because he wasn't in when I called back.

I spotted O'Conor, working both sides of the parting crowd, and then Kershaw's steely gray mop as his heron legs carried him up the steps onto the dais, followed by Peggy and the dog. After a few last handshakes and shoulder squeezes, O'Conor bounded up the steps after them. I saw Endicott standing just below the platform, but there was no way to get close to him.

Lynn Daniels, her back to me, stood dwarfed next to James as they both stared up at the mayor. I wondered how she'd react when I told her what I'd told Endicott; wondered if she'd laugh as he had. I hoped not, because then I was going to take it to the papers, and I didn't want to see it on the funny pages. I also wondered if she'd laugh when I told her the other thing I'd been playing with all morning, something I hadn't shared with anyone. I didn't think so, although I thought she might start civil commitment proceedings.

O'Conor grabbed Kershaw's hand and held it in his own. Strobe lights flashed, and I wondered if Peggy could feel them. Then the mayor dropped Kershaw's hand, cleared his throat, and requested quiet. The hubbub succumbed, gradually, until only the occasional cough marred the silence.

"My fellow citizens." A pause, a searching look over the crowd, though it was unlikely O'Conor could see past the floodlights into the murk. "Only days ago, I appeared in this hall to introduce to you the distinguished men and women who had agreed, at considerable personal sacrifice and acting in the highest traditions of public service, to investigate allegations that the Boston Police Department, as a direct result of the mismanagement and malfeasance of the Commissioner of Police, Francis Flanagan, had become a rogue force, actively threatening the well-being of large groups of our citizens and contemptuous of our ordered liberties."

He paused again, slicked his hair, resumed. "At that time, I assured you that the Mayor's Commission on Civil Justice, chaired by Eliot Kershaw, who is respected throughout the world for his integrity and dedication to the public good, would proceed in a thorough, expeditious, and—above all—dispassionate and objective manner, and would report its conclusions objectively, unswayed by popular passions or political considerations.

"Regrettably, recent developments have made it imprudent to await the commission's official report before taking remedial action. Mr. Kershaw contacted me yesterday and advised me that in his capacity as chairman, he, alone among the commission members, had been regularly and fully briefed by the investigatory staff. Owing to the highly inflammatory situation provoked by the premature release of the commission staff's findings, he offered to release *his* conclusions, subject to the caveat that his fellow members have yet to be briefed.

"In view of my pledge to you at the outset, Mr. Kershaw has not advised me of the substance of the conclusions he has reached, beyond confirming that, in light of the regrettable but ultimately fortuitous disclosure of the staff report, he felt his views would underscore the need for prompt action against the responsible official and contribute to the healing process."

He stopped and looked in the direction of a tiny band of Flanagan stalwarts, standing at the edge of the crowd with doleful expressions and a few WE BACK DAP signs crudely lettered on torn cardboard. "Given the lingering expressions of support for Commissioner Flanagan among some segments of the community, and the likelihood that they would continue to foster social unrest unless dispelled immediately, I concurred. Such is Eliot Kershaw's standing and experience, I have no doubt that when the full record is available, his views will command a solid consensus, both within the commission and throughout the Boston community."

O'Conor paused and looked down at the lectern. When he resumed, it was in softer tones, tinged with sorrow. "In my three terms as your mayor, nothing has caused me greater personal pain than learning that a man I appointed as the city's highest police official had not only allowed but encouraged individuals within the police department to indulge the darker side of their nature, turning that instrument of justice into a tool of oppression. That an exemplary young man lost his life as a result is a burden I will carry the remainder of my days."

He stopped, swallowed, gripped the lectern. When he continued, the satin voice gave way to a halting rasp, low and contrite. "I accept whatever judgment you, the people of Boston, feel fit to render regarding *my* responsibility for this tragic turn. You can render no judgment heavier than the one I already bear. However harshly you judge me, though, do not let your faith in our safety forces flag. A few—very few, I have no doubt—men indulged and encouraged by the dark passions and ruthless ambition of Francis Flanagan must not be allowed to stain the spotless record of the almost two thousand honorable men and women of the Boston Police Department, who risk their lives daily that we may breathe free of the scourge of fear."

He threw back his head, dropped his hands, and when sound again emerged, it was from the mighty instrument that had brought him so far. "I pledge to give you a police department ably and honorably led, as vigilant in its pursuit of law-breakers as it is in its commitment to the law."

O'Conor bathed the first rows in the light from his emerald eyes, captured the upturned faces and caressed them with a gaze so tender, so empathetic, that a shudder rippled across half a dozen onlookers. "And finally, I am today *demanding* that the governor honor his campaign rhetoric by making available *without further delay* sufficient funds to add three hundred uniformed officers to the force, *or prepare to yield his office to one who will!"*

He stood immobile, accepting humbly the applause that burst out of the mass before him, then silenced it with a sober look and an upraised hand. "And now, Eliot Kershaw."

There was a new spring in the old man's step as he stepped to the microphone and deposited a thick, spiral-bound volume on the lectern. "Thank you, Mr. Mayor." The mayor returned the head-bob and retreated, but only by inches, remaining well within camera range.

"The mayor has alluded to the distribution of a *purported* staff report and the distress it has occasioned. In order to correct whatever misapprehensions may have been created by the dissemination of this document, I asked my chief investigator to furnish me with the *actual* results of her analyses. I have those with me today." He squared the report before him and continued. "In addition, as the mayor said, I have been fully apprised throughout of the substance of her review of all police misconduct allegations since Commissioner Flanagan assumed office."

O'Conor's was not the only jaw to drop at the reference to an "actual" staff report, but his was the only face to draw a blind woman's triumphant stare. He looked back at her in something approaching bewilderment.

Kershaw went on. "Few crimes are more offensive than betrayal of the public trust by a public official administering his or her office to the detriment of the citizenry. Aided by experienced investigatory personnel, I have reviewed allegations that Police Commissioner Francis Flanagan has betrayed the trust reposed in him.

"The evidence was subjected to such verification as our able chief investigator thought appropriate. The results of those efforts, as well as my conclusions and recommendations, are detailed in this report,"—he tapped the binder on the lectern—"copies of which will be available to the press and public immediately following this session."

Kershaw took a sip of water. "I will now read my summary of the staff's findings." He opened the report, smoothed the page with his right hand, and deposited a pair of half-glasses on the end of his long nose. Clearing his throat, he began. "After careful consideration of the record, I conclude that there is evidence—compelling evidence— that this city official has knowingly abused his office for political gain. I recommend that this official be removed from office and that the evidence be presented to the appropriate law-enforcement authorities for criminal prosecution."

A great peace settled over O'Conor's face as Kershaw's words sank in. Kershaw shut the report decisively, strobes lighting the hall like fireworks on the fourth as a mounting drone poured out of the audience.

"Mr. Kershaw, Mr. Kershaw . . ." The reporters in the front row thrust microphones like beggars soliciting alms.

"No questions, I'm afraid." He turned to the mayor, who was wearing a sad, stricken look. "Thank you, Mr. Mayor."

The mayor stepped up to the microphone. "On behalf of the people of Boston, Eliot, may I express our gratitude to you. I am gratified that, whatever the origins of the *purported* draft,"—he looked uncertainly at Peggy—"the conclusions are unaffected, confirming the propriety of my actions against former Commissioner Flanagan."

"*Mr. Kershaw!*" The mayor broke off abruptly as every head swiveled to the dazzling Una Selkirk, one knee on the dais, electric-blue skirt ridden up over fishbelly thighs. She grasped the podium and, with a grunt into her microphone that sounded like the last stage of birthing, heaved herself onto the platform. Grasping the lectern, she clambered to her feet, smoothed her hair, flicked on the stage grimace, and grabbed Kershaw with an intensity that suggested he'd leave his arm behind if he tried to pull away. "Eliot, just one question. What did Commissioner Flanagan—"

"Now, really. It wouldn't be appropriate. If you'll read the report . . ." He looked about for help from the rooted onlookers.

"Report! My audience doesn't want to wait for some report. I've got three hundred thousand people out there who have a right to know: what did Commissioner Flanagan *do*? Just sum it up, Mr. Kershaw. For me? Puleeze?" She pulled on her fetching, little-girl-lost face, the microphone weaving two inches from Kershaw's chin.

"Oh, my goodness." Kershaw looked flustered, his bow tie's jiggle mirroring his agitation. "My goodness. S'pose I should have learned better than to expect you people to report accurately. Never said Commissioner Flanagan did anything; said 'read the report.'" He pulled his arm from her clutch with surprising vigor and started to walk away.

"But you said"—she looked frantically at her notepad—" 'there is compelling evidence this city official has abused his office for political gain.'" Goggle eyes roamed over Kershaw's face. "It *was* Commissioner Flanagan you were investigating, wasn't it?"

He turned back, shook his head. "His administration of the department, certainly. And it quickly became clear that Commissioner Flanagan is doing a first-rate job—first-rate—as his handling of the unfortunate event the other evening should have made obvious. Reminds me of—"

"But then who *is* the official you were referring to?"

Kershaw looked at her as though she'd just burst in on him in his bath. "Why, the mayor, of course. Man has no character at all. Wanted to sell off the public purse for private gain. Suborned a member of this commission. All down on tape, you know. Read it in the report." He gave a curt nod and trotted off-scene with a sprightliness that would have done credit to a man half his age.

chapter 39

NO ONE IN THAT ROTUNDA WILL EVER FORGET the moment as first one, then a dozen, then hundreds of voices came together in the anthem that rolled out of the crowd and broke like waves upon the dais and the stricken figure of Conor O'Conor. And though I could see his mouth moving, animal reflexes summoning unheard words of denial, explanation, expiation, accusation—all the tools of the political man—my mind still holds a fixed picture of the small, pale face of a boy in short pants, standing before Gehenna, viewing a sight more ghastly than even the sisters, who'd tried to tell him, had been able to paint.

I had no interest in the auto-da-fé; as I turned away, Una Selkirk was jabbing her electronic phallus at O'Conor, her mask twisted by the orgasmic rictus a man in his death throes brings her breed. The prophetic voice of Reverend James, soaring over even that great chorus, was already declaring to all who would listen the vindication of his faith in Francis Flanagan and the certain retribution that awaited the evil little man who had bound his people's fate to corrupt ambition.

Whatever O'Conor had done, it was no uglier than the spirit gripping that hall. I left it behind as quickly as I could, bolted for the street, and greeted it joyfully, reveling in the comfort of ordinary people doing ordinary things.

An old woman pushing through a trash barrel, tucking odd bits in a string bag. Offering her a dollar for a broken lamp. Strolling on, another trash can, recycling the lamp. Pigeons pecking at an old man's scattered love; a cool mist, the matching steam from the gilt teakettle over the Golden Kettle's door; the ferris wheel in Eric Fuchs's Hobby Shop; rows of stately cigars in Ehrlich's window; noisy boys stirring the Common's sod; the Garden's brash mums, daring frost to do its worst; swan boats softly swimming, only days until hibernation; the beckoning glow of the Ritz Bar.

"A Special, Henry."

"Right away, Mr. Nichols."

"Better make that three, I think. Will you join us?"

I heard the voice at the same time I felt the dog's nose in the seat of my pants; whirling, I almost knocked the owner over.

"I've told you not to do that, Leba—just because you like it doesn't mean that people do."

"How did you know I was here?"

"When you lose your vision . . ." She smiled.

"Really."

"We followed you."

"You and Leba?"

"She has many talents, but she's not Rex the Wonderdog. Sowell saw you leaving; he led us."

I looked around and spotted Endicott at a corner table. He waved, and I returned it, tentatively.

"Why?"

"I thought you deserved an explanation."

"You don't owe me anything."

"I got you wrong. I don't like to do that."

"We'll take the drinks over there, Henry." I led the way over to the table. Endicott and I shook hands. "Quite an afternoon, Mr. Nichols."

"Nase, please. Did you know?"

Endicott flashed a look at Peggy. "Yes, I knew."

"How did it work?"

"Better let Peggy tell it."

We waited while a waiter unloaded the stemmed glasses; the carafes of clear liquid; the little dish of olives, onions, and lemon peel; the silver salver of peanuts. Endicott poured for Peggy.

She hunted out a peanut, washed it down with martini, looked off into space, if only inwardly.

"Peggy?" Endicott laid his hand gently on her forearm.

"Oh—sorry. Where should I begin?"

"The beginning?"

"The beginning? I don't think so; not today." The tight, red curls bobbed. "No, not the beginning. A trial never starts with the beginning; that would take forever. Let's just start with what we need to convict. Let's do a closing argument, summarizing the evidence.

"Yes." She drew herself up, as though approaching the jury box. She took another swallow of her drink and laid her hands on the table. "Let's say it began with a phone call. Yes, that's as good a place to start as any." Her hand curled around the glass, and for a second I thought she was going to retreat into some private place, but then she tossed her head and started to talk, and it was as though she opened with "Ladies and gentlemen of the jury . . ."

"It started with a phone call from my uncle. Three days after the Whitmore boy was murdered. Wouldn't I join him for dinner, it had been so long, so much catching up to do, so on.

"Strange, I thought—quite strange. You see, my uncle and I, we have a . . . distant relationship, have had ever since I left for the school for the blind. Never any harsh words, the occasional dinner with supporters, a bit of chitchat about the career, that sort of thing—but no one-on-one." She turned a peanut in her fingers, bit the end, held the rest in front of her mouth as though it were something larger. "So I thought, *He wants something, wants something from me.*" She swallowed the nub, took another drink. "I liked that, wanted to know what it was. And so I accepted.

"His driver comes for me, takes me to the house." She drained the drink. "The house where I grew up.

"The housekeeper has been given the night off, and we will have a tête-à-tête, because there is no rich divorcée or widow to be Conor's hostess, no elegant couple from the North Shore to ensnare in the cult. And this is also odd, uncommonly odd, because if it were my funeral, Conor O'Conor would consider it criminal waste not to make it serve double duty.

"So there we were, alone again in that house on Front Street, me and Uncle. He is charming and solicitous, devotedly attentive, as he serves drinks, grills the steaks, every inch the devoted, surrogate parent—and a consummate actor he is." She touched the glass and Endicott filled it with the residue from the carafe. Her manner said, "Be there; see this; see it as I did."

I began to understand her success with juries, her edge over defense counsel. She lived in a world of word-paintings, where her adversaries would always be strangers. Now she painted for us, taking us back, into the present. I glanced at Endicott. He returned the look, shook his head; I held my peace.

"'How is work?' Her boss, the DA, tells him she's the best prosecutor in the office, her future holds no limits, he's so proud of her, perhaps he can be of some assistance? And now she *knows* he wants something, for Uncle *always* expects payment—there are no gifts, only debts.

"He plays the light conversationalist, the witty raconteur.

Does she think the orchestra sounds the same now that Ozawa's gone, has she heard what Tip O'Neill wanted on his tombstone? He flatters her judgment. Does she think the tax levy stands a chance, is Parker a good man for the council slot? And she thinks, 'What is his agenda? What does he want?' Because she knows this man, knows him better than anybody, knows that he *always* has an agenda, that there is no idle chatter, no interest in any subject but the one that looks out from the mirror while he practices spontaneous expressions, which she spied him doing, back when she could see.

"Finally, after dinner, he edges around to it. Let us go into the den, enjoy the warmth of the fire, a little cognac, perhaps. She feels for an armchair, but he steers her to the couch. She senses he is leading up to his proposition, and she has the dog with her, so she does not resist."

Peggy's lips narrowed. She rested her fingertips briefly on the edge of the table, gathered herself, took a deep breath. She felt for the glass, shook the last drops down her throat, continued while I signaled the waiter.

"He eases himself onto the other end of the couch, his weight sinking slowly, carefully, no sudden movement to alarm the blind lady. He clears his throat. Has she heard about this boy killed in Roxbury, this fine young man tragically, *savagely* murdered?

" 'Yes,' she says, 'I heard about that,' wondering where this is going.

" 'A policeman was seen with the boy just before he was killed. A policeman could be the killer.'

" 'Yes,' she says, 'I heard that. That's very possible.'

" 'Some people are concerned that the police may not try hard enough to catch one of their own; concerned that they'll cover up a murder committed in the heat of a Blue Tornado raid.'

"She knows that the police will bend heaven and earth to find this man and take him down if he did this, but all she says is 'Yes, some people think that, but what can you do?'

"He says he's thinking about appointing a commission, an independent citizen's group to monitor the investigation, but he isn't sure."

"She knows he is always sure, never floats an idea without first knowing his own mind, but she says, 'That's a good idea—why wouldn't you?'

"He grows quiet, until she feels him slide closer to her. And she holds her pose, doesn't flinch, doesn't sidle away, even when he rests his hand on her knee, drops his voice, that wonderful, warm, seductive voice. 'You know, Peggy, you're the only family I have. You've been like a daughter to me.'

"'Oh,' she trills, 'What a nice thought'—safe, because irony is not a voice he knows. Uncle Conor has never perched above himself, imagined a world existing outside of himself, a world where he could be mocked.

"'Tell me—what do you think of Dapper Flanagan?'

"'What do I . . . think of him?'

"'Well, do you think that he's gone . . . overboard with this program of his? That maybe the police department is a little . . . out of control, even . . . threatening to our . . . minority citizens? Is it possible that he's . . . pandering to people's . . . baser instincts?'

"And she has to stifle a laugh, it has such a campaign ring to it, that phrase. How many times had he practiced it in front of that mirror? She reads her uncle like a book, knows him as well as anyone can claim to know him, knows that in his entire life, he hasn't spent thirty seconds worrying about abstractions like due process or equal protection; knows that if he is worried about Dapper Flanagan, it has a political spin to it, knows Uncle is building up to what he wants from her, wants to help him get there.

"So she appears thoughtful, hand on chin. 'Why,' she says, 'I never thought about that. I suppose I thought, "Maybe the police are just doing a better job now."' And she adds, 'And gee, Flanagan seems awful popular with the cops I talk to, and the victims I talk to, witnesses and such—why, I get the impression that maybe a lot of people are pretty happy with Dapper Flanagan.'

"And he winces; she feels his pain, begins to understand, even as he continues. 'I'm worried about Flanagan. He's a . . . a Neanderthal!'

"'A "Neanderthal." Hmm. He *is* sort of a throwback, isn't he?'

"'Exactly. I knew you'd see it . . . Oh, I'm sorry, I didn't . . . I shouldn't have . . .'

"And he's something he never is—at a loss for words—because he has alluded to her blindness, and he has not done this before, not since it happened, because it sickens him, causes a physical revulsion. She felt it from the beginning, *loves* it. 'But I *do* see it, see it perfectly. I understand exactly what you're saying.' And she does, you see: Conor O'Conor, mayor of Boston, rising political star on the national horizon, is afraid; afraid of a simple man he had plucked out of the heap because he thought he knew him, thought he knew his limitations. But he had made a mistake, because he had spent so much of his life spotting men's weaknesses that he had been blind, far blinder than she, to the threat posed by a simple man who could not be easily shed and who would do his duty without calculation.

"'I understand *exactly* what you mean, Uncle Conor—but what should *we* do?'

"And he liked that, the *we*, as she knew he would; that was why she used it. Reassured, he continues. 'It's that a lot of people are drawn to Flanagan's kind of quick fixes, but they don't see that they don't get to the root causes of crime.'

"She nods, feeds him a straight line, the drivel she's heard him mouthing at suburban fundraisers: 'They think that by arresting criminals, you cut down on crime; they don't realize that poverty and racism are behind it.'

"She worries she may have gone too far, sung out of tune, hears the faint doubt in his voice. 'I thought maybe you were pretty old-school that way, Peggy.'

" 'Oh, I am, I am,' she hastens to add, 'the way *you* are. But we can't *break* the law to enforce it.'

"He likes that, likes thinking he's seen as tough on crime, tries 'can't break the law to enforce it,' so she knows she'll hear it in a speech soon.

" 'Why not fire him, Uncle Conor? Maybe this isn't the kind of man who ought to be running the police department.'

" 'I wish it were that easy. God damn it, I wish I could.' He lifts the hand from her knee, smacks it against the other hand."

The polite hush of the Ritz Bar was broken by the sound of her hands smacking together. The dog looked up, smiled benevolently, sank its face back on its paws. " 'I would in a second, but he can be removed only for cause. Otherwise, he's in for over three more years. God knows what he can do in that time.' And he adds, as an afterthought, 'What ideas he might get.'

" 'Of course,' she says, understanding *everything*, 'I forgot. And I suppose the people who *like* what Flanagan's doing, who don't see how . . . dangerous it is—why, they wouldn't understand if you tried to remove him. I mean, even if you could.'

"And he yells—something she'd never heard before— yells like a man in pain: ' "Tried to remove him"'? Why, the *Clarion*'s running editorials talking about what a great mayor he'd make!'

" 'Oh, don't worry,' she says, 'they always endorsed you before; I'm sure they will again.'

" 'God damn it, I can't take that chance. If I'm going for governor, I can't be tied to a bunch of inner-city red-necks; I've got to be able to articulate a truly . . . *progressive* approach to urban problems without worrying about getting jumped on by some *Neanderthal* mouthing simplistic catch-phrases for the parishioners to echo.'

"And there it was: there were people he needed to climb the next rung, and people he didn't need anymore, but it wouldn't do to leave the refuse with a potential voice. Ergo, Flanagan had to be destroyed. My uncle is a logical man, you see?"

She took another peanut, brought it to her mouth, put it down. "After that, it was child's play."

Her hands moved to her glasses, touched them, repositioned them on her nose, her voice small and distant. "Playing with a child." She drifted away, chuckled, came back, may-it-please-the-court voice once more in full control. " 'You're right there,' she says. 'You're going to need big money to run for governor, too; better not to have Flanagan's supporters nursing a grievance. Best if they decide Dapper let you down, I think.'

" 'Exactly,' he says. She feels his eyes on her. 'Peggy—' And his hand moves down from the top of the couch, rests on her shoulder; his fingers toy with the hair at the base of her neck. 'What would you think if this commission had a . . . broader mandate than just making sure the police do a thorough job with the Whitmore murder?'

"She knows she musn't vomit—it would spoil the moment—so it's a spider, a horrible, hairy spider—but only a spider, not his hand—and the feeling passes. 'But what would it do?' she says, although she can see it as clearly as if she had twenty-twenty vision.

" 'Suppose . . .' he says, as though it's coming to him on the spur of the moment, although of course he's thought out every nuance, every angle, played it through a thousand times before. 'Suppose I said that because of the Whitmore tragedy, we might as well address certain questions that have been raised about Flanagan's stewardship of the department, and we want this commission to look at that and prepare a report? Sort of settle the issue, once and for all? Adding that I have complete confidence that Flanagan has been doing a wonderful job and will be fully vindicated, of course.'

" 'Of course. But what,' she says, 'if this commission sees things the same as the . . . people who have become such

enthusiastic Flanagan supporters? It could even result
in . . . a ringing endorsement for Flanagan.'

" 'Well,' he says, and she could feel his eagerness, '*I* would
decide who serves on the commission.'

" 'True,' she replies, 'but it won't do any good if they're
all . . . the kind of people you need next year. I mean, some
of the public thinks Flanagan's critics are, well, opposed to
him precisely *because* he's doing the job he . . . should be
doing. Wouldn't you have to appoint at least *some* people
Flanagan's supporters trust, so if *they* should condemn
him . . . ?'

" 'You're right—you're so damn right.' He keeps the hand
on her shoulder but draws back, pauses, looks at her.
Admiration has *weight*, she realizes, can be felt, gives
power. 'But Peggy, how could you be sure, then, that their
conclusions would be . . . supportable?'

" 'Ah,' she says, 'perhaps *I* could help'—knowing, of
course, that he had that in mind all the time, else why come
to her in the first place? And she explains to him about use-
of-force reports and Review Board records and how . . .
judgment might bear on . . . selection of the data and how
it's . . . interpreted. 'After all, none of these people you'd
appoint would be experts. They'd need . . . *help* understanding the record, putting things in context.' And she
feels his eyes on her, knows he is thinking how clever she
is—she is his girl after all.

" 'I knew you'd understand. I wish my advisors had your
political instincts,' he says, and he tousles her hair. And this
time, she does flinch, but he's too absorbed to notice.

" 'How could they? They weren't raised by you, Conor.'
And before he can tousle her hair again, she adds, 'Yes,
maybe I could help . . .'

"And he says, 'I was hoping you'd say that. I'm sure you
can. With your experience, you could help these people
reach an . . . informed judgment.'

" 'I'm sure I could.' And she seals the bargain the way
that will give her absolute credibility with him: 'Of course,

with that kind of exposure, I'd be a logical candidate for the DA's job.'

"And he studies her face again, then gives a little chuckle, and says, 'You know, I do believe Martin is getting a little long in the tooth. And the women's groups would love it.'

"'So,' she adds, 'would the handicapped. You'd probably get national attention.'

"And he pauses, then chuckles again—nervously at first, then getting comfortable with it. 'Damn, you're sharp. You're right—you're a two-fer.' And he laughs out loud, squeezes her shoulder, kisses her cheek.

"And she makes herself reach out, find his face, touch it, hold her hand against it. 'You *have* treated me like your own. Now *I'll* take care of *you*.'"

"Now do you understand, Nase?" Endicott's voice held a little wonder; after the story we'd just heard, I could understand why.

I was watching Peggy and the dog work their way to the door and didn't answer right away. The handsome people in their pinstripes and pumps couldn't tear their eyes away, any more than I could. Leba moved through them with the same indifference she'd worn at the Oyster House. So did Peggy, for that matter.

"Why she did it, yes. How's still a little unclear."

"How was easy, as long as O'Conor thought she was on his side. She had to keep him thinking that, until it was too late for him to stop it. That's why we coopered up the dummy report to show him."

"How did Kershaw fit in?"

"He was O'Conor's Good Housekeeping Seal of Approval. Peggy would produce the indictment; Kershaw would have no reason to question it, and his endorsement would go a long way in selling it to the suckers. Only Peggy met with him, decided right away that whatever else had slipped, the character hadn't. So she told him what was up."

"Why not just go public with it up front?"

"I gather that was Kershaw's first reaction, too. But then what? Peggy pointed out that O'Conor would just deny it, say she'd misunderstood him. He'd come back with another team and do it anyway. No, she had to play along until they had O'Conor cold."

"So the idea was Kershaw would control the process, while Peggy fed O'Conor?"

"Right. That's why he insisted Peggy report only to him."

"And Finn was O'Conor's anchor in the parishes?"

"Exactly: no-nonsense guy, calls it like he sees it, made all kinds of noise about liking what Flanagan was doing. When *he* said Flanagan had to go, people weren't going to question it. Southie, Charlestown, the white ethnic groups—they'd figure O'Conor had no choice and wouldn't turn on him. In return, O'Conor was going to take care of Seaside for Finn. Get the city to fill it with public offices, pay heavy rent."

"What'd Kershaw mean, it's all on tape?"

"After that night O'Conor first raised it with her, she took a wire every time she talked with him. Phone calls, too. At first he was real cagey—never said anything that couldn't be explained away. But after a while, when he figured everybody was playing their part and Peggy was in as deep as he was, he opened up. The night you came to my place? You'd heard Peggy reporting to Kershaw that she'd met with O'Conor that morning, showed him the draft report that was supposed to keep O'Conor happy till we finished with the real thing. She went wired. Played to his ego, led him over it. We have him laying out the whole thing."

"So *that's* what she meant when she told Kershaw it was crystal clear. Boy, did I get that wrong. Who leaked Peggy's draft to the press?"

"Has to have been O'Conor. Finn was pressing him pretty hard to get it finished. Peggy left a copy; he must have figured why wait. It really screwed things up—we'd figured on finishing the work, being ready with the facts, then tossing in the O'Conor deal for icing."

"Now you're saying 'we'—how'd you get in the program?"

"Sheer luck. Peggy made quite an impression on me, that first meeting. I decided to, ah, harass the help."

"There goes your Supreme Court appointment."

"Ah, well. Anyway, the next day, I called, asked her out for a drink. Said I wanted to talk about a paper I was working on. She didn't fight too hard."

"Probably drawn to your manly features."

"Told her I looked like Harry Belafonte."

"She believe you?"

"Asked me who he was."

"Going to hustle younger women, got to expect that."

"Yeah." He laughed. "Well, one thing led to another, and we've spent a lot of time together, the last few . . . days."

"She told you?"

"Well, she didn't just up and blurt it out. But one evening, I was at her place when the phone rang. She was taking a bath when her answering machine kicked in. Kind that puts the caller on a speaker? Her uncle. Says she should call him, wanted to know how it was going."

"After he had made a big point of how he was keeping out of it."

"Right. I thought it meant it was rigged for Flanagan, and I hadn't signed on for that. So I demanded an explanation, told her unless we did it by the numbers, I was walking. And talking. It got pretty intense. Finally, she told me what was going on. Played the tapes of her conversations with O'Conor, had me talk to Kershaw, showed me how the facts were really shaping up."

"So then you signed on."

"Sure—after I heard those tapes and saw that data. Especially after Peggy told me about that night at his place. I wanted to take the bastard down, wanted it bad."

"You did that, all right."

"Yeah. Feels great."

"Why not tell me when I came to your place that night?"

"Because Peggy said you were working for O'Conor. I didn't know what to think when you came around. Anyway, I'd promised not to say anything."

"Working for O'Conor? Why would . . . oh." The pieces dropped into place. "Because I had Finn as a job reference?"

"Right. So she was unsure about you from the start. And just when she'd decided you were all right, you told Peggy you knew about O'Conor's deal with Finn. That sure made it sound like you were another O'Conor plant."

"I wasn't talking about the Seaside complex. He was doing a *new* project and had told a friend of mine that he couldn't wait to bless Flanagan so he could get going on that. That's what I was talking about."

"Damn! Doesn't that beat all!" He laughed, a big, pealing sound. "Sorry I didn't clue you in."

"No harm done. But if my references made me suspect, why did Kershaw agree to hire me?"

"He didn't know about any of this when he hired you. Peggy didn't fill him in until the day before we all met in his office. Then they figured Kershaw couldn't just drop you, or someone might get suspicious."

"So that's why Peggy volunteered me for the Whitmore investigation—so I wouldn't stumble on to her game?"

"Yep. She figured the kids would be easy, but she didn't want you looking over her shoulder and reporting back to Finn or O'Conor. Told me you seemed like a *very* devious character."

"The woman's sharp."

"She is that. Gave Massachusetts one less lying, corrupt politician."

"It's a start. I actually felt a little sorry for O'Conor this afternoon. Now I hope he rots in hell."

"I suspect he will. Probably next door to Finn."

"She's an awesome person."

"She is that. Never met anyone like her."

"Tough, Irish Catholic blind lady, smart black guy with his own ideas—could be a pretty potent combination, even in this town."

"I'd never have to worry about a parking space, that's for sure."

"Peggy said she used to see. Do you know what caused her blindness?"

"Hasn't said. She did say he was sickened by her blindness, wouldn't get near her afterward. She was sixteen when it happened, living in his house. You heard her—what do you think?"

"Then it may be reversible?"

"Maybe. I'll work with her on that, she wants to. Doesn't, not sure it matters."

"Not the blindness, no."

He pushed to his feet and offered his hand. "Gotta be going. Got a date waiting in the lobby."

"Watch out for the chaperone—she's a real bitch."

It would have been nice to sit there in that dark room, watching the lights come on in the Garden across the way, listening to the soothing murmur of satisfied drinkers, the happy tinkle of ice against glass, but I had a few more hours before I could say I'd finished the job I'd taken on. I made myself get up and do it.

chapter 40

NASE! WHAT A SURPRISE. WHAT A PLEASANT SURprise. Come in."

"Your secretary said you were alone. Hope you don't mind my dropping by like this." I stepped into Lynn's small office and took a seat.

"Mind? I'm delighted. I was just reading this." She held up a copy of Peggy's report. "Have you seen it?"

"Nope, but I got the gist."

"You want a copy? I can have one run."

"Not unless it's got want ads."

"How about this one: 'Wanted—intrepid sleuth to accompany tired lady lawyer to dinner'?"

"Circle that one—I'll be first in line."

"You're hired. I'm off duty in five minutes."

"My turn to pay, so help me earn my last Kershaw Commission paycheck first."

"You're worse than a probate lawyer. Shoot."

"Are you sure you got to the church at seven-thirty the night Whitmore was murdered?"

She settled back in her chair, looking amused. "You *are* an intrepid sleuth, aren't you? Yes. I was worried I was late, so I checked my watch when I pulled into the lot. Seven-thirty on the button. Why?"

"Damn."

"Why, Nase? What does it matter now? The police have the man who did it."

"I know, but there're a few holes."

"What kind of holes?"

"Can you sit on this? I'd like to keep it out of the papers, for Mrs. Whitmore's sake."

"Sure, I won't say anything. What is it?"

"The kid was running drugs. He spent a lot of time hanging around the church this summer, and it's possible he was selling some of them there."

Lynn's face went white. She pulled off her glasses and rubbed her eyes. "Oh, God—that's terrible. Theo will be devastated."

"I'm sure he would be. Not the kind of PR he needs."

"I'll say, but what's it got to do with what time I arrived that night?"

"You'll think I'm nuts."

"No, I won't—promise."

"Okay, but don't say I didn't warn you. I told you someone was seen walking toward the church around seven-forty-five. Say the cop didn't do it, and that person was Whitmore?"

"Nase, we went through that."

I held up my hand. "Bear with me. See, it crossed my mind the kid could have been on his way to deliver the stuff to Corey Webster, and maybe *he* did it."

Her jaw dropped like a rock. "You *are* kidding?"

"Well, Webster was there that night, just before you got there, right?"

"Sure, but—"

"And he was at the church a lot this summer. Someone saw him there talking with Whitmore one night, and you mentioned he'd been in some drug trouble before. And I've still got some aches to remind me he's got a hell of a temper. Whitmore showed up without the stuff, maybe told Webster he was going to blow the whistle on him . . ." I trailed off and shrugged.

"Look, I've got no use for the jerk, but this is kind of . . . far-fetched, isn't it? He was gone when I got there, and didn't they peg the time of death at some time *after* seven-thirty?"

"Right."

"So he *couldn't* have done it."

"That's why I asked if you were sure when you arrived. If you'd been late . . ."

"Down, boy. It won't work. Sorry."

"He could have left James and hung around outside until after you went in."

"Nase, he'd left by the time I arrived."

"How can you be sure?"

"Well, the parking lot was empty, except for Theo's Lincoln, so he had to have left."

I paused to reflect on what this meant, but no matter how I replayed it, it seemed to come out the same: "I suppose he could have pulled around the corner and waited."

"Oh, man—you're obsessed."

"See, I told you you'd wind up calling me crazy."

"You got me. And speaking of getting me, you said something about dinner? Can't we talk about this over a drink?"

I wasn't sure how hungry I was going to be, but I'd promised, and Lynn looked ready to eat for both of us. "Sure—maybe we'll talk about it afterward."

The canted smile returned. "My turn for a crazy idea: how about dinner, we decide on what happens afterward . . . afterward?"

I liked the way she said it, no eye-batting or coyness.

"Best crazy idea I've heard in a long time—only I've got an even crazier one. How about we stop at James's church on the way?"

"James's church?" She eyed me quizzically. "Why on earth do you want to do that?"

"Just want to ask him about Webster—does he have any record when he was at the church, how he seemed that night, things like that. I can call, see if he's in."

"Oh, lord. This *is* crazy, but what the hell, right? Give me a minute to straighten up this mess."

I went out and used the phone on the secretary's desk to call James. I explained what I wanted and he agreed to see us right away, although he didn't sound as though it was all he needed to complete his day. Bernie Lawson, my next call, was a lot more chipper, because Dapper Flanagan was back in charge, and when I asked him to meet me later, his grumbles were only for form.

I'd just hung up when Lynn came out, looking fresh and pretty and not at all like a tired lady lawyer. "Let's go, crazy man. Get this out of your system. Then we can work on whatever's left."

chapter 41

WE STEPPED AROUND A PILE OF GRAVEL AND THE wheelbarrow Ben Crews had used to haul it. I rang the buzzer and waited, not eager for the meeting. "I hope he's in a decent mood."

"Relax." Lynn gave my arm a squeeze. "He's used to counseling the disturbed."

I couldn't think of a good retort, but he opened the door and saved me the trouble. "Good of you to see me, Reverend. You know Lynn Daniels, I believe?"

"Of course. Good evening, Lynn. Come this way, please."

We followed him down a basement hallway into a large office lined with pictures of James pressing flesh with various eminences. He shut the door, and the sound of organ music faded to a barely audible resonance coming through the ceiling, more felt than heard.

James noticed my glance and smiled. "Sister Goshade practicing. It does make a noise."

He settled himself into a large, upholstered, swivel rocker behind a heavy mahogany desk and leaned back, gesturing to two matching armchairs across from him. "I was a little surprised by your call, Mr. Nichols—I had assumed that your work was at an end."

I took one of the chairs, Lynn the other. "It is, Reverend. Just one or two things I wanted to wrap up before I move on, if you'll indulge me?"

"Very well. What would you like to know?"

"Corey Webster, Reverend—he was here quite a bit this summer, I believe?"

"Mr. Webster and I had frequent dealings. No more this summer than before."

"But he did meet with you at the church this summer?"

"Here and elsewhere. May I ask why—"

"He met with you here in your office the night Purnell Whitmore was killed?"

"Yes—that was the last time. What—"

"I take it, then, you're no longer working with him?"

"Let's say I decided he wasn't heading in the right direction. That disgraceful performance the other night in Mattapan confirmed it. Now, why are you asking me about him?"

"I'll explain in just a minute, I promise. First, would you mind telling me what time he left the night Whitmore was killed?"

"Oh, very well." He brought his tented fingers to his lips and reflected. "Seven-fifteen, I believe, or thereabouts."

"Before Lynn got here?"

"Of course."

"Now, I understand Lynn got here at about seven-thirty?"

"Seven-thirty sharp, I believe. Yes, I'm sure."

"Let me see." I did a mental estimate, shook my head. "No, that doesn't work."

"What doesn't work?"

"Well, Webster had fifteen minutes after he left you before Lynn showed up. He could have waited outside, but . . . no. Sorry—it just doesn't work. The times are wrong."

"Mr. Nichols, I have been patient, but now I must insist. Why are you asking me these questions about Mr. Webster?"

There was no good way to ease into it, so I didn't try: "It occurred to me that Webster could have been buying drugs from Purnell Whitmore this summer—when he came to the church to meet with you?"

James shot forward and braced his hands on the desk: "That's preposterous. That's the most—"

Lynn held out a restraining hand. "Now, Theo, just hear Mr. Nichols out. He has a reason for thinking this, even if I think it's as far-fetched as you do. His intentions are good, so please—listen to him."

I wasn't sure he was going to heed her, but he gradually eased back in his chair. "Very well—go on, Mr. Nichols. And I hope you have a very good reason for making these . . . unspeakable allegations about a fine young man whose mother has little to cherish but his precious memory." He rocked back, scowling at the ceiling, his fingers a little steeple at his chest.

I ran through it quickly, hurried to the conclusion: "So, putting aside the night Whitmore was killed, can you at least tell me if Webster was here these other nights Whitmore apparently had some business at the church?" I held out a list of dates I'd taken from Whitmore's desk calendar.

He took it grudgingly, looked at it for a few seconds, then pulled his own appointment calendar over. He ran his big forefinger down the pages while he glanced over at my list in his other hand. Then he pushed the list back to me.

"Mr. Nichols, Corey Webster was here on only three of those dates. I'm sure that's pure coincidence."

"I'm afraid you're right." I stood. "Do you mind if I use your phone? I promised Mrs. Whitmore I'd call her either way after I met with you. She'll be waiting."

His hooded eyes jumped open. "Mrs. Whitmore? I told you to leave that poor woman alone! I ought to—"

"I won't be bothering her anymore, Reverend. Please—I know she's anxious."

"Oh, very well—but this had better be the end." He settled back in the big chair and I pulled the phone over. I looked for Mrs. Whitmore's number in my pocket but couldn't find it. "May I use your Rolodex? I'm afraid I've lost her number."

I took his dismissive wave to be permission, so I pulled over the Rolodex and riffled back through the cards until I found Mrs. Whitmore's. I dialed the number I found there and waited half a dozen rings.

"That's odd—must have misdialed; sorry." I checked the card again and redialed. She picked up on the first ring.

"Mrs. Whitmore? I see. Okay. Thank you very much. Yes, it certainly does. I'll get back to you." I hung up.

James had been listening to my end. "You will *not* 'get back to' that woman. You've put her through enough. I told you—" He stood and started to come around the desk.

"Sit down, Reverend."

He kept coming, so I reached under my jacket and came out with the gun. "I said sit down." I raised it until the front sight rested right below his nose.

Lynn eased herself out of her chair, looking at me as though she'd just realized her date was the Hillside Strangler. "Nase, what are you doing?! Put that away."

"I don't think so." I waved the barrel and James lowered himself slowly back into the chair as I kept the gun on him.

"You'll regret this." His nostrils flared, the low words barely moving his mouth as they slid out.

"My guess is *you'll* have quite a few years to regret keeping Purnell Whitmore's pager number with his home phone number. Years you're going to serve for killing him."

His eyes shot to the Rolodex. "That's insane! I don't know what you're talking about."

"I dialed the second number you had written there. Mrs. Whitmore said the pager beeped. Is that how you'd let him know when you'd run out between regular visits, wanted a little toot before services?"

"God damn you. I—" He started to rise, saw my finger tighten on the trigger, thought better of it.

"Theo—be quiet! There's been some mix-up. Don't say anything stupid."

Lynn was looking from James to me and back again. "Just keep quiet and let me handle this. I'm sure it can be straightened out."

"Good advice, Lynn, but a little late—I'm willing to bet if we look at that appointment book, we're going to see the Reverend James was here every time Whitmore came by."

She settled cautiously back into her chair, looking at me as though I'd changed faces. "But that doesn't mean he bought drugs from him—that's insane!"

"No, he could have used that beeper to call him in for vespers, but I sort of doubt it."

I saw James's hands pressing against the rocker arms, biceps flexing under his jacket. "You get out of that chair, Reverend, I'm going to save the Commonwealth the price of a trial."

He glared at me, a cold, unblinking look, and I was glad I had the desk between us and the gun in my hand. "You figured the sweet ride you were on was going to end fast if Whitmore turned you in, right? I mean, this kid was going to blow it all away. No way, you said."

Lynn was shaking her head as though trying to rearrange her brain so it would work better. "Nase, even if you're right about the drugs, Theo *can't* have killed the boy—I was with him that night. Maybe it was Webster after all."

"Webster left here at seven-fifteen; Whitmore was alive at the other end of the alley at seven-thirty. Webster was gone when you got here at seven-thirty, right?"

"Yes, but . . ."

I shook my head. "There you go . . . Webster was long gone before Whitmore could have gotten here."

"He hid outside. He pulled his car around the corner and waited, like you said. He must have. You were right. It *must* have been Webster."

"Possible, I suppose. I guess we could ask him."

"*Ask* him? Of *course* you should ask him. Get the police in, see if—"

"But it would be a waste of time; he didn't do it."

"*What*? You *told* me you suspected him. You told me in my office, you said it here . . ." She tossed her head, as though trying to get sticky gears to mesh.

"I know. I lied."

"Nase, what the hell kind of game—"

"I figured I'd get more cooperation if Webster seemed to be my target. I'm skilled in the art of deceit."

"But if Webster didn't do it, then who—"

I pointed the gun at James's forehead, gray under a sheen of sweat. "You're looking at him."

She was, but with disbelief. "But . . . he was with me that night."

"No, ma'am—not when he killed Whitmore, he wasn't. *Afterward*, he was with you. Right afterward. But you weren't with him when he did it. Good thing, too—make you a murderer, if you had been."

"But he couldn't have—you said so yourself. The times don't work. If Whitmore was alive at seven-thirty, and I was with Theo at seven-thirty, he couldn't have done it."

"Right."

"But then—"

"Not if you got here at seven-thirty—no way he could have done it."

"But I told you I did. *He* told you I did."

"I know."

"Well, then—"

"You lied. I never claimed to be the *only* one skilled in the art of deceit."

"*What?* Oh, man, have you gone off the deep end. Come on, Nase . . . let's not let your . . . fantasy spoil a nice evening. Let's go." She got up and reached for her purse.

"Lynn, Lynn—give it up. You *were* late. You got here— what?—eight o'clock, a little after? The rectory door was open; you walked in; there it was."

James was looking at me as though Satan had settled in my chair. "Let me guess, Reverend: Whitmore showed up hysterical, crying, the way he was when the cop left him. You've led him in here, you're standing there with him, and the kid's out of control. *He's going to blow the whistle on you! Some cop's given him two days to turn in his customers or his mother gets the whole story.* On top of that, Lynn is going to show up any second, and how could you know she'd turn out to be so . . . *pragmatic,* huh? You're going to be ruined, absolutely finished, all because you like a little blow from time to time."

I walked over to the wall and ran my hand across it. A few particles of coarse grit from the old mortar stuck to my fingertips. "What happened? You try to shake some sense into him, only he was standing a little close to the wall? That's only manslaughter. Of course, if you thought about it first, killed him to keep him from giving your name to the cop, we're talking murder one, Reverend."

James's eyes followed me back to the chair, little points of concentrated hate. I wiped my hand on the arm. "They'll compare this stuff with the particles embedded in his scalp, you know. The brickwork in the alley is filthy—this is nice and clean. What do you suppose the stuff they pulled out of his head will look like under a microscope?"

James wasn't going to answer, so I turned back to Lynn.

"Was he standing over the body when you walked in? Maybe the kid wasn't dead yet; James was still pounding his head against the wall?"

She said, "I mean it," but she stood rooted.

"I don't know, but I'd like to think you would have done the right thing if the kid had still been alive. But with him dead, then—might as well have *some* good come of it, huh? What was it you said, that night at Finn's? 'What're eggs for, if not omelets?' Whitmore was just a poor egg that was already scrambled—might as well make the omelet, right?"

"Last chance, Nase."

"You stayed here until it got good and late, huh? Talked social policy until James took the body out and loaded it on that wheelbarrow? Or did you use the time to work out the deal: you'll be his alibi if he ever needs one, and in turn he'll take you along while you redirect his talents towards more *practical* ends?"

She didn't say anything, just shook her head, and I went on, just free-associating as I tried to put it together. "That's why we got the new Reverend Theophilus James, debuting at that rally in Franklin Park, isn't it? You must have felt like a producer of a hit show, Lynn, built around some guy you'd found playing dinner theaters in the sticks. You did a hell of a job, too. You were absolutely right about what had to be done to get the reverend a larger audience. You scripted it, you directed it, and you owned the copyright. And the critics loved it. Were you building up to taking it on the road, Lynn?"

She was a tough lady, I'll give her that. I heard more pity than anger when she answered. "You *are* crazy. You've imagined this whole thing."

"Nope. You said his Lincoln was the only car here when you arrived. That meant you got here after the bus left."

"The bus left at seven-thirty. I must have pulled in just after."

"The bus didn't leave at seven-thirty, Lynn."

"Of course it did. The papers said—"

"Sorry, Lynn—the papers said the bus was *leaving* at seven-thirty. I found out yesterday the bus *didn't* leave then—supposed to, but the driver held it for ten minutes, waiting for Whitmore."

She blinked, only a couple of times, but enough to tell me she'd taken a shot and knew it. "The man driving the bus told me there weren't any other cars here when he pulled out at seven-forty. That told me you were wrong when you told me at dinner you got here on time."

She recovered quickly, practiced lawyer that she was. "Did it ever occur to you the driver was wrong about the time when he left?"

"Sure—that's why I talked to the kids on the bus. Half a dozen of them confirm him." She might have been a practiced lawyer, but the sudden tightening of her lips said I was becoming a practiced liar. "That got me wondering: had you just made a mistake about the time you arrived, or had you *meant* to get the time wrong? So I gave you another chance at it in your office, remember?"

I watched her replay it, silently, on the full lips that had seemed so attractive but now just seemed desperate. "Right—you remember: you stuck to the time, even threw in the bit about looking at your watch, so I knew it wasn't simply a mistake. You *wanted* me to believe you got here sooner than you did. And then, as you point out, just a few minutes ago, James backed you up on the time: 'seven-thirty *sharp*,' he said. Only one reason you'd get together on that lie."

"You've made this all up. I never said any of that. I'm sure, Theo, if you think about it, you'll recall I got here after eight. Remember—I got caught in traffic?" She seemed satisfied with the stunned look he gave her and turned to me with a confident, knowing smile. "Where's your supposed lie now?"

"With the new one you just invented." I pushed back my jacket and showed her the wire leading to the small of my back. "Little idea I picked up from Peggy Kiernan. Who I imagine will be talking to you pretty soon."

The smile faded as she turned for the door. "I'm sorry. It could have been fun."

I watched her back. "I'm sorry, too."

She got to the door but no farther, because Bernie Lawson and two detectives were on the other side of it. They escorted her back to the desk.

I holstered my gun and walked over to Lynn. "When you think about it, you're going to realize that as soon as the two of you are in separate rooms, whichever one talks first gets to deal. You're only in for accessory after the fact. I suggest you go first."

"I don't know what you're talking about."

I stepped closer, dropped my voice. "Once he gets a lawyer and they start working on it, he's going to know he can pull you in a lot deeper with the right kind of story. Like the kid was alive when you got here, you heard him threatening James and *you* slammed him into the wall. Doesn't have to be world class to cut into your bargaining position. On the other hand, if the rev told you he did the kid to keep him from talking, they can tag him with murder one. Might be willing to make you a nice offer in exchange. Think about it."

She let me watch the calculator work behind the eyes while we traded stares. She *was* a practiced lawyer, and there wasn't a lot to figure.

Bernie took her by the arm. She went with him, somnambulantly, three halting steps, then stopped. "No—wait." Her voice was low. "I want to talk to somebody. In private."

"You wish to make a statement?"

"Yes. There's been a mistake. I have some information pertinent to a homicide investigation. Perhaps I should have said something earlier, but I hoped that the responsible party would come forward voluntarily."

"You bitch! I'll—" James lunged across the desk. The two detectives wrestled his arms behind him and got cuffs on.

"Good girl, Lynn. You'll have that all worked up and ready for tryouts by the time you get to the station."

". . . have the right . . ."

"I guess this means dinner's going to have to wait, huh?" Lynn held out her wrists and looked at me over Bernie's shoulder as the cuffs went on. The lopsided smile was back, attractive as ever.

". . . afford a lawyer, one will be . . ."

"Afraid so. The afterward, too."

". . . can and will be used against you."

"It was just a crazy idea, Nase."

"About afterward?"

She shrugged. "Whatever." The detectives led them out. I thought Lynn might look back, but she didn't.

Bernie stayed behind. "Damn—James, huh? Why?"

"Whitmore kept James in coke. I don't know—maybe Webster was buying from the kid, told James he was a convenient source. Whitmore was going to make a delivery before hopping the bus for the outing when Hurley collared him. The kid thought about what Hurley told him, then went to the church. He must have told James he'd gotten religion, only not the kind James was selling. Maybe Whitmore told James he was going to roll him over; maybe James just couldn't handle the idea that he'd be walking around with that potential. Would have ruined James if it came out."

"Why'd the woman cover for him?"

"She figured he had his uses; Whitmore was dead; taking James down for it wouldn't change that."

"Pretty cold."

"She wanted to run with a pretty cold crowd."

"But what did she get out of it?"

I thought about my dinner with Lynn, the only one I'd ever have, and her answer when I'd asked the same question. "A place at the table, Bernie—a place at the table. And she was awfully hungry."

The Boston Hub
Editorial
September 15, 1994

KEEP THE PUBLIC IN PUBLIC HOUSING

Yesterday's announcement of a 200-unit housing complex between South Boston and downtown, to be called Shamrock City, comes as welcome news, especially since the units will be priced low enough for low-income families. We commend Acting Mayor Ianucci and his administration for working with the project's developer, Plato Frio Partnership, Ltd., to make it a reality.

We question, however, whether Shamrock City is really the model for future urban housing development some are claiming. We are particularly concerned by the city's proposal to permit residents of public housing to rent units in Shamrock City with vouchers they would receive from the city in lieu of the housing allowance they now get. Tenants would be allowed to purchase the units after three years, applying the accrued rents to the purchase price. They then would then be free to sell their units on the open market, inviting profiteering and turning public housing, a public responsibility, into private opportunity.

Furthermore, the administration's motives are at least open to question. As Professor Wanda Pryce-Jones of Tufts University says, "Is the purpose of this proposal to depopulate public housing of African-Americans, now a potent force in the projects? One may wonder."

It would be far better for the city to expand the existing stock of public housing, retaining it under public control. The bankrupt Seaside Complex, for example, could be converted into a large number of city-owned units, and we urge the City Housing Authority to acquire it, rather than undertake a questionable experiment at Shamrock City. People must come before profits.

chapter 42

I WALKED AROUND THE CORNER AND THERE THEY were: Bucky, whom I had expected, and the others, whom I hadn't. They all started waving and calling to me as soon as they saw me. It was Bucky's little surprise, and I was touched.

They were sitting at an outdoor café in Quincy Market, everybody as cheerful and upbeat as the beautiful, end-of-summer day. As I approached, they held up their glasses and smiled, and I had to swallow hard.

"Commissioner, Mrs. Flanagan."

His big hand engulfed mine. "You're a good man in a dust-up, Nichols. Maybe we'll do it again some time." He cast a glance at his wife, then winked at me.

She gave him a mock glare. "Your next 'dust-up,' Francis Flanagan, will be with me, and you'll need more than Mr. Nichols to save you then."

They were sitting with the Hurleys. Mrs. Flanagan was

cradling the baby, who was wearing one of those ridiculous sun hats mothers put on their babies, knowing they make them irresistible, even when they're drooling, as little John was.

Nora Hurley stopped snuggling against her husband long enough to jump up, run around the table, and throw her arms around me. "God bless you, Mr. Nichols. You saved our lives." Then she planted a big kiss on my cheek.

It wasn't a bad paycheck, and I filed it away to draw against the next time my self-esteem account was empty. "Thank you. You're back on the beat, then, John?"

Mrs. Hurley answered for him. "He is not!" She went back to her seat and snuggled in against him again as the color rose in his face. I hadn't been snuggled in a long while, and it looked good.

"Nora means I've quit the force. It just wasn't right for me." He glanced over at Flanagan. "Sorry, Commissioner."

The big man smiled: "Dapper, son. And that's just fine. It isn't for everyone, and it takes a big man to know when it's time to walk. You'll be rendering a fine service where you're going."

Hurley nodded. "I signed on with the City Recreation Department. The commish . . . uh, Dapper helped me get a job coaching kids in the after-school league."

Nora Hurley squeezed her husband's big arm. "He'll be able to help those children, Mr. Nichols."

"I don't doubt it." Mrs. Hurley's snuggle looked so good I thought of asking if I could get in on it, but instead I glanced at my watch; perhaps, I thought, if things worked out right, I'd have my own snuggle partner in a few hours.

I settled into a seat between Bucky and Sowell Endicott. Endicott and Peggy were being a little more circumspect than the Hurleys, but I saw there was some serious hand-holding going on under the table.

"So—what's next for you two?"

Endicott pulled Peggy's hand out from under the table and held it up so I could see the ring.

"It's a beauty—congratulations."

Her smile outshone the diamond. "We're gonna make babies, Nichols—lots of 'em. And when we're not making 'em, we're gonna be practicing."

"Nase, or Nason. And you've got me blushing again."

Endicott laughed. "She gets me blushing."

I turned to Eliot Kershaw, who was looking on with his head cocked to one side, more than ever the large bird. "Mr. Kershaw, it's been an honor to be associated with you."

"Honor's all mine, Nicholson. Damned lucky it turned out the way it did—could have been sticky, the fellow insisted on toughing it out."

"I'm sorry?"

"Constitutional crisis of the worst kind. Better he went the way he did. Real service. Still don't understand why he kept those tapes, though. Never would have got him otherwise."

"Oh. Ah . . . yes. I . . . follow you . . . now, I guess."

Suddenly, if I hadn't known better, I could have sworn one of the rheumy, washed-out old eyes winked at me. "Fellows like that, they always underestimate other people. Don't give 'em credit for having any brains—think they're the only ones got 'em. Mistake. Always make one. Sometimes it gives a chap a little edge, they think you're a little dull. Let their guard down then."

"Ah—quite." I studied him, but he'd mastered the poker face before I was born, and nothing I saw left me any the wiser.

I finally turned to my host. "Nice gathering, Buckster."

He beamed and pushed over a stein of beer. "Nobody had to have an arm twisted, Nase. You did good on this one, boyo."

To my embarrassment, this was greeted with "Here, here" all around. When it died, I said to Bucky, "It's working out all right, then, the housing project?"

"Like a dream." He leaned back and spread his arms expansively. "Can you see the Hanrahan, lord of the manse, riding through his demesne as cheering tenants doff their caps?"

"It is a vision. Think you'll be able to leave the sheep alone?"

"*Droît seigneur*, and all that. Perhaps a coat of arms: a flask or on a field *vert*, emblazoned with the family motto— 'We pride ourselves on our humility.'"

"I'm glad. You'll do it well."

"Finn's plan wasn't bad, once you forget about using the new project to subsidize Seaside. The properties I bought up came cheap, and the acting mayor said he'd get behind it, make sure the banks come through. With the housing vouchers, the city'll save money and the decent people will be able to get out of those hellholes they're locked into now, so it's a win-win. The Pryce-Jones crowd is apoplectic at the thought of losing some of their chips, so I must be doing something right."

"Nice of you to take on Mrs. Whitmore."

"Gonna take on a lot of Mrs. Whitmores—she's going to help me find them. They'll decide who gets a lease; these aren't people you shuck easy."

It was a beautiful day, a day prefiguring fall, sky as clear and blue as we make them in New England, and that's as clear and blue as they get. I looked up at the contrails coming into Logan and knew it would be time soon. I glanced at my watch and pushed back my chair. "I'm late. Got to get to the airport."

"You've got plenty of time. You said Rachel's not due in until six."

"Yeah, but there's something I've got to do on the way." I stood, reluctantly. "Sorry, folks, but I've got to run. But thank you all for turning out. It means a lot to me."

As I walked away, their good wishes followed. It was tempting to think about lingering, basking in the warmth of the good company of good people, but I just couldn't. If I hurried, there'd be just enough time before heading to the airport. I still had an idea or two, a few tricks left.

I got in my car, put my foot to the floor, ignored the blare of the truck behind me. It felt good to stick my head out into the wind, good to raise my cry, even if no one else heard it: "I know you're out there, Norman Wilkins—you can run, but you can't hide!"